CW00860437

GABON

MARIUS GABRIEL

This is a work of fiction. Names, characters, places, and incidents either are the product of the author's imagination or are used fictitiously, and any resemblance of fictional characters to actual persons living or dead, business establishments, events, or locales is entirely coincidental

Copyright © 2015 Marius Gabriel

All rights reserved.

ISBN: 1514717441
ISBN-13: 978-1514717448

MARIUS GABRIEL'S NOVELS:

THE SEVENTH MOON

"Few thrillers have as strong a sense of atmosphere and adventure as this fascinating tale." —Chicago Tribune

"[Gabriel has] a gift for suspense that can make you read 351 pages in a sitting."—The Charlotte Observer

HOUSE OF MANY ROOMS

"A sexy, gripping thriller that doesn't miss a beat."—Kirkus Reviews

"Gabriel offers up a profusion of surprising plot twists, relentless suspense and a humdinger of a climax. A spellbinding thriller that will keep readers riveted." —Booklist

"Bravo! This suspense thriller weaves an intricate web of lies and deceit. The reader is kept guessing around every turn. [House of Many Rooms] touches nearly every human emotion conceivable."—Rendezvous

THE MASK OF TIME

"Keeps you reading while your dinner burns . . . Great fun."— Cosmopolitan
"Turns on the heat at the start and doesn't let up."—Kirkus Reviews

THE ORIGINAL SIN

"Pulsing with romance, danger, and suspense . . . A compelling read."—Publishers Weekly
"Positively riveting ... A sexy, hard-to-put-down read." —Kirkus Reviews

MARIUS GABRIEL

GABON

1

Before he left Paris, Jean-Patrice wrote Justine what he considered was a blistering letter.

24 June 1899

My Dear Justine,

So it seems that all the vows and declarations of undying love were no more than the gasps of animal passion. After everything I gave you, did for you, you have not the bare humanity even to bid me farewell. You have used me shamelessly, taking your pleasure with abandon, giving nothing in return. No doubt I am of little interest to you now that your amusement is over, so I will not weary you with an account of the desolation, spiritual and material, which you have wreaked in my life. But I would like you to know, whether it means anything to you or not, that you have irreparably broken a true and loving heart.

He continued in the same vein for several pages, in places so enraged that he was barely able to form the words. His writing degenerated into a scrawl towards the end. Justine showed this missive to her husband, who read it and shook his silvered head.

"This time, my dear, you have surpassed yourself. That young fellow is truly on the cross."

"He has put himself there," she replied defensively.

"You have supplied him with the nails and the hammer." She picked up her Chinese fan at this point, as she so often did when she was accused of having behaved badly, fanning her cheeks and throat with swift beats like the wing of a nervous butterfly. "I have done what I can for him," Maurice proceeded, "but he is right. You have amused yourself far too much at his expense. You should have taken his nature into account. You are not judicious, Justine."

The beating of the butterfly grew swifter. She shot him a sharp glance from her bright, jade-green eyes (considered among the most captivating in Paris). She could certainly not reproach him with any disorder in his own private life. He had kept the same mistress for almost a dozen years now, quietly installed in a sober apartment where she – and the child they had in common – lived with the utmost discretion. By comparison, her occasional, turbulent affairs were conducted with no circumspection whatsoever; and often, as in this case, it was left to Maurice to impose a convenient solution on situations which had escaped from her control.

"I am not judicious," she agreed. Her voice was husky, déclassé, that of a chanteuse addicted to absinthe, maddeningly erotic in a woman of such elevated social standing. "But you must remember, Maurice, that there are fifteen years between us. I will learn judgment with time."

This delicate reference to Maurice's diminishing vitality, clinging as the powder left on one's fingers by a butterfly's wing, closed the exchange. He retreated behind the pages of his newspaper. She continued to fan herself energetically, cocking her head to catch the draft on her flushed skin but keeping her eyes fixed on the view of the orderly garden through the half-open window. The letter lay crumpled on the tablecloth between them.

And there they agreed to leave the matter, by which time Jean-Patrice was sailing for Africa on the *Marmotte*.

2

The whimper of the *Marmotte's* loose rivets and the groans of her worn decking provided a melancholy counterpoint to the grinding of Jean-Patrice's thoughts. The rhythmical surge of the ship, too, reminded him painfully of the movements of Justine's body in his arms, so he drew little consolation from the voyage. But he kept to the ship, refusing to be lured ashore by the delights of the ports of call – Algiers, Tangiers, Casablanca – which he imagined, or imagined he could imagine, perfectly.

At the edges of his self-absorption (and it must be said, for he was not altogether a young dog, his genuine suffering) he noticed how the shore changed from desert dune to straggling scrub, and then from scrub to a dark green forest, unbroken and apparently impenetrable, exhaling vapors that turned the sky grey and could be smelled a mile or two out to sea. The air lost its crispness and became sodden. The Equator loomed with an immense, oppressive heat. Nevertheless, each day he continued to dress himself as though for a Parisian promenade, defying the humidity in a suit with a waistcoat and a fob watch. He walked the deck endlessly, swinging his cane and occasionally prodding at splinters on the planking. He was a figure of some amusement to the other passengers, most of whom were seasoned Africa hands, lounging in loose cotton clothing, preferring to smoke and read novels in the deck chairs than to stir a limb between one meal and the next. He was so clearly new to Africa and to Life, striding (probably) to illness and death with his freshly shaven chin held high.

Justine's husband had been perceptive to speak of his being crucified. It was an apt metaphor. He felt himself to be nailed to his emotions, his flesh skewered, his soul pierced. He had loved her so much. He had been so convinced that this lovely young creature (so he thought of her) would be his alone. He had persuaded himself that her husband's wealth and authority weighed less in the balance than his own devotion and sexual prowess. After the gasps and whimpers, echoed mockingly now by the worn rivets of the coastal steamer, she had let him know that he was the first and only man to have taken her to those heavenly places where they had lain together, floating above the world. Looking back, he thought now she had perhaps flattered him to some degree, for the purpose of extracting from him even greater efforts.

Yet he had felt that he loved her with all the sincerity of which he was capable. He was twenty-seven, and no longer a boy. It was a man's heart he had given her.

"I gave her everything." He heard the words come from his lips at the dinner table, but could not take them back, or restrain others from spilling out after them. For the first time, he had made himself completely drunk, or perhaps the others had made him drunk for their amusement. The pressure in his head was intolerable, his treacherous lips were swollen. "I love her so much. I miss her so terribly."

The others watched him speculatively through their cigarette smoke. Nobody laughed. He tried to rise and upset his chair. "Excuse me."

Two fellow passengers helped him to bed. It was one

of these, the grizzled sub-manager of a timber company named Montpelier, who offered a few words of advice the next day when, too weak to stride the deck, Jean-Patrice lay greenly on a deck chair.

"Beware the fruit and the native women. Both can be poisonous. Eat nothing unless it has been cooked and drink nothing unless it has been boiled. Never trust a mulatto and never let your guard down. Have you a smoke?"

Jean-Patrice opened his case and gave the man the cigar he had asked for. He gazed dully at the dull sea, his head pounding. He felt he had crossed some line, not found on any map, which separated the old and civilized world which he had known from a new and horrible present. He heard the rasp of a match and smelled the tobacco.

"Never thrash a native too severely," the other man went on. "Their constitutions are weaker than you think and they may die. Then there will be the Devil to pay."

"I'm obliged to you," Jean-Patrice said in a hollow voice.

"Where are you to be stationed?"

"At Bassongo. A two-year posting."

"Know anything about the place?"

"Nothing except that it is remote. I am supposed to replace the Commissioner there."

Montpelier sucked the end of the cheroot, squinting at Jean-Patrice from lined eyes. "You will be among the Fang. They eat one another. And do other things."

"That was mentioned during the training."

The other man chuckled, showing brown teeth. "Where did they train you? In the Bois du Boulogne?"

"Excuse me." He rose to his feet, nauseous. His unsteady progress to his cabin was interrupted by a bout of retching. Fortunately, he had already emptied most of the contents of his stomach, but he was humiliated to glimpse one of the crew bringing a bucket and mop to clear the spattered deck after him. His knees were trembling by the time he reached his bunk.

The pain of missing Justine was a bee sting on the soul. He wanted release from this thing that nailed him to what he told himself he now despised, so he made himself drunk again at dinner the next night. This time the others, bored with his ramblings, were less sympathetic. The Captain made a cutting remark. He was left alone with the brandy decanter while the other passengers retired to the smoking room to play cards. A grinning steward marked each drink insolently in a notebook. Jean-Patrice was certain the man was cheating him, but he was determined not to stop drinking until the Justine who lived in his chest was drowned and harmless.

It was not an easy task. Laughing at the cheap brandy, she remained alert and cruel, illuminating, as if in a magic lantern show, the process of his destruction: his increasing demands, her alarm, the scenes he had made, the confrontations he had sought, the ultimatums he had delivered, long after he should have acknowledged that the game was over. She showed him how he had driven her to flee from him, hiding from his importunity. She lifted the curtain on his abysmal folly, turning up the lantern on a scarlet-faced Jean-Patrice, pounding on Justine's door, being answered by her courteous and dignified husband, a farce without laughter.

Presumption. Folly verging on madness. He leaned over the basin to vomit up the evening's cognac, shuddering. He had been so proud of having seduced the most desirable woman in Paris, a trophy worthy of his physique, his looks, his intellect. He had not counted on falling in love. On becoming enslaved, not to put too fine a point on it.

Jellyfish the size of footballs began to drift past the ship. Whitish, like blind eyeballs, they sometimes trailed venomous blue and yellow streamers yards long. Some of the passengers amused themselves by using the creatures for target practice, pounding away with their revolvers.

The bullets seemed to produce no effect on the jellyfish. Inert yet alive and travelling, they absorbed the shots and bobbed away on the greenish swells, carried by some purposeful current.

The mania for shooting persisted, having roused the passengers from their inertia. When the jellyfish vanished, they took potshots at logs and other flotsam. Fusillades broke the silence at odd hours. The shrewd purser had laid in boxes of ammunition in various calibers, which he now sold at stiff prices to the sportsmen. Occasionally a lucky shot would bring down a seagull in a shower of broken feathers. Though the Bureau had issued him with a revolver of his own, Jean-Patrice left the weapon in his trunk. He did not regard it as an implement of sport, but as a last release. In the vicinity of the Cape Verde Islands, a whale appeared. Frenzy swept the vessel. The passengers crowded at the rail, discharging ragged broadsides until they were all deafened. The creature appeared to be well out of range, but perhaps it took umbrage at so much ill will, for it sounded with a flip of its spreading tail and left the ocean empty.

As a consequence of this disrespect toward a monarch of the sea (according to the sailors) the *Marmotte* was battered by storms through the Gulf of Guinea. Like the large rodent after which the boat was named, she burrowed doggedly through the lumpy water. She pitched, she tossed, she rolled, she stood on her nose and then on her tail, throwing her passengers around their cabins. The bad weather did not leave them until Libreville.

3

Jean-Patrice was on deck in the predawn drizzle, nauseously smoking a damp cheroot, when a sailor jerked his head towards the port side of the ship and uttered the single laconic word, "Gabon."

He clung to the rail and stared. Gabon was revealed as a sullen, swampy coast, occasionally obscured by heaving swells that made the steamer wallow sickeningly. He fancied he could hear the roar of distant surf. Days of drinking had made his legs unsteady. Once he had started, he had been unable to stop. He had not been to the saloon in several days. Meals – and bottles – were brought to his cabin instead . He'd been made to pay for what he consumed in cash. He hadn't been insulted. He preferred to know that the bottles were his before he broached them. Nobody could then take them away. The empties rolled on the floor of his cabin, disdained by the stewards.

"When do we dock?" he asked the sailor.

"This time tomorrow," the man replied.

Was there time to get sober? He was uncertain as to how drunk he was. Very drunk, he suspected. His head hurt terribly. Perhaps twenty-four hours would not be sufficient. He retired to his cabin and resumed drinking.

The alcohol now tasted like vomit even before he brought it back up. It was the knowledge that she cared nothing for him that he found most unbearable. He was at the Equator (he felt it now like a vast iron weight) while she, in Paris, pursued her pleasures without bestowing a single thought on his fate.

He did not order any more alcohol, once he had emptied the last bottle, and was in a state of intermediate sobriety by the time he staggered ashore, preceded by his portmanteaus, which were carried to the Customs shed by a gang of half-naked Africans. They were the first black men he had seen. Truly black, they appeared to him, their skin like wet coal, shiny with sweat. He was fascinated. It was not until weeks later that he recognized that the skin of most Gabonese was, in fact, a rich brown. His initial impression of inky blackness had been hallucinatory, perhaps a metaphor of some kind, materializing from the alcohol he had drunk on the voyage.

The little town was shabby, studded with palm trees. The light on the estuary was like the sweep of a golden saber. A dozen fat cargo ships nuzzled at the wharf like suckling pigs. A warship of the French Navy was having her hull painted by sailors in rowboats. A gunboat was building up a head of steam to set off upriver, its funnel scribbling smoke across the limpid sky like a child's drawing. However it soon began to rain, persistently and mournfully, blotting out the morning.

The hotel produced in him the impression of a nightmare. The dining room where he ate two dreadful meals was all but deserted and had the air of a morgue, with worn steel implements and canvas table coverings. He was unable to eat the grisly dishes which he was served. He sat watching a large crimson centipede amble around his plate. His room was sordid, sleep made impossible, despite the mosquito net, by biting insects and flittering insects and other insects which shrilled piercingly in the darkness outside.

The initial interview with Gaston Malherbe, which took place the next day at nine, was not auspicious. The official was dressed in a colonial uniform with short sleeves and short pants, a type of outfit which Jean-Patrice had never seen before, revealing leathery limbs like those of a large turtle. Malherbe had also a somewhat reptilian jaw which he moved from side to side as he considered Jean-Patrice through his steel rimmed spectacles. Despite the bizarre uniform, he gave an impression of extreme severity and orderliness. His hair was cropped to bristles, as was his moustache. Jean-Patrice was aware that his own appearance had suffered during the voyage, and that he probably appeared seedy to the other man.

"Your reputation precedes you, Monsieur Duméril."

"I hope it is a good one," Jean-Patrice replied with what he felt to be a ghastly smile.

"It is principally a bad one. The Captain of the *Marmotte* tells me you were raving drunk from the first day of the voyage until the last."

"That is not quite fair. I did not begin to drink until we passed the Tropic of Cancer. I do not believe I raved." In the lengthening silence, he added, "I did not drink out of vice. I drank to forget my past folly."

Malherbe had a file before him bearing Jean-Patrice's name. His expression was cold. "I am not interested in your past follies, Duméril. The men who are sent here are almost invariably compromised at home. The scum of France is decanted on this shore to foam and froth."

Jean-Patrice felt his face flush hotly. "Monsieur le Directeur, I do not regard myself as scum."

"I am flattering you. The scum is that which is scraped from the top. The dregs are drawn from the bottom. We have both varieties here. In the colonial service, however, we are all assumed to begin with a clean slate. That slate must be kept clean. You may feel, when you reach Bassongo, that it is a place where indiscretions will not be noted. That could not be further from the truth. The forest has ears, Duméril."

"I understand."

"I would like to correct certain impressions you may have formed. You probably regard your posting to this continent as a punishment. It may not have occurred to you that far abler and more experienced men than you have been passed over for the appointment. Strings have been pulled on your behalf. There is considerable resentment against you in my department. With which sentiment, I might add, I have some sympathy."

"I am very grateful for the opportunity which—"

"Nor is this appointment a sinecure for the weak. If you continue to drink in the same fashion, the climate will kill you in three months."

"Sir, I intend—"

"Which might not provoke any overwhelming grief in the world at large, but which will cause even further inconvenience to France. Or is it of no use to appeal to your feelings of patriotism?"

"The drinking will stop," Jean-Patrice said. "And I am sincerely grateful for the opportunity to work in Gabon. If other men have been passed over, I will endeavor to demonstrate that my promotion was not unmerited."

Malherbe opened the file and used a desiccated flipper to sort through the pink sheets. "It is evident that you are a gifted young man. You took your degree well. You won competitions. The Minister awarded you the Silver Medal for your essay on Evolution."

"Yes," Jean-Patrice said. Those things seemed to have happened in another life.

"You were able to lay claim to administrative appointments. Your superiors have commended your diligence, your thoroughness and your wide interest in the sciences. So I ask you – for what is Gabon known?" While Jean-Patrice was still framing a sensible answer, Malherbe continued, "It is known for monkeys, cannibalism, a certain dark mahogany and an extremely poisonous viper with horns on its nose."

Relieved that his own faults were no longer under review, Jean-Patrice nodded solemnly and allowed his eyelids to droop a little. The days of drinking had left him with a constant throbbing in the temples and a feeling of exhaustion.

"It is one of these vipers, incidentally, which has bitten your predecessor in Bassongo, Hugo Joliet."

Jean-Patrice sat up a little straighter. "I'm sorry to hear that, Monsieur le Directeur. Is he...?"

"He is not dead. However, he has been somewhat indisposed. He is awaiting your arrival in order to hand over command before he goes on leave. He will introduce you to the local Chief. He will also show you around the district."

"I trust he will show me where the vipers are to be found," Jean-Patrice said, in an attempt at jocularity.

"The creature was in his bed."

"Ah."

Malherbe studied Jean-Patrice over the rims of his steel spectacles. "You appear vigorous enough. But it is what is upstairs that counts. It is customary for young men such as you to spend a few years of penance in Gabon and then to leave the country as ignorant as the day they arrived. I may add in passing that the training you received in Paris was utterly inadequate. I urge you to make some effort to understand the native mentality during the next two years. It will benefit you and perhaps also the natives under your command."

"I will try."

"There has been an outbreak of smallpox at Bassongo."

"Indeed?" Jean-Patrice smiled weakly. "The place appears to be a terrestrial paradise, Monsieur le Directeur."

"I do not see that it is a matter for inane humor. European traders, penetrating into the remote forest, brought the disease with them. As one interested in Science, you comprehend the nature of an epidemic?"

"A little."

"You understand what inoculation is?"

"Of course."

"You will be responsible for the inoculation of the village, which consists of some six hundred huts."

Jean-Patrice was taken aback. "Personally?"

"You will be shown how the vaccine is prepared and administered. It is a simple process. A child could do it. At Bassongo, you will choose a vaccinator from among the native population. You will, in turn, instruct this native in the procedures. It will be best to select from among those who were educated by the missionaries. Despite the dubious influence of the Church – all thinking men must surely be atheists, Duméril – they are the most assimilated of the natives."

"Is there likely to be any resistance?"

"Superstitious minds invariably resist progress. Yet what French child or adult does not nowadays bear the vaccination mark on his arm?" Malherbe lifted his sleeve to show the pitted mark. "This little badge is greater than any holy medal. It is the stamp of science. When men see that their children are no longer slain or disfigured by smallpox, they have proof undeniable. Not magic, Duméril. Not religion, or mumbo-jumbo or sorcery. Science! Through science, the white man conquers disease and death."

"But, Monsieur le Directeur, if there were to be any opposition—"

"You will command a unit of ten native policemen," Malherbe said. "They will know what to do."

"I see."

The instructions continued. Aside from the vaccination program, he was to encourage the native Gabonese in their progress towards civilization. He was to report any incidents that might disturb the peace of his district. He was to listen to the complaints and grievances of the local population and to inform Malherbe of all actions taken to redress those grievances.

There was no actual industry at Bassongo. Elephants were scarce, so the ivory trade was sporadic. The valuable okoume tree did not grow in the region; the nearest lumber camps were at Medoneu. There were no rubber plantations and the local bananas were not of export quality. The river ran past the village, but the landing was shallow. A road was being driven through the rainforest from Medoneu to Bassongo. When it reached Bassongo, the place would acquire much greater importance.

In the meantime, Bassongo was a tranquil backwater enlivened only by the smallpox outbreak and the presence of the Fang, invaders from the deep forest, whose predilections for witchcraft, cannibalism and conquest ran counter to the civilizing trend. The Fang interfered with the Beti; they stole the Beti women and ate their children and discouraged them in other ways. Should he encounter such incidents, he was to suppress them. Communication would not be difficult. After almost half a century of colonial rule, nearly every native in Gabon spoke at least some French. He was dismissed.

As he left the building at midday, he lit a cheroot to try to dispel the sense of doom which the interview had given him. He idled, watching stevedores loading the boats. The warehouses, filled with mahogany and ebony, ivory and bananas, rubber and cocoa, were evidence of the country's material richness. But the fabric of the little town was rotting clapboard and rusty tin, on the point of being swallowed by the rampant vegetation that took over where everything else left off. He did not yet have a sense of being fully in Africa. Rather, he seemed to be in some intermediate zone, where Europe was slowly being ingested into the dark continent, as the limbs of a gazelle might be seen disappearing into the body of a python.

He felt he was being suffocated with the heat and the humidity. His clothing was absurd. The European civilians he saw on the streets all wore sailor-like costumes of ducks and linen jackets. The white clothing appeared rather soiled – the pavements were mostly rickety boardwalks suspended over the churned mud of the streets – but at least seemed cool. There were few European women to be seen, most of them missionaries with complexions ruined by the climate. The native women were very colorful. Some wore long print dresses and colored scarves tied around their hair, which varied from long and fluffy to short and woolly; others wore fashionable European outfits and carried parasols. He found them generally to be very handsome, with full mouths and high and rounded cheekbones. They seemed proud, though some smiled at him. Were any of these women available? Were they the poisoned fruit of which Montpelier had spoken?

He paused in a market where native goods were being sold to languorous Europeans. There was woven cotton of surprisingly fine quality, ivory combs, gold jewelry of great delicacy and lightness, wooden sculptures of people and animals. His eye was caught by a model of a boat, very cleverly made. It represented a native canoe with several rowers. Each rower was ingeniously carved and could be removed from the boat, along with his oar. At the front of the boat was the self-important figure of a European, wearing a pith helmet and a bow tie. It had all been intricately painted and he was taken by its naïve charm. He bargained for the piece and bought it.

A heavy mist now descended, blotting out the higher parts of the town and bringing long, sweeping gusts of rain. No matter which way he held his umbrella, it was of no use. His clothing was soon soaked. His fashionable shoes let in the water. Looking down, he could see the shape of his feet in the lusterless and sodden leather, which felt fragile enough to tear. He had not come equipped in any way for Gabon.

When he reached the hotel, he was hungry and went to the dining room. The miasma from the kitchen was repulsive, making him stop in the doorway. A voice complained behind him,

"It smells like a whore's laundry."

He turned to glance at the speaker, a red haired man of about his own age, whose face bore the pits of severe acne. "It is not very alluring," he agreed.

"I'm going to get a beer and a sandwich in the bar."

He followed the stranger to the bar, a drab male retreat, paneled in the handsome, dark Gabon mahogany of which Malherbe had spoken. It smelled of extinguished pipes and spilled beer. Others had congregated there and were eating on their feet, propped against the bar in various negligent attitudes. He ordered a glass of wine, his first drink in three days. From beneath a glass bell, the barman produced sandwiches of tinned ham. They began to eat. His companion was wearing a crumpled linen suit of the sort he coveted.

"Where can I buy an outfit like yours?" he asked.

"This was made by a Chinese tailor in the next street, if you're so enchanted with the cut. You're Duméril, aren't you?"

Jean-Patrice winced. "You are about to tell me that my reputation has preceded me."

The other took a deep draft of his beer and wiped his ginger whiskers with a checked handkerchief. "I'm Tosti. I was in line for Joliet's post in Bassongo."

"I see. I'm sorry."

Tosti shrugged. "I suppose you'll be dead in six months and then I'll step into your shoes."

"Do I give so little appearance of fortitude? I wish for both our sakes I were not here to impede your career."

Tosti finished his sandwich in two gulps. "Come. I'll take you to the Chinese and see that he doesn't cheat you."

"Much obliged."

While the Chinese tailor took Jean-Patrice's measurements, Tosti prowled around the little shop, fingering the piles of fabric. "You made a fool of yourself over a married woman in Paris," he said in his abrupt way.

"So it seems."

"And your reward is Bassongo."

"You make it sound like Eldorado."

"I don't have your advantages in life," Tosti retorted. "My Eldorado is different from yours."

"I have had few advantages. I was orphaned as a child. My father left only enough money for me to be modestly educated."

"So who pulled the strings for you?"

"My mistress's husband."

"How comfortable." Tosti glanced at Jean-Patrice, who stood in his underclothes with his arms extended. "Yet you have advantages. You're built like Hercules and handsome enough to get a woman like that. I never will."

"I don't recommend the experience," Jean-Patrice said dryly. "My life has been ruined."

"Fellows like you are never ruined. You're froth, I'm dregs."

"I recognize the taxonomic classifications of Director Malherbe."

"Damn Malherbe."

Yet, as they got drunk together that afternoon and evening, he began to find it difficult to maintain the pose of a martyr. The frank envy which Tosti evinced for his exploits was consoling on one side. On the other, he was starting to feel that he had been something of a beast. He had been invited into decent homes, he the fatherless, the interloper. He had been made much of and praised for achievements which were, frankly speaking, well within his capabilities. He had gazed boldly on the wife of a grave and reverend signor and found her comely. He had sought her out in parks and other pleasances and had leaned over her, strewing the perfume of flattery. He had shown pretty attentions, given gifts, made assignations. He had, in short, seduced her for his pleasure and then been caught in his own honey. The mother of golden haired children!

The wife of a superior, whose graying temples he had desecrated with horns! Had he not deserved to do penance by bringing the salubrious light of science to those who dwelled in a great darkness?

Tosti, by contrast, had fled some provincial town after accumulating more debts than he could pay back. He had been engaged to a decent young woman, so he said, whom he had been forced to give up. She no longer answered his letters.

"They're beautiful, the native women," Jean-Patrice suggested to Tosti.

"You need money for these city women," Tosti replied glumly. "They're expensive. They wear the latest gowns and carry silk parasols. And if they get angry, they poison one. Up in the country, things are different. Malherbe is married to a mulatto, you know."

"Is he, indeed?"

"Ruined himself. Nobody has spoken to him outside the office for years."

"What's she like?"

"Never met her. But if you're in the mood, there's a house near the Battery. A German woman with a piano."

"Is she young?"

"About sixty. But jolly. You'll see. I'll take you there, at my expense, of course."

"Very kind of you."

A man who had been listening to their conversation, leaned over. "You're a lucky dog," he growled. "Bassongo is a plum. They leave you alone there. No telegraph. No railway."

"Nothing at all, in fact," Jean-Patrice said facetiously.

"And no damned missionaries."

"There used to be a mission there," Tosti explained, puffing on his cigarette. "A Belgian priest and some nuns. The priest died and the nuns went away."

"Better for you, Duméril," the other said. "Missionaries are trouble. The gunboat comes every month or two, if the captain feels like it. You're an Emperor."

"Over what?" Jean-Patrice said. "Over fever and savages?"

"Enjoy it while it lasts."

They drank to the new Century, approaching swiftly with all its freight of marvels and wonders. The bar began to clear at nine, leaving them clinging to the rail like the last survivors of a shipwreck. Jean-Patrice's head was throbbing, his diction slurred. "If Malherbe sees me like this, I'm through. I swore I wouldn't touch a drop."

"Damn Malherbe – and his mulatto wife."

Nevertheless, they retired to his room with a bottle of gin and passed successively through hilarity, melancholy and suicidal self-pity. Luckily, little furniture was damaged in the course of the evening and nobody complained of the noise. Long after Tosti had slumped, snoring in the armchair, Jean-Patrice remained awake, despairing. The only door where he could find solace for his pain was now closed to him forever. Love, he decided some time before dawn, was the most deadly of all diseases, far deadlier than the smallpox.

4

Malherbe presented him to one of the prophylactic calves the next day. It was a restless, piebald beast with a rolling eye and a liver colored muzzle which drooled copiously.

"It has been retro-vaccinated with the cow-pox bacillus, vaccinia," Malherbe said. He indicated the bluish vesicles all over the animal's small udders and belly. "This serum now contains the antitoxins which inoculate human beings against smallpox."

"By serum, you mean pus?" Jean-Patrice asked, studying the creature's festering pocks with some repugnance.

"Serum is the medical term," Malherbe snapped. "You yourself were inoculated as a child with this material, as was I and every other Frenchman alive."

"Yes, but I did not realize ... well, you may call it serum, Monsieur le Directeur, but it is pus in layman's terms, is it not?"

Malherbe was increasingly annoyed. "The vaccine is a precious gift from Nature herself, Duméril. The English practice vaccination using human lymph, thereby transmitting scrofula, tuberculosis, syphilis, leprosy, diphtheria and other hereditary taints throughout their unfortunate population. The inhabitants of the British Isles will probably be extinct in a generation or two, or reduced to a degenerate race of shambling and diseased imbeciles. We use only calf lymph, which carries no contamination. Now, please attend."

A state trained native vaccinator was on hand to demonstrate the process. He was an androgynous young man of about twenty-two or twenty-three named Albert, the product of a mission education and as assimilated as Malherbe could wish, wearing French clothes and horn rimmed spectacles through which he peered admiringly at Jean-Patrice's height and profile. He displayed the instruments of his mystery: tools for scraping serum from the calf, phials for separating it into doses, glycerin for preserving it, cases of lancets with which to scratch the arms of his subjects. Jean-Patrice dubiously inspected a tube of prepared serum.

"And they accept this willingly?"

Albert pouted. "It is sometimes necessary to explain certain things. But they accept willingly, Monsieur." However, on closer examination, it emerged that Albert had never taken part in any mass inoculation of tribal peoples. His patients had been restricted to the parasol carrying citizens of Libreville.

"What if they refuse?" Jean-Patrice pressed Malherbe.

"In Europe, the scourge of smallpox has died out in exact proportionality to the generalization of efficient vaccination. The same phenomenon will doubtless become apparent here in Africa. What mind could be so primitive, so resistant to logic, so trammeled in superstition and darkness as to deny such evidence?"

"Indeed," he murmured, reflecting that since the smallpox had been brought by whites in the first place, the privilege might not be so apparent to certain obstinate minds.

It was Jean-Patrice's turn to draw serum from the calf under the critical eyes of Malherbe and Albert. The creature's hooves were tied and it was laid on its side, gasping hoarsely and looking outraged at this indignity. As Jean-Patrice inserted the scraper into an especially nasty-looking pustule on the animal's belly, it uttered a hopeless cry, which echoed around the shed where it was kept.

"I think I am hurting her," he said.

"She is only calling for her mother," Albert tittered. The glass collecting tube filled with yellowish, bloodstained pus. "Good, good!" Albert said, and when Jean-Patrice pricked his finger and sucked it, slapped his wrist playfully. "Monsieur must not suck unless Monsieur wishes to risk a vaccinial eruption!" Albert was enough of an assimilé to make no bones of his effeminacy, Jean-Patrice reflected.

Over the next days, Jean-Patrice learned how to separate the serum into doses by drawing it up into small, capillary glass tubes, each containing enough to treat one person. The tubes were sealed with glycerin to prevent contamination. He also learned how to administer the vaccine. Some rather sullen natives were on hand for him to practice upon. There were various techniques, he learned. The lancet could be dipped into the serum before making a cut on the arm of the patient, for example. Or a puncture could be made with an ivory instrument and the serum rubbed into the wound. It was not necessary to make a deep incision. A superficial incision was sufficient. His natives submitted to his attempts grudgingly.

"Monsieur will be issued with an official calf of his own and a supply of vaccine," Albert told him. "When all is ready, Monsieur will vaccinate the calf. In a few days, the vesicles will appear. When they are ripe, the vaccine can be collected."

"The creature becomes a mobile medicine cabinet, Duméril," Malherbe said, his spectacles glittering. "You will in time train several vaccinators, who can reach the more remote areas."

The image persisted in Jean-Patrice's mind of eager, assimilated natives wandering the forests of Gabon with lancet in hand and drooling calf behind. The process, as Malherbe had said, presented little to challenge to the intellect. It was the ease of eventual administration which carried a question mark.

"If the calf should recover, die or run away," Albert pointed out, "Monsieur can make another official calf by vaccinating it with the serum."

"It is an endless chain of science," Malherbe said.

An endless chain of pus, Jean-Patrice thought. The mechanics of inoculation were less edifying than he had assumed.

He remained in Libreville a week. On Saturday night he accompanied Tosti (as his guest) to the house of the German woman, Fräulein Hanne, whom he did not find jolly at all, though she was certainly fat and able to play Träumerei with a wistful air on an out-of-tune piano. They tossed a coin for first go. Tosti won and Jean-Patrice sat drinking his Bock in the parlor. He was growing bored with Libreville and becoming impatient to go upcountry. The sooner he began the sooner he might be sent back to France. He was learning to suppress his thoughts of Justine. He simply forced his mind to stay away from the subject, directing it to anything else, no matter how banal. It was the only way to survive – not to think of her at all. It was a policy from which he expected some success.

Tosti emerged gloomily from the bedchamber, fastening up his pants. "Couldn't do anything," he said. "Don't know what's wrong with me."

With a feeling of resignation, Jean-Patrice drained his glass and went into the boudoir. Fräulein Hanne was reclining on the bed. She had changed into a negligée. One large breast spilled from the top and the bottom had been drawn up to reveal a sparse nest of blonde curls between her fat thighs. "Come, liebchen," she said. "Show me what you've got." She was pinching with her finger and thumb in a little flat tin, ogling him in a way that might have been comical, had he been feeling gayer. With a sigh, he unbuttoned himself.

"Oh, such a lovely schwanz." She snorted snuff into both nostrils and rolled her eyes back in pleasure at the action of the tobacco. Her body was as smooth and plump as a blancmange. She crawled across the bed to him on all fours and took him in her mouth. Her tongue was warm and busy. Jean-Patrice attempted to believe that there was something erotic in her ministrations. She disgorged him to sneeze loudly, twice, then resumed.

"Thank you, but I don't think I'm in the mood, after all," he said courteously after a decent interval.

"Don't be discouraged, liebchen. Look what you are missing." She lay back and spread open her sex with her fingertips. It had all the appearance of a well-cared-for organ. "Look closer. Don't be shy." He tried to imagine the moist, pink thing lodged in another body, belonging to another woman, the entrance to another soul. "There you are," she said. His schwanz had risen to the occasion. He settled on her. She guided him inside. "That's my boy. After all, I am the last white woman you will see in a year or more. Off you go."

"Thank you." He pumped away without any great enthusiasm, trying not to remember that all of Libreville had been here before him. Somewhat to his own surprise, he felt his climax approaching.

"That's right," Fräulein Hanne cooed. "Are you going to do your business inside or out?"

"What's the difference?"

"Inside is five francs more."

Mindful that Tosti was paying for the evening's entertainment, he gasped, "Outside, then."

"Schön. Eins, zwei, drei." A short while later she coaxed a copious – and as it turned out, surprisingly expensive – ejaculation from him onto the wobbly pudding of her belly.

"She charged me full rate even though I didn't do anything," Tosti complained as they walked back to the hotel to get drunk. "I take it you managed to perform?"

Jean-Patrice was feeling melancholy after the event. "I thought of Justine."

"And I have sponsored your orgasm. Really, my dear fellow, you have quite a knack of getting others to pay for your pleasures."

"Don't be unreasonable, Tosti. You invited me. And I was as economical as I could be."

His last meeting with Malherbe, shortly before his departure for Bassongo, was more inspiring than the first had been. Malherbe took the opportunity to expound his generally optimistic views of Africa.

"Africa is the continent of the future, Duméril. The vastness of its mineral resources, the beneficence of its climate, the innocence of its peoples, the richness of its soil, its accessibility to trade, all proclaim this. In fifty years, perhaps less, this continent will have become the New Eden. It will be rich beyond the dreams of the present, its people blessed with health and wisdom. One must believe, of course, in the Africans' capacity to be civilized. I do so, passionately. I see it everywhere. There are obstacles, of course. The invasions of the Fang, the persistence of ancient evil. Africa is not so big since the Germans arrived, shouldering us at every turn. The sacrifice is great but the altar is a noble one, Duméril. Do you not believe it?"

"Yes, Monsieur le Directeur, I believe it," he said. But as he did so, he doubted that he would ever share either Malherbe's idealism or the rapacious greed of those who had built the warehouses on the docks.

Malherbe favored Jean-Patrice with his humorless smile. "I'm sure that Tosti and the others have congratulated you on securing a post which appears to offer ample scope for idleness and sloth. I leave you with this thought — that every position in life offers as much opportunity for achievement as the holder chooses to grasp for himself. I commend to you a little courage, a little persistence, a little diligence. And—" He raised an admonitory flipper. "A little abstinence."

The smoke-blackened gunboat had chugged down the river a day or two earlier and was now ready to depart again. Jean-Patrice's belongings were carried on board. His very own prophylactic calf, known only as No. 5 (which was branded on her rump) was hoisted onto the deck, wailing, and penned behind the wheelhouse. Tosti, who had taken an unaccountable liking to Jean-Patrice, came to see him off. There was a heavy swell on the river. Jean-Patrice clung to the stern machine gun mounting and watched his friend's figure receding on the quayside. Tosti waved his checked handkerchief, appearing now and then to apply it to his eyes. Then the boat rounded the first bend in the river. A luxuriant green python swallowed Tosti, Libreville and the wider world beyond.

5

The journey to Bassongo took eight days. In that time, Jean-Patrice had an opportunity to appreciate some of the difficulties of climate and geography which Gabon presented.

The coastal area had been a paradise. The hinterland was dense and wet beyond any imagining. The heat which had been supportable in Libreville became, with this humidity, steadily unbearable. The river was majestically broad at first, its banks relatively clear of vegetation. There was evidence of human life to be seen – crops, sometimes a handful of dugout canoes spread like the fingers of a languid hand on the bank, sometimes settlements of low huts, whose children waved and called in shrill voices. But as the stream narrowed and grew deeper, these reassuring signs vanished. The river began to be hemmed in by towering walls of rainforest, monotonous and suffocating. Huge trees shot into the sky. The gloom beneath them was choked with undergrowth, tangled, untidy and dense. At times they had to pass so close to the banks that branches scraped the sides of the boat, darting through any open porthole into the cabins and leaving green leaves scattered on the bunks.

Crocodiles and hippos slid off sandbanks at their approach. Occasionally they would encounter natives in dugout canoes, selling fish or fruit. It rained several times each day, drenching squalls that brought a little temporary relief from the heat; but the subsequent humidity was an even greater torment. There seemed to be no air to breathe. It was sucked out of the lungs, leaving one gasping and exhausted by the slightest movement.

They reached confluences which revealed to Jean-Patrice that the land through which they were travelling consisted of an archipelago of densely vegetated islands caught in a web of rivers, lagoons, creeks, swamps and other waterways, made turgid by the incessant rain. It was bewildering. Even the pilot of the gunboat, a native in a soiled uniform, often appeared to lose his way, necessitating a laborious retreat from streams which grew hopelessly shallow or choked with vegetation. Perhaps he was incompetent; or perhaps the country itself changed endlessly as the water shaped it, and was never the same two weeks running.

The calf occasionally had paroxysms of bawling, extending a violet tongue and rolling her eyes back in her head. Nothing Jean-Patrice could do appeared to comfort her.

The commander of the gunboat, a grizzled shellback in his fifties, showed no interest in Jean-Patrice and curtly rejected all attempts to open a conversation. It was hard to imagine that this impassable forest could harbor any human enemy, but he scanned the banks constantly through his binoculars and kept the small cannon and the machine guns manned.

"Is there any danger?" Jean-Patrice asked the gunnery lieutenant, a younger man who was a little more disposed to talk.

"The Fang are on the move," the lieutenant replied and was apparently pleased with the dramatic sound of this proclamation, for he repeated it before strutting away.

Jean-Patrice found a little shade under the drooping tricolor and wiped his face with his handkerchief. His new suit of pale linen was crumpled and malodorous already; likewise his panama hat. Insects of countless variety and monstrous size maddened him. If Justine could see him now! His policy of not allowing her to enter his thoughts, successful for the last few days, broke down. He imagined her, cool and exquisite, bestowing her promises on some new favorite. Some creature scuttled along his scalp. He snatched off his hat and crumpled it in his hands, wishing on her a hideous old age, malignant diseases. She had sent him into this stinking hell to rot and die, unseen and unmourned. He saw himself wasting of some tropical malady while savages with filed teeth jeered at him; or raising his trembling revolver to his own temple in the woeful hours before dawn. It was nothing short of murder.

Bassongo, however, eventually materialized some three hundred miles up the river, a rickety landing built on a shoal of sand, with straggling huts behind. The water at the landing was too shallow for the little gunboat's draft, so it moored out in the channel. A flotilla of dugout canoes streamed across the river towards them.

"That scoundrel Joliet will be around somewhere," the young lieutenant informed him. "We'll be back to pick him up in a month. Good luck with the vaccinations." He chuckled a little. Jean-Patrice shook hands with the commander and his officer and clambered gingerly into one of the canoes. After the stable deck of the gunboat, it rolled alarmingly. No. 5 was now lowered into the river, bawling piteously, lifting her face above the water in terror. Jean-Patrice clung to the animal's halter from a dugout beside it, and so they proceeded to the landing in a zigzag fashion, the calf paddling wildly in one direction and the natives rowing determinedly in another.

Looking back, Jean-Patrice saw that the dugouts were having difficulty with the bulky boxes. One of his portmanteaus fell in the river. Luckily, it floated and was recovered. Far more seriously, the large government trunk also fell into the river, where it sank like a stone and vanished. Natives paddled around the spot, peering down and chattering, but displayed no inclination to enter the brown water. It had contained tinned provisions, medicines, most of the lancets and phials for the inoculation program, the revolver and all the bullets. This grave loss was inauspicious. The gunboat had already retreated around the bend and there was no help to be expected from that quarter.

By the time he reached the landing, a welcome party had been assembled. In place of the ten native policemen he had been promised, there appeared to be only three, standing to attention in uniforms of shorts and baggy shirts with epaulettes. They were barefoot and carried sticks as though they were rifles. There were also eight or nine women from mid-teens to middle-age, who sang and clapped melodiously. Their beaming smiles revealed that none had filed teeth. To the contrary, their teeth were more perfect than any Frenchwoman's he could recall. All wore long print skirts but some were naked from the waist up. Their breasts swung in time to their movements. He tried not to stare. Days had passed since Fräulein Hanne and he was keenly aware of his carnal lusts. Were any of these ladies available? Was this Malherbe's poisoned fruit? There was no sign of Joliet. He stood to attention beside the shuddering calf, watching the performance as gravely as he could. When the song came to an end amid scattered laughter, many of the women picked up infants and began to nurse them, smiling shyly at him.

An African man now approached him, carrying his wide-brimmed hat in both hands. Like the others, he was barefoot but wore long trousers and a white jacket buttoned up to the neck. He had marshaled the three policemen behind him.

"I am Raymond Mbangu. I am head servant of the

Residency. Welcome to Bassongo."

"Delighted to meet you." Jean-Patrice extended his hand. The man seemed surprised by the gesture but took Jean-Patrice's fingers in a limp and cool-palmed salutation. In turn, he presented the three policemen. "Hyppolite Mokamo is the corporal. These are Hyacinth and Narcise Raponda." The men saluted smartly. Jean-Patrice shook hands with each of them.

"I thought there were supposed to be ten?"

"There has been illness, patron. And accidents."

"I see. And Monsieur Joliet?" he enquired.

Raymond smiled and made a courteous gesture. "I take you to him." At his command, the porters hoisted Jean-Patrice's luggage and followed them. Mbangu wore a moustache and had a parting carefully shaved into his hair, producing a spuriously European stamp. His features were large and somewhat frog-like, with protruding lips and bulging eyes. His naked feet were also large, with splayed toes.

"Is Monsieur Joliet still sick?"

Raymond laughed heartily. "Oh no, patron. Monsieur Joliet is a very strong man. He is completely better."

"I'm glad to hear it. Did he arrange the singing for me?"

"Those are my wives," the other man said, beaming.

"What! All of them?"

"Yes, patron. All of them."

"And your children, I presume?"

"And my children, yes. I am not Gabonese, patron. I am Loango, from Moyen Congo. I bring my family with me."

"I congratulate you on your family." No poisoned fruit there, then. Jean-Patrice felt dejection close in on him. Bassongo could not be called anything but a wretched hole. The dwellings were all in native style. The disintegrated state of many allowed him to see exactly how they had been constructed – unbaked clay plastered onto a bamboo framework and roofed with raffia palm fronds. Among the puddles and the mud, chickens, goats and a few pigs wandered.

The opposite bank of the river was hemmed in by a high, rugged cliff, richly overgrown with luxuriant vegetation which had taken root in every crevice and break, festooning the sandy stone with fronds and ferns and trees, some of whose branches cascaded almost down to the surface of the water while others blotted out the sky above. The looming presence of this natural feature lent the village a somewhat oppressive atmosphere. And he was to remain here for two years! He, the silver medalist, habitué of the opera and the theatre, the symphony and the lofty, echoing public library, a man of culture and taste!

"My trunk fell in the river," Jean-Patrice said gloomily to the large corporal.

"I saw. Very sorry, Monsieur le Commissaire." His voice was deep.

"It's extremely urgent that we recover it as soon as possible."

The corporal's face was blank. "Yes, Monsieur le Commissaire."

It was easy to tell Hugo Joliet's house – it was the only two-story building in the village, a fortress-like structure made of grey mud bricks with small windows and a rusty tin roof, no doubt brought at considerable expense from Libreville. It had a small garden with a mud brick wall. Also, there was a six-pounder cannon outside. This piece of ordnance, with its huge wheels and corroded barrel, appeared to date to the Napoleonic period. The house was dark and relatively cool. His trunks were set down with a crash on the wooden floor, but there was still no sign of Joliet. Raymond led him up the staircase. In contrast to the humble materials of the walls and roof, all the woodwork in the Residency was well carved from black mahogany heartwood, including the staircase, the doors, and the four poster bed where Joliet lay.

The fetor in the room was overwhelming. Jean-Patrice realized he had smelled it from outside the house and had assumed it arose from the rotting soil. Joliet was almost naked. His body was skeletal, the midsection sunken between the cliffs of the ribs and the pelvis, the arms dangling like sticks. Jean-Patrice felt with a thrill of horror that the man was already dead, until he slowly turned his gaunt face away from the wall to face the room. His eyes were points of dull light in dark hollows.

"Thank God," he whispered on seeing Jean-Patrice.

"My dear fellow, this is dreadful," Jean-Patrice exclaimed, seeing that the right leg ended at a filthy bundle of rags around the knee. The surviving thigh was dark red, with black tendrils extending under the skin from the amputation, like primitive tattoos, crawling up the pale body. Another filthy bundle covered Joliet's genitals. Crouching on the floor at the side of the bed was an African child who held a glass of water. She lifted Joliet's head carefully with one hand and gave him the water. He wet his lips and made a gesture with one arm, the hand inert.

"Sorry about the stink. Blood poisoning."

"I have morphine in my baggage," Jean-Patrice said, remembering helplessly as he said the words that the trunk in question was now at the bottom of the river.

"No pain. Anyway, have some morphine left. Sit, Duméril."

Jean-Patrice took a chair. "Thank you."

"Cover your nose."

"If you don't mind, I will," he replied and pressed his handkerchief to his nostrils.

Joliet continued to stare at him with sunken eyes, his emaciated face stretched in a kind of smile. "Don't be perturbed. On the mend now. Viper bite, you know."

"They told me. In your bed?"

Joliet nodded slowly. "Put there."

"Deliberately?" Jean-Patrice said in revulsion.

"I believe so."

"By whom?"

Joliet closed his lids. They were so thin that Jean-Patrice could see the other man's irises slowly moving around beneath them, examining the images his thoughts produced. Jean-Patrice was so convinced that the man's death was imminent that he remained in his chair even when Joliet's breathing indicated he had slipped into unconsciousness. While he waited for the man to wake or breathe his last, Jean-Patrice looked around the room. Wasps had built dozens of mud nests in the high corners, on the roof beams and against the glass of the little windows. He could see the insects darting to and fro and wondered how poisonous their sting was. Geckoes scuttled upside down. Floating strands of gossamer from countless cobwebs glistened as they caught the light. There was a large cupboard and a dressing table but little other furniture.

He looked at the child beside Joliet's bed. She squatted on her hunkers, never taking her large, liquid eyes from Joliet's face. She wore a green dress printed with red roses. There was something quietly desperate about her pose and the intentness of her expression. He looked over his shoulder. Raymond Mbangu was standing patiently at the door, wearing a polite smile. His confidence in the strength of his employer appeared sadly misplaced.

Jean-Patrice was himself floating into sleep when Joliet awoke. Again, the girl gave him a tiny sip of water. He laid his hand, dark red and unnaturally large because of the thinness of his arm, on the girl's head.

"She is called Sophie," he said, holding Jean-Patrice's gaze. "Look after her."

"I will."

"Best solution, Duméril. Suits everyone. You'll see."

"Don't worry, Joliet." Anxious that these cryptic speeches appeared to be exhausting Joliet's meager store of energy, Jean-Patrice rose and carefully lifted the bandages around the other man's stump. What he saw made his gorge heave. "Who performed the amputation?"

"Schultze. German doctor. We're close to the border here. He'll pass by in a month or two."

"The infection is overwhelming your body. You should have gone back to Libreville on the gunboat. If only it had stayed a few hours."

"Makes no difference." He still had his hand on Sophie's head. "She's a good girl. They take care of it. If she becomes pregnant."

"Pregnant?"

"She goes away. A few days. Comes back right as rain."

He glanced at the child. "My dear fellow, I don't think..."

"Best solution," Joliet repeated, becoming agitated. He tried to raise one crimson hand. "Listen to me. She was chosen."

"Calm yourself." Jean-Patrice sat back down, blocking his nose with the handkerchief again. He stared at the fragile line of Sophie's neck. Could this child possibly be Joliet's concubine? She seemed hardly more than thirteen, her slender body crouched like a gazelle hiding from danger. The dress with its gay roses seemed suddenly pitiful to him. He wondered if she had ever seen a rose, or ever would. The girl's hair had been teased into a fluffy halo. The ends had been bleached, perhaps by the sun, to a reddish brown. He noticed tears sliding down her smooth cheeks and realized that Joliet had died.

"Shit," he said.

He got up and inspected Joliet, trying to still his rising panic. There was no doubt about it. The girl Sophie was crying silently but bitterly, clinging to the bony red hand of the dead man. Raymond appeared genuinely surprised. He had come forward and was looking down at Joliet, scratching his cheek and repeating the word, "Sorry," quietly at intervals.

Jean-Patrice wandered around the Residency, feeling dazed. What was he to do? The rooms were high ceilinged but largely empty. There was a second bedroom, a bed made up in it with a mosquito net, evidently for his own use. Someone had taken the trouble to remove most of the wasp's nests. The mud crust outlines remained on the walls and beams. In this place he was destined to spend months, years, perhaps the rest of his life. One day it would be his emaciated corpse lying on a bed, wept over by a corrupted child.

Something grunted and shuffled. He suddenly became aware that there was another presence in the room. He glimpsed a hideously deformed individual with a grotesque face, attempting to conceal itself behind a cupboard. He exclaimed in horror, his skin crawling. The misshapen creature scrabbled away, using its great strength to pull the cupboard in front of it.

He turned and encountered the burly figure of Hyppolite, the corporal, who had come up behind him. "There's someone behind the cupboard!"

"Monsieur le Commissaire, it is Chloë."

"Who is Chloë?"

"She is a gorilla. A young female. Hunters shot the mother. Monsieur Joliet bought the baby. He has raised it himself."

"My God." He peered around the cupboard, seeing a brawny back covered in dense, dark fur. He recoiled. "This is horrible."

"Monsieur le Commissaire, we must bury Monsieur Joliet."

"Immediately?"

"Tomorrow will be too late. He is already—" Hyppolite made a curt gesture and touched his nose.

"And the gorilla?"

"She will not do anything. She is civilized."

The word seemed an extraordinary one to him. "Civilized?"

"Nobody can come back to the village until Monsieur Joliet is buried. It is bad for him to stay. Very bad."

"Very well," Jean-Patrice said, feeling that he was in some endless nightmare. "Let's bury Joliet."

6

It had begun to rain again. Jean-Patrice stood huddled in his cape, watching Hyacinth, Hyppolite and Narcise dig in the red earth behind the village. About fifty of the villagers had come, the women wailing, the men impassive. It was not a very great turnout, he thought, for the representative of the colonial authority. Perhaps Joliet had not been admired. Or perhaps this immense forest was indifferent to the death of yet another white man.

Joliet's body had been sewn into a canvas parcel. He helped the policemen lower it into the pit, which had already started to fill with water. He climbed out of the grave and heard himself intoning the Lord's prayer, then the Hail Mary. He paused and looked around. Rain poured from a sky like mother-of-pearl. There were crosses to be seen here and there, sagging at crazy angles, but no names were written on them. He wondered how many of his predecessors were interred in this place. Perhaps all the District Commissioners of Bassongo lay in this red earth. The next grave would probably be his. Raymond stood holding his hat, staring into the hole, still with the air of one taken unawares. Jean-Patrice noticed Sophie behind him, crouching as she had done beside

Joliet's deathbed. She was holding the huge leaf of some forest plant over her head like an umbrella. He could not see whether she was still weeping but he suspected she was. In the more distant gloom, he could see the figures of others, their faces monstrous, with huge eyes and snarling mouths. Were they wearing masks? Headdresses? The rain intensified, blotting the vision out.

"That's it," he said to Hyppolite. "All over." He took a shovel and threw the first clod of mud onto the corpse. The others joined in quickly. Joliet's mortal remains disappeared into the clay.

An elderly, important-looking man was now ushered forward by Raymond, wearing a long cloak embroidered with shells and beads. Several younger men vied with each other to hold umbrellas over the dignitary's grizzled head. A heavy metal chain hung around his neck.

"The chief of the district," Raymond said. "Chief Obangui."

Jean-Patrice took the old man's hand in his. "A pity we meet on such a melancholy occasion." One of the young men, whom Jean-Patrice took to be his sons, translated this greeting. "Tell the Chief I would be honored if he would come back to the house. We can talk out of the rain, at least."

The old man assented to this and they tramped out of the muddy graveyard to the Residency. Jean-Patrice decided to hold the audience on the veranda, where a group of imposing chairs in native style were grouped. He investigated Joliet's cupboards and discovered in a cabinet some bottles of British gin, all unopened. Whatever his other vices had been, Joliet had not been a drunkard. "Bring these," he instructed Raymond. "And some glasses."

The meeting was cordial. They drank several glasses of neat gin. Obangui's eyes began to shine in their nests of wrinkles. Jean-Patrice felt his head spinning. The Chief's sons watched him constantly. They carried short swords at their sides. Should they wish to, he reflected under the influence of the gin, they could in a moment dismember him and throw his limbs into the river. It was rather puzzling that they did not. Perhaps they thought that his head, like Orpheus's, might sail down to Libreville, singing a tale of murder, and bring the boat with its Maxim gun and cannon.

He took the opportunity to ask the Chief whether there were any complaints he should deal with. The Chief waved this away and extended commiserations, through his sons, for the untimely death of Joliet. Jean-Patrice thanked him and expressed the hope that the government of Bassongo could be conducted prosperously between the tribal authority and the colonial power. Obangui endorsed this wish with a dry and ironic smile. It seemed to Jean-Patrice that they were soon on good terms despite the somber nature of the occasion.

"I intend to begin the vaccination program as soon as I can train a vaccinator," Jean-Patrice announced. "It had occurred to me that it might encourage the people if the Chief himself were to be the first to be inoculated."

"What does that mean?"

He explained about the incision and the pus. There was some confabulation. The Chief glared at Jean-Patrice and declined the invitation indignantly. Feeling that this had been a social gaffe of the worst sort, Jean-Patrice apologized hastily.

Later, when Obangui and his sons had gone, he regretted not having made Joliet's funeral more impressive. He could have read, at least, a verse from the Bible. Events had overtaken him, as they had done Raymond. He went to see about accommodation for the official calf. Raymond showed him a stall which had been prepared in the rickety stable where Joliet's horse was also housed. Jean-Patrice had been told that horses lived no more than two years in the country. This one appeared to be reaching the end of its tenure; it was painfully thin, its hammer head hanging down, its hoofs in a decayed state with the wet.

He recalled his own glossy bay mare in Paris, which he had been forced to sell before coming to Africa. How proud he had been of her, how proudly he had proclaimed himself a judge of horseflesh! How carefully he had taken care of her with his own capable hands. This was a sorry bag of bones, painfully reflecting his changed circumstances.

The only fodder he found prepared was a mess of green, wet vegetation, obviously recently cut. There was neither hay nor straw. "This food is unsuitable," he told Raymond. "That's why she's so thin. She needs proper fodder, or she'll starve. So will the calf. Is there corn grown locally?"

"Yes."

"We'll need a few buckets to start with." He examined the horse. The animal, a mare, had in addition to its state of malnutrition a number of swollen, festering abscesses all over her body. She was so weak that she barely flinched as Jean-Patrice probed these. One of the few heirlooms that had been handed down to him was a family Bible with gloomy engravings, whose fly leaf recorded the births and deaths of Dumérils going back to the 17th Century, the deaths of his own parents making the latest entries. This creature resembled the steeds the engraver had assigned to the Four Horsemen of The Apocalypse.

"The road," he asked, "from which direction is it coming?"

Raymond gestured to the north. "From Medoneu."

"How far away is it now?"

"Close."

"Can we walk there?"

"Too far. But the patron can take the horse and see for himself."

"The horse? She would die if she had to carry me a hundred yards."

"Oh no, patron," Raymond said cheerfully, "this is a very strong animal."

Jean-Patrice glanced at him ironically. "If I ever hear you say that about me, I will know my time has come."

Raymond chuckled. "Yes, patron."

He looked around. The sun was setting behind the great trees, staining the sky the colour of fish blood. Darkness was coming. "My damned trunk!"

"In the river, patron."

"I know that. It must be got out of the river."

"It is lost."

"Can't the policemen get it up?"

Raymond spread his hands. "Sorry. The local men believe there are evil spirits in the water. They cannot swim there."

"There are medicines in the trunk. And all the tins." He did not mention the brandy or the revolver.

"Sorry, patron."

"Where are the nearest whites?"

"In Medoneu."

"Is there nobody any closer?"

Raymond gestured. "Germans, across the border. They come, sometimes."

He sighed. "Who were those people at the cemetery?"

"Which people?"

"The men wearing masks and long cloaks."

Raymond looked sly. "I did not see, patron."

They went back to the Residency. Some women had come into the kitchen. He could hear them chattering and laughing as they cooked. The smells that emerged were strange and uninviting. Raymond lit some palm oil lamps and began to lay the table. Jean-Patrice poured himself a large glass of gin. He shook bitters into the spirit and drank it neat, standing at the small window. A few flickers of cooking fires were visible in the darkness outside. He felt exhausted.

A soft grunt made him turn around. He had forgotten

the gorilla. The creature was in the doorway, leaning its weight on its knuckles and brawny forearms. Its small, introspective eyes met his for a moment, then it looked away, smacking its lips. He called for Raymond to deal with it.

"She does not like to be alone," Raymond said. "She always ate with Monsieur Joliet. Now she misses him."

"Oh, God."

The gorilla shambled forward and hauled itself into a chair at the table. She sat looking around as though in truth expecting her former master to appear.

"You see?" Raymond said, smiling brightly.

"I would like her taken away."

"She will cry, patron."

"Let her cry. Lock her up."

"She will break the door."

The creature was quite large and no doubt extremely powerful, even though it was a juvenile. Chimpanzees, he had heard, made lively and intelligent pets which could be trained to perform before an audience. This gorilla seemed neither lively nor intelligent. It presented a melancholy aspect, with its massive brow and its face like a Greek tragic actor's mask, made of black leather and stitched onto the body of a wrestler. The huge, gaping nostrils and sad eyes were those of some remote ancestor of Man, left behind by the process of Evolution. It was pathetic and terrible. He noticed that there were flat, hairy but unmistakably female breasts with sloe-like nipples on the burly chest. Jean-Patrice averted his gaze from the horrible sight. "Does she bite?"

"She never bit Monsieur Joliet."

"What does she eat?"

"She likes milk and bananas."

"She is not carnivorous?"

"No, patron. She eats very little. Supper is ready."

He sat at Joliet's – his – table to be served. He was now the Commissioner of Bassongo, lord of all he had

44

found in this house of horrors. There would be no transitional period. It behooved him to acquire the dignity of the position. He would eat many more meals in this dark room. He composed himself to present an appearance of authority, his back straight, facing the gorilla.

Chloë was served first, he noted. A bowl of warm milk and a hand of bananas were placed in front her. She lifted the bowl and sipped the milk slowly and loudly. His own meal was a kind of stew. He took a mouthful. It was the most unappetizing thing he had yet eaten in Gabon.

"What meat is this?"

Raymond searched for the French word but could not find it. He bared his incisors and imitated the motion of some scurrying, questing animal.

"Pig?" Jean-Patrice suggested.

"Not pig, patron." He went into the kitchen and came back with a long, black-and-white striped quill.

Jean-Patrice touched the needle tip. "Porcupine?"

"Yes, patron. Porcupine."

"I saw pigs and chickens in the village."

"But those are for weddings." His expression said that the white man's appetite would empty the village of livestock in a week. "Very expensive. The hunters bring bushmeat. Much cheaper."

"Antelope?" Jean-Patrice suggested hopefully.

Raymond groped for the French words. "Monkey, lizard, snake, bird, frog and what-what." He glanced at Chloë somewhat apologetically. "Also gorilla. They find many animals in the forest. They smoke them over sticks and bring them here."

That explained the tarry quality. "Are there fish in the river?"

"Yes."

"Please get some fresh fish for me for tomorrow, Raymond. And take this away."

He sat with his gin, watching the gorilla eat. Apart

from her slurping, her manners were almost dainty. She ingested everything slowly and apparently with little appetite. When she'd finished the milk, she peeled a banana with her teeth, which he saw with some consternation were huge and very sharp. She exuded a faint smell, mammalian and not altogether inhuman. She avoided his eyes. He tried to find something companionable about her presence. Perhaps once he had learned not to be afraid of her, he thought, it might be almost like having a large dog which insisted on a place at the table.

Raymond brought him coffee. "Tomorrow we will raise my trunk from the bottom of the river," he said. He'd become aware of the distant sound of a drum beating out a strange rhythm in the night. "What is that sound?"

"It is the talking drum, patron. The witchdoctor's drummer is telling the people that Monsieur Joliet is dead and that you have come."

"Do those beats signify words?"

"Exactly, patron."

He found the beat disturbing. It seemed to tickle something deep in his chest in a way he did not like. He drank the coffee, left Chloë with her bananas and took the bottle of gin up to his room, deciding that a little Dutch courage would be necessary to face the coming night.

He examined the bed minutely for snakes. Finding none, he climbed in with the bottle. He lay back on the musty pillow and stared up into the darkness, fighting down the sense of panic that had awakened in him again. He was troubled by the idea that, in the darkness, hostile things had begun to creep towards him on all sides. It was a childhood fear that had returned in full adult force. He must ignore this foolish delusion.

Geckoes and other creatures scrabbled for survival among the beams. The drumming continued in the distance, riding up and down the scale in complex patterns. The witchdoctor was finding a great deal to say. A large moth flew into his face, brushing him with the powder from its wings.

He could hear a man's voice murmuring in the house. At first he assumed it was Raymond's. Then, with a shock, it dawned on him that the voice was coming from Joliet's room and that the voice was Joliet's voice – or rather, Joliet's croak. He recognized it. His skin crawled in horror.

Absurd, he told himself. Joliet was lying in the mud in that forlorn graveyard. This was the thrumming of some insect. Or the wind in the roof. Yet it seemed to him that Joliet's dry voice murmured on, giving instructions or orders in the darkness. He had heard of men who, though dead, were reluctant to quit their old places and occasions, who returned from the other world, unquiet spirits. But these were absurd tales.

A click at the door made him sit up, his heart thudding. Something was slithering towards him. This was no delusion. He groped for the friction flashlight at his bedside and wound the handle. He switched it on. The dim beam illuminated the figure of the girl, Sophie. She was naked. He saw that although her breasts were childlike, the hair between her legs was an adult tangle.

"Sophie!"

She stared at him for a moment, then came forward. "Patron."

"What are you doing here?"

The bed creaked as she got in beside him. She smelled faintly of wood smoke and sweat. She laid her fluffy head on the pillow and looked up at him. Her eyes were dark and liquid. The dim light of the flashlight was already failing. Darkness seeped in. "I'm afraid, Patron."

"Afraid of what?"

"Monsieur Joliet."

"He's dead, now. And you must go to your own bed." She did not reply, but he felt her hand slip between his legs. Skinny fingers investigated his genitals. He removed her hand firmly. "No, Sophie. I don't want you."

She nestled close to him, half-seductive and half-innocent. "Monsieur Joliet is there," she whimpered. "I want to sleep beside you tonight."

"It's impossible. Please go to your room."

Her hand stole back to caress his thighs suggestively. "Tomorrow?" she asked.

"Never, Sophie. You are not for me." He was aware of sounding like the heroine of a melodrama, but his arousal made it imperative he get rid of her. He pushed her out of his bed and heard the thump as she landed on the floorboards. He wound the handle of the flashlight. When the little bulb glowed into life again, she had gone. He thought he heard Joliet's voice in the next room, croaking reproaches. Then there was only the distant patter of the drum.

He lay restlessly, ashamed of his erection yet unwilling to take advantage of it for self-abuse. That this was Africa and not Paris did not mean he could abandon all ethics. She was a child. Yet Joliet had used her. Impregnated her. He remembered the bony red hand resting proprietorially on Sophie's head. He saw in his mind the tight knots of Sophie's pubic hair. Justine's hair in that place had been silky. He had delighted in its softness. She had allowed him to groom it carefully with her ivory hair brush, watching with her secret smile as he crooned over her. He would part the satiny curtain and then —

And then the enslaver had been enslaved. He groaned aloud. The bee sting on his soul throbbed anew. His thoughts clacked along the old tracks for a while, dragging their burden of resentments and bitternesses, then ground to a halt. It made no difference to Justine or anyone else to curse his fate. He simply had to endure it. He must let the past fall away and deal with the present, no matter how dreadful, or he would go mad. Tomorrow he must sort through Joliet's possessions and arrange for them to be sent back to Libreville on the gunboat. There were probably relations. He remembered the strange smile on the face of the dead man, and shuddered.

He paused in his plans. He could hear movement in the corridor again. Not the pad of a girl's feet, but the distinctive click of knuckles. It was not a quadruped, he reminded himself, but a quadrumane, the highest order of Mammalia after the bimanes, of which man was the type and only species. A kind of cousin, then.

He recalled at that moment that his little library was also in the trunk, the nucleus of books which he had been relying on to keep him sane in this place. His Darwin, his Voltaire, his Homer. All at the bottom of the river.

A heavy, powerful body climbed onto the bed and curled up at his feet. His toes encountered coarse fur. He recoiled. The animal began to snore almost at once, exhaling the smell of milk and bananas.

7

He was awakened by a crash on the tin roof which made his heart leap into his throat. He scrambled out of bed. Cautiously, he peered out of the window. The dawn light was pink. He could see white curls of smoke rising from the village huts. A furry grey body hurled itself past the window, followed by two more in quick succession. He glimpsed black paws and faces, long tails. The remainder of the monkey troupe thundered across the roof and into the trees. He watched the animals disappear among the shaking branches. One of them would no doubt appear pungently on his table by and by.

He had, at least, survived the dreadful night.

He turned and saw Chloë yawning at the end of his bed, showing her large, sharp fangs. Sprawling and stretching on his bed, she displayed her body in all its ugliness, barrel stomached, with powerful limbs and hands like well-worn black leather gloves. The female parts of her body were especially disturbing to him. There was a certain combination of strength, deformity and femininity which he found repellent. That they shared a common ancestor was not comforting. This thought reminded him that he had to rescue Darwin from the bottom of the river today. He exclaimed in annoyance. The ape looked up. For the first time, she met his eyes for more than a few seconds. He saw that her gaze was clear and compassionate, somewhat mitigating her hideous appearance. He turned his back on her and dressed. Her toilet consisted of minutely scratching herself, grunting softly in her own language as she examined her fur. He wondered whether she had fleas. Although he acknowledged that her presence had given him some comfort and had helped allay the terrors of darkness, he was determined not to spend another night with her. It was too much.

He breakfasted, with the gorilla in attendance, on a bowl of fufu, plantain porridge, a native dish which he had come to like. Raymond brought coffee. "The child came to my room last night," Jean-Patrice said.

"Which child?"

He glanced at Chloë having the strange sensation that this conversation was not for innocent ears. "Sophie."

Raymond smiled. "Sophie is not a child."

"How old is she?"

"Eighteen years."

"I don't believe you."

"It's true."

"Nevertheless, I don't want to her to come any more."

"She loves you, patron."

"Oh, don't be absurd," he snapped. Raymond's ingratiating smile disappeared. He made an effort to be civil to the man. "Whatever her relationship with Joliet may have been, she is of no interest to me."

"Patron, this is very difficult. It is better to speak of these things with a little knowledge."

"I promised Joliet I'd take care of her. I don't want her to suffer in any way. What did Joliet pay her?"

The other man's expression had become sulky. "He did not pay. She was his wife."

He had a vision of himself leading Sophie to Malherbe

in her rose print dress and demanding a widow's pension. "Married, in a church?"

"Married, but not in a church."

"You can find her work in the house, if she wants it. In the kitchen, perhaps."

"She cannot go in the kitchen. It is forbidden."

"Forbidden? What kind of wife is she, then?"

"A wife in the bed only."

"Well, she can't be my wife in the bed. I'll pay her something. She can go home."

"This is her home," Raymond replied sullenly. "If you send her away, you will shame her." He paused. "And me."

Jean-Patrice glanced at him over his coffee cup. "Are you telling me she is your daughter?" Raymond made no reply. Enlightenment dawned. Now was not the time to tell the man he was an immoral old pander. "I don't wish to shame you or Sophie. But I must choose who shares my bed."

"And who will the patron choose?" Raymond asked ironically. "The patron cannot go into the village and choose any woman he likes."

"The same rule applies in Paris. I was speaking hypothetically."

Chloë grunted and smacked her lips to indicate that she wanted more milk. Raymond poured it into her bowl. "Here they believe the whites are ghosts of the dead come back to eat the living. No woman will lie with you. To lie with a white man is death."

"Sophie doesn't believe this, I take it?"

"She is educated. She can read."

Jean-Patrice grunted. "Ah, yes. Well, thank you for your solicitude over my private life, but perhaps I can survive without a woman for a year or two. Now we must get my trunk from the river. We need ropes and the three officers."

"The men will not go in the river," Raymond said, his

face closed. "They believe there are ghosts under the water."

"This is not a joking matter," Jean-Patrice replied irritably.

"It is not a joke, patron. They believe the monster will swallow them. They will not go."

He rapped the table sharply. "Call them, please."

Raymond shrugged and went to summon the three policemen. They came into the room with guarded expressions, the two spindly brothers flanking the stalwart Hyppolite.

"You know that my trunk fell in the river," Jean-Patrice began briskly.

"It was very heavy, Monsieur le Commissaire," Hyppolite said in a growl. "It was not our fault."

"I am not assigning blame. But it must be recovered."

Blinking anxiously, Narcise peered around Hyppolite's broad shoulder. "We cannot go in the river, patron. There is a great water snake."

"And you believe that!"

"Yes, patron! It has been there for many years. Our grandfathers remember it. It is very, very dangerous." The others nodded.

"You live on the bank of this river," Jean-Patrice said, "and yet you will not venture into the water because you believe a monster lives in it?"

"We did not always live here," Hyppolite said in a surly tone. "Our village was fifty miles away. The whites made us come here and build another village, so we could work for them."

"When we came, the snake was already in the river," Narcise added.

"And the whites never gave us work," Hyppolite concluded.

Jean-Patrice stared at them. It was an impasse. What would Voltaire have done? He would perhaps have sided with the exploited aborigines and have written an impassioned pamphlet, On The True Monster Of The River. And Darwin? Darwin offered more inspiration. Practical and empirical, that excellent man would have rolled up his sleeves.

"Then I'll do it myself. The ghosts won't trouble me, since I am one of them." He rose. "And Raymond, I don't want this animal sleeping in my bedroom any longer. Please make her a nest or a bed in some other room and lock her in at night."

Raymond shrugged. "She will not be happy. She always slept with Monsieur Joliet."

"Monsieur Joliet seems to have been an unusual person," Jean-Patrice said shortly, "but I do not feel bound to maintain his charming eccentricities. Please see that it is done."

8

He took off his clothes on the shoal, watched by half the village, the children solemn, the women giggling behind their hands at his pale nakedness. The grinning policemen paddled him out into the channel in mid-stream, to the spot where he had seen the last of his trunk. He peered into the water, which was more sinister in appearance than he had remembered. "These are inconvenient superstitions," he muttered to himself. "Ask them to keep the canoes in the same place as far as possible," he told Hyppolite. He looped one of the ropes around his shoulder and slid over the side of the dugout. Under the shadow of the overgrown cliff, the water was colder than he had anticipated and the current stronger. He took a breath and dived.

The depths of the channel were murky. He could barely see his own hands. He touched the muddy bottom and groped, stirring up dark clouds. When his breath ran out and he was forced to surface he saw that the current had already washed him twenty meters down the river. He swam back to the dugouts, where dark faces peered down at him, and dived again.

It was an exhausting process. Each dive meant an

increasingly tiring swim back to the dugouts. He had drunk rather a lot of alcohol over the past weeks. It had not done him any good. He had always prided himself on his physique. As a boy in the country, he had been vigorous. He had pawed in the valley and rejoiced in his strength, like the war horse in the Book of Job. He had wreaked havoc among the country maidens. In Paris he had frequented a gymnasium where he boxed and fenced against a grim old maître d'armes. He rode well, swam strongly. He was (so he thought) a fine figure of a man. Enslavement to Justine – and then alcohol – had sapped some of his strength. He began to feel cold, the muscles of his shoulders and neck aching. The trunk eluded him. He anticipated the humiliation of arriving back at the village, naked and empty handed, his penis shriveled with the cold. But his groping fingers finally encountered a metal corner protruding from the ooze into which it had settled. With the last of his breath burning in his lungs, he dug into the mud, found one of the carrying handles, and tied the end of the rope around it. He burst from the surface of the water, gasping, and clung to a dugout to recover his breath.

"Got it," he panted.

Within half an hour, the trunk, streaming muddy water, was balanced on one of the dugouts. They paddled it carefully to the jetty and carried it to the Residency. The women formed a line along their route, spontaneously singing and clapping. Jean-Patrice turned to Raymond. "They seem happy."

"They are singing for you," Raymond replied.

"What do they say?"

Raymond listened. "The song is about the whiteness of your skin."

Feeling there was something Homeric about this, Jean-Patrice was pleased. He opened the trunk in the little yard behind the kitchen. The vaccination equipment was undamaged, being mostly steel or glass. He dried and cleaned the lancets carefully. However, the paper contents of the trunk were in a sorry state. He laid out Darwin, Voltaire and Homer in the sun, without much hope that they would recover. *The Descent of Man* had suffered, in particular, being an English edition, printed on very absorbent paper. *The Origin of Species*, in the translation by that most extraordinary of women, Mademoiselle Clémence Royer, had fared better. His editions of Voltaire and Homer were very cheap paperbacks bought during his University days and were half-dissolved. The cardboard boxes of ammunition for the revolver had fallen to pieces altogether, as had the medicine packages. The labels of all the tinned goods had also sloughed off and disintegrated. Some of the tins could still be identified by their shape as containing, for example, asparagus or sardines, but most were now unidentifiable except by empirical trial.

He took the revolver to pieces, cleaning and oiling each part. Raymond, Hyacinth, Hyppolite and Narcise cleaned the bullets one by one. Since the discussion about Sophie, the steward had been unsmiling, his eyes downcast. Rejecting the girl as a concubine had probably inflicted a serious loss of prestige on him.

Jean-Patrice broke the silence. "What did Joliet mean by saying the snake was put into his bed?"

Raymond shrugged. "He was making a joke, patron."

"It was not a very opportune moment for a joke."

Hyppolite, the corporal, spoke up. He was a tall, strongly built young man with deep tribal scars on his cheeks. He reminded Jean-Patrice of certain young men he had known at school who excelled at sports and had physical strength in abundance, resulting in a manner of arrogant superiority. He was the only one of the policemen who matched Jean-Patrice himself in stature. "Monsieur le Commissaire, snakes come into the houses, hunting for mice and rats. When they have eaten, they fall asleep in warm places. Sometimes in the bed."

"Sometimes in the patron's boots," Raymond added

with a malicious glint in his eyes, "and what-what."

"That must reduce the boredom of life. What happened to the snake, by the way?"

"It escaped."

"Indeed? Didn't anyone try to kill it?"

Hyppolite lined up the bullets in gleaming rows. "The people believe the oganga can make herself into a snake in the night if she wishes. Or a monkey, and ride a man to death." The others muttered.

"Who is the oganga?" Jean-Patrice asked.

"The oganga wipoga. She is the witchdoctor." Raymond jerked his head. "In the bush."

"The tins have no labels," Narcise said. He was the smallest, and very short-sighted, and was peering at his work with his narrow forehead corrugated into a frown. Though he and Hyacinth were brothers, he was the only one who could write. Jean-Patrice had considered him for the post of vaccinator, but his extreme myopia made him unsuitable. "How will the patron know what is inside?"

"It will be a surprise each time. That will also reduce the boredom of life. Likewise the medicines. And perhaps also the pistol. Let's try it out." He reassembled the revolver and loaded it. They all went outside. He cocked the weapon and took aim at a tree trunk some ten meters away. The policemen backed away to a safe distance. As he pulled the trigger, he wondered fleetingly whether the pistol would jam and explode. They could bury his one-armed corpse next to Joliet's one-legged one. There was a thunderous report. The pistol kicked in his hand and a wet scar appeared in the bark of the tree. He lowered the revolver slowly, his ears ringing. It was the first time he had fired it since he had been given it in Paris. He recalled the thoughts of suicide which had run wildly through his mind and imagined the ruin of his skull. He snorted the cordite fumes out of his nostrils. His prospects were not perhaps brilliant, but so far he had not stooped to that folly, at least.

"And now," he said, "I will inoculate you all." He prepared a lancet. Raymond steadfastly refused to be inoculated. The three police, bound by the discipline of their calling, suffered it dubiously but without flinching. When he had put plasters on the scratches, he felt pleased. "Let's open one of these anonymous tins. Whatever is inside, we will eat without protest. Is that agreed?"

They agreed, amused. He opened one of the larger tins. It proved to contain cooked pears. They ate, saying it was good. To Jean-Patrice, the flaccid segments had no more than the faint memory of a flavor, compared to the vivid tastes of the tropical fruits that grew all around in such profusion; but perhaps novelty added something, or perhaps they were simply being polite.

It had been a day of achievements; he climbed into bed with a sense of satisfaction that night. His muscles ached. He would get back into condition. He decided to stop drinking, a decision he had had taken several times before. The darkness no longer seemed so horrifying. He felt more sense of belonging, less terror. He was able to doze. An unearthly wail startled him into wakefulness. Chloë had been locked into a storage room as he had instructed, with some blankets and a bunch of bananas to keep her company. She had been quiet for an hour but now had begun to howl. Her cries contained so much desperate sorrow that he felt his skin crawling.

The wailing turned into short, sharp screams, now accompanied by a heavy thumping. It sounded as though she were pounding on the door. The house echoed with it. The screams were piercing and jagged, aimed at him. Sleep was impossible. The creature was an anarchist. He grabbed his riding crop and went downstairs in a fury. He unlocked her door, prepared to show his displeasure with a good thrashing. The animal flew to him and clasped his legs in her long arms, her chest heaving as if with the sobs of a child. He stood looking down at her, astonished by the intensity of her emotion. She wanted only tears to be human.

"Chloë," he said, "it's all right."

She reached up and took his hand in her leathery fingers, pulling him urgently along. Bemused, he allowed her to lead him back up the stairs to his bedroom. He got into bed wearily and allowed her to take up her place at his feet. For some time he listened to her whimpering, gasping sounds that were so like the shuddering of human sobs. How empty life was, he thought, how cold and dark and void the interstellar regions. Love was the only salvation he had ever found, the warmth of a certain pair of lips, the sweetness of a certain voice, that magical thrill which filled the ether between two persons, like a comet arriving from the remotest depths of space, unexplained and inexplicable. Was it possible that this grotesque animal perceived this in some way? Were her emotions in any way parallel to his? *The Descent of Man* was drying, but already he could see that most of the pages had glued themselves together and could not now be separated. If Darwin had discussed such issues, the answers were sealed in there until he could return to civilization and buy a new copy. He turned the subject over in his mind for a while as the gorilla settled. Then he fell asleep.

9

The somber task of collecting Hugo Joliet's possessions occupied some hours of the next morning. He found a convenient wooden tea chest to pack away the remains of the man's life. The clothing was a simple matter; the former District Commissioner of Bassongo had kept most of his clothes in a single cupboard. These were easily folded by Raymond and packed into the chest together with assorted hats, shoes and gloves. In the bedside drawer there was a small collection of valuables – a gold watch, a gold chain, an onyx signet ring, spectacles, a pearl handled pocket knife, an expensive fountain pen – and a wallet containing money, which Jean-Patrice put into a manila pouch and sealed with wax. He found a crooked, makeshift crutch which the dead man must have used to get around before his final illness. Thinking this a rather gruesome relic, he gave it to Raymond to burn. There were some also carved walking sticks, a whip and a sword which might give comfort to the man's widow (if he had one) or relatives.

Somewhat less likely to give comfort to any possible heirs of Commissioner Joliet was his journal, a large, leather bound volume which Jean-Patrice discovered under the dead man's bed. On opening this, he found that it contained a large number of pornographic photographs, together with what appeared to be a register of Joliet's sexual activities.

The photographs showed native women, mostly naked, some wearing a few minimal garments. At first Jean-Patrice thought they were the usual photographs of bare-breasted tribal women which caused such interest among ethnologically-minded tourists. But it was not so. Joliet himself figured in several scenes, wearing his shirt, waistcoat and jacket, but with his trousers around his ankles, participating in various acts of bodily fellowship with the women.

Joliet had entitled his journal, *Liber Libidinorum*, The Book of Pleasures. Jean-Patrice perused this catalog of sexual activity with amazement. The variety and number of female partners was in itself astonishing. Short and tall, fat and thin, old and young, all had been grist to the mill of Joliet's appetite. Had they all been drawn from Bassongo? All wore the same blank expressions and somehow all conserved some kind of gravity in the photographs, despite the indignity of their postures. Jean-Patrice had never conceived of such postures, such contortions. They seemed extraordinarily perverse to him. Joliet wore an expression of complacent satisfaction as he inserted a root-like male organ into various orifices. The backdrop was invariably the same: a misty scene of a Grecian temple.

The text, written in a small and somewhat crabbed hand, recorded an interminable sequence of exploits, using pseudo-medical Latin terminology, together with details of the women's behavior and the intensity of the pleasure he had derived from them. The women themselves were identified only by their initials. On one day, Jean-Patrice saw, Joliet had recorded no less than six orgasms, one "very good," three "satisfactory," one "painful," the final one (unsurprisingly) "poor – little result."

Jean-Patrice leafed through page after page, musing.

Over a year or two, Joliet's antics mounted up to an impressive total. It was hard to associate these concupiscent activities with the emaciated creature he had seen expire. It was, however, somewhat easier to see why someone might have introduced a poisonous snake into his bed – someone like F., for example, whom Joliet noted as possessing "very rounded buttocks" and having that day "cried constantly during *coitus per rectum*." There was a suggestive photograph to accompany this entry.

How had Joliet managed to get any work done? Where had these acts been recorded? And who had developed all these obscene photographs for Joliet? It was a mystery.

He turned a page and found himself staring at Sophie, her slender body yielding to a gross act with Joliet. He slammed the journal hastily shut, disturbed. Why had Joliet been so insistent he couple only with Sophie, a pebble on the beach, so to speak, whilst this great ocean lay all undiscovered before him? And what about the belief that whites were ghosts come to eat the living?

After a moment, he reopened the *Liber Libidinorum* and turned to the end to see whether Joliet had recorded the circumstances of his snakebite. The last entry concerned someone identified as V., and noted that in the evening there had taken place "*coitus per vaginam* – satisfactory; *fellatio* – v. good." Here the obsessional record of copulations ended abruptly. The succeeding pages were blank. The man had noted and scored every one of his sexual climaxes, but not the bite that had killed him. He had maintained a complete silence through his illness, the amputation of his leg and the succeeding deterioration that he must have known was leading him to the grave. Presumably sexual activity had ceased during this decline.

Jean-Patrice closed the book again. He could hardly send this catalogue back to tearful relations. Perhaps he should burn it. But he did not feel he had the right to. He put the thing away on a shelf, feeling slightly nauseous. He determined never to open it again. Well, perhaps he would glance at it, later on, out of scientific curiosity; but it hardly made up for the loss of *Candide*, the *Odyssey* and *The Origin of Species*.

Later, exploring the Residency with Chloë for company, he found a solution to the mystery in the cellar, which smelled strongly of photographic chemicals. One wall had been crudely painted with the Greek temple scene with which he was now so familiar. There, too, were the chair and couch which figured in the photographs. There was a camera on a tripod (an Ernemann "Tropical" Klapp) together with developing equipment. All of Joliet's hobbies, photographic and amatory, had been pursued down here, under the house.

There was also an old iron safe in which were a large quantity of silver coins of various eras and places, used to trade with the natives, ten rifles for the policemen, some ammunition, and two kegs of powder for the cannon. He almost decided to have these removed, not liking the idea of sleeping over enough gunpowder to blow himself and Residency sky high. He would never have cause to fire the damned thing. There were no balls for it, in any case. Was he supposed to maintain the authority of France with that relic of Marengo or Waterloo?

He had neglected to issue a death certificate for Joliet. He found the requisite form in a desk in Joliet's study and filled it out. He could supply the date of Hugo Joliet's death, but not that of his birth. Under Cause of Death he wrote, "Septicemia Due To Snake Bite." He folded the certificate into an envelope and laid it on the desk to give to the captain of the gunboat when he returned. The missing birth date troubled him. After a little thought, he took another death certificate and filled it out in his own name, filling in his date of birth but leaving the other details unwritten. This second certificate he placed back with the blank forms, where it would be found if it was needed.

The study also contained a medicine chest. From this

he took a scalpel, a large bottle of iodine and some other things he needed. He called Hyppolite Mokamo, who was the tallest and strongest, and went with him to the stable.

"Does she have a name?" he asked Hyppolite as he hobbled the mare's legs.

"Adeline."

He lit a cheroot and clamped it between his teeth. "Hold her head." He was not looking forward to the operation, but if the beast died, he would be stuck in this abysmal village for the rest of time. He chose to begin with the largest of the cysts, on Adeline's lean flank, and cut into it with the scalpel. The mare rolled her eyes and attempted to kick, but the hobble held fast. A quantity of malodorous slime poured out of the swelling as he cut it open. The wretched animal shuddered and swung her head. Hyppolite had to use all his strength to hold her. Jean-Patrice dug into the wound with the forceps and, with some difficulty, pulled out a leathery grub. He examined it, seeing the sharp mouth-parts that had allowed it to burrow its way into its host's flesh. Hyppolite grimaced. Jean-Patrice crushed the thing to a yellowish pulp under his boot. He cleaned out the wound with iodine and sewed it partially closed, leaving an opening for drainage.

"Hyppolite, we need to get the police up to strength," Jean-Patrice said, as he began on the second abscess. "Three men is too few. We will have to recruit seven more."

"It will not be so easy," Hyppolite replied.

"Why not?"

"They call the police *beni oui-oui*," Hyppolite said frankly, "the yes-yes men. They say we are toys of the whites."

"Why did you join, then?"

"Narcise joined because he is weak and his eyes are so poor, he cannot see to fish or farm. But he can write. Hyacinth joined because Narcise is his brother. Me, I joined because I am strong." He laughed heartily. There were a number of problems, which Hyppolite attempted to explain. For one thing, the post of policeman carried little prestige. What would happen, should any of the native police be required to take action against a member of the village, who would certainly be a neighbor and very likely also a kinsman? Such a confrontation could only end badly, and no decent person would put himself in a position which might lead to it. The pay, too, was small. It was not sufficient to lure most villagers away from more manly occupations such as hunting or fishing, which could make a man prosperous and respected, if not rich. Finally, there was the question of possible danger, should a state of war or insurrection arise. Armed only with rifles and absurd European names, what would a handful of native police do? In short, the game was generally not regarded as worth the candle.

Jean-Patrice listened carefully, squinting against the curling smoke of his cheroot as he plied the curved needle. "We need to address the young. Where are all the strong young men of the village?"

"They are at initiation camp, in the bush. They stay there for three months. They are circumcised and taught about the ancestors. When they return, they are men."

"And when do they come back?"

"In the New Year, patron."

"We'll have a recruiting drive then," Jean-Patrice decided. "Hold her head again."

He extracted another parasite from Adeline's shivering flesh. This one appeared to belong to a different species, or perhaps it was merely at a different stage of development. He crushed the thing underfoot.

He extracted in total twenty-three burrowing parasites from Adeline's flesh. He then attended to her hoofs, cutting away as much of the rot as he could. The mare had no shoes; he would have to deal with that as best he could. He and Hyppolite were both dripping with sweat.

"I'm going for a swim to cool down," he said. He

walked down to the river and stripped off. He plunged into the water and swam a few strokes. When he looked back, Hyppolite was standing uncertainly on the bank. Jean-Patrice waved cheerfully. Slowly, Hyppolite began to undress. He was the strongest man in the village, as tall as Jean-Patrice and, if anything, even broader. He joined Jean-Patrice in the water, his powerful shoulders gleaming. "Aren't you afraid of the water spirits?" Jean-Patrice asked, feeling they had formed a rapport of sorts.

"I used to be a Catholic, patron."

"Used to be?"

"Not anymore."

"Did you abandon your faith when the missionaries died?"

"Yes. There was nothing left."

"Why didn't you help me get my trunk that day?"

"I am not afraid of ghosts. But I am afraid of the crocodiles."

"Are there crocodiles?" Jean-Patrice asked casually.

"Of course. Every year they take goats, sometimes children or women who are washing clothes. But they will not attack you."

"Why not?"

"They don't eat white people."

Jean-Patrice looked at the man to see if he were being humorous. It was hard to tell; Hyppolite's face was like granite. They emerged from the water. "Monsieur Joliet," he said as he dressed, "seems to have had a lot of lady friends."

Hyppolite's expression did not change. "A great many."

"They were all from Bassongo?"

"Most."

"Raymond told me that the women wouldn't lie with a white man because they believe we are ghosts."

"That is true,"

"Then can you tell me how Monsieur Joliet convinced

so many women otherwise?"

Hyppolite lips curled. "Monsieur Joliet was a very strict officer."

"What do you mean?"

"He enforced many fines. And taxes. People in Bassongo have little money to pay."

Jean-Patrice winced. "So all those women – they were coerced?"

"He told them they could pay the taxes with something other than money."

"But that is hideous!"

"The women had little choice. They said he abused them, then stole their souls and put them in his black book."

"And nobody complained? There was no opposition?"

"To whom would they complain?" Hyppolite asked dryly. "As for opposition, Monsieur Joliet had us to enforce his will."

"You mean the police?"

"Yes."

"I can't believe you supported Joliet in this," Jean-Patrice exclaimed. "No wonder they call you the beni oui oui."

Hyppolite shot him a bitter look. "It was our duty. And behind us were the soldiers from Medoneu."

"It was a systematic rape, Hyppolite. The people of Bassongo must have hated Joliet. And you."

"There have been worse Commissioners than Monsieur Joliet."

"That is hard to imagine." He buckled the revolver to his side. A thought struck him. "Do the people of Bassongo anticipate that I will behave in the same fashion?"

"The people of Bassongo are waiting to see how you will behave."

Jean-Patrice grunted. "However I behave, I will not be as bad as that." He caught Hyppolite's look. "You may rest assured."

Hyppolite shrugged indifferently and said nothing more. He was clearly angered by Jean-Patrice's criticism. As they walked back to the Residency, Jean-Patrice reflected that Hugo Joliet had bequeathed him a large number of very thorny problems. How was he expected to govern the town in such an atmosphere as this? How would he attract recruits to a police department with such a reputation? Much was now becoming clear to him, and he liked none of it.

10

The lingering presence of Joliet in the Residency was a particularly unpleasant feature of his situation – not just as a bad memory, but rather as a present nuisance. There were suggestions that Joliet was still obstinately in occupancy: the smell of Joliet's rotting stump at the dining table, taking away Jean-Patrice's appetite, or Joliet's hoarse voice muttering at night in his room, something which always made the hairs on the nape of Jean-Patrice's neck stand up.

He decided to take action against these disagreeable phenomena. He ordered the Grecian mural to be scrubbed off the wall. It was done, and the wall appeared blank for a day or two, but the next time he went down, the columns of the temple had begun to bleed through the plaster again; and eventually the whole scene reappeared, though blotchier and less distinguishable than before.

The photographic equipment was evidently expensive, made of mahogany and brass, and would have to be sent back to Libreville along with the rest of Joliet's possessions. Jean-Patrice had no desire to learn any of the processes himself. Raymond dismantled the tripod and the other contraptions and put them in a crate. There was also a collection of glass negatives, kept in little cardboard boxes. Holding these to the light, Jean-Patrice could see, imprinted on the plates, the ghosts of Joliet's victims.

"We're going to burn these things," he told Raymond. "I want rid of them."

He and Raymond made a bonfire, which was not an easy proceeding, due to the endless rain and the scarcity of dry wood. They threw the boxes onto the flames. The plates cracked, the bromide coating flaring violet. At length, all that was left was a pile of smoldering and blackened splinters.

"What is Sophie doing?" he asked Raymond, poking at the cinders.

"She cooks my food."

"You should find a husband for her."

Raymond looked sullen. "She will not find a husband now."

He had caught glimpses of Sophie in the village. She no longer wore her green dress with the red roses, but a shabby yellow frock that had clearly been handed down from a much bigger woman. She looked dirty, her hair uncombed. She did not look at him, but slipped away each time he saw her. She had about her an air of degradation now, despite her youth. She struck him as something that had been used up and discarded. He had a vision of her drifting into the life of a common prostitute, being used by brutes, declining into disease and an early death.

"Will you ask her to come and see me, please?"

Raymond eyed him warily. "If you wish, Monsieur le Commissaire."

He began to look for a vaccinator he could train. It was not so easy. Those to whom he explained the process recoiled in horror from being associated with it in any way. It was difficult to explain vaccination in appealing terms. He could not even find anyone willing to undergo the operation. He tried to tempt some children with sweets, but when he produced the lancets, they ran away, screaming. He felt that whatever he attempted, the evil reputation of Hugo Joliet preceded him and poisoned his endeavors before they could begin.

He wondered how many of the women who passed him in the village, their faces averted from him, had been abused by Hugo Joliet; how many of the men had been forced to endure the mistreatment of wives or daughters. He felt as though tainted with the wicked deeds of his predecessor.

In fact, the only person who did not avoid him was the madman, Ndoumou, who remained on the outskirts of Bassongo, like a half-tamed dog, often completely naked. Jean-Patrice had a weakness for the insane. The convent school he'd attended as a boy had adjoined a lunatic asylum, also run by the nuns. To his schoolfellows, the strange people next door had been objects of terror or mockery, but he had found in them some kind of kinship. He had sometimes climbed over the wall to be among them. Some were glad to see him, especially the women, many of whom had left children on the outside.

With Ndoumou he felt the same kinship. His hair and beard jutted from his thin head like a ram's fleece as he paced and counted invisible things with his skinny fingers. His far-reaching, burning gaze struck Jean-Patrice forcefully. One day, Jean-Patrice sat down beside him and, without ceremony, scratched his arm with the serum. The madman examined the wound briefly and without interest. After this, he disappeared for several days. However, he eventually returned, with the characteristic pock mark already healing on his arm; and so the light of science had been brought to the least illuminated of Bassongo's population.

Adeline recovered better than he had expected from the brutal surgery. He managed to get some grain and made a bucket of mash for her each day to supplement her diet of weeds. She began to look less death-like. She still had no shoes, but he was told there was a blacksmith nearby who could make some. He reflected that the ground was so soft and moist in this season, during which it rained at least three times a day, that she could perhaps do without them if he was careful with her. At least the abscesses drained and healed.

The mare became healthy enough to saddle. He began to ride around his domain and learned that Bassongo was much more extensive than he had thought. The houses by the river formed only one part of a large settlement, a patchwork of little suburbs, so to speak, separated by groves of bananas, fields of vegetables and thick forest

Further up the river, he noticed one afternoon a rusty iron cross protruding above the bushes and turned Adeline's head to investigate. The track to the cross was overgrown. It appeared not to have been used in years. He had to hunch over the mare to protect his face from the whipping branches.

He emerged into a clearing. The cross had been set on top of a small mud brick church, now crumbling, its tin roof sagging on rotten beams, its doors and windows missing. Beside it was a ramshackle building which bore the hallmarks of a small schoolhouse. It, too, was without door or windows. Beside it was an arch in which hung a small, corroded bell. There were other structures, now too buried in eager young trees and waist-high grass to make out. This was the mission where all the missionaries had died of fever.

He opened his water bottle and drank, surveying the melancholy scene. It was a fitting monument, he thought, to the white man's endeavors in Africa – poorly conceived, doomed to early failure, and now left to rot in the forest. Were his own projects to meet the same fate?

Something barked at Jean-Patrice. A large monkey was glaring at him from a branch, its face scarlet and blue. For a moment, he and the creature stared into one another's eyes, then the thing bared its tusks and leaped away.

He rode slowly around the decaying buildings,

absorbing the not unpleasant sense of long-abandoned enterprise. The place was peaceful, at least. Certainly, none of the inhabitants of Bassongo came here any longer.

Behind the church his nostrils caught a stench of putrefaction and he found himself looking down on a tangle of human bones. He dismounted and peered closer, seeing the dome of the skull, the dull gleam of a mother-of-pearl rosary tangled among the finger bones. These were the remains of the priest, he decided. He could see the rotting black stuff of a cassock. The roots of a nearby tree had heaved him out of the red earth, only half-digested. Termites had eaten the coffin and persistent rain had further exposed the remains.

The stink of the place was oppressive, deterring him from any attempt to re-inter the corpse. In any case, he had no spade. He remounted, making a mental note to arrange a burial party. As he rode away, he looked over his shoulder. The priest, poor devil, looked rather as though he were trying to climb out of his grave.

He rode through the outskirts of Bassongo, picking up a train of naked children who ran after his horse excitedly. In the market, baskets of fruit and vegetables were piled in displays. There were stalls selling simple imported goods: bolts of Indian cloth, shiny machetes and hatchets, bars of yellow, blue and red soap, tins of cooking oil.

At a crossroads outside the village, he came upon several rows of clay pots, drying in the sun. The potter, a woman, was seated on the ground, working on a bowl as he arrived. Her skirt was pulled up to expose her strong brown thighs, which were splayed around her work. Something about her made him stop his horse. His entourage of children stopped too, looking at the woman as though trying to see what had arrested him. She did not look up at him, concentrating on the bowl. He felt a warm pleasure at her grace, then grew aware that the vessels all around her were also graceful, with rich curves despite their slender walls, and elegantly simple decorations. Some were huge, big enough for her to have climbed inside if she had wished to. Her arms were slim. Her hands, wet with slurry, moved deftly, shaping the rim of the bowl.

At last she looked up at him. He felt something contract sharply in his heart. She was a beautiful woman. She had a full, African mouth and dark, almond shaped eyes, her rounded cheek bones giving her face a heart shape. Her hair was tied in a red scarf. She wore silver rings in her earlobes. She was as old as he, or perhaps a year or two younger. She cocked her head on one side as if reproving him for his stare.

"I am Jean-Patrice Duméril, the new District Commissioner."

She folded her slim arms. "I did not think that you had dropped from the moon."

She spoke good French, though he was not very pleased at her pert answer. "How much for that bowl?"

"You cannot have it."

"Why not?"

"This bowl must be baked, Monsieur." She spoke like a person of education, without humility. "There are others here that have been baked."

"I want that one."

"Why this one?"

"Because I saw you make it."

"Ah, well. If it pleases you." She dug her thumb into the soft clay, making an oval imprint near the rim. "There, now you'll know your pot. Come back in one week. It will be baked."

"Did you make all these pots?" he asked.

"Yes. Did you make all these children?"

He looked at the small fry clustered around Adeline. "Yes, every one."

"I don't see your thumb print on any of them."

He felt he was not being very witty. "You still haven't told me the price of the bowl."

"I'll tell when it's baked."

"When will you bake it?"

She turned to look at the rows of clay vessels she had made. "On Sunday."

"May I come and watch?"

"Are you going to impose a tax on pottery?"

"My interest is aesthetic, not administrative."

"Ah, aesthetic." She rinsed her hands in the battered tin of water that stood beside her. Her fingers were slim, the palms rose colored. Then she rose, shaking down her skirt to cover her legs. She put her hands on the small of her back, arching her spine to take out the stiffness. She was taller than most Beti women, rather wiry than plump, her legs long and slim.

"Are you finished?" he asked.

"It's time to eat, Monsieur."

"May I come on Sunday?"

"I cannot prevent you. You are the District Commissioner." She turned away. Her back was straight and strong. He watched her walk to her house, which stood alone. She disappeared into the dark doorway. He had wanted to engage her in conversation, but he had been dismissed. He suddenly recalled the *Liber Libidinorum* and kicked the unoffending mare's ribs in anger. She obviously thought he was propositioning her in the manner of Hugo Joliet. Damn Joliet! The first interesting woman he had met since leaving Paris, and that leering ghost had come in the way.

Fuming, he rode back to the riverside. He stripped off his clothes and led the mare into the shallows of the river. The grateful animal lay down in the cool water and rolled and he did likewise. When he looked up, Ndoumou the lunatic was sitting on the bank, hugging his thin knees. Jean-Patrice emerged from the water and sat beside him. "I'm losing my wits and you've already lost yours," he said. "I don't know which of us is better off, old fellow."

The madman scrabbled in his bag and produced a papaya and a small knife. He cut the fruit carefully in two and scooped out the black seeds. Then he passed half to Jean-Patrice. It was the first sign he had given that he acknowledged Jean-Patrice's existence and Jean-Patrice was touched. They ate together in silence. The fruit was sweet and perfumed. The river was busy today. Rafts drifted downstream, huge but simple vessels made of planks lashed together with a piece of mat for a sail, so heavily laden with ebony logs that their decks were awash; at each end a pilot used a long pole to keep in the channel. In between these great freights, the villagers paddled with piles of yellow bananas and parcels of food wrapped in banana leaves. Occasionally the lashings came loose and the pilots needed help in securing them again. There was little he needed to do – the Beti worked out all questions of work and payment among themselves. He left Ndoumou counting the papaya seeds in the sand.

He encountered Raymond when he got back to the Residency. "Who is the woman who makes pots at the crossroads over there?"

Raymond gave him a dry look. "That one? She is called Catherine Atélé."

"She appears to be educated."

"She was brought up by the missionaries. But she ran away from them."

He thought of the abandoned schoolhouse, the silent bell. "Is she married?"

"She is a widow. Her husband drowned. The missionaries said she was cursed by God."

"Very Christian of them. So she can read and write?"

"Yes. She was a teacher of children."

"Why does she live outside the village?"

"Potters and blacksmiths must always live outside."

"How's that?"

Raymond lifted his shoulders. "They dig in the ground, where the spirits live. Their hands are unclean. Only a woman can make pottery. Only a man can work iron. Only a blacksmith can marry a potter and only a potter can marry a blacksmith. If others go with them, they may be killed by the spirits."

"There's a blacksmith nearby."

"He has asked her. But he already has three wives. And she does not like him. She supports herself, so she has no need of a husband." He smiled slyly. "Besides, if she married again, she would always be pregnant. And then her pots would leak."

"Why?"

"A potter who is pregnant must leave a small hole in every pot she makes, otherwise her womb may close up and she may die in childbirth. Nobody will buy pots from a pregnant woman."

"Another inconvenient superstition." But he stored the woman and her name in his memory.

He shared his lunch with Chloë. It was slowly becoming more natural to him to eat with the animal. Her table manners were delicate. Her company, indeed, was in some ways consoling. She was not obtrusive and did not have a dog's ways of asking to be petted or begging for tidbits. It was apparently his intellectual companionship she enjoyed. She did not seem to want to leave the house except for the calls of nature. Having answered these, she would return quickly inside, though she would often stare out of the windows rather wistfully. She greeted him with quiet satisfaction when he came home and if she were separated from him in the house, she would soon make her way to where he was. At night, in particular, she could not bear to be alone. She would follow him anxiously from room to room. Leaving her in the darkness was a great cruelty. He did not repeat the attempt to make her sleep alone. He, too, was afraid of the dark. There was comfort to be taken in her presence. But he was not a du Chaillu; sharing his life with a young gorilla presented daily inconveniences. From what he could understand from Raymond, she must be two or three years old; probably old enough to make her own way in life. He determined that the animal should be returned to the forest to rejoin her species. Her mother might be dead but surely there were aunts and uncles who would take care of her?

11

"The patron asked to speak to Sophie," Raymond said to Jean-Patrice one morning. "She is here."

"Good. Tell her to come in."

Sophie came into his study with downcast eyes. She was wearing her pale yellow frock, pinching the seams between her fingers and thumbs.

"Hello, Sophie," he said. "Are you well?"

"Yes, patron."

"I see you in the village sometimes. Your father says you are helping him at home?" She nodded. "What else do you do?"

"Nothing." Her gaze was sullen, almost blank. He wondered who had "chosen" her, as Joliet had put it, to fulfill the role of courtesan. Her arms and legs were slender, her feet, in battered white sandals, were small and dusty. Her features were fine, with full lips and flaring nostrils. Her breasts were minimal. There was about her something haunting, something at once delicate and carnal. Perhaps it was this virginal quality that Joliet had appreciated, even though (according to Hyppolite) he had been able to coerce so many others. Perhaps it had indeed been a kind of marriage, with an appearance of conventionality and a steady undercurrent of infidelities?

"I wanted to give you this." He held out the envelope. She took it from him and held it awkwardly, hesitantly, as though he had asked her to post it and she were not sure where the post box was. "Look inside."

She opened the envelope and saw the sheaf of ten-centime notes inside. Her expression did not change.

"The money is for you to keep," he said.

"Yes, patron." She seemed neither pleased nor offended.

"I hope you can use it to make your life better. You could buy some things to sell in the market, for example, and make an income."

"Nobody will buy."

"You don't know that until you try. Or perhaps you could get something nice to wear, so people will notice you." He saw that she wore a string of blue and white glass beads around her neck and a simple copper ring on one finger. She had no other adornment. He remembered the sight of her naked body by the dim gleam of his flashlight. "Anyway, it's quite a lot of money."

"Yes, patron." She put the envelope in her pocket without thanks.

"You shouldn't be idle. Your father told me you're educated. Can you read and write?"

By way of an answer, she came to his desk and picked up a pencil that lay there. She stooped over the blotter and wrote, slowly and carefully, Sophie Mbangu, female, 18 years of age. Her handwriting was rounded and immature. He caught the smoky smell of her skin as her arm brushed his. The frock hung loose on her slender frame and he glimpsed the curve of her breast, the brush of hair in her armpit. He averted his gaze. "And you can do sums?"

"Yes."

"Then there must be many ways you could earn money."

She shook her head. "Nothing."

"Can't you find work?" She shook her head again. "Why not?" he asked. "Is it because you were Commissioner Joliet's—" He hesitated over the word. "—wife?"

"It is because I was double."

Her voice was so soft that he thought he must have misunderstood. "You were double?"

"I was two." She held out her hand with her first two fingers pressed together. "When I was born. My mother had two."

"Oh." Understanding came upon him. "You were a twin? You had a sister?"

"A brother."

"And where is he?"

"He died."

"And because of that, you cannot find work?"

"Yes."

"I don't understand."

The girl – perhaps he should think of her as a woman, if she were not lying about her age – licked her lips with the tip of a rose-colored tongue, eyeing him speculatively. She stood swinging her hips slightly from side to side, a movement that was childlike and suggestive at the same time. "I can work, patron."

"What can you do?"

"You know what."

He sighed. "Sophie, that work is over. And don't you understand? It is not work for such a young girl. It's shameful."

He had said the wrong thing. For the first time, her smooth face showed an expression, a flash of displeasure. Her mouth turned down. "I am not a child. You have seen me. You know that."

"Then you should have a family of your own." Too late, he remembered Joliet's words. They take care of it. If she becomes pregnant. She goes away. A few days.

Comes back right as rain. She had stopped swaying. She was looking from under her thick eyelashes into a corner of the room, as though she saw something there. Perhaps she was just waiting to be dismissed. He sighed. "If you can think of something you would like to do, come to me. Not as – not as a wife, I mean. Just ask me if you need help."

"Yes, patron." Without any sign that she was grateful for the gift or that anything he'd said had affected her, she left him, melting away like a cat. He was left with a feeling of shame, as though he, like Joliet, had taken advantage of her in some way. He had been wrong, he now thought, to have summoned her and spoken to her, made her a gift of any kind. It implied something that he did not wish to examine too closely.

On Sunday, normally the dreariest of days, he awoke with the pleasant feeling that for once there was something for him to look forward to. He had made an appointment – of sorts – with the potter, Catherine Atélé. He was eager to see her again. She had aroused his curiosity. And today he could assure her that his interest in her was not of Commissioner Joliet's brand. In fact, today he could dazzle her with his wisdom and experience of the wider world beyond Bassongo.

His meager wardrobe had suffered since he had come to Bassongo. His own sweat had bleached all his khaki shirts on the chest and back; and the laundry run by Raymond's wives had worn out the fabric of everything. However he dressed with care, putting on a slouch hat and boots to look, as he hoped, masterful. He rode out to her house feeling more optimistic than he had done for weeks past.

By now, the collection of pots had changed in colour to a variety of dry, pale grays. He found her carrying the vessels into an open field behind her house, assisted by two old women. Once again, she had her skirts tucked up, showing her long, shapely legs, which he noted with pleasure. He dismounted and greeted her.

"May I help?"

"If you are careful," she replied, slightly breathless.

He joined in the work, carrying the larger pots to the field. There, she was heaping them on a sort of raft of branches. Nearby, he saw that she had gathered a large stack of dry wood and vegetation. "Where is your kiln?" he asked her.

"I don't have a kiln," she replied.

"Then how will you bake your pots?"

"Wait and see," she replied with some irritation. Her face was pearled with sweat and there were dark patches on her dress where it had soaked through. Her attention was concentrated on her work. He watched her with covert appreciation, wondering why such a vital, handsome woman had not attracted blacksmiths from far and wide.

"All your pots have round bottoms," he commented. "They'll all fall over unless someone is holding them."

"I would prefer it if you left your aesthetics at home."

"The issue is a practical one." She ignored him and arranged the pile of pots with great care, studying the placement of each pot intently, moving some pieces several times until she was satisfied. He lit a cigar. "I suppose this lot represents many days of work?"

"I suppose you will continue to ask foolish questions all morning?" she retorted.

He was amused by her snappishness. "I will be silent."

"You may speak, if you are sensible."

"I can't guarantee that. But I would like to be useful."

"Then I need your arms and not your tongue."

"They are yours, Madame."

She pointed. "Will you bring the dried leaves, please?"

He obeyed, helping the old women to carry the bundles of rustling straw. She packed these around the pots, her hands deft and quick. When he attempted to place some of the stuff himself, she pulled it out impatiently and re-laid it. After all the pots were covered with leaves, she began spreading the firewood over them, slowly heaping it up to make a large pyre, walking round and round, pulling a branch out here, pushing more wood in there, turning her head on one side in a characteristic pose to consider her work. He continued to be amused, but he was also impressed. Simple as her materials were, she knew what she was doing, and was going about it with sureness and precision. Once again, he had the feeling that she was far better at what she did – at her life – than he was.

"Why do you stare at me like that?" she asked, bending down to move one of the larger branches.

"I am simply admiring your thoroughness."

"Aren't you thorough in your work?"

"As a matter of fact, I was just thinking, with some shame, that I am nothing like you."

"Perhaps you don't go hungry if your work is badly done."

"Perhaps that's it." She had such life, such beauty! Such a one would be a sensation in Paris, he thought. Imagine if he were to meet Justine, say in the Jardin des Tuileries, with Catherine on his arm. What a coup that would be! The remembrance of Justine cast a momentary shadow over his happiness.

At last she had the stack the way she wanted it. She held out her hand. "Can you give me a match?"

He handed the matches over. She lit a dry leaf and moved around the pyre, touching the straw in various places. Flames began to lick upwards, almost invisible in the bright sunlight, but giving off a coiling shimmer of heat. The old women retreated, covering their heads and faces with their shawls. Smoke began to rise. Soon the bonfire was hot enough to drive Jean-Patrice back, but Catherine kept close by, pushing logs further into the flames with a stick. At last she could not bear it either, and she came to him, gasping. He offered her his water flask. She tipped it up and poured a stream into her open mouth.

"I thought you were going to catch fire."

"Sometimes the wood moves. It can break the pots, or fire them unevenly. You can lose all your work."

She handed his flask back. He poured water onto his handkerchief to soak it. "Please allow me." He mopped her face to take away ash and cool her skin. Her almond eyes looked back at him warily. "I was told that you are called Catherine Atélé and that you were a schoolteacher at the mission."

"You must first have asked questions to have been told those things."

"Yes, I asked about you."

"Why?"

"I am interested in you."

She raised her eyebrows slightly. "Indeed? And what else did you learn about me?"

"That you may only marry a blacksmith."

She laughed. "Poor me! If I believed in that superstition, I would be very sad."

"Why did you leave the mission?"

Her face closed. "I married a man who was not a Christian," she said. "My husband didn't want me to worship the white men's god. So we went away to live with his clan."

"And then?"

"He died. I came back to live in this village."

"Why didn't you continue teaching?"

She was plainly irritated by his questions. "This is like a catechism. I didn't continue teaching because by then the missionaries had gone. And I couldn't start a school all by myself. I teach a few children now and write letters for people. But I have to support myself from day to day, so I taught myself to make pots."

"How did you begin?"

Catherine shrugged. "I picked up clay in my hands."

"Just like that?"

"It was not hard."

"I could not do it. You have a wonderful talent. Everything you make is beautiful. But now you live outside the village, all alone."

She watched the flames pouring from her bonfire. "Perhaps the village prefers that I live outside, all alone."

He smiled at her. "Are you so difficult?"

"Very difficult."

"Then perhaps it suits you to be alone, too."

"Yes. It does."

"And yet you're an educated woman. It's sad to see you so isolated."

"Sad for whom?"

"Well, for me, I suppose."

"What am I to you?" she asked, with a sparkle of amusement in her eyes. "Are you a blacksmith?"

"Nothing so useful. But I am given the task of vaccinating the population of Bassongo. Do you know what vaccination is?"

"I've heard of it."

He showed her the scar on his arm. "A scratch is made on the arm. There is a little fever and then one is protected against the smallpox. Everyone in Libreville, white and black, has already had it done."

"And what does this have to do with me?"

"I have to train a vaccinator. Someone to prepare the serum from the cow and administer the inoculation. It isn't complicated. There's a salary. More than that, it is a service to humanity."

"A service to humanity! You are very eloquent."

"Well, a service to Bassongo."

"I am not so indebted to Bassongo that I feel the need to do it a service." She went back to the fire to move a log that had slipped out of the flames. A column of smoke was rising high into the clear blue sky. He watched the fluid movements of her body, feeling that she was rising in his estimation with each tart answer. And as he learned to understand her beauty, so she appeared more and more beautiful to him.

When she returned, dusting her hands, he said, "You are literate and responsible. I think you are perfect."

"I am very imperfect, Monsieur."

"Well, imperfect as you are, perhaps you could come to the Residency one day? I can show you everything there."

"Perhaps." She gestured at the fire. "But you can see that I am busy. These must be taken to the markets. It will be some days before I am free."

"Yes." Her fire, after a few minutes of intense heat, was collapsing into a mountain of cinders now, heat glowing red through the ash. "Is that sufficient to bake all the pots?"

"It appears to have worked for the last thousand years or so," she said, straight-faced. But he saw the gleam in her eyes and the rounding of her cheeks that indicated a suppressed laugh.

"You think I am patronizing you. But if you were to build a kiln, you would be able to control the firing very accurately. And you would obtain much higher temperatures."

"And what would that do?"

"Well, the clay would vitrify. The vessels would be much harder."

"Would that be progress?"

"They would last longer. It's the way it's done in Europe. I happen to have seen it done," he added. "There was a large pottery factory in the town where I was born."

"But this is not Europe."

"Why are you laughing at me?" he complained.

"Perhaps Monsieur should consider the humble African pot more carefully before wishing to change it."

"What should I consider?"

"Because the clay is not vitrified, and the bottom is round, we can put our pots on the fire and cook in them, and they won't crack. If we carry water in them, the clay absorbs a little and keeps the water cool. They balance on our heads easily when we need to carry them. In every kitchen there is a little corner with sand, so the pots can be put there – and so, Monsieur, they do not fall over."

"You make me feel foolish."

"Folly and ignorance are different things."

"Much obliged to you," he said wryly.

"In addition to this, a kiln would need a lot of fuel. Our pots are baked using only a small amount of dead wood, which is easy to gather. You whites love to cut down trees, but we blacks seldom do so, and then only after we have consulted the spirit of the tree. To kill a tree in order to bake a pot would be very wasteful. And quite un-African." The pile of ash was sinking lower and lower as it burned up, revealing the humps of the largest pots, like fossilized dinosaur eggs. "Now they will cool down slowly for the rest of the day. That will make them stronger. Except this one." She went forward and carefully lifted a smaller pot out of the coals, using her stick. She took it some distance away from the fire and laid it upside-down on the earth, dusting off the fine coating of ash. She took a container of some dark liquid and, using a brush made from a handful of straw, sprinkled a few drops on the pot. The clay was still extremely hot and the liquid hissed and evaporated, leaving circular stains. She continued to sprinkle, turning the pot carefully, until it was covered with a free design of concentric circles, like agate. He watched, bemused both by the simplicity of the process and the skill with which it was used. "Why is that one so special?" he asked.

"Don't you recognize it?" she asked. "This is the one you wanted." She indicated the oval dent near the rim. "There's my thumb print."

When the bowl had cooled, he picked it up and examined it. It was now dark, marbled and glossy. She had taken great care over it. "I don't think I could find anything more lovely in Paris."

"You may take it back with you and astound them," she said.

"I will, unless I end up in the graveyard next to Joliet," he replied. "Thank you for teaching me."

"You appear to be a satisfactory student."

"How much is the pot?"

"I will have to think," she said. "Next time I see you, I will tell you the price." She left him to go and tend to her fire. He put the bowl carefully in his saddlebag and mounted the mare. Before riding away, her looked at her one last time. She was standing by the pile of ash, looking at it as though deep in thought. He wondered whether she had forgotten him already. But he had issued his invitation and now he would await the results.

He returned to the tranquil companionship of Chloë, who was not beautiful, but who was considerate of his feelings and did not make him feel such a fool. She was waiting for him in the entrance of the Residency, grunting with quiet satisfaction at his return. "It's a lovely day, Chloë," he said. He held out his hand. "Let's take a turn in the garden."

The gorilla hesitated, then took his hand trustingly. He led her outside into the sunlight. If she was to rejoin her family, she had to get used to the world beyond the Residency. Blinking somewhat anxiously, she allowed herself to be conducted around the garden. Her tight grip on his fingers slackened after a while. She began to show some interest in the plants. At last she let go of his hand and ambled over to a tree. Reaching up with her strong arms, she tore off a small branch and sat down to browse on the leaves with evident pleasure. He was surprised. So she was a leaf eater, as well? Her diet of milk, bananas and cooked vegetables, while perhaps suitable for her baby years, was clearly insufficient for her needs. She was a growing quadrumane and her appetites had evolved.

He stood watching her, feeling a pride that was – he hesitated to frame the word in his mind – paternal. He noted the tree she had chosen. She ate slowly but constantly, and with evident pleasure, seated on her ample buttocks, looking around her placidly. Somehow in this pose she acquired a kind of dignity which she did not have perched on a dining chair and sucking milk out of a bowl. All in all it had been, he felt, a day of progress and learning.

12

Two days after this, he was startled by the shriek of the gunboat's whistle. His first thought was that he had stopped being aware of the passage of time. Weeks had passed imperceptibly. He had been a soul in limbo. Hyppolite and Narcise rowed him to the gunboat in one of the dugouts. He clambered onto the deck, carrying the bag with his reports to Malherbe and some letters home. The policemen carried Joliet's few possessions. The grizzled shellback received the news of Joliet's death with the utmost indifference.

"At least he had the decency to wait for your arrival. Did you issue a death certificate?"

"It's in the bag. Natural causes. Although as he was dying, he said the snake had been deliberately introduced into his bed."

"Feverish," the captain grunted. "Anything else?"

Jean-Patrice felt empty. Anything else? He had spent a season among savages, without seeing another white face except that of a dead man, sleeping with a gorilla and eating porcupines. What else was there to report? Certainly not the *Liber Libidinorum*, which he had retained. "Nothing else."

"You will see us in mid-January or the beginning of February," the captain said.

He suppressed an exclamation. "So long?"

The man looked at him coldly. "There is nothing to bring us up this reach of the river. You can manage for that time, I take it?"

"Of course," he said with a hollow smile.

The Captain gave him the bag from Malherbe and bade him a curt farewell. The young lieutenant helped him off the gunboat. "How many inoculations have you performed?"

"My three officers. And one civilian."

"Who is the civilian?"

"A madman."

"Excellent progress," the other replied with irony. "Have you considered your appearance, Duméril?" he asked.

"What is wrong with my appearance?"

"Your hair, to begin with. Who cuts it?"

"I have been cutting it myself," he replied with as much dignity as he could summon up.

"You are not an octopus. Ask one of the native women to cut it for you. Are you settled in that department, by the way?"

"Which department?"

"Someone to share your bed."

"That is my business," he said stiffly.

"Well, take care you are settled. One can easily go crazy in these surroundings."

"I have not yet gone crazy."

"And you should shave more often. It is important to give the right impression to the natives, my dear fellow. You might be able to inoculate some sane people if you did not resemble a madman yourself." He favored Jean-Patrice with a superior smile. "Don't let yourself go, Duméril. A white man should never let himself go."

Jean-Patrice sat rigidly in the dugout between the two

policemen, infuriated by the brief encounter. He did not look over his shoulder when the gunboat whistled, though he longed to watch it out of sight, as a marooned pirate might gaze at his comrades abandoning him on a desert isle. He was determined to conceal his loneliness at all costs. Are you settled in that department?

He opened the bag from Libreville at his desk. It was bulky, but most of the bulk was made up of some Paris magazines, well-thumbed and many months old, which he set aside for later reading. From Malherbe there was a laconic circular about certain diseases of cattle and humans, the collection of taxes in February, and other departmental matters. There was a box of vile Manila cheroots from Tosti. There were also some letters from home. One of these, he saw with astonishment, was sealed in a pale lime green envelope. It was a hue with which he was extremely familiar. He stared at it for a long while, then tore it open.

My dear Jean-Patrice,

Your letter was very painful to me. I'm not perfect, but I don't think I'm the monster you portray. I loved you, in my own way, with as much passion as I am capable of feeling. I'm sorry it wasn't enough. But you know, relationships such as ours have certain limits. One cannot easily transgress those limits, no matter how one may yearn to.

You must admit that you also had your fun with me. You set out to win me as a corsair on the Barbary Coast might have pursued a little caravel, laden with spices and silks. You boarded the caravel and you plundered the spices and the silks to your heart's content. The caravel rejoiced in your plunder, my dear, she did indeed sigh with delight. But then, like a cruel corsair, you wanted to sink the caravel. Was that sensible?

I have a husband and four children. You wanted me to leave everything and live in some pirate bay with you for evermore. But one cannot change one's life so easily. What would my children have done in the pirate bay? What would I have done? We would have sunk in all senses — sunk from grace, from society, from comfort. You would have found that the pearls soon lost their luster and the silks tarnished. I would no longer have been the rich caravel you admired so much, but a drab hulk at anchor — and you would have ceased to be the romantic corsair and would have become a sad landlubber staring at the sea from a tavern window. I do not want to think of that.

Perhaps if you had been more patient, less impetuous, more guileful — ah, but then you would not have been Jean-Patrice. But perhaps even Jean-Patrice can change?

Our love was sad at the end. I wish it had been otherwise. We must both do penance for our sins.

Whatever you may think, my penance is sincere. I care about you and miss you greatly. I know that the abundant gifts which a loving Creator has bestowed on you will bring you great success in Africa. Two years will soon pass. You will return, I sincerely believe, triumphantly to your motherland. Perhaps then we may meet as friends and perhaps by then you will have learned to forgive your affectionate

Justine.

He read the letter a second time. Was that all she had found to say to him? Was that all the apology he was to receive for having destroyed himself at her altar? This was a schoolgirl's essay, with its elaborately extended metaphors and trite conclusion! Jean-Patrice felt the blood rush to his face. Enraged, he snatched up paper and a pen and began to dash off a reply.

My dear Justine,

And did you not promise – no, swear on all that was holy – that you would be mine alone? Did you not vow a hundred times that you would go with me to the humblest refuge, so long as we could be together? I am not guileful and cunning, as you want me to be. I believed the words you spoke!

Your penance and mine are very different, as our loves were very different. Are you denying yourself coffee-cream and petits fours at Charbonell, or saving Maurice the cost of a new hat with a stuffed hummingbird on the brim?

Your talk of a heroic return to France is fatuous. "Two years will soon pass!" How easily those words flow from your pen! Your years must, like your love and your penance, be very different from mine. Here the time crawls like

He threw the pen down. What was the point of these inanities? What could he say to her? That, even if he survived and got back to Paris, he would always be the man who had seduced a Director's wife and was sent to the jungles to perform nobody knew what pointless expiation?

His career, such as it was, would bear the mark of this hiatus, like the rings of a tree that had suffered through bad winters. Men would snigger behind his back, no respectable woman would look at him. Yet to remain here, in the colonial service, never hearing decent music or having a decent conversation or eating a decent meal, was to accept a living death. He would grow old and yellowed and turn into a leathery turtle like Malherbe, waving an impotent flipper at lusty young scoundrels freshly decanted on this shore to froth and foam; and going home each night to eat with a mulatto wife and contemplate his own meaningless.

He heard the murmur of Joliet's voice upstairs. His flesh crawled. This was becoming too much. And then, the stink of Joliet's rotting stump slowly pervaded the room, nauseating him.

A leathery hand slipped into his. Chloë clambered into his lap, putting her long arms around his neck and laying her massive head on his chest. She weighed nearly as much as an adult woman. Perhaps she was moved by his despair. Tentatively, he put his arms around her. She was warm, muscular and hairy. The zoo smell of her fur was better, at least, than Joliet's supernatural putrefaction. She lay there for a while, grunting peacefully, until he shooed her away.

He went to the mirror and peered at himself. He looked gaunt. He had lost weight. His self-administered haircuts had seemed successful to him but then, he could not see the back of his own head. And he had not shaved himself as diligently as he should have. Was he starting to look like Ndoumou?

He put his shaving kit and the scissors in his pocket and went out to saddle the mare. As he rode, he thought over the letter Justine had written him. Taken at face value, it was so reasonable, so warm. The words were kind. Why had it wounded him so deeply? Because it had contained so much truth about himself?

Yes; her touch had always been as delicate as a butterfly's wing, but as accurate as a poniard. She understood him better than he understood himself, in some ways. He did not like being shown his own folly. At least she had done it as affectionately as possible.

There was something in him that had always wanted far more from her than she could give. Was it because he had lost his mother before he could even know her? He had never lacked for the company of women. They were drawn to him. Why had he chosen to fall so deeply in love with a married woman, when all the world was before him? Why had he destroyed his life so readily?

He arrived at the crossroads. Baked pottery stood in rows around the house but there was no sign of the potter.

He dismounted, tethered the mare and went to the doorway of her house, calling her name. "Mam'selle Atélé?"

She came to the doorway, wearing a white dress, her slender arms bare. Her loveliness was painfully sad to him. He felt emotionally destitute, his strength eroded by weeks in this awful hole. He stared at her blankly until she frowned.

"What is it, Monsieur?"

"I came to ask a favor." He produced the scissors and razor from his pocket. "Can you cut my hair and shave me?"

She examined the implements dubiously. "I am not a barber."

"You're an artist. It must be much easier than making a pot." She looked as though she were about to refuse and he played his last card. "I have no-one else."

She shrugged. "Very well. I can try."

"Thank you."

She stepped back. Jean-Patrice took off his hat and entered. The house was cool. As his eyes adjusted to the subdued light, he stared around him. One wall had been decorated with dozens of hand prints, arranged in neat rectangular patterns, sometimes ochre on white, sometimes white on black. The other three walls were covered in tribal masks. He was at first bewildered by the extraordinary collection of faces which looked back at him, some snarling or grimacing threateningly, others mimicking the serenity of sleep and death. He tried to pick out something in common, but the carvings were as varied as Africa itself. Some of the faces were naturalistic, as delicate as the neoclassical sculpture currently in vogue in Paris. Others were simplified into geometric designs that only resolved themselves into faces when one's eyes allowed them to. These were, to him, more savage than the animal snarls. They were disturbing. He groped for the word. They were abstract.

Catherine watched him as he walked through the rooms of the house. Each room was decorated in the same way, with the imprint of her right palm, the fingers outstretched, and with dozens of human faces carved in the shapes beyond any European imagination.

"Where do all these masks come from?" he asked in wonder.

"I rescued most of them from fires."

"Why were they being burned?"

"The first thing the missionaries do is make their converts burn their old beliefs," she replied. "Everything is piled on a bonfire and goes up in smoke. That way, even if the converts get disillusioned with their new God, there is nothing left to go back to."

"So you darted into the flames and pulled out these?" he said, smiling.

"I burned my hands many times."

"I don't know how you sleep with all these faces glaring at you." The rooms were spotless. He looked at her single bed, low on the floor, a crucifix hanging on the wall above it, a Bible and a few other books on a shelf. The house spoke of a woman at peace with solitude and her own company. It smelled of her and of her skin. He reached out and laid his right hand over one of her palm prints, covering it. "This pattern is beautiful."

"It's only the print of my hand. Take off your shirt, Monsieur."

Jean-Patrice stripped to the waist and sat on the stool she gave him. He felt her fingertips run experimentally through his hair and caught his breath. It was the first time a woman had touched him in weeks. Gooseflesh spread across his body, hardening his nipples. She began to cut. "If you had kept Sophie, she would have done this for you."

"Does the whole of Bassongo know everything I do?"

"Except the deaf," she said. She moved in front of him. He could smell her skin, sweet and womanly. Her warmth made him giddy, her closeness overwhelmed him. He wanted to put his arms around her waist and bury his face against her breasts.

"She should find a husband," he said.

"It will be difficult. People believe Joliet's ghost still possesses her."

"That is superstitious rubbish," he retorted. "Are you no longer a Christian?"

"I'm telling you what others believe, Monsieur, not what I believe."

"She told me she was born a twin but that her brother had died."

She was silent for a while. "He didn't die. He was killed at birth."

Jean-Patrice was appalled. "Why?"

"Twins are accursed. They are monsters who don't have souls. If they're allowed to live, they will swallow up the whole village. The oganga buried her brother alive. The mother was sent away to a village in the forest, where the mothers of twins have to stay without men, in case they bear any more monsters. For a man to mate with her now is punishable by death."

He looked at the savage faces that hung all over the walls, grinning at him cruelly. "And Sophie?"

"The oganga kept her alive for a special purpose."

"To be the concubine of white men?"

"It's considered a better fate than death."

"Is it?" he said. "Have you looked into her eyes?"

Catherine answered him calmly. "Yes. I taught her to read and write."

"Your oganga kept her alive but made sure that she knew she was doomed, only fit to service the lust of soul eaters. It doesn't matter in her case, since she doesn't have a soul."

"Why are you so angry with me?"

"Because you talk so calmly about these hideous superstitions. You may defend African ways of baking a

100

pot, Catherine, but you cannot defend that."

"I did not give you permission to call me Catherine."

"You are very starchy."

"I don't try to defend superstition. But since white men come here, and men need women, you are also part of the problem. A woman always needs to be found for the patron. Some men want more than one. Sophie had her uses. I see you pull a face. Your morality is very tender. Much easier to say that blacks are savages than to admit that whites are immoral. And it's easy for you to say these practices are hideous. You were not born here."

"No, indeed. If I hadn't hauled my own trunk out of the river, it would be there yet." He saw her smiling. "What is so funny?"

"I watched you that day." Her eyes sparkled. "They made up a song about you. Now they call you by the name of the song."

"What's the song called?"

"Culblanc." She covered her mouth with her hand and laughed out loud, almost closing her eyes.

"White Bum? Does everyone call me White Bum?"

"Every time you dived under the water, we all saw your backside." She was laughing so much that she had to sit on the stool beside him. "It isn't meant to mock you."

"I'm not so sure," he said ruefully.

"Culblanc is the name of a water bird. It also has a white backside and it dives, as you did. Don't be angry. All white men are given nicknames, you know."

"I see. And what was my predecessor called?"

She hesitated. "He was called Mchwa."

"And what does that mean?"

"It means a termite."

"Why did they call him that?"

"For many reasons."

He watched her laughing, enjoying her beauty, the vitality in her. "None of them complimentary, I presume?"

"The mchwa makes an ugly red pillar of mud in our fields."

"Is that what Joliet was like? An anthill? An obstruction?"

"In some ways."

"He behaved abominably."

She did not take the opening to discuss Joliet which he offered. "You're not like other white men."

"How am I different?"

"You don't think you're a god." She glanced at him mockingly. "Or do you?"

"I'm just a man. You can see that."

"If you're not a god, then what gives you the right to come here and rule us all, one man over many hundreds?"

"I don't know. I didn't ask to come here."

"Yet you came."

"I had little choice."

She resumed cutting his hair. "Did you do something very bad, to be sent to this terrible place?"

"Bassongo is not so terrible," he said, as though he had not been cursing the place half an hour before.

"They say that Culblanc stole the wife of an important man in his own country. He had to be sent away to avoid a scandal."

He recalled Malherbe saying the forest had ears. "I believed she would leave her husband for me, even though I am much poorer. Culblanc is a very foolish man sometimes."

"Culblanc is a man who doesn't accept things as they are. That is both good and bad. You dived to the bottom of the river to get your box. With all the bottles of brandy inside."

"They say that, too, do they? That I'm a drunkard?"

"They say you're lonely." She took the brush and lathered his face. She tilted his head back and began to shave his chin. He looked into her face. Her skin was astonishingly fine, seeming to be covered with microscopic

102

flecks of gold dust which caught the light. Her mouth was full, the skin of her lips covered with tiny, soft wrinkles. He felt that in some way, he was seeing humanity for the first time, meeting something alien yet profoundly familiar. He was under a spell. There was an erotic thrill to feeling the razor at his throat. He barely felt the deft scrapes of the steel, yet he was aware that she held his life in her hands.

She finished and held the bowl of water while he rinsed his face. She took a broom and began to sweep the clippings of his hair into a pile. Children were crowding at the door by now, peering in wide-eyed at the sight of the half-naked Jean-Patrice being trimmed by Catherine Atélé the potter.

"Thank you," he said, putting on his shirt. "Have you decided about the vaccinations?"

She studied him with her almond eyes. "I am still thinking. I can't say now."

"Tell me how much I owe you for the bowl – and everything else."

"That can also wait."

"I hope the price won't keep going up every day."

"Half of Bassongo owes me something. Why not you?"

"I would like to live in a house decorated with your hand prints," he said inconsequentially. He rode back to the Residency. The air was cool around his cropped temples. He felt that he looked presentable. More than that, he felt she had helped to lighten a leaden weight that had been hanging on him, bending him almost to the ground with despair.

13

He had given up the idea of replying to Justine's letter. There was nothing he wanted to say to her. The shipwreck of their relationship (to continue her maritime metaphor) lay like an immovable hulk on the coral reef of his consciousness, emerging or submerging as the tides of his mood fluctuated. Until the waves battered it to pieces, so to speak, its sullen presence had to be accepted.

In the meantime, there was work. It was not work of an elevated sort, true, involving as it did the counting of things and the listing of things and the cataloguing of things, but its very tediousness was a relief from his thoughts – and perhaps a way to comfort himself and keep his terrors at bay. He was seated at his desk in the study, writing, when a soft murmur made him look up. Sophie had come into the room, making one of her silent, feline entrances. She was wearing the green dress with the red roses again today and her hair was teased out around her face.

"Good morning Sophie," he said. "You walk so quietly."

"Good morning, patron."

He was wary, feeling that the teased hair and the

printed roses meant business. "Why have you come to see me?" She held out the envelope he had given her a few days earlier, showing him that it was empty. "You are asking for more money?"

"Yes, patron."

"But Sophie…" He laid down his pencil. "I gave you quite a lot of money last time. Have you spent it already?"

"Yes."

"On what?"

"I gave it to my father."

Jean-Patrice was irritated. "The money was not intended for Raymond. I told you that. It was for you."

"For what?"

"To buy a new dress, for example."

"I have this dress already."

"I can't keep giving you money to hand over to your father. That is not an arrangement I want."

She looked at him without expression. Knowing what he now did about her, he found that her blank gaze was disturbing. Perhaps if someone was raised not to believe they had a soul, that spiritual organ did not develop. Or perhaps there were oceans of suffering behind that impassive mask. "What arrangement do you want, patron?"

"I don't want any arrangement."

"But you gave me money. And you said I must come back when the money is finished."

"I did not say that. I said—" He sighed. "I should not have given you money. It was wrong."

"You let that bad woman cut your hair." She frowned. "That was foolish, yes."

"Why do you say that Mam'selle Atélé is a bad woman?"

She made a click of scorn between her teeth. "Mam'selle Atélé!"

"She was your teacher, wasn't she?"

"Oh, she is clever, that one." Sophie spoke with

contempt. "She likes white men. She will make you run and run and run. You don't want me, but you want that one. Why? I am younger and prettier. I am for you. That one will take your hair to the oganga and make juju." He had not seen her show so much feeling before or speak at such length. "She will make you sick and die."

He couldn't help smiling. "I don't think Mam'selle Atélé will make juju with my hair."

"She will take your hair to the witchdoctor," Sophie said with emphasis, "and they will mix your hair with the earth from a grave and they will put it in the stomach of a doll. And they will hammer nails into the doll. And then your spirit will belong to them."

"Well," he replied tolerantly, "I hope I am proof against such sorceries."

"That one is not for you. I am for you." She slipped her arms around his neck and slid onto his lap like a cat, looking into his face. The scent of wood smoke from her skin made him dizzy. Her eyes glistened. "I am not so ugly."

"You are not ugly at all." He tried to ease her off his thighs but found that his hands were encountering more of her supple body than he intended to touch. She kissed his cheek in a way that was daughterly – or was it motherly? "Please, Sophie."

"No, I am not ugly," she murmured. A warm, wet tongue probed the corner of his mouth in a way that was neither motherly nor daughterly. Her body seemed to mould itself to him like something adhesive. Her mouth travelled to his ear. Her breath was hot and moist. "Monsieur Joliet was so ugly," she whispered confidentially. "But you are not ugly." Her tongue probed the sensitive passage of his ear, producing a thrilling sensation that scuttled down his belly like a lizard.

This was like the temptation of St. Anthony, he thought with a groan. He recalled the Abbé Fouquet, his old headmaster, illustrating the way St. Anthony had raised his hands to Heaven, crying out, "Oh Lord, who may escape from these snares?" and how the Almighty had replied, "Humility shall escape them."

"What did you say, patron?"

He managed to extricate himself from her slim but surprisingly tenacious arms and rose, dislodging her. His erection was extremely discomforting. "I said, I have something to show you."

"What?"

He looked around blankly. His eye lighted on a colorful object, the model boat he had bought on his first excursion in Libreville. "This is rather clever. You see? The little men can be taken out and lined up next to the canoe, holding their paddles. This white fellow looks something like me, except more handsome." He offered it to her uncertainly.

She investigated the carving, moving the oarsmen around, changing their positions. Her fingers were careful. The fox-like expression that had come over her face began to fade.

"Do you like it?" he asked.

"Yes, it's pretty."

He was relieved that she had been distracted, at least temporarily, from her project of seduction. "Then you may keep it."

"For me?"

"Yes."

She seemed pleased. It was hard to believe that she was eighteen. She looked more like a child of twelve who had no toys. He ushered her to the door, trying to strike the fatherly note. "I have work to do, Sophie. You mustn't distract me."

"Don't go to her again."

"Mam'selle Atélé? She's useful to me. And you have no right to tell me whom I can and cannot see, Sophie."

"You will be sorry." She gave him a glittering look from the tails of her eyes. "You will regret. Yes."

"That is my business."

She shrugged her skinny shoulders and departed, absorbed in the carving. She had forgotten her request for money. He was aware that he had not yet found a permanent solution to the problem of Sophie, but he was happy to have given her something that pleased her. Her jealousy was amusing and yet also pathetic. He would have to see about finding work for her.

The ancient gun that squatted in front of the Residency piqued his interest. To be District Commissioner of Bassongo was not a great position in the world, to be sure; but to have custody of a cannon possessed a certain schoolboy romance. He examined it. The breech and bore were somewhat corroded but still functional. The trucks, made of mahogany, had resisted the gnawing of termites. In theory, there was no reason why the thing should not fire. The tools for maintaining the cannon were in the cellar. He ordered his police force to mount a cleaning party. Stripped to the waist, he and Hyppolite spent a morning cleaning the oxidation from all the working parts with a wire brush and oiled the bright metal, while Narcise and Hyacinth painted the spokes of the wheels.

"Has this gun ever been discharged?" he asked.

"Nobody remembers," Hyppolite replied, after conferring with the others.

"It was probably last fired against the Duke of Wellington," Jean-Patrice said, peering down the bore. "But in principle, it is operative."

"Does the patron wish to fire the cannon?"

"Perhaps."

"Against whom?" Hyppolite enquired cautiously.

"Well, not against anyone in particular. As a demonstration."

"A demonstration of what?"

Jean-Patrice did not answer. He had looked up and seen Catherine walking across the open yard towards them. She wore a long print dress, as most of the younger women did, but she moved like no other woman he knew, with grace and pride, her arms held a little way from her body, her long legs swinging. She stopped in front of him, ignoring the other men completely.

"I've come to see how the inoculation is done. "

He felt the importance of the occasion. "Excellent," he said briskly. "Let me make myself decent." He ordered the others to finish in his absence and heard them murmuring behind him as he walked away. After rinsing his torso, he put his shirt back on and conducted her to see No. 5, who was stolidly munching in her stall. "This is the prophylactic calf. We begin by making a cut in her skin. We break open an ampoule of serum and rub the vaccine into the cut. A few days later, festering sores develop all over her belly."

"Poor animal."

"They don't seem to mind too much." He looked at the calf speculatively. "And perhaps it's a better fate than being turned into veal cutlets. Certainly, it confers a greater benefit on humanity."

"That must be a consolation to her," Catherine said. "And what does one do with these festering sores?"

"Ah, they contain the effective matter, the antitoxin. We use that to inoculate the population." He took her back to the house to show her how to separate the serum in Joliet's study, which was now to serve as a laboratory. She stopped short as she encountered Chloë in the entrance. "Don't worry," he said. "She's tame."

"I've seen her before," Catherine said warily. "But she was very small, then. She's much bigger now."

"I'm going to return her to the forest."

"That may not be so easy," she replied, watching the gorilla embracing his legs. "She loves you."

He was embarrassed at the gorilla's display of affection. He tried to disentangle her from his legs. "It's foolish, I know, but we are friends of a sort."

She studied him. "I don't think it's foolish."

"Well, one gets lonely," he said, shamefacedly. He hoisted Chloë onto his hip. She was immensely heavy, but he liked striking the fatherly note. "I take her into the garden every day so she can get used to the outside and learn what leaves she likes to eat. Each time she stays a little longer. I think that in the end she'll just wander away."

"She will run up to the first hunter she sees and he will kill her."

He was shocked by the grim remark. "I didn't think of that."

"Smoked gorilla meat is expensive, especially the hands and arms. And witchdoctors pay well for the skulls. The skins are sold in Libreville to Europeans. She represents a lot of money for an ordinary person. She's learned to trust humans. It would be very easy to kill her."

"You are right," he said gloomily. "She is yet another of the problems that Joliet has bequeathed me. He seems to haunt the place. I hear him talking, at night. Smell him. And in the house I found things, disgusting things—" He paused, aware of sounding and looking unhinged, with a gorilla on his hip and a wild light in his eye. "I'm sorry. You must think me mad."

"It's a grave metaphysical problem," she said gravely.

"You are mocking me."

"You sound like a superstitious African," she replied, "not a rational white man."

"I suppose I do."

She smiled slightly. "Don't worry. Everyone in Bassongo knows that Commissioner Joliet has not yet reached the underworld."

"Really?"

"The spirits of the dead are sometimes reluctant to leave their old places. They have to be guided."

"And how does one do that?"

"You need to enlist the aid of some frightening spirits to chase him. And the spirits of some pretty young girls to lure him."

"The carrot and the stick?"

"Otherwise he'll keep hanging around, making life unpleasant for you."

"Perhaps he wants his *Liber Libidinorum*," Jean-Patrice mused.

"His what?"

"He took photographs. Of an obscene nature. They're all stuck into a sort of journal. No point worrying about it now. Come and see the laboratory." He put Chloë down and took Catherine to the study, where he showed her the equipment, explaining how it was used. "The serum can be kept liquid and sterile for some time in these phials, using glycerin. When one is ready to inoculate a victim, the phial is opened. This little knife is dipped into the serum and then a scratch is made on the patient's arm, so the serum goes under the skin. The left arm is the best spot, high up enough so the patient can't suck the scratch."

"And then?"

"Then the patient gets a mild dose of cow pox. It can be uncomfortable for a day or two. The scratch festers and then heals. It develops into a typical pock mark, like this one on my arm. But now the patient is immune from smallpox. There is no more risk of death, blindness or disfigurement."

She looked up at him. "It seems simple."

"Yes. I told you it was. Do you accept the position? The salary is not very high, but—"

"Yes, I know. I will be a benefactress of humanity."

"Exactly."

"I'll think about it."

"Good. The problem is that people seem reluctant when I try to explain it. Apart from the policemen, I've only been able to vaccinate Ndoumou."

She considered. He saw that the pupils of her eyes were slightly oval, rather than round, something he had never noticed before. "Perhaps you should not explain too much. Talk of pus and poison will frighten away the superstitious. And you will have to start with someone who is not mad, or a policeman, to show that it has no ill effects. You may as well begin with me."

He smiled. "All right. The vaccinator has to be vaccinated." He dipped a clean lancet into a phial of serum and considered her slim, brown arm. "I'm afraid this beautiful skin is going to be scarred."

"Better than having my face look like a wasp's comb after the smallpox."

He took her arm in one hand and leaned forward, drawing the blade down the fine skin. There was a drop of blood. She inspected the scratch. The flawlessness of her face fascinated him, with its large, leaf shaped mouth, perfect nose and slightly tilted eyes. There was something almost Egyptian about the way her head was poised on her long neck. He prepared a plaster and applied it over the scratch. "There. It's done."

"Thank you, Monsieur le Commissaire. And now I have a scratch for you." She took a small piece of folded paper from her pocket and gave it to him. He opened it, Her writing was heavily slanted but neat, every letter formed with care:

1 pot	2 francs, 10 centimes
haircut	3 francs
shave	1 franc, 50 centimes
total	6 francs, 60 centimes.

"The haircut is somewhat expensive," he said with a note of protest.

"It was difficult. I had never done it before."

"But I was hoping – well, one's hair grows, you know. I was hoping that you would cut it once a week or so."

She raised her eyebrows. "You are finding many duties

for me, Monsieur," she said dryly. "I am not a barber."

Discomfited, he went to get her the money. With Justine de Marigny he had been imperious, a tyrant whose every whim had to be indulged. Infractions had incurred his grave displeasure and condign punishments. With this black woman he was unaccountably humble. But perhaps she had a presence that Justine, for all her sophistication, lacked. And perhaps, in his present abject state, he was learning humility. He counted it out carefully into her hand. "Remember, you will get a mild fever now," he reminded her. "The place will itch. You mustn't scratch. Just rest for a day or so."

She nodded. "I wish you luck with the ghost of Monsieur Joliet."

He wanted to ask her when she would come back. He was already dreading her absence, the seeping in of loneliness, the little supernatural scratchings and murmurings of the departed Joliet. But he held his peace. She was not a woman to be hustled.

He walked with her as far as the cannon and said goodbye there. He was aware of the looks the policemen gave him and wondered if they were laughing at him. The cannon was now gleaming, so he dismissed them.

Later, he lit one of Tosti's cheroots and sat with the pot she had made in his hands, turning it slowly to study its rich curves, caressing with his fingertips the velvety burnish that was so like her skin.

Raymond came to see him in the afternoon. Lately, his face had taken on a permanently sour cast. He expressed his displeasure in the sulky ways of a servant – slamming doors, crashing crockery unnecessarily, neglecting to perform certain duties. Jean-Patrice felt it was beneath his dignity to confront the man about his grievance, but today Raymond had the air of one ready to speak.

"What is it, Raymond?" he asked.

"Patron, why do you give Sophie toys?"

He looked at the man warily. "She seemed to be happy

with the thing."

"She is not happy. She is home crying. You insult her. You insult me. Sophie is not a child – she is a woman! She doesn't want toys. She wants woman's things!"

"By that, you mean money?"

"She needs a man, patron. She needs you."

"I have already spoken about that, Raymond. You must accept my decision."

"She cannot work in Bassongo," Raymond said, glowering at Jean-Patrice with his discolored eyes. "She cannot marry. What is she going to do?"

"She is your daughter. You must look after her."

"I have many daughters! I have many children, you know that. Sophie has no mother anymore."

"Yes, I have been told that."

"She was a bad woman. She has gone. Now I am left with Sophie. All she does is stay at home crying, crying, crying." He spread his hands. "What can I do? She has a mouth that asks for food. Where must the food come from?"

"I gave her quite a lot of money not so long ago. She told me she passed it on to you."

"Yes!" Raymond nodded eagerly. "If the patron does not want her, then the patron must pay the same every month."

"That is out of the question," Jean-Patrice retorted. "I can't afford that, for one thing. For another, I do not accept that I am responsible for her."

Raymond's mouth hardened. "Joliet left her nothing."

"I have no control over Joliet's finances, Raymond."

"You sent all his things back on the gunboat!"

"Of course. I had no right to give the girl anything from his estate!"

"But Joliet asked you to look after Sophie!"

"I have already told you that I am not bound by Joliet's wishes," Jean-Patrice said, his temper rising. "I am sorry for Sophie, but I have no arrangement with you or anyone else about her. I decline to be made responsible for her upkeep."

"Then why did you give her money the first time?"

"I gave her the money in the hope she would be able to use it for something practical."

"She is good only for one thing," Raymond said.

"I have no use for that thing." He controlled his temper. "I can offer her work in this house and pay her a small wage. She can eat here as everyone else does. But I cannot pay large amounts of money for her on a regular basis."

"Monsieur le Commissaire—"

"There is no more to be said," he interrupted, cutting the protests off.

Raymond departed, his frog face inflated with dudgeon. He could blow himself up until he burst, for all Jean-Patrice cared. He was starting to dislike the man intensely.

The next day, as he left the Residency, he heard a voice call, "Patron!" He found Sophie standing behind a shrub near the door. Her head was hanging but he could see that her face was swollen from at least two blows, one across the mouth, that had puffed her lips, another on the right eye, that had left it dark and swollen. So that was why the girl had been "crying, crying, crying." He recognized the injuries as deliberately public ones, designed to show the village Raymond's displeasure and embarrass the patron.

"Did your father do this?" he demanded, lifting her chin with his hand.

She kept her eyes down. "You said you would help me."

"I am not going to give you money."

She scraped the sole of her sandal in the dust. "I don't want money. I want to go to my mother."

"Where is she?"

She gestured vaguely. "At the forbidden village. Not far. One hour with the horse."

"You want me to take you?"

"I am afraid to go on my own. Nobody will come with me."

"Have you told your father you are going?"

"He will beat me again if I tell him."

"He will not beat you again," he replied grimly. "I'll see to that."

"Will you take me?"

He was about to refuse, but stopped. Perhaps this was a chance to get rid of her. If she remained in Bassongo, a thorn in everybody's side, the situation might become intolerable. Raymond would ill-treat her and the fault would be laid at his door. He sighed. "Very well. I'll take you on the horse."

Sophie brightened. "We must take food for her."

He went with Sophie to the kitchen. Two of Raymond's wives were chattering in there, but when he and Sophie entered, they fell silent and sidled out with lowered eyes. He allowed Sophie to choose some provisions, a sack of maize flour, a sack of beans, a bunch of bananas.

Jean-Patrice saddled the mare and loaded the food in her saddlebags. Perhaps this was for the best. Giving the boat to Sophie had been a stupid, impulsive act. What a fool he had been! The generous white man, giving toys to the African, toys which turned out to be unexpectedly dangerous.

"Did he beat you because of the boat?" he asked.

"He said I should have brought money."

"I'm sorry, Sophie. It's my fault."

She did not reply. He mounted and pulled Sophie up in front of him. She was nervous on the horse. Her body was slight and supple against his, pressed intimately between his thighs. He tried not to think of the implied eroticism of their position. He felt her hair brush his face and caught the smell of palm oil.

"Are you sure you know the way?" he asked.

"Yes, patron." She pointed. He guided the mare in the

direction she indicated, past the mission. He thought of the priest's skull, slowly emerging from the red clay as if for a breath of air, the bony fingers still clutching the rosary. The mare grunted under their weight but did not otherwise complain. Sophie's slim body bumped against his as she swayed to the mare's gait. She was like a wraith in his arms.

Some way past the mission, she pointed to a track which swerved off into a forest of spiky palms with tall inflorescences, which exuded a strong, sticky smell of resin. The scent grew almost overpowering as they rode through the palm forest, burning Jean-Patrice's throat and make him feel headachy.

At length, after riding for an hour, the mare began to snort and flick her ears. The smell of resin had given way to the unmistakable smell of human habitations – smoke, refuse and excrement. He judged they were about five miles from Bassongo now. They came to the settlement, on a low-lying piece of marshy land, no more than a handful of broken-down huts near a stream which snaked slowly towards the distant river.

Surrounding the village was a paling made of wicker hurdles, now half-rotted. At intervals, wooden masks had been set on posts. These, roughly carved and streaked white with the remnants of kaolin clay, were unmistakably threatening; they had the glaring eye holes and bared teeth of skulls.

"What are those?" he asked Sophie.

"They are warnings that this is a forbidden village. No man can come in."

"Then I had better leave you here."

"You may come in because you are white."

He felt a pang of apprehension as he rode into the place. It seemed deserted though smoke was rising from a patch of ash and a pestle leaned abandoned in a mortar. Refuse lay everywhere. He could see clear through some of the huts, whose roofs had collapsed. There were no chickens or other village animals, not even a dog to bark at them.

"Mami!" Sophie slid off the mare and called in a low, cautious voice. "Mami! Mami!" At length, a woman's figure appeared from the bush, keeping a careful distance. Sophie beckoned. The woman walked slowly towards them. "That is my Mami," Sophie said to Jean-Patrice with a hint of pride.

He dismounted and unloaded the provisions that they'd brought. There was no show of affection in the two women's greeting. They did not touch each other, but stood talking quietly. Sophie's mother had once been very pretty. Indeed, she seemed to be no more than thirty, but she was dirty, thin and exhausted-looking. She wore a worn-out singlet and a tattered frock. Her breasts made sharp peaks in the singlet but otherwise the cast-off garments hung on her as on a dead branch. She had something of Sophie's listless, emotionless manner, her eyes holding no light, her expression fixed. She appeared indifferent to her daughter's swollen face. It came to him, as he watched them murmuring to one another in their own language, that they both reminded him of the "strange people next door" from his schooldays, the psychiatric invalids among whom he'd played as a boy. There was a certain type of melancholy despair which produced this appearance, these mechanical movements of an automaton. After a while, the woman turned her empty eyes and face to him.

"She cannot stay here. She must go back."

"She wanted to be with you."

"You see what this place is. There is nothing for her."

He looked around, regretting that he had not had the foresight to bring more food. "How do you survive here?"

"We grow a few things. Sometimes people leave food on the road for us. If we try to go out, they kill us."

"How many of you are there?"

"There were ten of us last year. Now eight. They

killed two who ran away."

"And your only crime was having twins?"

The woman looked away from him. After a while she said, "At least Sophie is alive. You must take her back to Bassongo."

"Her father has started to beat her."

"It is better to be beaten than to starve." She frowned at him. "Why don't you want her?"

"I don't know," he said helplessly.

"She will do whatever you want."

"I want nothing. I am unable to use her as though she were an animal."

"She could be your friend."

He thought of Catherine's fiery spirit and conversation. "I am trying to help. I don't know what to do for her."

"You can take her to your house, even if you do not use her."

"How old is she?"

"How old do you think?"

He felt the question was a trap. "I think she is too young to come to my house."

She gestured at the desolate huts. "Is she too young for this?"

He grimaced. "Does everybody have these beliefs about twins?"

"Missionaries would take her," the woman said, shrugging indifferently. "They try to save these children."

"There are no missionaries left. I would like her to find work of some kind. Is there nothing she can do?"

"Nobody will eat what she cooks, nobody will buy what she grows, nobody will drink the water she brings or the beer she brews, nobody will take her to his house. Nobody, nobody, nobody." There was a gleam in the woman's eyes now, but it was hard and cold. It seemed even a kind of gloating. "She is a ghost, as I am a ghost and you are a ghost."

"I am not a ghost."

Her lip curled. "You are worse than a ghost."

"Whatever I am, she is just a child," Jean-Patrice retorted. "She is innocent."

"Innocent!" the woman sneered. "I saved her! Now look what she does! It is her fault, blanc. Everything is her own fault."

"That is cruel and unjust."

"Do you know what it cost me to save her life?" The woman struck herself on her temple with the heel of her hand, indicating he was crazy or a fool. "You know nothing!" Jean-Patrice saw that two other women had crept out of the bush where they had been hiding, even dirtier and thinner than Sophie's mother. They approached as stealthily as jackals, squatting to tear some of the bananas off the bunch they had brought. Without turning, Sophie's mother uttered a sharp command. The women fell back. One, having devoured the banana, started gnawing the inside of the peel. Sophie's mother kept her eyes on Jean-Patrice's. "If you give him money, he will not beat her."

He was about to tell her that he would not be blackmailed by Raymond, but the idea seemed inane hypocrisy in this desolate setting. "I will speak to him," he said.

The woman nodded. "Take her back, now. She cannot stay here."

"Mami?" Sophie moved as though to embrace her mother. With unexpected strength, the older woman thrust her away. Wailing, Sophie clung to her mother's thin arm. The two women struggled for a moment, their faces contorted with different emotions. Then the mother rid herself of the daughter and slapped her face hard. The movement shook one of her lean breasts out of the singlet. She tucked it back, glaring at Sophie. She spat a phrase in her own language. Then, without another word, she picked up the bags of flour and beans and walked away.

"Mami!" The woman did not turn despite the broken

note in Sophie's voice. The girl had started to cry, as she had done at Joliet's deathbed, silently and hopelessly. Jean-Patrice felt sick. He tightened the girth and got back into the saddle. Sophie buried her face against the mare's neck, clinging to the animal.

"We must go," he said gently. "You can't stay here." She allowed him to pull her up onto Adeline's back. Her body, which had been pliant during the ride to the forbidden village, now felt like a disjointed marionette. Her head hung down as though too heavy for her thin neck. She sobbed in silence. What had she been hoping for? Some tenderness from a mother to whom she had been only a curse? Some gesture of solidarity in the face of a monstrous injustice?

"I'll send somebody with food for them once a week," he said. "I cannot have them starving five miles from my house."

He rode past the furiously grinning masks and back into the palm forest. Where did the guilt lie? With savage superstitions? With his own intrusion into this world? Perhaps there was some evolutionary advantage to the killing of twins. Perhaps they placed too many demands on the mother. Yet women had two breasts. Twins survived in ancient times. Castor and Pollux, Jacob and Esau. If only he could consult Darwin on the subject. Eerie as they were, twins did not seem to be outside the bounds of natural phenomena as would be, for example, a child with two heads. There was refuge from despair in such scientific speculations.

As he passed through the resin-heavy forest, he turned and glimpsed Hugo Joliet, standing among the palms. He was supporting himself on a crutch, the stump of his thigh dangling, one bony, red hand raised in valediction or warning.

The shock was so great that Jean-Patrice felt as though he'd been struck in the heart. With his skin creeping, he turned the mare around and went back to look again.

It was not Joliet, of course, but a dead tree, its heart eaten out by termites, which had built a pillar of red mud among the crooked branches. He stared at it, trying to recover the vision of Joliet that his brain had created. He could not; all he now saw was a dead tree, but his memory held the vivid details, even down to the strange leer.

"I saw him too," Sophie whispered. "I see him everywhere." Her thin fingers bit into his arm. She was trembling. "He follows me all the time."

"It was a tree."

"It was him!"

He made no reply, but rode on back to Bassongo. Reluctantly, he gave Sophie a little money when they arrived. "Tell your father to come and see me at once," he ordered.

In the study, he took Joliet's leather bound journal from the shelf where he had put it. The thing was heavy, expensively bound, the thick leather cover embossed with a fancifully entwined H and J. Joliet had filled almost half of the cream vellum pages with his notes and photographs. Jean-Patrice turned the pages, his eye drifting across the endless records of sexual encounters, the photographs that were at once lewd and prim. The images were pornographic, yet the stiff poses and blank expressions were absurd. But then, were not most sexual acts absurd when one viewed them clinically? Did they have any dignity if there was no emotion in them?

The identities of his partners (if that was the word) were invariably concealed behind initials, while other details were punctiliously annotated. Thus Q had "submitted to every instruction" while Y had "eyes closed during 6 mins coitus." Multitudinous copulations and pleasurings, reduced now to a little dried ink on paper. There was no clue here to the mystery of Joliet's nature, or human nature in general. Was this catalogue the reason Joliet still haunted the Residency?

Raymond appeared at the door, looking surly. "I am

here, patron."

"Listen to me, Raymond," Jean-Patrice said briskly, "because I have a couple of things to say to you. One is that if you beat Sophie again, I will dismiss you instantly."

"Patron! One cannot tell a father not to beat a child!"

"Secondly, I have been to see Sophie's mother."

Raymond recoiled. He frowned and protruded his lips. "It is forbidden. You should not have gone."

He ignored this. "I was disgusted by what I saw. She is your wife, the mother of your child. You leave her to starve in rags while you are fat as butter!"

"That one is a bad woman," Raymond muttered.

"That is rubbish. She committed no crime."

Raymond glared at him. "It is better to talk of these things with some understanding."

"Twins are normal. There is nothing evil about them — or the women who bear them. I cannot change your beliefs, but you should not remain a slave to superstition."

"I already divorce her."

"I don't care about that. From now on, I want you to make sure she has enough to eat. Send food to her."

"If the patron want to send her food, then the patron must pay," Raymond said sulkily.

"Nonsense. Do you think I don't know how much your wives steal from the kitchen? There is food to spare in this household. A sack of flour and a sack of beans every week. Do you hear me?"

"I hear," Raymond said sulkily.

"I will check, and if I find her hungry again, you will have me to deal with."

There was no response. He saw that Raymond was eyeing the *Liber Libidinorum* with a cynical eye. It was open on his desk, at a page which showed a particularly repulsive photograph. He closed the book, feeling that his elevated moral position had been somehow undermined. "That will be all," he said firmly. Raymond sidled out, smirking.

14

He awoke the next morning to a complete silence in the Residency. There was no clatter from the kitchen, no sound of Raymond's voice. The village was hushed. Chloë was sprawled at his feet, still fast asleep. Perhaps it was a holiday of some kind, or perhaps there had been a death. He rose and shaved himself. While he did so, Chloë awoke and went through her own toilet of muttering, scratching and grooming her fur. She did not have fleas, he had found, but appeared to have an almost pathological fear of small insects, even ants. Her grooming seemed to be based on an anxiety that some infestation might appear. He dressed and went downstairs, followed by Chloë, still yawning sleepily, walking on her knuckles. The house was empty. None of the staff had come to work. He put on his hat and took the gorilla outside to relieve herself in a deserted world.

Or not quite deserted. Three men were standing by the cannon outside the Residency, peering into the bore and talking quietly among themselves. Their appearance was that of the forest, not the village. They straightened as he approached, turning to look at him. He was struck by the combination of barbarism and nobility in their appearance.

They were alike enough to one another to be brothers, burly men wearing no clothing but red loincloths. Two carried long muskets which were at least half a century old, the third had a sheaf of spears.

Jean-Patrice's heart sank. He had left his revolver at his bedside and these men presaged imminent trouble of some kind. His policemen had evaporated. He cursed them inwardly for their cowardice; they would be skulking in their huts, no doubt. The village beyond was utterly deserted. A heavy silence had settled on Bassongo.

The tribesmen had lavished narcissistic care on their appearance, their hair stiffened with clay into ornate coiffures, decorated with the brilliant feathers of tropical birds. Two of the three had nostrils pierced with silver rings, from which strings of beads were looped to their ears. They stared at him boldly.

"Yes, patron!" the biggest of the men greeted him.

He tried to maintain a resolute appearance in the face of their insolent curiosity. "Good morning. What is it you want?"

"Where is Monsieur Joliet?"

"Monsieur Joliet is dead. I am the new District Commissioner."

The tribesman uttered a grunt of surprise. They turned to one another and conferred in their own language. All, he saw, had teeth filed to auger points. Their faces appeared to express equal parts of cunning, humor and ferocity. A pungent smell of wood smoke and male sweat came from them. He saw them pointing with interest at Chloë. "What do you want?" Jean-Patrice asked firmly.

The man indicated a long canvas bundle which lay at their feet. "You buy?"

"What is it?"

The man squatted and began to unfasten the bundle. It was the size and shape of a woman's body. It almost exactly resembled the bundle in which Joliet had been buried. The inner folds of canvas were blotched with patterns of dried blood. A stink of rotting flesh invaded his nostrils. These savages had surely not brought him a human corpse? Unaccountably, he thought of Catherine Atélé. Jean-Patrice felt his heart grow icy.

The last folds of canvas were thrown aside. He found himself staring at two large elephant tusks nestled together. The stumps still had gobbets of elephant adhering to them, but the ivory was magnificent, creamy and smooth. Chloë, disturbed by the sight or the smell, set up a loud grunting of protest. The men glanced at her with heavy, yellow eyes.

"How did you kill this elephant?" Jean-Patrice asked.

The man grinned and lifted his musket. "We are hunters."

"You are Fang?"

The men laughed, sharp teeth gleaming. "Yes, we are Fang," one replied, slapping his powerful chest. "You buy?"

He had been given a schedule of prices for ivory. It was becoming scarce and he had been instructed to buy every scrap he was offered. It was to be paid for in silver. He led them to the back of the Residency where the scales stood. The tusks were heavy, a sign of quality. He checked the schedule and offered them exactly the price which was specified. He had expected them to haggle, but they nodded in satisfaction.

He now had to retrieve silver from the cellar. If they wanted, these men could fell him with a musket ball or a spear thrust and take everything in the strong room – silver, weapons and powder. The axiom that no Fang would ever harm a white man appeared a fragile hope at this moment. These Fang had not treated him like a god.

"Wait here," he told them. He went into the house. It occurred to him to get his revolver, but he decided against it. It would be a sign of weakness to come back armed, and in any case the pistol might not protect him against men capable of killing an elephant.

He returned with the coins to find them waiting patiently. They had thrust the tusks into the soil, base down. "The ants will clean," one of them grinned, pointing. Jean-Patrice stared at the insects which were already bustling around the flesh. At times of stress, odd fragments from his schooldays would surface in his mind. Now the tribesman's words recalled to him the warriors of Achilles, called in Greek the Myrmidons, the Ants. They must have looked something like these black men – grim, vain and brutal. Musing over the thought, he paid the men, counting the silver out carefully. The leader, whom he now thought of as Achilles, folded the money into a pouch and tucked it into his loincloth. Then he put his arm over the muzzle of his musket, and rested his chin on it, staring at Jean-Patrice with yellow eyes. The other two waited expectantly.

"Patron!"

"Yes?"

"The whites are taking our brothers."

"Which whites?"

The man jerked a thumb over his shoulder. "In the bush. They steal our brothers to make the road."

"What do you mean, 'steal?'"

"We are not Beti. We are not slaves of the whites. We are Fang."

He felt threatened by their postures, which had grown belligerent. "What can I do? I am not making the road."

"You are white. The other whites are your brothers."

"Not all whites are brothers." There was a silence. Three pairs of eyes considered him, black stones set in amber. He felt they thought he was a liar, evading the issue. "There is nothing I can do," he repeated. "You must complain to the Commissioner of your own district."

Achilles nodded slightly as though this were the answer he had expected. "You buy more ivory?"

"If you bring it, yes."

"We will bring." The man pointed at Chloë, who was

seated under one of her favorite shrubs, eating a breakfast of leaves. "Sell me that one, patron."

"She is not for sale."

He held up a finger. "I give you one tusk for that one."

"She is not for sale," he repeated brusquely.

The hunter grinned, showing his pointed teeth. "You love her, eh?"

"Yes."

"When you don't love her any more, you sell to us."

"I will not sell her." They considered one another. The Fang were heavily armed. The muskets were ancient things, crudely repaired with iron bands, but their greased and businesslike appearance showed they were in working condition. Each of the men carried a heavy bush knife at his waist, capable of hacking through dense forest. The smallest of the men carried ten or twelve throwing spears with sharp blades.

Achilles tilted his head back and looked at Jean-Patrice over his flaring nostrils, his heavy lids lowered, expressing superiority. He held up his finger again. "One tusk."

As they turned to leave, another of them – perhaps Patroclus, the beloved comrade of Achilles – said, "Tell your brothers not to steal our brothers."

He made no answer. He watched them walk back into the trees, the feathers nodding brightly in their headdresses.

For an hour after their departure there was silence. Then Bassongo slowly came to life, people emerging from their huts or filtering back among the trees. Smoke began to curl up from the cooking fires. He waited in a cold fury until Raymond and the three policemen reappeared. They arrived at the Residency in a group, looking very ill at ease.

"Where did you go?" he demanded.

"We were hiding," Raymond said frankly.

"From three hunters?" Jean-Patrice said bitterly. "Is that all it takes to make you run away?"

"There were five more," Raymond replied. "They

stayed in the bush, watching. They had guns."

He was outraged. "And you left me alone to face them?"

"They will not harm a white."

"How do you know?" he snapped. "You make these pronouncements, Raymond, but I no longer believe what you tell me." He turned on Hyppolite Mokamo. "And I expected more of you, Hyppolite. You are the corporal. I did not think you would run at the first challenge."

Hyppolite looked surly. "I was not afraid for myself, Monsieur le Commissaire. But nobody can make trouble with those people. They come back in the night with guns – and worse things."

"Vipers that crawl into men's beds? Ghosts that swim in the river?"

"They are wizards."

"They are merely savages with muskets," Jean-Patrice retorted. "And you are an assimilé with a bolt-action Chassepot. You should have confronted them." He dismissed the policemen and they left, muttering among themselves. He had to recruit more men. It was essential. He could not manage with so few. But the young men were not yet back from initiation camp. This Africa moved at its own pace; here nothing could be hurried, nothing expedited. One simply waited for the right conjunction of affairs. If one died of old age or a viper bite in the meantime, then that was the way it must be. The force of inertia was ancient and immoveable.

Still fuming, he mounted Adeline and rode over to Catherine's house. Her pots lay in front of the house but there was no sign of her. Her door was slightly open, so he went inside the house.

"Catherine?"

"I'm here."

He went into her sleeping area. She was lying on her bed, half-conscious. She was pale, her face drawn, and for a horrible moment he had a memory of Joliet's last moments. He knelt beside her bed and drew the blanket away from her. He laid his hand on her brow and felt the fierce heat of her fever. Yet she was shivering as if with cold. She turned dulled eyes on him.

"You said it would be nothing."

"This is not normal." The arm he had vaccinated was swollen. He peeled the plaster carefully away from the vaccination and found a torn and weeping blister. He could see other blisters on her flank. His heart sank. "You have a vaccinial reaction."

"My head is bursting."

"How long have you been like this?"

"Since the night of the vaccination."

"Who has been looking after you?"

"There is nobody." She whimpered as he lifted the blanket to examine her. "I'm so cold! Please go away and let me sleep!"

"I can't leave you here, Catherine. You must come to the Residency, where I can take care of you properly."

She shook her head, closing her eyes and huddling back under the blankets. He was agitated as he cantered back to the Residency. What if he had killed her with that all-too-casual jab of the lancet? He'd been told that this reaction was extremely rare. Why had a sullen fate decreed it should take place in her? Was it some cosmic joke?

He sent Hyppolite and Hyacinth to fetch her and prepared his own bed to receive her. He did not want to put her into the bed in which Joliet had died. Then he scoured the medicine bottles which had survived immersion in the river. All of these had lost their labels and it would take a chemist or a doctor to tell what the contents were; but one he recognized by its aniseed smell as wine of opium. He set the bottle aside; likewise the iodine.

They brought Catherine to the Residency on a litter, complaining weakly at the jolting, her eyes half-closed. He lifted her in his own arms and put her in bed, then put a tablespoon of the opium between her lips. She choked a little, but swallowed the stuff. Her teeth were chattering though it was a hot, humid night. Raymond came soundlessly into the room and looked down with disdainful eyes at Catherine.

"Have you chosen, then, patron?" he asked with an ironic smile.

"There's no question of that," he snapped, "Can't you see she is sick?"

"I see, patron." He had brought towels at Jean-Patrice's request and he laid these at the bedside.

"You must take Chloë," Jean-Patrice commanded. "Let her sleep with you, or she'll cry."

"Yes, patron." Raymond took the gorilla by the hand and led her out.

Jean-Patrice unfastened Catherine's dress. She tried to protest, pushing his hand away, but he soothed her. He found a dozen of the vesicles on her smooth skin, most of them on her sides and hips. Perhaps there would be no more. These he dressed with iodine. It would relieve the pain, though at first it stung enough to make her whimper and bite her lower lip. When he had done, he pulled the blanket around her. She rolled onto her side. The paregoric was now starting to take effect. She began to snore a little. She looked absurdly young. Her expression habitually held a natural authority; that had ebbed away now, revealing something soft and vulnerable beneath.

He pulled the chair up to the side of her bed and made himself as comfortable as he could for the night. He did not know exactly why he should do this. He had heard of nurses spending the night at the bedsides of the sick. As a child, lacking a mother, he had often fancied that, had she lived, she would have sat up at his bedside when he was sick and watched over him. He'd even had dreams, or feverish fancies, that he had seen her shape there. In any case, it gave him some comfort to be close to Catherine. If she died, he might as well abandon the inoculation program altogether. And he would lose the only friend he had in this place.

He turned the lamp down low and looked at her sleeping face, her lids heavy, her temples sparkling with sweat. Could he call her a friend? The word was not one he'd used often in his life. He'd had few friends. The quietness and solemnity of the night had inclined his mind to reflections. He remembered himself as an intensely romantic boy, yearning passionately after princesses and fairy queens. He'd been compelled to hide this idealism deep inside; it did not belong in the world he'd inherited. There were no fairy queens at boarding schools and boarding houses. There was little sweetness of any kind in the life of an orphan whose small affairs were preordained, administered and paid for by a trust. All that which was sweet and romantic in his own nature had been a closely guarded secret, one which he had seldom shared and had come eventually to almost forget, as one might forget a small sum of money put into an account during childhood; but as such small investments do, it had grown to a surprising amount by his twenties. He had lavished much of this largesse on Justine in an outpouring of affection and desire that had swept them both off their feet. But the vault was not empty. He had much more to offer.

Catherine was restless, muttering incoherently in her sleep and crying out from time to time in a voice of anguish. He dozed now and then and once awoke to find her also awake, or at least, with her eyes open. He leaned forward stiffly and spoke to her. She did not reply. He lifted the lamp and looked carefully into her eyes, dreading he would see the ulcerations that could blind her. He gave her a little more of the paregoric to drink. She gazed back at him for a while, her eyes drifting across the features of his face as though she did not recognize him. Then he saw her pupils dilate under the effect of the morphia salts and she slowly sank back into sleep. In the distance, he heard the patter of the witchdoctor's drum start up, broadcasting its complex rhythms.

15

He was awakened by the rising heat of early morning. He had been sleeping with his chin on his chest and his legs sprawled out. Catherine had her back to him, the blanket drawn around her. He went quietly around the bed, to find that her eyes were open. Her hands were clasped against her breast.

"How do you feel?" he asked, laying his hand on her brow. Her skin was hot and rough. Her eyes were still glazed with the effect of the morphine. She spoke in a dry whisper.

"I dreamed so many things."

"It's the paregoric. It brings visions."

"When did I come here?"

"Just last night."

"It feels longer. A long time. I must go home."

He eased the bedclothes away from her body. The vesicles were still angry and weeping. "You're not well, yet. You can't go until the blisters begin to heal. But you look better, I am glad to say."

She covered herself again, her fingers clumsy. "Were you awake all night?"

He smiled. "I had intended to be, but I dozed off."

He gave her water and she drank. He could see how weak she was. "Are you still in pain?"

"These things itch and ache at the same time."

"They affect the nodes of the nerves. I'll dress them with iodine again later." He gave her another sip of water. "You called out in the night."

She lay back. "I called for my child. I believed she was alive again." Her eyes lost their focus, as though she were once again looking into a dream. "There was a strange thing – she had grown, even though she's dead. She was older, taller. She was so beautiful."

"As you are."

"My time is past."

"Do you really believe that? How old are you?"

"Twenty-seven."

"I am the same age."

She turned away from him. "It's different for a man. And I have been widowed and have seen my child die. Something dies in you, too, when that happens. You no longer want to live, not in the same way as before."

"I have felt that way too. Although your grief is far greater than mine." He hesitated. "Perhaps we can find a way to help each other want to live again."

"You shouldn't have brought me here. I don't want a man."

"I didn't bring you here to seduce you," he said gently. He saw that her lips were cracked. He applied Vaseline to them with his fingertips, feeling them soften and yield.

She pushed away his hand. "I don't want to be touched and stroked. I want none of that."

"I am not trying to touch you in that way. You should eat something now."

"I can't eat. I would like only some tea."

"Of course." He rose.

"You're very kind," she said quietly as he left the room.

He turned at the doorway. "Not at all. I don't want anything from you. But you can't hold back life,

Catherine, no matter what has been lost. It will swell and build behind your dam and then spill over and flow around the sides and continue on its way, even if the course is more crooked than before."

"You are very eloquent."

"You will not forget, but you can't die yet, either." He went down to the kitchen and found Raymond, looking sullen. He asked him to take tea up to Catherine. The man gave him a sour look. "The patron has chosen. I said it was so. But the patron has chosen badly."

"What do you mean?"

"That one is no good. She is rotten fruit."

"I do not plan to make her my lover."

Raymond sneered. "There is only one reason why a black woman goes to a white man's bed."

He felt a lofty contempt. "Do you suppose I would take advantage of a sick woman?"

"Even rotten fruit can be eaten by a hungry man."

"You are insolent and a fool."

"Does a white man take every black woman to his bed when she is sick? My daughter is young and clean. She has not been educated by missionaries – or spoiled by them." With that he turned his back on Jean-Patrice and went into the kitchen.

Jean-Patrice walked out into the bright morning with the slightly unreal feeling of having slept little and fretted much. He went to the stables to check on the mare. The animal seemed pleased to see him, tossing her head and whinnying. He patted her neck, uttering a few soothing, meaningless words. The scars he had made in her hide were healed now, the first feathers of russet hair starting to grow over them. The calf was placid, her nose running as usual, her saliva green with the cud she was chewing.

He walked down to the landing and stood staring at the high cliff that hung over the river, trailing its creepers and ferns into the water. The sky was piled with moist-looking cloud, framing patches of duck's egg turquoise sky. There was no evidence on the river's brown surface of the deeper currents that ran purposefully to the distant sea. But there had been more slaughter of great trees upriver. Raft after raft drifted past, laden with trunks that must have towered once like the columns of Corinthian temples, now lashed together, headless and rootless and bearing the laconic chalk marks of European factors. Occasionally the pilots would pause to buy food or drink at Bassongo. Most often, they passed by.

He opened his silver cigar case, now badly tarnished with the humidity, and lit one of the misshapen cheroots that Tosti had sent him. The strong Manila tobacco failed to soothe his restlessness.

He turned and found Hyppolite at his side. "How is the woman?" the corporal asked.

"She's sick. But she'll get better."

"They are saying she spent the night in your bed."

Jean-Patrice laughed shortly. "Yes. But not in the way everyone seems to think."

"In what way, then?"

"There was nobody else to care for her – and it was the vaccination which made her ill." He paused. "She's different from the others."

"Oh yes." Hyppolite's eyes were heavy-lidded and glittering. "That one is clever, patron."

"You don't like her?"

"Sometimes it is better to be simple than clever."

"I think she's a good person. Women who live alone have to be hard, sometimes."

"Sometimes women have to live alone because they are hard."

"You are in an aphoristic mood, Corporal. I think she would be a good vaccinator. Do you have anything against her?"

"Nothing."

"You say that in a tone as if you meant the opposite."

"If the patron thinks she is good, then she is good."

"She can read and write. She's responsible. Women do this kind of thing better than we do. Is that not so?"

"It is so."

"Then what is the problem?"

"She is beautiful."

"And – ?"

"And she is beautiful. Nothing more."

"I am trying to follow you, Hyppolite, but you are being cryptic. Do I understand you to say that Catherine Atélé is not a good candidate? And that you suspect I am under the spell of her beauty?"

"I say nothing."

"She is not well-liked in the village – is that it?"

"People say she is proud," Hyppolite conceded.

"Her pride is one of the qualities I like most about her."

"Then you must admire her greatly, because she has plenty," Hyppolite observed dryly. "She thinks she is too good for Bassongo."

"Perhaps she is."

"Many people think her arrogant and heartless."

"Those are the qualities of a good leader."

"If you say so, patron."

He offered the man a cigar. Hyppolite accepted it and they smoked in silence for a while. "You know that Sophie's mother lives at the forbidden village?" Jean-Patrice asked at last.

"Yes."

"Have you been there?"

"Men are not allowed to go," the corporal replied.

"But you know the conditions there? They have nothing to eat and their houses are falling to pieces."

Hyppolite nodded slightly. "I know that."

"It is a disgrace."

"If a woman has had twins, she may have twins again. That is why they are not allowed to be with men."

"But they should not be compelled to live in squalor

and misery. I want to send a couple of builders there to repair the houses and thatch the roofs. The woman can go out of the village every day while the men are working so they need not meet."

Hyppolite looked doubtful. "People are afraid of those women."

"I have been there," Jean-Patrice replied, "and they are the most wretched creatures imaginable. There is nothing to fear there." But he remembered the leering, blood red figure of Joliet among the palms with an inward shudder.

"The builders will have to be well paid. They say there are evil spirits there."

"The spirits may be happier when the roofs are fixed," Jean-Patrice said, "and I will pay well. Please arrange it."

Jean-Patrice returned to the Residency at mid-morning to dress Catherine's blisters. She was asleep. He touched her brow. She felt cooler. The crisis had passed in the night. He drew the sheet away from her shoulder and saw that the blisters were not so angry-looking now. No fresh ones had appeared. He prepared swabs of iodine and dabbed the lesions gently. She stirred into wakefulness, twisting away from his hands.

"Let me do this, Catherine," he said. "There will be less pain and less scarring." She acquiesced and lay on her belly, her head turned to one side as he dressed the vesicles. She smelled of sweat and of something else, something disturbing and feminine. Perhaps she used perfume of some kind, or some fragrant oil. She stared at the wall dully, without whimpering, though the iodine must have burned. "Did you have any more dreams?" he asked.

"None."

She did not meet his eyes as he tended to her. She was ashamed of her nakedness, he thought. "When I first saw you, you were not wearing much more than you are now," he said, hoping to console her.

She did not smile. "If I had known you were coming

that day, I would have been less naked."

"I lost my shame early in life. I was always with other boys. And adults did not tolerate shyness in us, not even the nuns. They called it affectation. So I learned to be clothed, even when my body was naked. Nakedness is in the mind, I think. The ancient Greeks went naked all day long, if one believes their statues and ceramics. One day perhaps I will be able to show you pictures of Greek pottery. You would be interested. The things you make are very fine." He turned her on her side to address the blisters on her abdomen. He glimpsed with guilty pleasure the springy triangle between her thighs and, realizing that he had been babbling like a fool, fell silent.

When he'd finished, he sat beside her for a while. She was disinclined to talk, her mouth sullen or sad, he could not tell which. "Are you in pain?" he asked.

"I feel as though something inside me has broken."

He was struck by her tone. "The paregoric leaves this depression," he said. "It's nothing, it will pass. If you need more, you can take some tonight. But we must be careful with it. It creates an addiction easily."

"Yes."

"Perhaps I sounded superficial when I said to you last night that life cannot be held back. I don't say it glibly. I lost my parents when I was a child and I was raised by people who had little love for me. There have been times when I have wanted my life to stop – either because I was so happy that any change could only be for the worse or because I saw no hope."

"You haven't lost a child."

"No."

"That pain does not go away."

"When did you lose her?"

"While she was a baby. She would be seven now."

"And her father?"

"I don't want to talk about him."

"He is dead?"

"Yes."

"I should not have asked. Forgive me."

"This woman of yours, in Paris. She made you suffer?"

"Compared to your suffering, that was light. At the time, though, there was a peculiar torment in it. I pursued her because she was the greatest prize I could see. I look back and see how completely without scruples I was. I cannot pretend that I was motivated by love for her. I wanted to conquer her. My youth had been hard and I had finally reached a position where things came to me. I won medals, secured good positions, made conquests, both romantic and in other ways. She was frivolous and pretty and bright. I felt I deserved her, so I set out to win her." He smiled. "But I stayed one minute too long in her arms. I found that I no longer wanted an affair. I wanted her to run away with me. Of course, she laughed in my face. I could not believe that she would not renounce her wealthy husband and her position in society to live in a bachelor apartment with me. I was very arrogant. I can see in your eyes that you think I am not a very good person."

"I do not judge you."

"Well, once love has taken hold of a human heart, it does not let go easily. It clings like a thorny briar. The more you try to tear it out, the more it lacerates you. You continue to love someone long after you learn that they are narcissistic and superficial. How does one explain that? For a long time, I have been sick with love. I believe that healing comes when one accepts one's own blame. I have tried to do that."

She made no reply to his speech, in which he felt he had revealed more of his nature than he should have done. He waited patiently with an illustrated magazine, idly perusing the dense columns of text and the advertisements for patent medicines and ingenious devices of all kinds, his eyes drifting over the photographs of beauties and dandies and powerful old men. Revolutions were being spoken of in cold and distant places. Sarah Bernhardt had enjoyed a huge success playing Hamlet. A different world was turning, elsewhere.

Eventually, Catherine's eyes closed and she drifted into sleep. Her hands, which had been clenched, curled open. He lifted one gently, careful not to wake her, and studied it. As so often, he had the sense of seeing humanity in a new perspective. Was it simply the colour of the skin? Was the gulf wider and deeper than pigmentation? The skin was a soft brown on one side, the veins rising in places like dolphins breaking a smooth sea, the transition to the pinkness of the palm quite sudden. He looked at the little scars on the delicate knuckles, the short, oval nails. He recalled the way this small hand had formed the rim of the pot, the slurry oozing between her sure fingers. It was a practical hand, a hand which worked for its living. He wondered what it would be like to be caressed by it in passion.

Catherine slept most of the day. Each time he went to look at her she had moved her position, but her eyes remained closed and her breathing was steady. It began to rain in the early evening, heavy drops like the notes of a xylophone on the tin roof, with a sostenuto of thunderous cellos and basses muttering softly in the distance. She awoke and tried to get up, disoriented after the fever and the opium.

"I want to wash myself," she said restlessly, "I cannot bear to be dirty."

"Tomorrow would be better."

"I cannot bear it!"

He could not soothe her, so he asked Raymond to prepare some hot water and, when it arrived, helped her to the galvanized iron tub which he himself used. He sat behind her, pouring the warm water over her shoulders and back with a jug while she soaped herself. She seemed too weak to hold her head up and let her face hang over her breasts, the nape of her neck slim and fragile.

He helped her rise from the bath and wrapped a towel around her. It was dark now. He lit one of the palm oil lamps. The delicate light attracted a moth from outside, then another, then a ring of fluttering insects. The rain was loud on the roof, the air hot and humid. Catherine sat on the bed, drying her hair. A pale yellow moth settled on her naked shoulder, vivid against her dark skin. He stared at the gently stirring wings as though mesmerized. "Do they really believe that whites are ghosts come to eat the living?"

"It's true."

"But you were educated by missionaries."

"If it's not true in one sense, then it's true in another. The whites have come to Africa to devour. Your gods eat our gods. Everything of value is cut down or killed or torn out of the earth for you. Your ships carry it away and bring back more whites. Each time you reach deeper, until in the end there will be nothing left."

"But we also bring good things."

"What?" The moth fluttered away as she turned, wincing at the lesions in her side. "Even your medicine kills us."

He took the iodine and dabbed the blisters, feeling the futility of the treatment and the truth of her words. "Your culture is also flawed. I went to the forbidden village with Sophie. Those women have been assigned the cruellest fate for nothing more than being fertile. I've sent a party of workmen to rebuild their houses and clear the land, but they have to live in isolation for the rest of their lives. Is that moral?"

She shrugged. "What is morality? The nuns taught us that there is a benevolent Creator who loves each one of us. But he doesn't care about us, or he wouldn't kill so many of us. He made us and our world and then he forgot about us. Or maybe he's amused by our suffering."

"Then what do you believe in?"

"Those who loved us once – if they don't disappear

after death, then they love us still. They watch over us here on earth – our mothers and grandmothers and great-grandmothers. When we give birth, they are beside us. When we give milk to our children, their breasts fill our breasts. And when we die, they are waiting to welcome us."

"I hope that may be so."

"Are you a believer?"

He finished with the iodine. "I was raised by nuns, like you. Like you, I doubt whether there is a gentle God in heaven. I've been to séances in Paris where people accept much the same things as you, or pretend to. Tables rock, violins are played by invisible fingers, one feels ectoplasm brush one's face. All theatre, I imagine. I am a sceptic. I believe in Darwin. In my final year at University I wrote an essay on Darwinism. It won an important prize. That's my religion, I suppose – Darwinism and self-interest. Now I'll make you something to eat."

"With your own hands?"

"With my own hands. I'll open a tin."

In fact, he opened three. One he knew to contain asparagus. He opened it in homage to her, since it was one of his few luxuries. The other two were surprises; one contained three partridges squeezed together in a wine jelly, the other sweetened condensed milk. He carried them up to her and laid out the food on her bed. She inspected it in a doubtful manner.

"Is this what people eat in Paris?"

"You have to use your imagination." She tried the asparagus but made a face at the taste and would not repeat the experiment. She picked at the partridges without enthusiasm. However the condensed milk pleased her and he was glad to see her spooning it up. He supposed it would restore her strength as much as anything else. "You approve?"

She smiled. "I love sweet things."

"I'm glad to see you smile again. You've been very

bad-tempered."

"If I stuck a knife in your arm and made you sick and covered you with sores, you would be bad-tempered too."

"I didn't come to Gabon to plunder, Catherine. I am not innocent, of course. But my motive wasn't pure greed. They might as well have sent me to Indochina or Tahiti for all I knew or cared of Africa. But now that I am here..."

"Now that you are here, what?"

He smiled. "Now that I am here, I am here."

The storm rolled overhead, thunder rattling the iron roof like hammer blows. The glare of the lightning froze each drop of rain at the window. They sat without speaking as it passed away. Her eyelids were drooping. The air had cooled and he covered her with the sheet. "You can sleep now."

"You don't need to sit with me all night again."

"I'll just stay a little while." He watched her sink into a peaceful sleep, then himself nodded off. He slept for some hours and woke to see her lying with her back to him. It was still raining. He covered her again. This time he slept deeply. When he next awoke, it was dawn and both the rain and Catherine were gone. He stared blearily at the imprint of her body in the mattress, feeling a keen sense of loss. He lay down where she had lain, listening the metallic notes of the iron roof as the rising sun heated it.

An hour later, he heard the soft thud of Chloë's knuckles on the floor. The animal clambered onto the bed and lay beside him, putting her head on his chest as though consoling him, or perhaps reproaching him for his infidelity. He stroked her fur gently.

He didn't go to Catherine's house again, knowing by her silent departure that she wanted to be alone for a while. It was in any case a busy few days. The river was crowded each day with rafts and barges. As though there had been some great battle of giants in the forest, the truncated corpses came down, lashed in monstrous bundles, sometimes half-submerged in the stream. The villagers paddled out eagerly to these passing hulks, their dugouts piled with food, doing a brisk trade. The river was swollen with rains, its surface dirty with foam. The roughness of the water had its effect on the rafts; several had come unraveled and arrived at Bassongo in a half-disintegrated state. He had to supervise the lashing of the logs again. As he stood watching the work, Catherine came down to the river, walking with her old swing and pride and grace again, her head held high. He watched her approach, feeling the deep physical pleasure he always had in seeing her move.

"You appear to be better," he greeted her.

She showed him the mark on her arm. "It has healed. They all have."

Jean-Patrice inspected the mark. "Have they left scars?"

"Nobody will care if they have."

"Nobody who loves you," he said, smiling. "The bloom of health is in your face again. I'm glad to see you well." He gestured at the floating rafts of logs. "Things torn out of Africa by whites, as you said. Do you remember saying that?"

Her eyes glinted. "I remember everything."

"We were somewhat melancholy, I think."

"We were serious."

"We advised each other very sagely on various topics. I think we became friends."

"That's one way to put it." She seemed to struggle for a moment. "You looked after me with great care. Don't think I'm ungrateful."

"I do indeed think you very ungrateful," he retorted. "You complained constantly. You snapped and snarled like a leopard. If you get sick again, I shall be much more wary about taking you on as a patient."

"I won't get sick again. I never get sick."

There was a certain arrogance in her manner which

both amused and impressed him. "You have your existence well under control, it seems."

"Perhaps it will be you who gets sick and I who will have to look after you. Then we'll see what sort of patient you are. Priests and doctors are always saints, it's the patients who are 'difficult' and 'ungrateful.' One side gets all the glory, the other side has to endure misery, unwelcome pity and usually be very dirty into the bargain." She did look, indeed, like a kind of human leopardess as she spoke, her golden eyes sparkling. "One side is fully clothed and maintains all their dignity. The other side has their backside on show and whines all the time. The relationship isn't a very just one."

"Yes, well, one side gets to sleep in the other side's bed while the first side has to lick his wounds in a chair all night."

"I am trying to thank you for your kindness."

"I am trying to accept your thanks without incurring any more bites or scratches."

"I will not bite or scratch unless you show me kindness."

"Then I will have my chair and my whip at the ready."

"So long as we understand one another. I'm ready to start the inoculations," she said.

He made a gesture of tipping an imaginary hat. "You have the heart of a warrior, Catherine."

"I need the money," she replied.

"I have been thinking about this," he said. "I want to capture their attention. I'll fire the cannon."

Catherine stared at him in surprise. "The cannon is a hundred years old. Even I can see that!"

"It should work. We'll use a light charge and fill the barrel with red, white and blue rags. That ought to make a fine display. What do you think?"

"You assume that Africans must be treated like children," she said with some irritation. "I think they'll come without having the tricolore shot into their faces from your cannon."

"I think the cannon will create excitement."

"Especially if it blows you to pieces."

"Assuming it doesn't, the effect will be dramatic. What have we got to lose? I, for one, can hardly make a bigger fool of myself than I already am. We'll have a show. A feast." He warmed to the idea. "There'll be food and drink. Music. Dancing. We'll give a display of marksmanship with the rifles and let the men try a shot or two as well, once they've had the vaccination. We'll give prizes. And we'll offer incentives to the first twenty people to be inoculated. A dress for the women, a new machete for the men, something of that sort. You can give a speech, Catherine."

"They won't listen to speeches, least of all from me."

"You are frowning."

"Inoculation is a serious subject. I don't see why there need to be bribes, a cannon, a feast and all that."

"Leave that side of it to me. I have the popular touch." He rubbed his hands together. "We are getting somewhere at last. This is capital! The first thing is to inoculate the calf."

He enlisted the aid of Hyppolite and went to the calf's stall. They tied her hoofs together and pushed her on her side, bawling loudly. Jean-Patrice found a patch of bare skin on her belly and made a scratch with the scalpel. He rubbed an ampoule of the serum into the wound. The die was cast.

The glow of achievement persisted all evening, until he got into his bed and heard Joliet's voice begin muttering in the bedroom next door. He tried to dismiss the sound as a hallucination, or the cry of frogs or geckoes. But his flesh crawled nonetheless. As he drifted into sleep, he heard Joliet break into a long, low, mocking chuckle.

16

Having inoculated the calf, there was now a period of waiting for the animal to develop vaccinia, together with the abundant pustules which would supply the antitoxin. Catherine went back to her pottery, arranging for her wares to be sent to market, and he had no excuse to pester her. Jean-Patrice decided to do a fuller round of the district and reach the road.

He packed his saddlebags with water and provisions, prepared to spend a night away from the Residency if necessary. He set off very early to take advantage of the cool, which was relative – two o'clock in the morning could be as hot and humid as an August afternoon in Paris. He rode past the abandoned mission, catching a glimpse of the rusty cross above the leaves and wondering how far the Belgian priest had emerged from his grave by now.

His first call was at the forbidden village. He passed through the palm forest, noting that the rank inflorescences were now withering and beginning to spill crimson seeds like drops of blood. The choking smell had decayed into something softer and more insidious. He had sent Narcise to supervise the repair work and he was pleased to see, when he reached the village, that the men were already at work. Three of the five huts had been re-plastered with mud and re-thatched and now presented quite a respectable appearance. The remaining two were in the process of repair. There was no sign of the women.

Narcise came to greet him. "Good morning, patron."

"Good morning, Narcise. I see the work is getting along famously."

Narcise peered at him earnestly. "The men want to finish and go back to Bassongo. They don't want to stay here anymore. They say there are ghosts and demons here."

"Have you seen any?"

Narcise produced from his pocket a tattered Bible distributed by the missionary society. "I have this."

"And does it protect you from seeing the ghosts and demons?"

"I see them. But they cannot harm me."

Jean-Patrice smiled. "And what do you see?"

Narcise glanced over his shoulder at the workmen and lowered his voice. "The old patron. Monsieur Joliet. He walks around with his one leg and his crutch."

"Interesting," Jean-Patrice remarked laconically. He did not add that he had also seen the peripatetic Joliet in this vicinity, but he was moved to reflect that superstitions were odd things. They seemed to pass from one person to another like microbes, taking on a life of their own. No doubt the conformation of the rotted tree trunk just outside the village was to blame. Seen from a certain angle, in a certain light, it produced an impression on the ocular nerve that evoked the figure of a one-legged individual. This, in turn, provoked the memory of a real individual who had suffered the loss of a leg. The general credulity of the population did the rest. He had been shown cunning drawings of that sort. If one stared at them long enough, a leering face appeared, or a beautiful woman turned into a skull, or some other hidden design suddenly manifested itself.

He went to inspect the huts. The men were sullen and uneasy and did not disguise their resentment at being asked to perform this work. They were doing it thoroughly, however, and he was satisfied. They had also cleared away the rotting refuse that lay everywhere. The place looked no less a prison, but at least it was not a squalid one. He had breakfast with them as the sun rose.

"Where are the women?" he asked Narcise.

"They hide in the bush while we work. They come back to sleep when we leave. We do not see them. Sometimes we hear their voices."

He looked at the thick vegetation all around. "It is a hard life for a woman."

"Twins are bad, patron," Narcise whispered. "They are evil spirits."

"You say this with your Bible in your pocket?"

"Even in the Bible, twins are bad. Adam and Eve were twins."

He laughed. "Were they? I don't want to argue with you. But this seems unjust to me."

It was already growing very hot, the sun glaring down from a white sky. After they had eaten, the men got reluctantly back to work, sweat pouring down their naked backs. Jean-Patrice mounted Adeline and left them, promising to pass by on his way back. He set off into the wilderness with a pleasing sense of achievement, of having left the world a little better than he had found it.

It was ferociously humid, the air almost too moist to breathe. Sweat dripped from his chin. He was soon alone in a sea of high grass. The going was slow; he let Adeline feel her way lest she put a leg in a hole. A lamed horse in this wilderness might mean death.

Since coming to Gabon he had grown reconciled to the thought of his own death. It had terrified him at first (though there were things that frightened him more); but loneliness had changed him, made him more accepting of his mortality.

He would have been hard put to define the change in all its ramifications, though he felt it clearly enough. It seemed to him, for one thing, that he was less self-regarding. He did not think about himself as much as he had once done. That was why death was no longer so frightening – or so remote. He was more in the world and less in himself.

His affair with Justine had revealed deep flaws in his nature. He looked back now at his own outrage and sense of grievance and saw how foolishly he had behaved. What right had he had to be outraged and aggrieved? She had made promises and said extravagant things, it was true, but women said these things in love. Every man knew that. They were written in water. She had given him what she had been able to give. Instead of accepting it gladly, he had wanted more and more, forcing her into concessions she had not wanted to make, until at last she had cried, "enough."

It had been his first deeply felt emotion but he had not been ready for it. He had showered her with love; but what, after all, was love worth? Did madmen not love? Murderers? Love was the devalued currency of the world, worth nothing in itself, expressing only that most infantile of human cries, I want! I want! I want!

He had been untried, despite his twenty-seven years. He had believed himself to be many things – courageous, fair, decent. The shell of that egg had been cracked, first by Justine and then by Africa. The slippery, unresolved contents had spilled out. He would now see what he really was, of what stuff he was made.

He had been pleasantly surprised, at least, by the pragmatism he had so far displayed in Gabon. That was something. Faced with a problem, he had tackled it head-on, unthinkingly. Yes, that was something. And here he was, riding through the wilderness alone, devoid of fear.

Well, not devoid of fear. When he stopped and looked

around him, the terror came rushing in from all sides, crushing his heart. So alone! So isolated! A crawling speck in a vast landscape not marked on any map, unknown to the civilized world. All those terrors of childhood – cannibals, lions, serpents, crocodiles – all were real here, not illustrations in a book or phantoms under the bed.

"Under the bed," he muttered. He had taken to talking to himself – or to Chloë, which was much the same thing – rather a lot. The sound of his own voice was comforting. "Under the bed, under the bed, under the bed."

He plodded doggedly on, searching for the pioneer spirit, the lust for new horizons. The trouble was, he had liked his old horizons well enough. He had none of the bitterness towards his native land that the true pioneer must feel. Paris was like a golden dream to him now.

The sun roasted his shoulders and thighs, burning his hands till they were swollen and red. The miasma of the mare's sweat rose around him, attracting a cloud of flies that tormented his face. He pulled his hat down low and sat it out, losing himself in the swaying motion like a victim yielding to the overwhelming power of torture.

The Road (it had assumed capital letters in his mind) was approaching from the north. It was being built along a valley, forming a kind of river of grass between the dark masses of tropical forest. Using his compass and the directions he had been given, Jean-Patrice was reasonably certain that he was heading in the right direction this time. His principal landmark, a blue mountain peak on the horizon, shimmered in the heat, occasionally seeming to disappear altogether. He stopped at midday in the shade of a clump of trees. His clothes were drenched with sweat and he felt nauseous and weak, his heart racing because of the loss of salts. He was too hot to eat anything, but he drank from his canteen and sprawled on the baking ground. Adeline hung her head and dozed. He closed his eyes, seeing jagged red and black flashes. He must be careful not to get sunstroke or it would be all over for him.

He managed to stop himself from vomiting and losing his precious water. He, too, slept for a while. When he awoke, he felt better and resumed the journey.

At around three in the afternoon, he saw a smudge of dust in the still air up ahead and felt he must be approaching the road now. He had come further than anyone had said he would have to go. The road was a long way from reaching Bassongo.

Half an hour later, he breasted a rise and found himself looking down on the roadwork at last. The Road! He halted the horse and stood staring at it. It was there, all right, no more than a red ribbon of raw earth like a wavering cicatrice through the vegetation. He tried to assess his feelings. What had he expected? A pavement of gold? There it was, the scar of civilization, a link to freedom, an escape, a way out, a connection between one dot and another on the empty map of Gabon. He exhaled a deep sigh of relief. Something of his claustrophobia lifted. A road went somewhere. It had a purpose. Be it ever so humble, a road contradicted the anarchy of nature. Emerging from the dark forest, it snaked across the valley and petered out below him, where a group of men had camped under a pall of dust and smoke from fires. He rode Adeline carefully down the slope, singing nonsense songs of relief to himself. As he approached, he was challenged by an African guard with a rifle.

"I am Jean-Patrice Duméril, the District Commissioner of Bassongo," he announced proudly. The man seemed unimpressed and escorted him to the camp with his rifle at the ready. A very dirty and unshaven white man in boots and a khaki uniform emerged from a tent, staring at Jean-Patrice with bloodshot eyes.

"Who the hell are you?"

Jean-Patrice dismounted and repeated his name and title. "I've ridden from Bassongo to see the work."

The man hoisted his braces over his shoulders and looked Jean-Patrice up and down. "In this condition? Where's your guard?"

"I brought no guard."

"You must be insane."

"There is only one horse at Bassongo, you see."

"Horse? The men will run next to you."

"Not in this heat," Jean-Patrice said, laughing. "They would die."

"If they die, you leave them where they fall," the other retorted. He held out his hand. "I'm Carbonell, the road engineer." His grip was hard, his palm calloused. He was a short, muscular Catalan with a fierce little head which seemed to have been compressed from the top and the bottom, so that his lower jaw thrust out pugnaciously like a bulldog's, while his brows beetled down over a pair of darting black eyes. He pulled a flask out of his pocket and thrust it at Jean-Patrice. "You must be insane," he repeated. "You'd better have a drink."

It was early in the day for alcohol, but Jean-Patrice swigged, his mouth filling with a fiery, raw brandy. It was oddly refreshing. He exhaled, half-expecting to see flames shooting from his mouth. "I'm very glad to see you. It's been a long ride."

"Forty-three miles as the crow flies," Carbonell said, swigging from the same flask. "What did you expect to find?"

"The road, at least."

"You have found it." The man turned and waved his hand. "There it is, and it's a bitch."

"May I see?"

"May you? By God, you may. Come." Jean-Patrice followed Carbonell as he stamped along, his boots kicking out in a bandy-legged strut. This trait, together with the large revolver he wore at each hip, gave him a Wild West air. A second white man, taller and older, but similarly unshaven and dirty, was supervising the native laborers.

"We've got a visitor," Carbonell rasped. "This is Duméril, the new man at Bassongo. My overseer, Jaworski."

Jaworski, evidently a Pole, had a hard, thin axe of a face. He inspected Jean-Patrice suspiciously. "What does he want?" he asked with a thick accent.

"He likes roads."

"He can have this one," Jaworski muttered. He carried a heavy, braided whip coiled in one hand. To Jean-Patrice's dismay, he now uncoiled this instrument and almost casually struck a heavy blow at the naked back of the nearest African. The leather curled around the thin shoulders, making the man lurch and leaving a glistening stripe in the brown skin. Jean-Patrice now saw that the laborers were chained by their necks in groups of four or five.

Despite the heat, he felt the sweat evaporate coldly on his skin. The chains formed long loops between the men as they worked, rattling constantly. They moved with a kind of exhausted care among the clouds of dust. They had evidently become expert at avoiding tangles, which could cause severe injuries, and attract the overseer's whip. Nor were the men all young – some were middle-aged, with pot bellies and stick limbs. Some appeared to be no more than adolescents. All wore expressions of blank despair, their eyes glazed, almost like the eyes of dead men. Some had been set to clearing away trees, others were digging the culverts on either side of the road. They were wearing rags so filthy and ancient that all had taken on the same ochre colour. He watched in silence as a group of four hauled the tangled roots of a tree out of the crimson earth. He noticed that the collars had made deep chafe marks on the men's necks, some ulcerated and running.

The tree emerged with the reluctance of some vital organ being wrenched out of a living body, something not meant to be seen, the woven roots bleeding as the men hacked at them with their bush knives. At last, the horror tore out. There was no sign of achievement in the empty faces. The men began hauling it to one side. Another gang began to fill the wound.

He found his voice. "Why are they chained by the throat like this?" he asked.

"Why do you think?" Jaworski growled. "Do you imagine there would be one left here by tomorrow morning if they weren't restrained?"

"This is the most abominable cruelty."

Jaworski merely spat, but Carbonell chuckled. "You cannot be cruel to a thing, Duméril. These are things, not men."

"Are they criminals?"

"Of course," Carbonell said, and winked.

Jean-Patrice walked slowly down the line. There were perhaps fifty laborers in the gang, all chained in the same way. They loomed out of the dust like phantoms, and vanished again. Now and then he encountered an African guard with a rifle, and at the very end, another white man, who looked up from the map he had been peering at to stare in astonishment at Jean-Patrice. By now, Jean-Patrice was too sickened to bother with introductions. He ignored the European. The very light of the sun had been darkened by the clouds of dust. Stumbling with exhaustion, the chained figures dug in the earth in silence, not a word or a groan coming from their mouths. The only sound was the tearing of roots and the rattle of the iron chains. This was a vision of Hell, complete with the damned and their devils.

He recalled the Fang hunter: The whites are stealing our brothers. He had not understood. How could he have understood? He felt shame now that he had shrugged off their plea for justice.

He returned to the head of the line, plodding heavily through the soft earth, with his head down. He was walking, he realized, on the Road. His Road. The Road he had dreamed of. The roads of Africa were being built in this way, by such as these lost souls. The thought was terrible.

Carbonell was waiting for him. "Why the face?" he demanded. "Don't you like what you see?"

"I have never seen anything like this," he replied. "How long do these men serve in these gangs?"

"A few months," Carbonell said. He produced a cigarette and put it between his lips. "Then they go free."

"But many must die in their chains?"

"That is an inconvenience, certainly."

"Where do they come from?"

Carbonell lit his cigarette. "They are doing nothing, sitting in the bush. They may as well work for their living for a season or two."

"So they are forced laborers."

The man shrugged. "I do what the Government tells me to do."

Jean-Patrice stared at the roiling, hellish agglomeration of suffering and degradation, making its way slowly towards his village. "How long before you reach Bassongo?"

"Depends on how many laborers they give me. If they keep the supply up, eight months. If they can't catch enough, another year. Your sleepy little place will wake up when we get there, I can tell you. Business will be brisk. What happened to the other fellow at Bassongo, what was his name, Joliet?"

"Dead," Jean-Patrice replied briefly.

The other smoked reflectively without commenting. "Eight months," he said again. "Then my contract here is up. If I live that long."

"You will die here," Jaworski said, appearing from the dust like a hatchet-faced old Mephistopheles. "You will die here and I will have the task of heaving up a pile of stones to keep you in your grave."

"You see?" Carbonell said with equanimity. "You see how they hate me?"

"You are an ugly dog," Jaworski replied.

"But I bite," Carbonell said. "I bite Jaworski, Jaworski bites Hainault and Hainault bites the niggers. So long as I get the first bite, I don't care if they hate me."

There was no choice but to spend the night with the road builders. The sun was now low, peering bloodily through the dust. The chink of the chains slowly faded as the dusk gathered. The guards walked down the line bawling. The chained men squatted in groups, making fires to cook whatever wretched meal they were given. The white men sat on camp stools around a fire pit where one of the guards prepared a pot of beans for them. A bottle of cheap brandy was passed around. Jean-Patrice drank deeply, wanting to numb himself. Hainault, the third white man in the engineer's party, produced a banjo and strummed a few songs, singing half under his breath.

Jean-Patrice threw his head back and stared up at the swimming stars. They were like silver fish in black water, his drunkenness magnifying their cold fires. Hainault's tuneless voice was a lonely, sad sound. He could bear it no longer. While the others ate, he wandered off into the darkness. The glimmer of charcoal fires illuminated the faces of the laborers, savage and mournful, as they brooded over their meal. Each held a lump of porridge cupped in one hand, picking at it with the other. There was no talking; perhaps it was forbidden, or perhaps there was nothing for these hopeless men to say to one another.

But later in the night, as he lay sleepless on his bedroll, he could hear the sound of men weeping and the endless coughing of the sick. It was hard to sleep. He was awoken some time before dawn by two shots. He sat up. There was no further sound, but he could not lie there anymore. As the grey light stole down the hillside, he rose and saddled up Adeline.

"Going already?" Carbonell had come of his tent and was pissing against a tree, his sharp little eyes on Jean-Patrice.

"I have a long ride ahead of me."

The other man grunted. "Have some coffee, at least."

He sat with the three road builders, drinking strong, bitter coffee as the rim of the sun appeared, like the crack of a furnace door. The enforced labor was already in progress, the chink of chains ringing out. The stark figures of the men began to fade into the red dust. "I heard some shots," he said.

Jaworski refilled his tin mug. "One of them got clever," the Pole said. "Used a sharp stone to saw through his collar and tried to escape. The other niggers stopped him."

"They stopped their companion from escaping?"

"If one nigger from a work gang escapes, the rest work without food till they starve." He smiled thinly. "Tonight they'll get double rations."

"And the man?"

"I shot him myself."

Riding back through the wilderness, his thoughts were very different from those optimistic reflections of yesterday. Today, he felt the purposelessness of his existence, of everything that he had done or had happened to him. The faces of those men, chained like animals, haunted him. So did the casual brutality of the overseers. What was he doing here among such men? In two years he would be almost thirty, his youth over. He was presumably meant to redeem himself during this period. What great feats could he accomplish here, in this no-place in the middle of nowhere? What eyes would watch him fail or succeed? Even if he and Catherine managed to inoculate every soul in Bassongo, he could not bring himself to believe that he would have altered the course of human destiny in any way that mattered. Every good deed he did was cancelled out by such as Jaworski. Nobody in the outside world cared whether one native – or ten thousand – lived or died or was enslaved. The natives themselves appeared not to care. And how many millions more were there, inaccessible in this endless wilderness, buried in their own indifference? The concept of destiny, or fate, or God, of any kind of purpose, seemed absurd.

He reached the forbidden village by the late afternoon, sick and drained with the heat. There was nobody in sight. The work had been completed; Narcise and the others had departed. He did not go into the village, feeling that his presence would be an intrusion. He squirmed at the idea of being offered thanks. As he took the road back to Bassongo, he glanced at the termite tree, half-willing it to metamorphose back into Joliet. The man's appearance would have been almost welcome. But Joliet refused obstinately to appear, and he went his way alone.

Adeline, scenting home perhaps, broke into a trot despite her exhausting day. As he jogged along, Jean-Patrice suddenly felt he understood the meaning of Joliet's leather bound journal. The thing was a trophy. Other men took home from Africa the stuffed heads of animals or cases of butterflies. Joliet had been planning to take that book. During the reflective latter part of his life, in some orderly French department, he would open its pages and recall the flaring heat of Gabon, the red days and nights spent taking his pleasure from dark skinned women who had wept and submitted to his lust. That was his memento of Africa.

Was everything the white man did in Africa based on exploitation and theft? Perhaps there was a Darwinian explanation, the domination of a more primitive species by an evolved one. In the absence of God, subtracting the supposition of a moral universe, there was nothing either good or bad about that. It was simply Nature. Rape, nature. Slavery, nature. Murder, nature. Extermination, degradation, mutilation, vileness of every kind, all nature.

But could one make God absent himself? Perhaps it was not so easy, and there would be a dreadful price to pay at the end of it all. Perhaps a vengeful deity (or a vengeful Nature) would appear from the clouds one day and smite. Or perhaps things would just keep getting worse and worse.

17

In the end, they were unable to accommodate all of his great plans for the day. There was no demonstration of marksmanship, since it was considered risky to put the weapons in the hands of the general public. But a village band was assembled in front of the Residency, playing a variety of instruments, including a balafon, a huge xylophone made with hollow gourds of various sizes, pounded by two indefatigable old men. Raymond's wives, who formed the village choir, sang and clapped alongside. Jean-Patrice had ordered gourds of beer and palm wine to be brewed as well as the slaughter of eight goats and a number of chickens, which were now roasting over the coals. Clouds of fragrant smoke drifted into the morning air.

The calf had been vaccinated and had dutifully developed a satisfactory quantity of ripe pustules. Jean-Patrice and Catherine had worked day and night to prepare cases of capillary tubes. They had carried the Residency's kitchen table outside for Catherine to use. The glittering trays of lancets, with their alarming appearance, had been discreetly covered with a sheet. They would be unveiled at the proper moment. Catherine wore a dress he had not seen before, black with large gold flowers, and looked (as he thought) like a queen. She wore a turban of the same fabric and long earrings which dangled on each side of her long, slender neck. Over the table fluttered a banner which she had painted with a human face, weeping and covered with red dots, to symbolize the affliction of smallpox, together with some lines in Beti, which he could not read.

The ten new machetes and ten new dresses had been bought, and were laid out temptingly. He had also prepared a Vaccination Ledger, in which the names and clans of the inoculated were to be written down by Narcise, whose writing was the neatest despite his myopia. Its blank pages shone like untarnished youthful hopes in the sun. Inoculation would begin, he had planned, once the cannon had been fired. He would discharge the gun when he judged the time was ripe. Hyppolite was stationed beside it to ensure it was not tampered with.

Despite all these enticements, the morning passed quietly. A few people arrived to stare and talk and then drifted away. There was no sign of Chief Obangui, who had been especially invited. Without him, success was very uncertain. He began to fear that the day would be a fiasco.

"Will they come?" he asked Catherine.

She gave him a sympathetic smile. "I'm sure they will."

But an obstinate indifference reigned. A pair of hadeda ibises cawed loudly on the roof of the Residency, a sign, Raymond noted with relish, of impending catastrophe.

Then, at around midday, there was a commotion. Two men wearing colorful robes arrived, beating on brass gongs and chanting. These were the heralds of Chief Obangui. Jean-Patrice felt a thrill of hope. Villagers began to appear from the huts. The crowd grew. Some rhythmic clapping began. Finally, Obangui himself arrived waving a fly whisk and shuffling along between his sons. He was wearing a cloak with elaborate trimmings of embroidery and beads and a tall headdress. Jean-Patrice was deeply relieved to see him appear. Apparently beloved by his people, the old man was seated in pride of place, smiling benevolently under the shade of banana leaves held by his sons. A grandchild brought him the choicest cut of the largest goat, together with a calabash of palm wine, which he drank in one heroic draft, to great applause.

Eating, drinking and dancing began in earnest. Jean-Patrice greeted the Chief formally, and sat watching the celebration with Chloë seated on his lap. The gorilla seemed calm and interested in the spectacle, though she would not let go of him. He, on the other hand, was nervous. It remained to be seen whether anyone would consent to be inoculated. Otherwise, he would have made a fool of himself, and have spent rather a great deal of his own money, in vain.

The music grew louder, the voices of the women sharper and more piercing. It was a brilliantly sunny day. A very pretty woman danced up to him, swaying her hips and holding out her hands. He lifted Chloë in his arms and allowed himself to be drawn into the dance. There was laughter and cheering as he arrived in the circle with the gorilla clinging to him. He felt his own absurdity, in boots and a hat, but did his best to imitate the sinuous dance steps of the men. The rhythm was complex, the music confusing. He knew they called him White Ass and considered him a figure of fun, but he did not care. It was the most carefree hour he had spent since arriving in Bassongo.

Breathless, he escaped at last and went to stand beside Catherine. "What do you think?" he panted.

She leaned back in her chair to look up at him. "You can ride and swim, but you can't dance."

"I don't mean that. I mean, are we ready to start inoculating?"

She considered. "Perhaps better sooner than later. The men are already getting wild."

"Then I'll fire the cannon." He passed over Chloë,

who accepted the transfer with some reluctance.

He and the policemen rolled the cannon forward. They'd prepared a charge which he had calculated from one of the almanacs that had survived immersion in the river. Too light a charge could apparently be as dangerous as too great a one. He hoped that there would not be a catastrophic end to the day. The idea had begun to look less wonderful than when he'd first dreamed it up. The ancient barrel might fly to pieces, killing more of Bassongo's population than the smallpox, but there was no going back at this point.

An unexpected problem now presented itself. Hordes of naked children, becoming aware that the cannon was about to be fired, ran up in great excitement and began to clamber all over it, hanging from the muzzle and peering into the bore eagerly. Dislodging them was not easy. No sooner had he lifted one wiry little body off the gun when two more had clambered up. It took the bellowing of Hyppolite to make them run back, giggling.

They fixed the wheels and the train of the weapon. He elevated the barrel as far as it would go. The music died down. There was an expectant hush. Jean-Patrice inserted the fuse he'd made into the touch-hole and pushed it down. His heart was thudding. He lit a match and glanced at Hyppolite. Hyppolite shrugged. "Vive la France," he said.

"Hyppolite, with those words, which may well be your last, you have become not merely a beni oui-oui but a full assimilé." He struck a match and lit the fuse. The gunpowder sputtered, then caught. Spraying yellow sparks, the fuse disappeared rapidly into the touch-hole. There was a brief silence.

The concussion, when it came, was so great that Jean-Patrice felt certain the barrel must have burst. The ground seemed to leap under his feet, the breath was knocked from his lungs. Deafened and blinded, he coughed in the billowing black smoke that had blotted out the light.

Burning fragments stung his arms and face, threatening to set light to his clothes. He beat out the glowing worms that wriggled across his shirt. The smoke rolled away, revealing that the ground he'd chosen had been too soft: the cannon had driven itself backward into the yielding earth. The carriage and wheels were half-buried. It would take shovels to dig it out again. But the barrel was intact. And he could see figures dancing all around, though he could hear little as yet, except a shrill sound as of cicadas on a hot summer's day in the countryside. Fluttering down from the heavens were hundreds of blue, white and red rags from the tricolor bundle that he and Hyppolite had carefully constructed. The firing of the cannon had been a success. Though several children were lying on the ground, these appeared to be stunned, rather than injured. He found Hyppolite in as scorched a state as himself. The two men hugged one another, laughing. Narcise, appearing blinder than ever, stared up at the sky, open mouthed.

As his hearing returned, he found that the band was playing with redoubled energy. Those children who had not been blown flat were running around, snatching at the colored shreds of cloth that continued to rain down from the sky. Screaming in terror, Chloë galloped up to him and hurled herself into his arms, her powerful arms locking around his neck tightly. He looked at Catherine's table and saw that an old woman had arrived and was baring a wrinkled arm. As he watched, Catherine vaccinated the woman in a businesslike way and presented her with one of the new dresses. The old woman gave her name to Narcise and hurried away with her prize. This instantly drew a crowd to the table, villagers jostling one another to be the next. He saw Catherine assert her natural authority and put them into an orderly line. He felt a flush of pride on her behalf. She was magnificent, he thought.

Reeking of gunpowder, Jean-Patrice sat beside the half-sunken cannon to watch and comfort Chloë. The bush knives and dresses soon ran out. It made no difference. Those who had been vaccinated dragged those who had not to the table. Parents brought their children, children brought their siblings. The queue at the table grew so long that Jean-Patrice abandoned his cigar and went to get a chair. He sat down beside Catherine, rolled up his singed sleeves, and set to work with a lancet.

"How did you like the cannon?" he asked, as he vaccinated his first patient, a shrinking young girl.

"I never want to witness anything like that again," she replied.

"I thought it was colossal."

"You are a boy."

"Well, it worked."

"They would have come without the cannon." But she was smiling at him. "Your face is black, Monsieur."

He looked up to find that Sophie had arrived at the table. He was pleased. He made the scratch on her slender arm He fixed on a plaster. "You are protected against the smallpox now, Sophie," he said. "I'm glad you came." She gave him the smallest of smiles and melted away again.

The dancing continued. When the goats and chickens had all been eaten, they roasted yams and brought fufu and maize bread. Jean-Patrice and Catherine sat side by side, vaccinating a seemingly endless line of villagers. Some demanded Catherine, others Jean-Patrice. They came from near and far, some brought by the music or the cannon, others afraid of the smallpox and genuinely eager for protection. Some brought babies, too young for the vaccine. Some went straight to the back of the queue and asked to be vaccinated again and had to be sent away, disappointed. Others arrived with the marks of smallpox already in their faces; it was of no use to tell these they were now immune, so they vaccinated them with a tiny dose of the precious serum and entered their names in the book.

Obangui steadfastly refused to be inoculated, declaring that he was immune by virtue of his royal blood. However two of his sons were privately inoculated by Jean-Patrice when their father's attention was diverted. The sun beat down and the humidity of the day intensified. They kept working until their arms ached and their clothes were soaked with sweat, their voices hoarse from repeating the formula to each patient, "In two or three days the place will swell and begin to itch. Do not scratch. Lie down and sleep if you have fever. Come to the Residency if you are very ill."

Around them, the feast grew wilder. Jean-Patrice saw men becoming so drunk that they could hardly walk, falling to the ground and being unable to rise. Then, among the crowds, he caught sight of the nodding feathered headdresses of Fang hunters. Uneasy, he tried to keep them in view. There were four or five of them, as far as he could tell. His view of them was obscured by the crowd, but he caught glimpses of naked, muscular torsos, spears and muskets.

"I'm going to see what they're doing."

Catherine, who had also seen them, nodded. "Be careful."

He made his way through the crowd of sweating, fuddled faces. The sour smell of beer and the bitter smell of sweat were everywhere. The smiles had given way to those blank expressions he particularly disliked, the "strange people next door" look. He had the feeling that the feast was running out of control. Obangui had by now melted away with his sons. There was an atmosphere of dangerous despair now. Or perhaps the feeling was within himself?

He was dismayed to find one of the Fang, a small man with an elaborate necklace of animal teeth, feeding Chloë with plantains. He took the gorilla into the Residency and locked her there, ignoring her plaintive cries.

He found two more of the Fang hunters drinking beer

from calabashes. The villagers were keeping clear of them. He recognized them as Achilles and Patroclus, the men who had brought the ivory. Achilles rolled his eyes at Jean-Patrice but did not put down the calabash until he had drained it. He wiped his mouth with his forearm and belched in satisfaction.

"Yes, blanc!" he greeted Jean-Patrice.

"Have you come to be scratched?" Jean-Patrice asked.

The man grinned, showing his pointed teeth. "Me, I am too frightened of the blanc's medicine," he replied.

"How many of you have come?" Jean-Patrice demanded. The men shrugged. But Jean-Patrice could see the grim figures of the other Fang moving among the crowd and calculated there were perhaps ten of them, probably the same party which had brought the tusks. "If you want to eat and drink, you must be inoculated."

"By the woman?" the big man replied contemptuously.

"I will inoculate you myself," Jean-Patrice said. "There is no pain."

The other man had a piece of goat in his hand, still dribbling blood. He chuckled. "No pain, blanc?"

"The knife is very small."

"Your knife is small?" Achilles slapped the heavy-bladed machete that hung at his belt. "Our knives are big. You cut us and we will cut you." He tore off a piece of meat with his filed teeth. His lips shone with blood and grease. Their eyes were mocking, assessing, knowing. They were waiting for him to challenge them. Once again, however, he was alone. There was no sign of Hyppolite or Raymond. His heart was beating faster.

"Very well," he said calmly. "I agree. Come to the table. I will cut you and then you can cut me."

Their expressions changed, becoming wary. "For true?"

"Yes." If he could succeed in inoculating Achilles, who appeared to be the natural leader, the others might follow suit. "Come with me." Patroclus tossed aside the gobbet of meat and wiped his hands on his naked belly. They followed him to the table. Seeing the Fang, the villagers moved aside hastily. He saw Catherine's alarmed expression but kept his own face calm. He prepared a lancet and turned to the big man. "You first."

"No." Achilles thrust his shorter companion forward with a grin. "This one first, blanc!"

Jean-Patrice took Patroclus' sinewy arm, and neatly scratched the skin. By now they had run out of plasters. "That's all."

Patroclus looked at him speculatively. "Nothing else?"

"Nothing. The place will itch. Don't scratch. In a few days it will be healed and you will be protected from smallpox."

The man grunted. "Now I can cut you?"

"If you want."

Grinning with his pointed teeth, Patroclus pulled the machete from its scabbard and grasped Jean-Patrice's wrist in strong fingers. He jerked Jean-Patrice's arm straight and raised the machete high above his head. The blow would sever his arm at the elbow. Some of the women in the crowd screamed and ran away. The men backed off, muttering. Jean-Patrice felt his bowels cramp. The man's face looked crazy, his eyes gleaming. His taller companion was watching avidly. What insanity had led him to entrust his life to an Iron Age warrior, drunk on beer and his own arrogance? Whites like Carbonell were forcing his brothers to work, chained throat to throat, shooting them like dogs when they tried to escape. He forced himself to remain immobile, staring into the black eyes steadily. He sensed Catherine rise to her feet and hoped she would not try to put herself in the way of the heavy blade.

"You got magic, blanc?" Achilles asked. "Maybe you will grow a new arm, eh?"

The moment stretched. Then the man swung the blade down with a deep grunt. The metal thudded into Jean-Patrice's biceps. Catherine screamed. But the hunter had turned the blade at the last moment so that it was the flat, and not the razor edge, which struck him. The blow was a weighty one, and numbed his shoulder at once. The two Fang burst out laughing at Jean-Patrice's expression.

"You are lucky, blanc," Achilles said. "You got magic."

Jean-Patrice pulled his wrist out of the man's grasp, trying to conceal the fact that his whole body was shaking. "Now you," he said.

"Ah no! Not me."

"Are you a coward, while your friend is brave?"

The big man stared at him, his smile fading. "If I cut you, I will cut for true."

The numbness was turning into a throbbing pain that spread up into his chest. "I will take that chance."

"Jean-Patrice!" Catherine said quietly and urgently.

"They have come here and have eaten our food and drunk our beer," he said in a steady voice. "Now they must be scratched."

Achilles shook his head. "You are lucky one time, blanc, maybe you will not be so lucky another time."

Jean-Patrice was growing tired of being called blanc. He prepared a second lancet. "Give me your arm, negre."

The big man's eyes glittered with anger. He turned away from Jean-Patrice and examined the scratch on his companion's arm. He spat on his palm and rubbed the little incision. "This is nothing," he said contemptuously. "This has no power. You are joking with these people, blanc. Your little knife does nothing." The two men turned and shouldered their way through the crowd without looking back.

Jean-Patrice sat down heavily. His arm ached and he felt weak. Catherine put her arms around him. There were tears in her eyes. "Why are you so stupid?" she said.

Narcise was grey with fear. "Patron, these people are dangerous. Not for games. You understand?"

"At least I vaccinated one of them. The others might follow."

Catherine's arms were tight around his neck. "They are different, Jean-Patrice. They smoke hemp. They eat plants in the forest that give them visions and make them worse than drunk. You can never know what is in their minds. They are like madmen sometimes. Please understand."

"I can't sit by and let them do what they want."

Now that the Fang had left, the crowd was moving back to the table. There was no time to discuss the folly or otherwise of his action. They resumed work.

By early evening, they were all exhausted. The serum ran out, which was just as well, since the lancets were by now all blunt and needed re-sharpening. Narcise, too, was running out of ink and shaking his swollen writing hand ruefully. Several pages of the Ledger were now covered with his neat script.

"We have to stop," Jean-Patrice said. "We'll make more serum tonight and fix the blades. Tell them to come back tomorrow. We'll start again at two in the afternoon."

Catherine rose wearily to her feet and addressed the waiting crowd. There were some cries of protest, but the queue slowly dispersed. Darkness was settling. People started to drift away. The sky was the swirling, red, fish-blood colour that reminded him of his first night in Bassongo.

As they packed up the table, he caught the sound of guffaws of laughter and a strange, thin screaming. He peered through the gloom and the smoke. The Fang hunters were standing in a semicircle around the dying fire. He made his way tiredly to investigate. At the centre of the group, he glimpsed the ragged, shaggy-haired figure of Ndoumou. He realized that they were tormenting the madman with spears, driving him to walk on the glowing coals with his bare feet. It was from him that the eerie shrieks were coming. Jean-Patrice had never heard him utter a sound before. He thrust his way furiously into the circle. He grasped Ndoumou's arms and pulled him away from the hot ash. "This is not sport," he snapped at the men. "Go back to where you came from."

Laughing and with no sign of shame, the Fang closed around him, muskets and spears bristling. "Where is the monkey, blanc?" someone called.

"Give us the idiot."

"Give us the monkey!"

He was too angry to pretend indifference. Ndoumou trembled against him, hobbling on his blistered feet. "I was told the Fang are brave," he said tightly, "but you are cowards. All of you."

The men fell silent. He led Ndoumou through their ranks. When he was a few paces away, the laughter burst out again. He ignored it. Keening, Ndoumou broke away from him and fled into the darkness. Jean-Patrice called after him but he would not return. The band finally stopped playing and the old men carried away the balafon. The day was over.

They went into the Residency and sat around the dining table to take stock. Narcise counted the entries in the Ledger carefully. "Eight hundred and sixty-three," he said. "But many ran away without giving their names. Counting those, I think there must have been a thousand, perhaps more."

Jean-Patrice felt a sense of weary triumph. He himself, he reckoned, had inoculated only some three hundred of that total. It was Catherine, far quicker and defter than he, who had done the lion's share of the work. "You are magnificent," he said to her quietly. Someone brought some of the remaining fufu and yams from the feast and they ate together, talking about the day and the incidents that each had experienced. Catherine sat beside him, speaking little and eating almost nothing. He felt the presence of her body against his, warm and increasingly pressing, until he looked at her and saw that she had fallen fast asleep with her head on his shoulder. He put his arm around her to support her. Hyppolite watched him with

174

heavy eyes. He let her sleep like that until she started into wakefulness and sat up, rubbing her face. He coaxed her into eating something before they started to prepare for the next day.

"By my estimation, there are two thousand people in the Bassongo area," he said. "That is, between three and four to each hut. It means we've inoculated about half of them. They won't come in such numbers as today, I suppose. We may have to go to the remoter parts ourselves to do the people who won't bring themselves here. In any case, there are many days of work to do. But it has been a wonderful beginning."

She nodded. "I hope none of them have the same reaction I did. That will be a disaster."

"What if the Fang come back tomorrow?" Narcise asked.

"Tomorrow I will have my revolver. You, Hyppolite and Narcise will have rifles."

"There are four of us," Hyppolite pointed out quietly. "And maybe twelve of them."

"It cannot be helped. We've started the program now. We have to continue. We can't let them intimidate us."

"Do not play games with them if they come back," Catherine pleaded. "You can never know what they are going to do."

They went to draw serum from the official calf by the light of a hurricane lantern and then worked until late in the study, Catherine separating the doses in phials and sealing them with glycerin, Jean-Patrice sharpening the lancets for the next day's work. She was absorbed in her task, but his eyes were drawn to her constantly. He loved the grace of her movements. She made the simplest actions seem beautiful. When she passed him, he drew in his breath deeply, searching for the distinctive scent of her body, which was hers alone. He tried to do this covertly but saw her glance at him on occasion. By midnight they had finished. She was heavy-lidded with tiredness.

"Would you like to sleep here?" he suggested hopefully.

"I'll go to my own house."

"I'll take you on the horse."

"That's not necessary. Hyppolite will walk with me." Hyppolite shrugged in a surly manner. It was useless to urge. He caught a mischievous gleam in her eye, as though she enjoyed thwarting him. He was aching to press his lips to that lush, soft mouth of hers. Instead, he said good night to her chastely at the door and went upstairs to his own bed. The machete blow had left a dark purple bruise across his arm. He remembered the moment of horror he'd felt as the man had swung the blade. Sleep rushed over him almost before he could pull his boots off. The deafening blast of the cannon woke him with pounding heart, making him sit up, before he realized it had been a dream. Chloë crawled into his arms and clung to him, grunting to be comforted. He petted her for a while. Then he lay back down and slept until dawn.

The next morning, a steady trickle of people began to arrive. There was no sign of the Fang. By midday, there were one or two hundred waiting patiently in front of the Residency. Jean-Patrice was delighted. Catherine set up her table and, with Narcise to take the names, began to vaccinate. She worked steadily all afternoon. As he went about the afternoon's activities, it gave him constant pleasure to keep her in view. She wore a pink dress today which he thought set off her complexion perfectly, and which could be seen from a long way off. He felt as though his life had a centre again, a pink centre with smooth, dark skin and almond eyes.

He set Narcise and Hyppolite to disinterring the cannon which had performed so manfully the day before. At mid-afternoon, the Fang hunters reappeared.

They came swaggering back into the village in a group, their muscular bodies oiled. As always, they were armed with their guns and spears. He felt anger and alarm at their persistence. They were like hyenas, sniffing at the village for weakness of any kind. What was it they wanted? He asked Hyppolite, but the Corporal merely shrugged. He had his revolver strapped to his hip and Hyppolite had his rifle, but he was aware that they were heavily outgunned and outnumbered. Today they ignored him, not approaching the table but prowling around the huts, pointing and talking amongst themselves. He could see them peering into doors and windows with the insouciance of men who saw no opposition to their wishes. He had locked Chloë in the house again but he felt anxious about her and sent Raymond to guard her.

"Three hundred and fifty so far," Catherine said. "They are coming from as far away as Medoneu. Some of them have crossed the river. There will be more tomorrow. And they're not asking about dresses and bush knives. They just want the vaccination."

"Any reports of illness?"

"Not yet. When they stop coming, it will be time to go out to the huts further into the bush."

"We can go together," he suggested, with visions of himself and Catherine sharing a tent in the wilderness

"It would be better if I went with the three police," she said gently. "Your place is here. Look there, Jean-Patrice." She pointed.

He turned to look. With finely honed predatory instincts, the Fang had found Sophie. They had a genius for finding weakness. The girl was standing in a circle of half-naked men. She wore her rose print dress and seemed more childlike than ever, her slim legs and arms pathetically frail next to their sinewy limbs. He could see the men grinning at her, one of them gesturing as he talked.

"Damn them," he muttered. "How do I get rid of them?"

"It's impossible, Jean-Patrice. They say this was their territory before the whites made the villagers come here. To them, we are trespassers."

"So they think they can take what they like?"

"Please," she begged him, "remember what I said yesterday! No more trials of strength with them!"

"I am hardly in a position to show my strength," he replied bitterly. With his usual finesse, Hyppolite had melted away and was nowhere to be seen. Jean-Patrice walked over to the group. His shoulder was aching from yesterday's blow . The revolver felt heavy on his hip and his heart felt heavy in his breast.

As he reached the men, he saw one of them take Sophie's arm and begin leading her towards the river.

He called out, "Sophie!"

They all turned to him. It was Achilles who was leading her away. "What do you want?" he asked Jean-Patrice brusquely.

Jean-Patrice ignored him. "Where are you going, Sophie?"

"She is going with us, blanc," the hunter said. "Go back to your woman and your little knives."

Sophie's face, as so often, seemed to show no emotion; but in her eyes he thought he could see the flickering fear of a crouching gazelle among hyenas. "I need you to help me at the table, Sophie," he said. "Come."

Sophie's eyes darted from face to face. She made no movement to get away from the big man, who held her arm. "Let her go," Jean-Patrice commanded.

"Eh, blanc, you don't let us play any games!" Achilles said with a harsh laugh. "This is not your business."

"Sophie is my business."

"Everything is yours, eh? The monkey is yours, the idiot is yours, the girls are yours. Your village, eh?"

"Yes. It is my village."

"What if we like to take it?" The men moved closer together, their eyes focusing on Jean-Patrice. He had the sense of a pack preparing to attack. Achilles fixed his bold eyes and taunting smirk on Jean-Patrice. "Do you want us to scratch each other again?"

"Let her go," he repeated. He laid his hand unequivocally on the butt of his revolver. He was aware that he had come to some kind of crossroads in his dealings with these men, and perhaps also in his life. He either had to demonstrate that he was willing to act, or stand by and watch them take Sophie away — and do what they wanted with her and with Bassongo. In his mind he saw himself pulling the revolver out of the holster and firing at the men before they could bring up their muskets or spears. He could kill at least some of them before they closed in on him. And then? He no longer cared. His anger and fear had formed a potent cocktail which surged through his veins. Something of this must have shown in his face, because the big man seemed to yield, moving back and releasing Sophie's arm. "You are angry, blanc?"

"Yes," he said tersely. "Come, Sophie."

Hesitantly, the girl detached herself from the men and walked towards him. As she passed the last man, he suddenly grabbed her wrist. Jean-Patrice was about to draw his revolver when the man looped a string of beads around Sophie's slender neck. There was a belly laugh from the others. He put his arm around Sophie and drew her to his side. She was trembling. He yanked the string of beads hard. It snapped off her neck and the beads scattered.

"À bientôt, blanc," Achilles said. "We will see each other again." They moved off, talking amongst themselves. Savages as they were, they had perfect physiques, proportioned like Greek sculptures of athletes.

"Are you hurt, Sophie?" he asked.

"No," she said.

"Were you afraid of those men?"

"A little."

"Don't let them take you out of sight of the village. Do you understand me?"

"Yes. I understand."

He wondered whether she did, whether she understood

the danger of drifting into a life of degradation and ending up floating in the river one night. "Go to your father."

Catherine was waiting for him in the darkness. "I'm afraid of those men," she said. "I'm afraid for you. They are interested in you."

"Why do you say that?"

"Because you are different." She took his hand, lacing her fingers through his. "You are not like Joliet or the others. They don't know whether you are weak or strong."

"I don't know that either," he confessed. "But I like holding your hand."

She laughed quietly. "I like it, too."

He and Catherine ate a simple meal together in the Residency. It was Sophie who served them. Raymond remained in the kitchen. He no longer made comments about Catherine's presence in the Residency, but his sulks and heavy eyes showed what he felt. Sophie moved silently, her eyes downcast, showing no emotion.

"That girl hates me," Catherine said, when Sophie had left.

"I don't think she has any emotion at all, Catherine."

"You don't see it, but it is there. Her father hates me, too. He's less important than he was. The village is laughing at him. He thinks I've taken his daughter's place."

"That isn't true."

"He believes it." She looked at the food on her plate in a doubtful manner. "He would poison me if he could."

"Nobody will dare touch you, Catherine."

"Not while you're with me. But you don't know what these people are like."

"There has been no impropriety between us."

"Is that what you think?" she asked. In the lamp light, her eyes were soft, her mouth bittersweet. The pink dress cast rich luminosities into her dark skin. "To you, your behavior is normal. But other District Commissioners are very different from you. A Commissioner doesn't eat at the same table with a black woman, even though he may use her body in the darkness. He doesn't talk to her as though she were a human being, an equal, someone he respects. A Commissioner does not take off his clothes in front of the whole village. He doesn't put a sick African woman in his bed and take care of her. No white man treats any black person with tenderness anywhere in Gabon."

"Tenderness?" he repeated, his voice altered. "There is only one person for whom I feel this tenderness, Catherine."

She leaned across the table and laid her fingertips on his mouth to silence him. "Don't say anything more, Jean-Patrice. Just listen to me. I am saying something important to you. You are kind and true, but very few people will understand your motives, black or white. Many will take your kindness for folly or weakness. Like those Fang men yesterday and today. They will laugh at you. And worse, you will put yourself in danger. A man who loves a woman too much is seen as weak."

He took her hand in his and kissed her knuckles gently. "I'm not afraid of what they may say or do."

"I am afraid," she replied simply. "I'm not brave, like you."

"But we can be friends."

"We can be friends," she said with a smile. "But when you show by your eyes that you want to kiss me, when you breathe in my scent each time I am close to you—"

"Oh, Catherine."

"Then you show that you want more than friendship. White men do not look at black women that way. A white man takes a black woman in the night, and during the day treats her as though she were a servant."

"You talk about these ugly things as though they were immutable laws."

"They are laws because this is the way whites are in Gabon." She withdrew her fingers from his. "You can't be different."

"I am different."

"You chose the wrong woman in Paris. Don't choose the wrong woman here."

"Are you the wrong woman?"

"Yes."

Jean-Patrice sat back in his chair, shaking his head in disbelief. "Whatever you say, I don't think you are indifferent to me."

"What does that matter?" she said with sudden passion. "My feelings for you, or yours for me, cannot be indulged, Monsieur."

"Am I Monsieur now? Just now you called me Jean-Patrice."

"Now you are Monsieur again."

"Why do you say you are the wrong woman?"

"Because you make me wrong. You treat me in a way that is wrong. In two years you'll leave Bassongo. Or be dead. I don't want to be another Sophie."

"I don't want that, either."

"Then you should not look at me as you are looking at me now."

He saw that her hands were trembling slightly. "I will never see you as another Sophie. I don't know how you can imagine such a thing. You must know that my feelings are deeper than that."

"I have never been to France," she said, turning her face away from him, so that he could see only the glow of the lamp light on the smooth swell of her cheek. "But I think the men and women there are very much as they are here, good and bad. Unfortunately for Gabon, only the bad ones are sent here. Africa is where they send those too cruel or too weak to be tolerated in France. They made a mistake with you, I think. They should not have sent you here. You do not belong with the other colonials." She rose. "But we can never belong to each other, either. They will not let it happen."

He sat at the table long after she had left, thinking. Was it impossible for a white man and a black woman to make a decent life together? In the colonial service, the relationship was by its nature a temporary arrangement for the man, to be discarded without a backward glance when no longer needed. One could not stay in the service unless one obeyed that rule. What decent woman would willingly enter into such a bargain? That was why girls like Sophie existed, to serve a need that was imposed on both sides. That was what Raymond had meant by saying it was better to speak of these things with a little knowledge.

And if he took Catherine back to France? That situation was so rare that there were scarcely any precedents to go by – a diplomat one heard of, who had married an Indo-Chinese, an engineer who had married a Malian, said to be a princess, and beautiful, things to be wondered at. It was hard to imagine how she would survive, away from Africa and her world, how she would bear being stared at and whispered about like some creature in a zoo. If he was falling in love with this woman, what future did they have together? He felt that he was entering another narrow street with no outlet, another relationship that had no possible happy ending.

He was awakened very early the next morning, even before the dawn, by Raymond shaking his shoulder.

"Patron! Patron! Sophie is gone."

He sat up in confusion. "What do you mean?"

Raymond began to cry, tears spilling down his frog-like face. "They have taken Sophie."

Hyppolite was behind him. "And Ndoumou, the madman," he added. "He is gone, too."

Jean-Patrice felt his stomach knotting. "Who has taken them?"

"The Fang took them an hour ago. They took them into the bush. They are gone."

"Get rifles from the strong room, Raymond." He rose and began dressing. Raymond shook his head.

"It is no use, patron. Nobody can find the Fang in the bush. And there are many of them."

"Don't be a poltroon. Saddle the horse." He went to the strong room and broke out rifles and ammunition for the three policemen. He also got his revolver, pushing fistfuls of bullets into his pockets. When he emerged, Raymond had saddled the mare. He gave the policemen the rifles, which they took very reluctantly. "Which way did they go?" he demanded, mounting up.

"I will show you," said Hyppolite with an unexpected show of resolution. Shouldering his rifle, he ran on ahead. Jean-Patrice followed at a trot, the mare grunting and coughing indignantly at the precipitate pace.

He plunged into the bush. There was a track, at first, but it gave out quickly and they found themselves in a tangled country of tall grass and scrub. Hyppolite ran at a crouch, following the trail, occasionally stopping to examine the grass and the trees. Jean-Patrice felt his heart thudding with anger: at the Beti, for their timidity, at the Fang for their arrogance, at himself for being taken unawares. And the gunboat was not due back for weeks. They had chosen their moment well.

"Patron!" Hyppolite had stopped, dangling his rifle by the strap, staring down into the grass. Jean-Patrice rode over to where he stood. Ndoumou lay face down at the foot of a tree, his arms outflung as though he were flying. Hyppolite turned him over carefully. His head had been crushed by a heavy blow. His poor, addled brains had been knocked out. His blood had soaked into the grass. "He is dead," Hyppolite said, looking up at Jean-Patrice.

Jean-Patrice dismounted and knelt beside the dead man. Grief choked him. He saw the little blunt knife lying near one of the outstretched hands. He recalled the taste of the papaya Ndoumou had shared with him on the riverbank. Ndoumou had tried to fight them and they had swatted him like a fly.

Hyacinth had been walking around. Now he returned.

"They have gone in different directions," he said. "These to the North and these to the East. If we follow, they will surround us and trap us."

As he said the words, the sound of a shot rolled to them from the rising sun. The men muttered amongst themselves in dismay. "They are warning us, patron," Hyacinth said. "Their guns are old but they shoot well."

"We should go back now," Hyppolite agreed.

Jean-Patrice drew his revolver and fired a shot at the wobbling red ball of the rising sun, aware that it was a stupid act. The report was not answered, but drifted into silence. His rage ebbed away slowly, leaving an ache of sorrow. There were so few people that he cared about in the world and now there was one less. They cut saplings to make a litter for Ndoumou. Then they turned back to Bassongo, carrying his body.

Catherine was waiting for him with her arms tightly crossed over her breasts. "I heard the shots," she said. He could see she was holding back tears with difficulty.

"I'm all right," he said shortly, "But Ndoumou is dead." He dismounted and began to unfasten the saddle

"I'm so sorry." She stood huddled, looking tired. "Why did they kill him?"

"I don't think they meant to. I think the poor devil struggled and they hit him too hard."

"And Sophie?"

"No trace."

Raymond uttered a wail of bereavement. "My Sophie! She is gone! They have taken my Sophie!"

"I am sorry, Raymond," Jean-Patrice said heavily.

"Sorry? What is your sorry to me?" Raymond turned a furious and tear-streaked face on Jean-Patrice. "It is your fault, patron!"

"How is it my fault?"

Raymond clutched at his head and pulled his own hair as though to tear it out of his scalp. "You would not take her! She is only good for one thing, but you threw her away! Now the Fang have taken her and I have no daughter!"

"You are always telling me how many other children you have," Jean-Patrice pointed out dryly.

"You laugh at my tears!"

"I am not laughing at your tears, but—"

"You must recompense!"

He was taken aback. "I?"

"You did not protect her. It was your duty. Now she is gone. You must recompense me for the daughter I have lost!"

"I will get her back."

"No. You will never get her back. She is lost forever." Raymond seemed beside himself. "Forever! You must recompense!"

Jean-Patrice felt a heavy weight settle on his heart. "This is not the time to talk of such things. Please stop this performance. I have to bury Ndoumou now."

The burial of Ndoumou was a melancholy affair. There appeared to be nobody in Bassongo willing to claim kinship with him. His thin body was wrapped in his own rags and laid in a trough at the far end of the graveyard, dug by the three policemen. He thought that he and Catherine were the only other mourners. But once again, he saw the figures in frightening masks, wearing shaggy raffia capes, moving among the trees. He asked Hyppolite who they were.

"They come to greet the ghost of the dead man," Hyppolite said, glancing around uneasily.

"But they look so menacing."

"If he is not driven away, he will stay in the village, among the people and places he remembers. That is bad, patron. He has to be chased down to the underworld, where he belongs."

"What will happen if he stays?"

"Bad luck." Hyppolite shrugged. "People will get sick, babies will be born dead. The fruit will rot on the trees before it gets ripe."

"Don't be angry with me," Catherine said in a quiet voice as they walked away from the grave. "Since we talked, you hardly look at me, Jean-Patrice. I did not mean to insult you."

"I am not angry."

"A man is always angry when he wants a woman and she says no."

"I am not angry," he repeated, "only sad."

"What are you going to do now?"

"I could ride to Medoneu. There are soldiers there. They could call the gunboat. People would be killed. It would be futile." He stood, thinking. "I want to talk to the witchdoctor."

"Why?"

"Isn't she the one who controls everything in Bassongo? Didn't she decide what Sophie was useful for? I want her to send a message to the Fang. Can you take me to her?"

"You don't understand," Catherine said. "She's dangerous."

"How can she harm anyone?"

"In a thousand ways."

"By turning herself into a viper or a monkey? Do you believe in that mumbo-jumbo?"

"No."

"Then can you ask her to come to me?"

She shook her head. "The oganga wipoga comes to nobody."

"Then I will go to her."

"If she doesn't want to be found, then you will never reach her. And she doesn't deal with whites."

"If you came with me, she would deal with me."

"I can take you, if that's really what you want."

"When can we go?"

"Come to my house tomorrow, at sunset."

He nodded somberly. They parted.

18

He came for Catherine the next day at sunset, when the sky was becoming bloody. She was in her kitchen and was preparing a meal.

"We should go," he said impatiently.

"We have to wait for the moon to rise," she replied. "And I want you to eat this before we go."

"Why?"

"It's better." He sat with a sigh and watched her prepare the food. Her hands were sure, her slim arms strong to lift pots and carry water. The glow from the charcoal illuminated her face from time to time, showing the curves of her cheeks and the line of her throat.

"I've never watched anyone make food for me before." He said the words without meaning to.

"And that woman you loved in France? Did she never make food for you?"

He shook his head at the idea. "She reigned in her salon, not in the kitchen. All sorts of important men came to eat at her house, but she didn't prepare the dishes."

"Were you important?"

"No, Catherine. I was very young. I was a nobody who worked for her husband. I don't know how she even came to notice me."

"Don't you? Important men are old and fat, have

white hair and wrinkled faces. You are not like that."

"What am I like?"

She stirred the pot. "Women look at you. When the village women saw you walk naked into the river, they said—"

"What did they say?"

"They said it was a pity that you were white."

He rubbed his face. "That is a great compliment, I suppose. I don't know how to shed my skin."

"You do not need to. They say other things about you."

"What?"

"They say that your hands are those of a man, but your touch is that of a woman. I felt the same thing when I was sick, and you cared for me."

"I was very afraid for you."

"I'm strong." She lit a palm oil lamp, which gave a soft, golden light. The rich smell of the food filled the house. She served the soup in bowls and sat opposite him, her knees almost touching his. The ghostly white prints of her hands on the walls seemed to glow as the darkness settled. The intimacy of the moment excluded all the other things in his life, the failures and the errors. Here, in Catherine's house, it did not matter what he had been. It mattered only that he was with her.

After they had eaten, she gave him a little bundle. "Hold her."

He unwrapped the little figure. It was a primitive thing, the wood worn smooth by countless hands, one of the legs broken off. The figure was female, naked, the breasts flat against the torso, the eyes closed, the hands cupping the umbilicus. "It's an ancestor?"

"From long, long ago. See, how she shows her navel? That is to tell the living that all of us are descended from her."

"It's a sacred thing."

"To me, yes." She took the thing reverently from him

and stared at it. "You see her breasts?"

"Yes."

"A woman's breasts tell the story of her life," she said. "They say how old you are, how many children you have had, whether you are still fertile. Whites admire breasts that are still high. But we Africans think breasts are beautiful that are flat and hang to a woman's navel, like these, showing she has given life to many children and will be remembered for generations to come."

He remembered the sway of Catherine's naked breasts. "I understand."

She took a little palm oil from the container and rubbed the small figure till it gleamed, whispering to it. Then she wrapped it again.

"What did you say to her?"

"I asked for her protection. She'll watch over us tonight and keep away evil ghosts. She's very powerful."

"I believe you."

"And—" She hesitated.

"And what?"

"I put something in your food. Something to protect you."

He smiled. "Thank you."

She combed her hair quickly, teasing out the soft, silky curls. He watched her with pleasure, admiring the tilt of her head and the turn of her neck. When she had finished, he took the comb from her and examined it. It was carved of a single piece of ebony, the handle a naked female figure, the tines delicate. "It was my mother's," she said. "We can go, now."

A yellow moon had risen over the tops of the trees. She guided him across a moonlit glade and into the forest. Here the moon shone fitfully through the branches as they passed under them. It was a hot, still night.

"How far is it?" he asked.

"Don't talk," she whispered. After that he was silent, trusting in her eyes to see roads through the forest which his could not. The only sound was the rustling of their feet through the ferns. At last she turned to him, her breath touching his cheek. "We are close now. Wait here. If she wants to see us, she will come."

They stood without moving. Catherine's body relaxed against his, molding itself to his shape. He took the friction flashlight out of his pocket and wound the little handle. Its light was too dim to even reach the great trees all around them. He put it away and held her close, closing his eyes, listening. Something was shuffling towards them out of the darkness.

"She's here," Catherine said quietly. "We must sit." She pulled on his arm. Jean-Patrice sat on the earth, as she indicated. The place was so dark that he could not see where he was, or what lay around him. A gleam of light showed between the tree trunks, growing brighter. He felt the hair on the back of his neck grow erect. Two figures emerged from the blackness. One was that of an old woman who laid her hand for support on the shoulder of a thin, naked man who held up a burning torch to light their way. They moved very laboriously. The old woman dragged one leg as though it were all but paralyzed. The naked man moved with a convulsive gait, like someone with a nervous disease. He'd expected that the witchdoctor would be dressed in some outlandish get-up, but she wore a plain, drab dress like all the other Beti women of her age. Round her neck were several strings of beads. Her hair was completely white. Despite her assistant's torch, she seemed to be groping her way forward. Jean-Patrice saw with a stab of pity that both of her eyes were milky with cataracts. She must be all but blind. He felt Catherine trembling beside him.

The oganga stopped a few paces from them and leaned heavily on the naked man, whose head hung down. She did not direct her pale eyes at them, but appeared to be looking into the air over their heads. She spoke in a harsh voice with a strong native accent. "They took what you did not want. Why do you ask for it back now?"

"She's just a child," he replied.

The old woman laughed shortly. "A child? I killed her three babies with my own hands. At least the Fang will let her keep her children."

"And Ndoumou?"

"What does an idiot matter?"

"He mattered to me. They must bring Sophie back."

"It was the whites who started this quarrel, not the Fang."

"I didn't come here on behalf of the whites or the blacks. I came on behalf of Sophie."

She turned her face towards him at last. "Why? None of the men of her village will marry her. Now she will have a husband."

"They killed an innocent man. They insulted Sophie's father. And they flouted my authority. I can't overlook all these things. If I call the soldiers, there will be more blood. I don't want that. If one of those men wants to marry Sophie, he must bring her back to Bassongo and we must all hear her say that she is willing to have him. Then they must ask permission from her father. They must pay the bride price that Raymond asks. And they must pay a fine for killing Ndoumou. I can understand they did not mean to kill him, but he is dead all the same."

"What fine are you asking?"

"They must return the price of the ivory which I bought."

"A lot of money. And if they refuse?"

"I will come to take back the girl and the silver myself."

"Silver, girls and ivory." The old woman swayed from side to side slowly, considering. The smell of something rotten drifted to them. "You talk like a man," she said at last. "Can you fight like one?"

"It would be better for them to do as I say."

She smiled in mockery. "Raymond is a dog. Why should they respect him?"

"They should respect Sophie. She's unprotected among the Fang, with nobody to stand behind her. They must bring her home and start again."

"And this one, who sits by your side?" the oganga asked, turning her face to Catherine. "What is she to you?"

"She is my friend."

"Only that?" The old woman sniffed. "I smell more than friendship. And she holds your hand like a lover." It was true. Catherine's fingers had knotted in his and were gripping tight. "She went from her own people to the white priest and then she ran from him to the bush. Beware that she does not betray you."

"I don't think she will betray me."

"You are innocent, Culblanc." The old woman chuckled quietly. "Your brothers call this land the white man's grave."

"I have no brothers. Or sisters. No mother and no father. There is only me."

"Africa is not for fools or cowards."

"I hope I am neither."

"I hope so, too."

"Will you send my message?" Jean-Patrice asked.

"I will send it," she said.

He reached into his pocket, touching the silver he had brought. "What must I pay you?"

"You will pay," she said, "in time." The old woman struck her assistant on his thin shoulder. They began to turn ponderously. For a moment the red light of the torch gleamed on the man's face; Jean-Patrice saw the wasted features and shaggy, mud-clotted hair of Ndoumou, a gaping hole in his brow. Catherine stuffed a scream back into her mouth with her hand. Then the pair became fire-rimmed silhouettes that shuffled back into the darkness. He watched the flickering light disappear among the trees, his heart galloping. The smell of rotting flesh was overpowering for a moment.

"She has Ndoumou," Catherine whispered, her voice

shaking.

"It was some trick," he retorted. "The old hag is full of them."

Catherine laid her hand swiftly over his mouth. "Hush! She hears everything."

"Let her hear."

"Please, Jean-Patrice!"

"Let's get out of this accursed place." He rose, pulling her to her feet.

On the walk home, he held Catherine tight against him. She was still shivering. He longed to run his hands over her body, claiming her as his own, and tell her it was just trickery, the malicious conjuring of a crone who heard all the village gossip and knew how to create illusions. But he, too, was afraid of the old woman and her white eyes and the thing that had held her torch.

The moon was high, a tiny brilliant disk overhead, by the time they reached her house. The street where she lived was silent and dark. At her door she turned, putting her palm of her hand on his chest to stop him. "You cannot come in."

"Don't you want me to?"

"That is neither here nor there. The world is full of wickedness. We should not add more."

"Would it be wickedness for me come into your house?"

"At night, in the dark, like a thief – yes."

"Catherine ... " He tilted her face to the moonlight and looked into her eyes. "I am falling in love with you."

He saw the sad mockery cross her face. "Still only falling?"

"Then you feel the same thing I do!"

"I don't think you feel what I feel, or that I feel what you feel."

He took her hand. She tried to pull away, but he bent and kissed the palm, then closed her fingers around the kiss. "Please don't think that I don't respect you, just

194

because I desire you. The opposite is true. You were very brave tonight. Thank you."

She nodded. She was still shivering. She seemed subdued and empty now. "I hope you get what you want. Goodnight."

He stood in the dark street for a long while after she closed the door, then got back into the saddle.

He found Raymond at the Residency. "I went to speak to the oganga wipoga tonight."

Raymond's frog eyes bulged. He froze with a tray in his hands. "What for, patron?"

"I asked her to send a message to the men who stole Sophie and killed Ndoumou. They must bring your daughter back here and pay a fine."

"A fine?"

"The full amount I paid for the ivory." Raymond stared at him, as though deprived of the power of speech. "I will get Sophie back for you, Raymond. If one of those men wants to marry her, he must say so before all the village, and pay bride price. Do you understand?"

Raymond nodded slowly, recovering his voice. "Yes, patron. I understand."

"Perhaps I have acted unjustly in this matter. If so, I want to set things straight now."

"Yes, patron," Raymond said again. His face was closed now.

The kidnapping of Sophie had cast a shadow over everything. Catherine continued to vaccinate new arrivals all week. Each day there were some two or three hundred waiting outside the Residency. A small colony also began to occupy the veranda, consisting of those who had experienced illness after the inoculation. They slept in rows, wrapped in blankets. Jean-Patrice attended to these himself each day, administering the treatment that each case seemed to require. Most recovered quickly and went away again. One, an old woman, died; but that he attributed to natural causes. The vast majority of the inoculated survived and thrived. By the end of a fortnight, three thousand people had been inoculated. Only a few dozen were arriving each day, now. Catherine had lost weight and was looking tired and drawn. The prophylactic calf, No. 5, primogenetrix of all these vaccinations, continued to chew the cud placidly in her stall. She was still providing adequate quantities of pus, but there was something different about her. It was as though she had attained a kind of dignity, a maturity, through what she had done for Bassongo.

As Jean-Patrice and Catherine drew pus from her one morning, Raymond came to summon him. A white man on a horse had arrived, preceded by two African soldiers in blue uniforms with red fezes, carrying rifles, and three porters with loads on their heads. The European dismounted. He was a short, fat little man, tightly strapped into boots, jodhpurs and a khaki tunic, with a large leather holster at his hip. He wore a pith helmet. A bushy grey beard framed a broad-nosed and somewhat bear-like face. He clicked his heels, his spurs jingling.

"Schultze, at your service. How do you do!"

Jean-Patrice shook the man's hand in a dazed way. "Schultze?"

"Don't tell me," the other replied in his strong German accent, "that you have forgotten our appointment? No goose in the oven? No plum pudding? No schnapps?"

"I'm sorry, but I don't—"

"That scoundrel Joliet! Did he forget to tell you?"

Understanding dawned. "You are the doctor, are you not? I'm afraid your patient died almost the moment I arrived here."

"Ach, so." Unexpectedly, the doctor burst into hearty laughter. "This explains everything. It must have slipped his mind. He had a pressing engagement elsewhere. He is to be forgiven, not so? Ha! Ha! Ha!"

Jean-Patrice smiled weakly. "I'm Duméril. Delighted to meet you."

"The delight is on my part, I assure you. Poor Joliet. Septicaemia, not so?"

"Yes. He was little more than skin and bone."

"Less, my dear Duméril, less — since I myself removed some dozens of those bones pre mortem." He counted on his fat fingers. "Patella, tibia, fibula, the tarsals and metatarsals and all the other constituents of the foot. Ha! Ha! Ha! My dear fellow, your face is a picture. Your poor predecessor and I made quite a cult of spending each Christmas together. He was to arrange the same tradition with you."

"Is it Christmas already?"

"Tomorrow, my dear fellow, tomorrow!"

"Well, of course, I will try to put together a suitable meal. I'm very sorry, but I've made no preparations for your arrival. I hardly knew the date, to tell you the truth."

Schultze inspected his face with a keen grey eye. "Bad, very bad. The date is of great importance. But I anticipated some such difficulty. Africa inculcates foresight, does she not?" He waved at his baggage. "I have brought wine, schnapps, marzipan cake, butter, almonds, ginger, dates, spices and I know not what all else. It remains only for us to select a convenient sacrifice from the village menagerie and our Christmas may proceed uninterrupted." He slapped his stomach. "I am, alas, a gourmet in exile. But let my fellows take my things up to my room and we will plan the menu." The house filled with the tramp of boots as the baggage proceeded upstairs. "Joliet, incidentally, is by no means restricted to Bassongo," said Schultze, peering down from the landing at Jean-Patrice. "The leg which I amputated — I took it back with me in alcohol to examine the effect of the venom under the microscope. The bite of the viper is a particular pursuit of mine. I still have it in my laboratory. One might say poor Joliet has a foot on both sides of the border, not so? Ha! Ha! Ha!!" The news of his patient's death appeared to have amused him immensely. "The man becomes the apotheosis of the European colonizer, straddling the continent! What is it that Shakespeare says? 'Why man, he doth bestride the narrow world like a colossus!'"

Jean-Patrice went to arrange stabling for the German's horse and accommodation for his entourage. The arrival of another European had disconcerted him. It seemed incredible that Christmas had come without his noticing the date. There were so few Christians in Bassongo, he supposed, that the day passed unmarked. He had not seen a white face in weeks. He had forgotten how intrusive and annoying white faces could be. He delivered the German's foodstuffs to the kitchen and ordered as sumptuous a meal as could be prepared for the evening.

Schultze had encountered Chloë and was very excited. "How much do you want for this animal?" he demanded.

"She is a pet. She's not for sale."

"I will pay you a good price. Better, perhaps, than you imagine."

"You are fond of gorillas?"

"I do not believe that a full dissection of a healthy individual has yet been performed, Duméril. Most specimens which reach museums are in a very decayed state. Mere skins. Think of it! So many questions that remain to be answered! What is the weight of the brain in relation to the human organ? The heart? The major glandular structures? How does the digestive system differ from our own? The muscular system? The fields of human and animal anatomy would be galvanized. I have all the equipment in my laboratory. A correctly performed and well reported dissection would catapult the author into the forefront of scientific achievement!"

"I'm sorry, Schultze," he said stiffly. "It's out of the question. The animal is a pet."

"Put aside sentiment for one moment, my boy," Schultze urged. "Think of the celebrity! Your name would also become famous!"

Jean-Patrice was adamant. At his guest's request, however, he accompanied Schultze on a tramp along the river, the doctor carrying a shotgun over the crook of one arm and wearing a fearsome bandolier of cartridges. "As a matter of fact," he said, "Joliet has left me rather a difficult legacy." He recounted the tale of Sophie and the Fang hunters.

Schultze snapped the shotgun closed and sighted at a nearby tree. "You were well rid of the girl," he said, his mouth distorted against the stock of the gun. "Why did you interfere?"

"I felt responsible for her—" The blast of the shotgun cut him off, making him start. A very small bird fell out of the tree. Schultze walked over and pocketed the trophy. "—for her welfare," Jean-Patrice continued. "It was Joliet's dying wish that I take care of her, after all."

"Those fellows will soon knock the sauce out of her. It doesn't do to cross the Fang, you know."

"I cannot permit my people to be kidnapped and murdered under my nose, Schultze."

Schultze pressed a fresh shell into the breech of the shotgun. "You are new to Africa. Take my advice, Duméril. Deal with the men. They in turn will deal with the women, the children and the madmen. You need not concern yourself about those." He threw the gun to his shoulder and sighted at another tree.

"I cannot agree. I—" Again, the discharge of the shotgun cut him off. He shook his head angrily, having lost the train of his thought. Schultze methodically pocketed another small corpse.

"A few more of these and we will have the makings of an hors d'oeuvre. There were also certain edible fungi which Joliet was able to obtain. The taste was remarkably like the European boletus edulis. Quite delicious. Have you come across these?"

"No," Jean-Patrice said shortly.

"Ah, well. You were about to say—?"

"I have sent my message through the oganga. They may choose to ignore it, but they had better do as I ask."

"They are unruly fellows, those Fang. I whip a dozen of them every week. It seems to have some effect. I think they enjoy it. But I do not cross them. If you want them to bring you more ivory, you had better let them steal a girl or two. Do you know what ivory is currently fetching in Berlin?"

"That is beside the point."

"Young man, I most earnestly advise you not to go beating among the mahogany forests, looking for this thrice cursed paramour of Joliet's. You will end up providing the entrée for some cannibal banquet."

"I believe they did it as a protest against the use of forced labor on the building of the road from Medoneu. Those men are chained like animals. It is a horrible thing."

"Do not waste any sympathy on those brutes," Schultze said briskly. "And you should not have issued an ultimatum. It was most unwise. Your force seems under strength. Lucky you have that big corporal. Between you and he, you could hold up the Pillars of Hercules."

"I plan to have a recruiting campaign in the new year."

"The Beti are not natural warriors. Now, those two fellows of mine are small, but tough nuts. Askaris. Picked them up in East Africa and they have been with me ever since."

Jean-Patrice began to answer, but once again, the shotgun cut him off. He decided to give up arguing with Schultze, at least until he had his bag of sparrows. When he had shot a dozen of the little creatures, the doctor appeared satisfied. On the way back to the Residency, however, he came across Catherine, inoculating the afternoon intake. He insisted on examining all of them for diseases. He was particularly interested in swellings, prodding at any limb which looked enlarged.

"A common lipomatoid tumor," he said in disappointment, dismissing a fat old woman with a swollen leg. He waved his monocle. "Elephantiasis, my dear chap, that's the rare one. I can show you photographs that would make your hair stand on end. I had a young fellow who got the disease in the testicles. They were swollen to the point where he had to push them around in a cart as if he were selling watermelons. In point of fact, I purchased one and removed it from its owner. The microscopic examination was fascinating. I am hoping to provide a definitive analysis of the disease for the medical fraternity. I may say without blushes that I know more about the condition than anyone else. I hope to have it named Schultze's Disease."

"Having big balls?" Jean-Patrice said ironically.

"Quite so. Should you see any native with such symptoms, I hope you will find a way to alert me. Or at least, take a photograph. Have you a camera?"

"No," Jean-Patrice confessed. "They are rather expensive toys."

"Hardly toys. In Berlin, I have seen the cinematograph, a camera capable of reproducing movement and life. The galloping of a horse, the dance of a lovely woman. Nature is revealing her secrets to us, Duméril, one by one. We need only open our eyes to see them." He stared at Catherine. "That is a damned handsome woman you have there. She knows what she is doing with the knife, too."

"She is wonderful," Jean-Patrice said warmly.

Schultze stroked his moustaches. "Do I take it from your tone that she shares your bed? If not, you may send her along to mine after supper. Ha! Ha! Ha!!"

He bit back a retort. "Perhaps you would like a rest now, Schultze. You must be fatigued." To Jean-Patrice's relief, the garrulous little German doctor assented to the suggestion and went on his way back to the Residency. Jean-Patrice caressed Catherine's shoulder. "He expects a Christmas supper tomorrow. I think he is more than half mad."

"What was he saying about me?"

"That I should send you to his bed. He has taken a fancy to you."

"Well, I have not taken a fancy to him. He assumes I am your concubine."

"I wish to God you were."

"I hope you don't mean that."

"I mean that I desire you with every breath I take. I wish you desired me half so much."

"You don't know what I desire."

"Do you desire me? Say it!"

"I desire — your welfare."

"You are essential to it," he said with a smile. "To maintain my welfare I require you in large doses." He kissed the velvety skin on the nape of her neck.

"I did not give permission for such intimacies," she said, evading him. But she smiled.

Feeling cheered, Jean-Patrice looked in at the kitchen and handed the little bundle of birds to Raymond's rather sullen-faced wives.

While Schultze snored, Jean-Patrice received a courtesy visit from Chief Obangui and his sons. "My father wishes you a very happy Christmas," the interpreter said. He was one of the young man whom Jean-Patrice had inoculated. "He says he hopes there will not be trouble in the area."

"Why should there be trouble?" Jean-Patrice asked warily.

"Over the daughter of Raymond."

"You mean, with the Fang?"

"They are our enemies, patron." He consulted with his father for a time. The old man spoke slowly, moving his hands slowly like ancient tree branches in the wind. "My father says that the girl is not worth making a quarrel with these people."

"If I allow strangers to come into my district and steal or murder whom they choose, where will it end? What sort of authority would I display if I stood by and did nothing while every pretty girl and every idiot was dragged away?"

The man frowned. "My father thinks the Fang will not obey your command. He asks, what will you do, then?"

"I will go to them myself."

"Alone?"

"With my police."

"My father does not want a war between the Fang and the Beti."

"There will be no war with anybody," Jean-Patrice retorted. "It is absurd to speak of a war. I expect those men to comply with my orders. The question of police action will only arise if they defy me. And any such action will be strictly limited."

The chief grew angry at the tone of Jean-Patrice's voice and muttered to his son. The young man leaned back and conferred with his father, never taking his eyes off Jean-Patrice's face. "My father says that if there is police action against the Fang, blood will be spilled. He says that you may one day ask yourself for what, exactly, the blood was spilled."

They gathered their robes, rose and departed.

Schultze's remarks about photography had reminded Jean-Patrice about the *Liber Libidinorum*, and the problem of what to do with it. He brought up the subject somewhat diffidently over supper, asking the German's advice as a medical man.

"An album?" Schultze asked, raising his eyebrows.

"Yes. But the subject matter is somewhat indecent."

"You mean bare breasts and so forth."

"Something more than that. These photographs are unique."

"You intrigue me greatly, my dear fellow," the German said, finishing his glass of wine with a smack of his lips. "I should be delighted to give you my opinion."

Jean-Patrice led Schultze to the study, where he showed his guest – not without misgivings – Joliet's journal. At the first photograph, Schultze's expression became blank for a moment; but he fixed his monocle in his eye and leafed through the subsequent pages intently. "Fascinating, fascinating," he murmured. "The man must have taken and developed all these himself."

"He had a complete photographic studio in the basement."

"There is more such material...?"

"I destroyed the remaining plates myself. There is nothing left but this book."

"A pity! A great pity! Ah, what a mind poor Joliet had, what an intellect!"

It was not exactly the reaction Jean-Patrice had experienced. "That is what strikes you about these images? That they proceed from the intellect?"

"Of course. It is an extraordinary undertaking. You don't see it?"

"See what?"

"This is no casual record of dalliances, Duméril. It is nothing less than an African Kama Sutra."

"I have no idea what that might be."

"The Kama Sutra," Schultze said impressively, his monocle gleaming, "is the ancient Sanskrit treatise on love."

"Oh, indeed."

"The wisdom of the ancient Hindus, distilled into a thousand erotic verses, describing each variation of pleasure, savoring each drop of honey, illustrating each position into which the bodies of man and woman can be molded during the act of love."

"I see."

"There is no question of it. Why, here is The Snake Trap. And this is assuredly The Elephant Posture." Warming to his subject, Schultze turned the album upside down for a moment to examine one of the photographs. "And this, if I am not mistaken, is the difficult and painful Lotus Position. Remarkable, remarkable."

"You seem to have some specialist knowledge

yourself."

"The culture of India happens to be one of my fields of research."

"You are interested in everything, it seems. But I meant personal knowledge."

Schultze smirked. "It is the duty of every man to have such knowledge at his fingertips, so to speak, just as every man should be able to distinguish between a hock and a rhenish, a claret and a burgundy."

"This seems a rather more obscure field of study."

"You think so?" He showed Jean-Patrice a photograph. "Have you never attempted this?"

"Never."

"Or this, the Nutcracker?"

"I am not a contortionist."

"Nor are you a connoisseur of the arts of love, it seems," Schultze said with a superior smile.

"I have had no complaints," Jean-Patrice replied, a little stiffly. "In order to satisfy myself – or the lady in the case – I have never found it necessary to attempt such postures."

"Yet such postures produce the most electrical excitement, the most intense of orgasms on both sides. One achieves a mystical union with the infinite."

"You have performed these acts?" Duméril asked with a touch of skepticism, for the doctor appeared somewhat stout to have accomplished the circumvolutions which were illustrated by Joliet, an unusually lean man.

"In my youth, in my youth. I have been terrible among the maidens, trust me. At my age, you know, the ardor is somewhat dimmed. I am at the time of life when one enjoys the recollection as much, perhaps, as the act." Schultze brushed his mustaches with his forefinger. "And now that we come to that, I am extremely grateful to you for presenting me with this remarkable compendium. The study of it will serve to pass many a weary hour when my day's work is done."

"I hadn't intended to present it to you," Jean-Patrice said cautiously. "I was asking your advice on what to do with it."

"And here you have my answer. As a doctor, as a student of anthropology, as the older man, I am a far fitter curator of the book than you."

"What does my age have to do with it?"

"Well, I rather wonder whether you are old enough to understand such things."

"I have some experience of women!"

"Of course, of course," Schultze said soothingly, "yet I can see that these images are already preying on your mind." Schultze had the book firmly tucked under his arm by now. "You should forget them – or they may fester and cause what we Germans call psychological harm."

"Oh, take the damned thing," Jean-Patrice said irritably. "I'll be glad to be rid of it, after all."

"My interest is moral and medical," Schultze assured him, patting the embossed cover. "I will make a detailed study. In fact, it is not impossible that from such a study I will be inspired to produce a monograph on morbid sexuality."

"Only, for heaven's sake be discreet with it. The women in those photographs are all local, you know."

Schultze chuckled indulgently. "Such an article would be published a long way from Bassongo, I assure you, and in the German language. I am acquainted, you know, with the Baron von Krafft-Ebing."

"I don't know him."

"No? You have not read the *Psychopathia Sexualis*?"

"I'm afraid not. But you agree, then, that this book of Joliet's represents a perversion of the sexual feelings?"

"Indubitably. But a magnificent perversion. One worthy of the closest study. Here we see obsession, exhibitionism, erotomania, even megalomania. Joliet is presented here as a modern satyr. I doubt whether one man in a thousand could have attempted what he has done."

"Well, it seems to have killed him," Jean-Patrice commented.

"That is an excellent point," replied Schultze. "Ha! Ha! Ha! It appears to have killed him, nicht wahr?"

"I wanted to ask you something. Did Joliet ever describe to you any unusual circumstances of his snakebite?"

The other man shrugged. "What circumstances could there be? These reptiles often come into houses and secrete themselves in warm places."

"Such as beds?"

"Exactly."

"Yet it seems odd for a snake to wriggle itself all the way down a man's sheets and then bite him in the leg."

"Nothing odd about it. I have found snakes in my boots."

"So it was altogether natural?"

"I don't understand what you are getting at."

"Joliet never spoke of it being a punishment of some sort?"

"Of course not! He was as rational a man as you or I." He clicked his heels and bowed. "With your permission, I will retire for the night, Duméril. The day has been rewarding but tiring."

"Of course. I hope you sleep well."

As Schultze mounted the stairs with his prize, Jean-Patrice had the feeling that the German had gained possession of the *Liber Libidinorum* by spouting of a lot of nonsense, and that he himself had been rather gullible. There was nothing about Schultze to suggest that he had ever been "a terror among the maidens" at any stage of his life, or that he had esoteric sexual knowledge from the ancient Hindus or anyone else. However, it was a relief to get rid of the thing at last, and when Schultze once departed back to the Cameroon, he would not need to think about it ever again.

He had put Schultze in Hugo Joliet's room, and he was interested to see whether the grim little chuckles and nightly soliloquies would manifest themselves while a living man occupied the room, and an old acquaintance, at that. He lay in his own bed, listening for any metaphysical disturbance from next door. None came. Joliet was silent. The only sounds came from Schultze, who snored loudly most of the night.

19

Jean-Patrice had lain awake for many hours, and not only due to Schultze's snoring, so he was glad to get up early. The cool of the morning was his favorite part of the day. He made his toilet before the sun was up and left the Residency freshly shaved and groomed.

He rode the mare to Catherine's house, admiring the dusky pink of the dawn, the slightly putrid scent of tropical fruit from the orchards of Bassongo. Everything was quiet and still.

Catherine's shutters were closed. He tapped on the door, hoping she was awake. After a while, she opened the door, holding a cloth to her breasts, her face and shoulders still soapy.

"You are the most important thing in my life," he said.

"And you are the most importunate man I know. I haven't even finished washing. Why are you here so early?"

"It's Christmas day. I want you to marry me."

"Today?"

"Any day you choose."

"You'd better come in."

Jean-Patrice went into the house. "Catherine, I love

you."

"I am going to continue with my morning wash, if you don't mind. Turn your back."

He obeyed, listening to the sounds of her splashing. "It's useless for me to pretend otherwise. I don't want a life without you. There is no life without you. You have become everything to me. I lay awake all night. The German snores terribly. But that wasn't what kept me awake. I could think of nothing but you. Of the life I want with you." He paused. He could smell her soap. It filled him with desire. "God knows I haven't been a good man. I've been a fool. I've made a mess of my life. But with you I will be different. You make me decent. Of course you have no confidence in me. Why should you have? You have seen me at my worst. If you can only believe that I can be better than this. Far, far better. I will look after you." He heard the sound of water being poured. He sighed. "I will love you. Not as I loved before. Not selfishly. I will love you—" He had run out of words. He listened. There was silence. "I can't say how I will love you. I don't know how to express it. But it will be pure and tender. As you wish it to be. As I hope you wish it to be. I want to be the man you wish me to be." There was no response. Jean-Patrice groaned. "You say nothing. Are you laughing at me?"

He felt her slim arms encircle his neck. "I am not laughing at you."

"Oh Catherine!"

"Don't turn around. I am still naked."

"Catherine—"

"Be still." He felt the soft warmth of her body press against his back. She laid her cheek on his shoulder. "You're a good man. I worry that you are too good."

"We'll leave this place. I don't want to stay in the Colonial Service, or even in the Civil Service. I want to take you back to Paris with me."

"And what will we do there?"

"I don't know. I'll open a tobacconist's shop."

"A tobacconist's!"

"Why not? I'm young. With you at my side I can make a success of anything."

"Even a tobacconist's?"

"Anything."

"And are there many Gabonese tobacconist's wives in Paris?"

"That does not matter. You will be a queen."

"A queen in exile. And you will be in exile, too. Nobody will talk to you, or buy your cheroots."

"France isn't like Gabon, my darling. Nobody cares about such things as the color of one's skin."

"Really?"

"In any case, I don't care what people think, and I hope you don't care either."

"But I care about you, my dear, and how happy you will be the morning after our marriage, and in a year's time, and in ten years' time."

"Then you agree that there will be a marriage?"

"I will think about it."

He felt his heart leap. "Catherine!"

"You may not turn around."

But he turned and took her in his arms and kissed her. Her lips were pillowy, billowy, cushiony, moist. He was trembling with joy. "Catherine, thank you, thank you. I love you."

"My tobacconist. My darling tobacconist."

He drew back to look at his prize. "You are so beautiful! Are you really mine?"

"I have only said that I will think about it." She kissed him again, making his head swim. Then she covered her magnificent breasts. "And now you must go. You cannot stay in the house while I am naked."

"But Catherine—"

She would brook no argument. He was compelled to leave her, averting his greedy eyes from her nakedness, and ride back home, his heart singing within him.

Raymond's wives had labored all afternoon to produce a roasted kid, together with various concoctions which Schultze himself had ordained and supervised. Jean-Patrice dressed himself for dinner with a jacket and tie, something he had not done since arriving in Bassongo. He had never felt happier.

Schultze was waiting in the dining room with a bottle of schnapps. He was wearing a white suit that his men had evidently recently pressed. He filled the glasses with great ceremony. "My dear Duméril, your country is a republic, so I hope you will not be offended if I propose that the first toast of the evening should be our German Kaiser."

Jean-Patrice shrugged. "It does not offend me in the slightest."

"To the Kaiser! God bless him!"

"To the Kaiser." Jean-Patrice raised his glass and drank the schnapps, which was pleasantly fiery.

Schultze smacked his lips and sighed with pleasure. "We Germans say wine is for children, champagne for men, but schnapps is for Generals." His grey eyes glinted. "Have you considered that, one of these days, we may find ourselves on opposite sides of a battlefield?"

"Who can say?" Jean-Patrice replied indifferently. He could hear the popping of fireworks outside, together with the cries of gleeful children. There were some Christians, at least, left in Bassongo. "The prospect of a modern war is hideous."

"All wars are hideous. Do you think the battles of the ancient Greeks were any less bloody than the war that is to come?"

"It is science which makes each war worse than the last."

Schultze grunted. "I think it is human nature which does that."

Jean-Patrice held out his glass to be refilled. "Then that should be our next toast. To human nature!"

"Shall we begin?" Schultze suggested when the toast had been drunk.

"We are waiting for Catherine."

"Your assistant?" Schultze fixed his monocle in his eye to examine Jean-Patrice. "She is dining with us?"

"Yes."

"Surely not!"

"She is late. But of course, that is the prerogative of a lady."

"You eat with her?"

"Yes."

"That is very strange. I never heard of such a thing. She eats with her fingers, does she not?"

"Her table manners are far better than mine, I assure. Better even than Chloë's, and she is very delicate."

"That is most droll," Schultze said coldly. "To sleep with a negress, yes. To eat with her? Never."

"I am the other way around. I eat with her but I do not sleep with her."

Schultze laughed shortly. "You French always do things the wrong way round."

"I certainly do. But for once I am certain that I have things the right way round."

"You did not ask my permission to bring this damsel to our Christmas table, Duméril."

"I do not need your permission," Jean-Patrice replied.

"Courtesy demands it. What if I do not choose to share my meal with a negress from the forest?"

"Then you may have a tray in your room."

"You're joking."

"Not at all."

"You jeopardize my esteem? For the sake of your concubine?"

"She is not my concubine."

"Then what is she?"

"She is my future wife."

Schultze stared hard, then allowed the monocle to drop

from his eye. "Your future will be an interesting one, my dear fellow."

Jean-Patrice was too happy to let Schultze's icy displeasure dampen his spirits. "Here she is, now." Catherine entered the dining room, looking, as he always thought, like a queen. He kissed her hand. Schultze contented himself with a click and a very stiff bow. "Shall we dine?" Jean-Patrice said. For a moment he thought Schultze was going to refuse. Then, with a shrug, the German walked to the table. Relieved – for he did not want to quarrel with the only doctor within a hundred miles – Jean-Patrice rang the little silver bell.

Raymond entered from the kitchen with a covered dish which he uncovered with a flourish, revealing the little birds Schultze had shot the previous afternoon, somewhat blackened, arranged in a circle. At the same moment, the glass in the window cracked. Jean-Patrice turned to inspect it with some irritation but could see no reason why the glass should have broken. He turned back to Raymond to demand an explanation and then noticed that something strange had happened to Schultze's face. The grey, spade-shaped beard had vanished, along with the chin which had supported it. In fact, Schultze's face now consisted only of two staring eyes and a bear-like nose. As he considered this, he saw a copious crimson stain spread down the German's immaculate shirtfront.

"Good God, Schultze," he exclaimed, repelled by this trick. Schultze sagged back in his chair. His tongue, appearing monstrously large, drooped plaintively out of what remained of his lower face.

Catherine gasped in horror. Jean-Patrice now saw that Raymond was cowering in a corner, the dish of little baked birds scattered on the dirty mat. The man's frog eyes were starting out of his head in terror. He also recalled now that there were no fireworks in the jungle. The popping he had heard had some other origin. The only explanation for these events was that someone had fired a weapon into the room and that the bullet had carried away Schultze's jaw.

"Catherine, get under the table and stay there," he said. She obeyed at once, without question. He stood for a moment, stupidly trying to remember where he had left his revolver. Then it came to him. It was in the pocket of his bush jacket, upstairs in his bedroom. He put out the lamp on Catherine's desk. He passed back through the dining room and put out the two lamps there as well. Before the darkness rushed in, he saw that Schultze was groping around the floor, perhaps looking for his teeth.

Jean-Patrice felt reality begin to vibrate in him, like the engine of a ship starting up on a placid sea. As he ran up the stairs, however, it was difficult to distinguish the relevant from the irrelevant in his mind. Relief that he no longer had to endure a Christmas dinner with Schultze confused itself with concern that the man's terrible injury might well kill him and puzzlement at who had shot him and for what reason. Puzzlement turned to anger. What sort of person would shoot at his dinner guest on Christmas? He found his revolver and filled his pockets with loose bullets. He also took the little friction flashlight from his bedside. He went back downstairs. He was now very angry indeed. He was in a towering rage, in fact.

Snorting with passion, he walked out of the front door, grimly determined to administer retribution. A bright moon was rising over the trees. He walked around the Residency and encountered, at the dining room window, the figure of a man. He was peering through the broken glass, trying to see inside. Jean-Patrice recognized him by his elaborate headdress and by the long musket he held as one of the Fang hunters. The man turned swiftly to face him, throwing the musket to his shoulder. They fired thunderously at the same moment. The flash of the muzzles was blinding. His ears singing, Jean-Patrice looked down at himself quickly to see whether he had been hit anywhere. He appeared to be intact, but the other man was now writhing and groaning on the ground. Jean-Patrice twirled the handle of the flashlight and shone the faint beam down on the Fang. The man's teeth gleamed in a contorted face. He was clutching at his naked chest. Through his crooked fingers, the spouting blood appeared black. Sobered, Jean-Patrice bent down to examine the wound. The action probably saved his life because a volley of shots erupted from the darkness. He heard the heavy musket balls buzzing over his head and burying themselves in the mud brick walls of the Residency behind him. Abandoning the wounded man, he ran back into the house and slammed the door behind himself. He bolted it. It was very thick mahogany. Would it resist musket balls?

His legs were now trembling beneath him. His stomach was starting to churn and ache. He was swiftly and violently sick. Recovering, he found the whole ground floor in darkness. Someone had turned out the remaining lamps in the house.

"Who's there?" he demanded, raising the pistol, his finger pulling back the trigger in readiness to fire.

"Patron?"

The voice was Hyppolite's. Jean-Patrice lowered the pistol and groped forward. With relief, he grasped the corporal's solid arm. "Hyppolite! Thank God."

"Are you hurt, patron?"

"No, but I shot one of them. In the heart, I think. They have shot Schultze in the face. They fired through the dining room window. How many of them are there?"

"We saw five. I think there are more. I don't know where Narcise is, patron. And Hyacinth is wounded."

"How badly?"

"His arm is cut with a bush knife. He went to tie it up. He'll come here if he can."

"And the rest of the village?"

"They have all run away, patron. They are hiding in the bush."

Jean-Patrice took the key to the strong room out of his

pocket and gave it to the corporal. "Get all the rifles and the ammunition."

He felt his way to the dining room, winding up the little electric flashlight. Using its dim beam cautiously, he found Catherine crouching under the table with Schultze, Raymond and Chloë. "The Fang are outside. Hyppolite is here. Hyacinth will come if he can."

"What do they want?" she whispered.

"The silver, I suppose."

"Will they kill us?"

"Not if we fight." They sat listening to the darkness. Raymond was whimpering. Chloë was trembling; her teeth chattered like a human being's. Jean-Patrice shone the electric flashlight on Schultze and saw that the German was doggedly bandaging his face with a napkin. His eyes bulged ferociously. .

"I shot the brute who did this to you," Jean-Patrice said to Schultze. "He's done for, at least. How are you feeling, old fellow?" Schultze groped in the pocket of his white jacket, now sadly blotched with his own gore. He withdrew a little notebook and a tiny silver pencil, and motioned Jean-Patrice to hold the flashlight over the paper. He scrawled several lines and thrust the notebook at Jean-Patrice. Jean-Patrice peered at it but, no doubt because of his emotion, Schultze had written in his native German, a language Jean-Patrice could not speak well. He frowned, trying to decipher the groups of consonants. "What does this word mean?" he enquired, pointing.

Schultze snatched the notebook back, rolling his eyes in disgust. He scribbled a fresh page, adding several exclamation marks in places, the pen digging into the paper. He shoved the notebook back at Jean-Patrice, who now read:

BARRICADE ALL DOORS & WINDOWS!!!
BARRICADE SELVES HERE
WITH DINING TABLE!!!

DON'T GO OUTSIDE AGAIN!!!

These suggestions struck Jean-Patrice as eminently sensible. He dragged Raymond from beneath the table. Together with Hyppolite, the three of them pushed a sideboard in front of the window and then, with some difficulty, for it was large and very heavy, turned the table on its side and created a kind of bunker with the chairs and the sideboard. It was like the preparation for some grim party game. While they did this, Catherine tried to help Schultze with the bandage he was trying to make. She plugged his shattered face with the napkin and tied a second napkin around it to keep it in place. He looked incongruously like someone suffering from a bad toothache. He nodded to thank her and began to write afresh in his notebook:

MY ASKARIS CIRCLING BEHIND ENEMY
WILL SURPRISE THEM SHORTLY!!!
ENEMY HAVE FLINTLOCKS.
WE HAVE BREECH LOADERS.
OUR RATE OF FIRE SUPERIOR!!!
BRING MY WEAPONS FROM MY ROOM!
BRING MY MEDICINE BAG!!!

The warlike tone of this message was heartening. Jean-Patrice had forgotten about the German's two East African soldiers, who had been billeted in the village. Perhaps they were indeed even now planning a counter-attack. He sent Raymond to get the German's guns and medicine bag while he and Hyppolite went cautiously around the house, pushing the heaviest of the furniture against the doors and windows. For the first time, he was beginning to appreciate the fortress-like structure of the Residency, with its thick walls and small windows.

The kitchen was abandoned, Raymond's wives having fled. The Christmas meal was marooned on the table, getting cold. They rammed the kitchen table against the back door.

Another window pane shattered and they heard the thump of the ball burying itself in the stucco. Jean-Patrice turned and saw that the bullet had lodged in the centre of the shadow which he himself was casting on the wall. He at once sank to a crouch, as though he had been shot. He motioned to Hyppolite to be silent and crept to the window with his revolver. His sense of outrage had returned. These brutes were trying to kill him. They had mistaken his shadow for the real thing. The mistake would cost them dear! He listened until he heard what he thought was a stealthy footfall outside. Then he rose and fired three shots out of the window. There was a shout. He was disappointed to hear that it had the sound more of surprise than of pain. He sheltered behind the wall, reloading the revolver, dropping several of the bullets in his fumbling haste. He heard a hoarse voice calling from outside.

"Patron!"

"What do you want?" he called back, surprised at the steadiness of his own reply.

"Give us Raymond." He recognized the voice of Achilles

He was puzzled. "Raymond?"

Several voices answered, "Yes, Raymond! Give us Raymond!"

"Give us Raymond," Achilles said, "and we make him tell you the truth."

"What truth?"

"We did not steal the girl. He sold her."

"Sophie?"

A chorus of voices answered, "Sophie, yes, Sophie!"

"He sold Sophie to us," Achilles' hoarse voice said. "We gave him silver. Now he say we stole her and we must pay a fine. Bad, patron! He is a liar!"

Jean-Patrice looked at Hyppolite. "Can that be

possible?" he muttered.

Hyppolite shrugged. "Yes."

Jean-Patrice finished loading the heavy revolver. "Why did you shoot the German?" he called.

"It was by accident, patron."

"An accident? To shoot an unarmed man through the window?"

"That man want to shoot Raymond. He aim badly. And now you have kill that man yourself, patron. It is finished."

"Finished?" Jean-Patrice exclaimed. "Are you mad? You killed Ndoumou. The doctor may die, too. You have all been shooting at us. You are all responsible. And where is Sophie now?"

There was a silence. Then Patroclus' sulky voice replied, "Sophie is here."

"With you?"

"Yes, with us."

"Then let me speak to her."

There was the muttering of men confabulating. "She does not want to speak now."

"They are lying," Hyppolite whispered. "They have eaten her."

This new and horrible possibility made Jean-Patrice shudder. "Would Raymond be party to such a thing?" he asked.

"With Raymond, anything is possible," Hyppolite said. "The Fang sometimes eat human flesh. It is part of their religion. And Sophie was no use for anything anymore."

"Patron?" The hoarse voice of Achilles was calling from outside the window. "Patron? What do you say now?"

Jean-Patrice tried to think, groping for the bullets he had dropped on the floor. "We have to talk," he said at last. "You must bring Sophie back so we can see she is alive. You must give up all your weapons and surrender yourselves. Then we will find out the truth of what happened. Those who are guilty will be punished. The innocent will go free."

There was some muttering in the darkness outside. Then a fresh voice spoke up. "Why you say we surrender? There are many of us and few of you. We can kill all of you quick."

"That remains to be seen," Jean-Patrice retorted. "And the more of us you kill, the worse it will be for you. The soldiers will come and will find you. They will burn your houses and hang you. Your women and children will starve. The best chance you have is to surrender to me and let me help you."

Somebody laughed scornfully. He could hear them talking to one another in their own language. He had spoken bravely but he was sickened by the thought of Catherine's danger. If their pitiful little force was overwhelmed, she would be at their mercy. He could not bear to think of what they might do to her. "If you don't shoot at us, we won't shoot at you," he called.

There was more muttering. Then a voice replied, "We don't shoot, patron."

"Let's barricade this window in the meantime, and get out of here," he said to Hyppolite. They heaved a cabinet in front of the window and crept back to the dining room.

Catherine threw her arms around him and held him with all her strength, burying her face against his throat. "I thought they had shot you."

The embrace was painfully sweet, even if it was the last he would have from her. Jean-Patrice kissed her face. "I spoke to them and told them to give themselves up. They are thinking it over." He shone the little flashlight on the others. Schultze was loading his rifles in a businesslike manner. But Jean-Patrice could see that he was bleeding heavily. His clothes were soaked with it. Raymond hunched behind the table, his knees drawn up to his chin. Jean-Patrice shone the dim light into his face. "They say they didn't steal Sophie," he said grimly. "They say you sold her to them for silver."

Catherine had been cradling the terrified gorilla in her arms. She turned on Raymond with a hiss. "I knew it! The oganga is right – you are a dog!"

Raymond's eyes gleamed yellow. "They lie."

"You wretch! They have nothing to gain from lying. You are the one who has lied, Raymond. You sold your own daughter and you lied to me. You made them take Ndoumou, too, for some reason of your own. What did they buy her for? To eat her?"

"They do not eat girls," Raymond said scornfully.

"You know that they do," Hyppolite retorted.

"Whether they will eat her or use her in other ways, you sold her like a lump of meat," Jean-Patrice said in disgust. "Your own daughter! They want me to send you out to them, so they can deal with you in their own fashion."

"They will murder me," he said hoarsely, hugging his knees.

"That is what you deserve," Catherine said in a tight voice. "Why should we die for your lies? Send him out, Jean-Patrice!"

"It's not so simple," Jean-Patrice said heavily. "People have been wounded and killed. There has to be an enquiry."

"This is Gabon, not France," Catherine said. "There doesn't have to be an enquiry! We just have to save our lives."

Schultze had prepared a huge syringe of morphine and some other drugs mixed. He bared his arm and gave himself an injection. Then he began scribbling in his notebook again. He passed it to Jean-Patrice.

THEY WILL KILL HIM &
THEN HAVE ONE LESS TO DEAL WITH.
HE CAN HOLD A GUN &
FIGHT FOR HIS OWN LIFE!
KEEP HIM HERE!!!

"I agree," Jean-Patrice said. "You can fight, Raymond, since all this is your fault." He picked up a rifle and gave it to the man. "If we get out of here alive, we can decide your fate. But you can be sure that if the Fang take you, you will pass a bad night."

"How could you do it?" Catherine demanded, staring at Raymond in disgust. "Your own daughter!"

"And you?" Raymond snarled back at her. "Didn't you sell your own daughter, too?"

Catherine was silenced. Jean-Patrice looked at her. "What does he mean? I thought your child died?"

She spoke very quietly. "My child is alive, Jean-Patrice."

"Why did you tell me that she was dead?" She did not answer, but turned her face away from the dim light of his flashlight. "I don't understand, Catherine."

"She bore the missionary's child," Hyppolite said. "She was his woman. They sinned with one another." He glanced at Catherine with dislike. "She ran away. Father Jacques took his own life. The nuns took the child with them. The mission was closed because of her. And him." He snapped open Schultze's shotgun and pushed a cartridge into the breech. "We abandoned our faith. There was no priest at Bassongo to celebrate the Mass any more. And none came."

Jean-Patrice stared at Catherine's profile. "When did this happen?"

"Six, seven years ago." Hyppolite passed the shotgun to Schultze. "She married a man from another village. That one died, too. She came back here and became a potter."

"I told you." Raymond sneered at Jean-Patrice. "I told you she was rotten fruit. But she likes white men, at least."

Soundlessly, Catherine threw herself on Raymond, clawing at his face. Jean-Patrice grabbed her arms. It took all his strength to pull her back. Her body was quivering with passion. "I am nothing like you!" she spat at Raymond. "It broke my heart to leave my child!"

Raymond cradled the rifle, chuckling softly and staring at the floor, but made no other reply. Jean-Patrice felt heavy. "Where is the child now?" he asked her.

"They took her to Leopoldville. They were Belgians. She's in a school there. I send money for her three times a year. That's why I took the inoculation work. But they never send me any word of her."

Jean-Patrice could not face any of this now. He shut it out of his mind and peered at his watch. It was ten o'clock. The whole night was before them. It would not be light for many hours. He thought of the Christmas meal congealing in the kitchen. His stomach rolled over with hunger. Yet how could they eat in the presence of poor Schultze, who would never chew again? He was now a gourmet in permanent exile. Perhaps they were all destined to never eat another meal, and he was being overnice. "You have to drink some water, Schultze," he said. "We must find a way of getting it into you."

Schultze scrawled in his notebook. Jean-Patrice read:

NASO-GASTRIC.
HAVE YOU INDIARUBBER TUBING?
ALSO, A FUNNEL
ALSO, A JUG.
1 L. WATER, A LITTLE SALT & SUGAR.

"I will get it," Catherine said.

Jean-Patrice gave her the flashlight. "Please be careful."

They sat in silence, waiting. Hyppolite peered through the barricaded window. "The moon is getting high," he said. "We will soon be able to see them better than they can see us."

Jean-Patrice nodded. "If the worst comes to the worst, and we can't defend the doors and windows, we can go down and lock ourselves in the strong room and wait for help. But there's not much space in there. Barely enough for the five of us. And no air."

Nobody seemed to relish the idea. He was beginning to feel insubstantial, as though his head were floating away from his body. The searing vividness he had experienced while firing at the enemy had faded away again. He thought of the man he'd shot, of the life-blood spouting between his fingers. Nausea threatened him again. He supposed this was what it must be like for soldiers in battle, this succession of madness, terror and boredom. Immediacy faded into speculation and then became dream-like. Why, he was quite an old veteran already. Two hours at the hands of the Fang had given him as much action as many soldiers ever saw. He had been fired upon and had given fire in return and had killed a fellow mortal, deliberately and (he flattered himself) coolly. And here he was, still alive, with his revolver dangling from his fingers and the smell of gunpowder in his nostrils.

And Catherine – but his mind shied away from Catherine. He did not want to think about that yet. She had the missionary's child. She was his woman. His nausea intensified. He gulped a little, trying to fight it down.

Catherine came back with the tubing and the solution. Schultze wrote some instructions. She knelt in front of him and began to feed the India-rubber tube into his left nostril. The tormented man quivered and groaned under the operation, his eyes streaming, his burly chest heaving.

"The tube is so thick," Catherine said in a tight voice. "We don't have anything else." Schultze grunted encouragement, guiding the tube with his own hands. Blood spattered from his face over Catherine. There seemed no point in resisting his rising gorge; Jean-Patrice went outside and was sick again. With his head spinning, he wondered whether they would all be alive by morning and what the new day might bring in the way of relief or fresh horror.

He rubbed his eyes and went back to the dining room. Catherine had succeeded in pushing the end of the tube down into Schultze's stomach. She was now attaching the funnel to the other end. Schultze himself appeared buoyant again, directing her with brisk gestures. The morphia cocktail had probably begun to take effect. She poured a little of the water into the funnel. They all watched by the wavering light of the flashlight. Then, with a gurgle, the water disappeared into Schultze. The doctor sighed with satisfaction. Catherine continued to dribble liquid carefully into the funnel. Hyppolite disappeared in the direction of the kitchen. There followed discreet chinks and scrapes. Schultze's Christmas dinner was being celebrated after all, though Jean-Patrice did not think it seemly to point this out. The corporal returned a little while later, wiping his mouth. Having been filled with water, Schultze rested, the rubber tube dangling from his face, his head in his hands.

Jean-Patrice motioned to Catherine to accompany him to the kitchen. The roast kid was on the table. Hyppolite had eaten one haunch. He carved the rest of the animal, which now struck him as a sacrificial lamb. They sat side by side and ate in silence.

"The tube was too thick," she said. "Poor man. As if he is not suffering terribly enough."

"You were very delicate," he replied. "I couldn't have done that." His own voice sounded dead in his ears.

"Do you feel differently about me now?" she asked quietly. "Have you stopped respecting me as you once said you did?"

"What does it matter?" he replied. "Your life is your own business, Catherine."

"Yes. But one's life is also the business of others."

"I wish you had told me the truth." It was too dark in the kitchen to see her expression properly. "I have never lied to you about anything."

"I wish I had too," she said. "I wish many things, now.

226

I will tell you what happened at the mission, if you want."

"Now is not the time or place." He did not respond to her caress. He felt benumbed. "It doesn't matter, in any case."

"It matters to me."

"At least I now know why you were reluctant to come to me. I suppose that is something."

A fusillade of shots from outside made Jean-Patrice jump to his feet. The firing continued for some time. He could distinguish the ragged boom of the Fang muskets from the sharper sound of more modern weapons. "Schultze's Askaris," he said in excitement. "It sounds as though they have the upper hand!" He ran back to the dining room. "You hear, Schultze?"

The doctor nodded. They went to the window and pushed the sideboard a little to one side, peering out through the slit. The moon was now high and brilliant. Jean-Patrice saw the figure of a man rise from the shrubbery, shoulder a weapon and fire. The long, flaring tongue of flame confirmed it was one of the Fang warriors. He aimed his own revolver without thinking and pulled the trigger. The man screamed. He dropped his musket and ran a few paces before pitching face-forward onto the ground. Schultze, leaning on the windowsill beside him, fired at the recumbent figure with his rifle, grunting with gratification as they heard a second shriek. He slid down to the floor to reload his rifle. Jean-Patrice remained staring out. He could see the flashes of the continuing gun fire but it was impossible to distinguish who was shooting at whom.

Catherine seized his free hand in both of hers. "Don't stand there," she begged him. He allowed himself to be pulled from the window. But he was listening to the shots with increasing disquiet. The flat crack of the Askaris' modern rifles was giving way to the old-world boom of the muskets. Soon the cracks were intermittent, the booms triumphant. "Only one of them left," he said to

Schultze. Schultze nodded in gloomy agreement. Then there was exclusively the sound of the muskets, falling away into silence. There could be only one interpretation.

"There are twenty, maybe thirty of them," Hyppolite said. "And Hyacinth and Narcise have not come." They pushed the sideboard back across the window.

After a silence, the hoarse voice called from the darkness outside. "Patron! You say no more shooting. You lie! Patron? You hear me? The two little soldiers, they are dead. Your policemen, they run away. What you doing in there, patron?" There was a chorus of mocking laughter.

"Send us Raymond," another voice shouted.

There was more laughter. "Yes, yes! Send us Raymond and the woman, we go away!"

"Send us Raymond and the woman and the policeman. Send us the black ones, we let the white ones live."

"Send us the blacks, the whites can live!"

"Give us the silver!"

"Eh, patron, give us the silver!"

"Give us the monkey!"

"Give us the monkey, patron!"

"Patron!" A new, weaker voice was calling from outside the window. "Patron, it's me, Narcise!"

Jean-Patrice peered through the crack, Hyppolite pressing up beside him. It was indeed Narcise. He was being held, half-naked, between Achilles and Patroclus. He peered at the Residency shortsightedly.

"Narcise!" Jean-Patrice cried out.

"Patron, they say they want the silver and the rifles," Narcise said. Jean-Patrice saw that there were several deep cuts in his arms and legs, dark ribbons of blood on his skin. His hands were tied in front of him. He was swaying with exhaustion. "They say you must give them the silver and the guns and then they go away."

"What you say, blanc?" Achilles shouted.

"Release that man to me," Jean-Patrice said, "and then

we can talk."

"No more talk! Give us the silver."

"Give us the guns, blanc!"

He tried to keep his voice steady. "I will give you nothing until you release my officer."

"Please, patron," Narcise begged. He was crying now, his thin shoulders shaken by sobs. "Do what they ask!"

Patroclus had produced a long machete, which glinted in the moonlight. He twirled it around Narcise's head.. "What you say, blanc? We kill this little man?"

Jean-Patrice remembered the heavy, numbing blow on his arm. This time the blade would not be turned aside. He aimed his revolver, but there was too much chance of hitting poor Narcise. "What shall we do?" he asked Hyppolite in anguish.

"I don't know," Hyppolite muttered through clenched teeth.

"I will give you twenty pieces of silver for that man," Jean-Patrice called out. "When you release him, we can talk again."

The two Fang men muttered behind Narcise's back for a while, apparently arguing with one another. Jean-Patrice waited, his heart churning heavily. Then Patroclus, almost casually, struck at Narcise's neck with the machete. The blade made a hollow thud as though it were striking a banana tree. Feeling that what he was seeing was impossible, Jean-Patrice tried to scream, but his voice failed him. Narcise staggered forward, his head half-severed from his trunk. The man swung the heavy blade again. Narcise's head fell neatly to one side. His decapitated trunk collapsed to the other, an irrevocable parting of the ways. Jean-Patrice found he was firing the revolver again and again. Schultze and Hyppolite both discharged their rifles, too. The two Fang men, unharmed, loped back into the darkness and vanished.

"Narcise," Hyppolite wept. "Narcise, my friend!"

Narcise's body was no more than a darker stain in the

darkness, barely discernible. A musket spat; the ball smashed into the barricade. Jean-Patrice tried to fire back but his revolver was empty now and the hammer clicked on a spent cartridge. Hyppolite pulled him away from the window. They both reloaded in silence. Jean-Patrice tried to blot out what had just happened, his mind still refusing to accept it as a real event. Catherine was sobbing aloud, clinging to Chloë. Jean-Patrice turned his fury on Raymond.

"You dog!" he said, slapping the man across the face. "Do you see what you've done?"

Schultze slumped wearily against the wall. Despite his extraordinary stamina, Jean-Patrice realized, the man was dying. With the recent exertion, the wound to his face had begun to bleed heavily. He was growing very weak. "You must rest," Jean-Patrice said, taking the German's rifle out of his unresisting hands. "If you continue to bleed like this, you will not survive the night."

Schultze pointed a shaky finger at the bottles of wine on the sideboard. Jean-Patrice hesitated for a moment, but there was no point in denying the wretched man. He selected a Burgundy and offered it to Schultze, but Schultze shook his head, stabbing with his finger at another, a deep red bottle which he himself had brought in his baggage. Jean-Patrice examined the faded label. It was a very old Hock. "This one?" Jean-Patrice asked, showing it to him. Schultze nodded, his eyes filling with tears of emotion. Jean-Patrice opened the bottle ceremoniously and poured the wine into a glass. "Your very good health, Schultze." He transferred the wine carefully into the funnel which Catherine held. It gurgled its way down towards Schultze's interior regions. It was impossible that Schultze should be able to taste any of this rare vintage. However, it was not until four glasses had been decanted into him that he made a gesture saying enough and slumped back against the wall, groaning. Catherine covered him with the tablecloth. He seemed to slide into a sleep. Jean-Patrice wondered whether he would ever wake again.

20

He prowled around the Residency, checking the doors and windows, peering out through the chinks. Everything was quiet. Nothing was stirring. He tried not to think of Narcise's head tumbling off his shoulders. It was better to think of the men he himself had killed. He had now killed two. One and a half, if you allowed that Schultze had finished the second one off. However, he had no sense of achievement. Each death added to the weight on top of him, making it less likely that he would ever get out of this alive. He was in a pickle. Between the wickedness of Raymond and his own inexperience and impulsiveness, he had landed himself in a real pickle.

He thought of the abandoned mission, the roof of the little church sagging through the crumbled beams. Well, he knew the story behind that now. The errant Father Jacques and he, the errant Commissioner Duméril, had loved the same woman and would both leave their bones here. And his endeavors would meet a similar fate to the missionary's. The cannibals outside would kill them all and burn the Residency. It, too, would be left to rot. As would he, beneath some anonymous cross or cairn.

Perhaps that summed up the white man in Africa.

Inexperience and impulsiveness meeting savagery. He pushed a cabinet absently closer to a window and heard a chuckle from the darkness outside. A voice said, "Eh, patron? What you doing in there, patron?" He did not reply. He wandered back to the dining room. Impulsiveness, he thought, in the sense of giving in to lust and greed, the sensual grasping of the slaver intoxicated by soft, naked brown flesh, the rapacity of the miner clawing diamonds out of the mud. Inexperience not simply of Africa, but of the self, of one's own capacity for corruption in the face of such overwhelming abundance. Savagery in the sense of the wildness of nature, untamed by niceties. And of course folly, pure human folly, unregenerate and irredeemable.

He sat down with the others. Catherine was crying, her face shiny with tears. The gorilla seemed dazed. She lay inert in Catherine's arms. Catherine caressed her as she would a wounded child. Schultze was snoring through his one unobstructed nostril. Hyppolite was still pushing bullets stoically into the rifles. He would load them all, then methodically unload them all and begin again. Raymond was lost in his own thoughts, his face sunken into frog-like folds.

"I feel ashamed of myself," Jean-Patrice said heavily.

"Ah, my dear." Catherine looked up. "You are a good man. You acted honorably."

"I acted arrogantly and foolishly. I cannot think of one of the Seven Cardinal Sins which I haven't been guilty of."

"Patron?" The mocking voice called from the darkness outside the window. "What you doing in there, patron?"

"Eh, patron? What you doing in there, patron?" There was a chorus of rude hilarity.

"I've just realized it," Jean-Patrice went on. "What a fool I have been, from start to finish! None of you would be here if I had not been such a fool." He sighed. "But more than that, I am simply ashamed of myself. Of what I am. Of my inability to change into something better."

"You are the best man I know," Catherine said, crying afresh.

"Probably your standards are not very high," he said gloomily.

"Jean-Patrice!"

"I don't mean to insult you. I just mean that here in Bassongo there are few opportunities for anyone to display the highest qualities of human nature." He cocked his head, pausing. He had heard a stealthy scraping sound from outside. He listened carefully. It was not repeated, but his senses were alert. "Hyppolite, watch the window," he commanded. "You, Raymond, go to the kitchen. Watch the door there. Shoot if you see anything."

He went quietly up the stairs. The windows on the top floor were very small; it would take a child to find an entrance there. But the roof was only tin, nailed onto beams. He prowled quietly between the two bedrooms, listening carefully. At times he thought he could hear noises, but he could not be sure. He scratched his temple with the muzzle of the revolver. If only Hyacinth would come, there might be a faint chance. They would at least present a more formidable enemy than they did at present. They might be able to hold out until

someone reached Medoneu to fetch the soldiers. That was, if anyone had thought to set off to get help from Medoneu. If everyone was not skulking in the jungle, miles away.

He listened. Silence. No sound of the oganga wipoga's drums, either. The old hag! She was keeping silent, of course. Delighted to see another white man bite the dust. *Your brothers call this land the white man's grave.* The old bitch was probably cackling in her cave or hovel. You will pay, in time. That'll teach you to bring your white man's medicine to my Bassongo!

He heard a scuffling sound over his head. His heart leaped in his breast. He looked up, eyes and mouth stretched wide. There was no doubt about it. Someone was climbing onto the roof. He heard voices hissing to one another. In terror, he saw the corrugated tin sheets bend under the weight of a man, and then a second. He watched the footsteps progress sideways, stopping when the tin creaked too loudly. They had found the wooden beams and were walking along them. The beams were stout, making it impossible for him to fire at them. He was shaking like a man with the ague. Since the siege had begun, he had not experienced real terror like this. Everything had somehow been unreal. This was real. His bowels had loosened. His throat was tight and dry, his heart beating so wildly he had time to wonder whether sheer fear would kill him before the Fang could cut his throat. There was a pause. More whispering. Then the quiet screech of metal on metal. They had found a loose sheet of iron. They were starting to pull it open.

He went underneath the place and pointed the revolver at the roof. There were six shots in the weapon. He decided to fire five of them in the pattern of the Five of Spades. He would leave the sixth one to be allocated later. He marked the spots with his eye and then began firing. His ears rang. Burning powder from the muzzle fell in his eyes. Over the deafening bangs, he could hear screaming. He paused on the last shot, panting as though he had run up a steep hill. He could hear hoarse cries of pain. He took careful aim and fired the last shot. The cries dwindled into whimpers and then died away. With trembling hands, he pushed the smoking shells out of the chambers and reloaded. He could hear something moving in a sluggish way on the roof, the sound a crocodile might make trying to emerge from a river. Then something rolled with increasing noise and speed to the edge of the roof, the crescendo breaking off suddenly. There was a faint, eerie wail. Then silence. He stared at the six neat holes that had appeared in the corrugated iron. Through three of them, blood was dripping quickly. He inspected the dark pool that had begun to form on the floorboards.

More blood on his head, on his hands. He fired another shot at the hole which seemed to drip the most. There was no response.

He went shakily down the stairs again. That made four. Or three and half, depending on how you looked at it. But there could be no such thing as half a man. If he and Schultze had killed a man together, they had each killed one man. That was how the law would see it in France. They would each be guillotined, if it was a case of murder. So it was four. He thought of Malherbe's leathery smile.

Hyppolite and Catherine met him at the bottom of the stairs. "You killed one, patron," Hyppolite said approvingly. "He fell off the roof. He is lying dead outside."

"There is another one lying dead on the roof, I think," he replied. "It's time you killed one of them, Hyppolite. I don't want to go to Hell alone. And please don't call me patron any more. I hate the sound of the word." He looked at his watch. It was past midnight. It would be light in four or five hours. He looked into the kitchen. Raymond was hacking at the roast kid. The animal was now half-consumed. The white bones were starting to appear through the pinkish meat. When the kid was finished, Jean-Patrice thought, they would have to fall back on the tinned goods. And there were not many of those left now. Raymond's cheeks bulged with each mouthful. He ate stolidly, ignoring them. "They may attack again. We can't all huddle in one room. We should guard the weak points. Raymond can stay here. Hyppolite, go with Schultze and watch the window. Catherine and I will go to the study. Each of us will shout for the others if there is any suspicion of danger."

He, Catherine and Chloë went to the study. The desk was covered with her phials of blood and serum, the lancets laid out in a glittering row, symbols now of futility. It was a substantial desk. They sat on the floor in its dark shelter. Chloë crept into Catherine's arms; Catherine lay with her head against Jean-Patrice's breast. He held her, inhaling the scent of her skin, slightly sweet, slightly bitter. Justine had always been elaborately perfumed. It had seldom been possible to know what her body smelled like except during the hungry intrusions of sex. This woman smelled of herself. Nature, untamed by niceties. Her hair smelled a little smoky. He remembered watching her comb it out. He closed his eyes and allowed his lips to touch the side of her neck. Here she smelled warm, milky. Here, at the throat, there was something sweet, a lingering of the soap she had used. The blue variety, favored by women over the carbolic red variety, used by men. At her temples there was the lamby scent of the day's sweat. Her eyelids were dewy; they, too, had their own intimate scent. He laid his cheek against hers.

"In the morning, soldiers will come," she whispered. "We'll be safe."

"It's many days' walk to Medoneu."

"Hyacinth will go on the horse. And the raft pilots will see something wrong. They will call for help."

"Nobody in Bassongo cares whether we live or die."

"Perhaps not me. But they like you."

"I doubt it. I'm just another detested white man."

"You make them laugh."

"That's something, I suppose." He caught the haunting aroma of something cooking. The corner of his mouth was against the corner of her mouth. She was motionless. He turned his head slightly. Her lips were softer than he had ever imagined. They pressed to his, warm and full, in the kiss he had wanted so much. Yearning swelled in him. He found himself trembling with desire now as he had trembled with terror a few moments ago. These peaks of emotion were so vertiginous, mountains in the landscape of his life, which he now saw to have been much flatter and duller than he had hitherto supposed. This was one of those nights, as described in the romances of his childhood, which would turn a man's hair white by morning.

She, too, was trembling. "Our lives should have been different."

"They are what they are." He kissed her again, the sweetness of her mouth so intense that he moaned aloud. Chloë whimpered beside them.

"I have wanted your kisses for so long," she whispered.

"Then why did you keep me away? You yielded to the missionary easily enough!"

She drew away from him. "I was nineteen, Jean-Patrice! He was forty. I did not even know how great the sin was."

"I'm sorry."

"He never kissed me on the lips. He would have thought that a degradation of himself. My husband did not kiss me on the lips, either. Your kiss is the only one I have ever wanted."

He sighed. "I shouldn't have spoken in that way." He touched her long, slim neck. "The Queen of Sheba looked like you, I think. I wish I were as wise as Solomon."

She was not mollified. "You have no right to judge me. You are also an adulterer. And I think you had less excuse than I."

"Much less." He smiled wearily at her. "Don't be angry with me. I'm just jealous of the other men who have touched you."

That seemed to make her even angrier. "You have no need to be. They are both dead. And I never desired to be touched. I wanted only to live a life of my own."

He sighed. His pockets were still heavy with the fistfuls of revolver bullets he had snatched up. He started to count them now but was unable to reach an accurate total. They were too slippery, too shiny. They slithered in his hands playfully. Two or three dozen, in any case. Better keep two, he thought, for the final exit. One for her and one for himself. He paused in his thoughts. Would she prefer to be shot than fall into the hands of the Fang?

And what about Chloë? He opened his mouth to ask her, but thought better of it. It was a difficult topic to open at present. He would cross that stile when he came to it. He longed to kiss her again, but it seemed not very likely she would let him. They sat in silence. The Fang were very quiet. He had anticipated a furious attack after having dispatched the men on the roof, but there had been nothing. Nobody had even fired at the house. He could hear distant voices, though, and occasionally some laughter.

He glanced covertly at Catherine. She was staring into the shadows. Her profile was so noble, he thought, like a queen from an Egyptian fresco. Her feelings were noble, too. He had insulted her in his stupid way. He would apologize. But not yet. He knew enough about women to wait until her temper had cooled before attempting any reconciliation. Yet it was hard that their last night together should be wasted in sulks.

He sniffed the air. There it was again, that haunting aroma. Smoke and sizzling fat. Something roasting over a fire. He went to the window and put his nose out cautiously. Yes. The insolent brutes were holding a barbecue. The night was redolent with it.

"They're having a feast," he said to Catherine. He inhaled appreciatively. "Can you smell it? They are certainly bold enough!"

Hyppolite had smelled it, too. He came into the study, followed by Schultze, now awake and very pale. "They are eating, Jean-Patrice."

"I can smell it."

Schultze, looking ghastly, scribbled in his notebook and showed it to Jean-Patrice.

THAT IS THE SMELL OF
ROASTING HUMAN FLESH.
THEY ARE EATING MY ASKARIS.

Jean-Patrice recoiled in horror from the idea. "Oh, the devils!" he exclaimed. Schultze nodded slowly, his eyes staring into Jean-Patrice's with the glaze of morphia upon them. The brown India-rubber tube wagged from his nose like a miniature elephant's trunk. The roasting smell, which had been pleasant, was suddenly choking, greasy and repugnant. "When they are hungry again," he said unsteadily, "they will come for us, too."

Hyppolite scratched his jaw. "They will call the rest of their village," he said. "By tomorrow they will be here."

"With their napkins around their necks," Jean-Patrice said. "We can't sit here like cattle waiting for the butchers. I'm going outside to scout."

Catherine stood up quickly. "No!"

"We have to know what they are doing and where they have camped Then we can work out what to do. It must be done."

"Please, Jean-Patrice," Catherine said, grasping his arm tightly, "don't go outside."

"I'll be very careful," he said, pleased at her concern. "They'll find all the palm wine they want in the village. Beer, too. They'll be too busy eating and drinking to notice me."

He was not altogether counterfeiting his bravery. The idea of being not only killed, but eaten too, had filled him with indignation. To sit in this hole was unbearable. Despite Catherine's implorations, gratifying as they were, he was adamant. After deliberation, he chose the kitchen door as the discreetest means of egress. They moved the table quietly away from the door. He peered out. The garden looked deserted, bathed in pale moonlight. "Lock up after me," he whispered. "Watch Raymond."

As he stole away from the Residency, he saw that the garden was littered with bodies. One belonged to the man who had fallen from the roof. It was sprawled in a dark pool next to the cannon. He inspected it and found it to be the burly corpse of Achilles, his abdomen torn by Jean-

Patrice's bullets. That meant Patroclus was probably dead on the roof. Their careers had come to a fittingly Homeric end.

The next was poor Narcise, his head some feet away from his torso, luckily turned away. Jean-Patrice did not care to see his face. The first man he had shot was still there, too. The savages had not even dragged their own dead away. The abominable smell of the cannibal feast blew into his face, filling him with revulsion. He could hear them carousing, shouting and laughing at one another. Trying to keep to the darkest shadows, he crept towards the sound of shouting, holding his revolver at the ready. The glow of the bonfire guided him, pouring sparks and smoke into the clear night sky. He could distinguish moving figures, silhouetted against the flames. The village itself was deserted. Everyone had fled. The Fang were in sole possession.

He concealed himself behind a hut to take stock. The Fang had camped between the Residency and the river, the only feasible means of escape from Bassongo. The place they had chosen was a level clearing beside a banana grove. He could see that they had hacked down several of the bunches, which were piled up beside other booty they had looted from the huts, iron cooking pots, clothing and the like. He got down on his hands and knees. His heart in his mouth, he crawled from hut to hut, getting nearer to the heat and the revelry.

At length he was as close as he dared approach. The bonfire was bright enough to illuminate the whole area and hot enough to sear his face. Something was roasting on an impromptu spit beside the flames. Jean-Patrice squinted against the glare. It was unmistakably the mutilated body of a man. The sickness of pure horror froze his heart, making his head spin. He forced himself to concentrate. He counted the figures as best he could. Hyppolite had been right. There were between twenty and thirty of them. They appeared to be circling around the fire, perhaps in some ritual dance. An idea was forming in his mind. He groped after it. It was a daring plan. But the sight of that poor, butchered human body on the spit made any plan attractive, no matter how desperate.

He backed away cautiously from the bonfire and made his retreat as stealthily as he could. He reached the Residency without meeting a soul, and tapped on the kitchen door. "It's me!" he hissed. They let him in. Catherine flew to him. The passion in her embrace made him think that perhaps he was forgiven. He gulped at the bottle of wine that Schultze passed him and related what he had seen. "I think there's a chance for us," he announced.

"Do you think we can escape?" Hyppolite said.

His idea was taking a bolder shape. "We can attack!"

"We are too few," the corporal said.

"But we have the cannon!" They all looked at him in astonishment. He held up a finger. "We've seen that it works. We have powder, two kegs in the strong room."

"How can we use the cannon, Jean-Patrice?" Hyppolite asked dubiously. "One cannot carry a cannon around as though it were a rifle."

"You and I are strong, Hyppolite. And it's mainly downhill all the way to the river. We can push it, as we did for the inoculation-day. While they're all drunk, we can wheel the cannon to a strategic position and fire at them. We might kill or injure two dozen of them, if we are lucky. They're in a clearing and they haven't posted any guards that I can see. Then we can attack with rifles. We can reach the river and get into canoes. By the time they recover, we'll be miles downriver."

The others stared at him with varying expressions. Schultze wrote briefly in his note book:

AND THEN?

"The river is full of natives selling food to the raft

pilots. We'll be able to survive. We'll keep paddling towards the coast until we find help. We simply have to put as much distance between us and the Fang as possible. Don't look at me as though I were mad. We don't even have to move the cannon very far. The further away from the target, the better. That will allow the shot to spread more widely."

"We have no shot, Jean-Patrice."

"We have no shot, but we can improvise."

WITH WHAT ARE YOU GOING LOAD THE GUN? Schultze scribbled with an ironic flourish. THE CUTLERY???

"I've thought of that. There is too much chance that forks and knives may get stuck in the barrel and burst it. It's only a six-pounder. No, I think we must use the silver."

"The money?" Hyppolite said in astonishment.

"There is rather a lot of it. Easily six pounds. Most of the coins are heavy. There are quite a lot of old Maria Theresas. She would make a nice hole in someone. I'm not sure about the aerodynamic properties of coins. I've been thinking about that. There would be a lot of resistance offered by the air against the flat side. But almost none against the edge. I think the lighter coins would tend to lift. But we could carry those with us to pay for food on the river, and load the cannon with the thalers and the ducats and heavy old pieces of that sort."

YOU HAVE GONE MAD, Schultze scribbled.

"I don't care," Jean-Patrice replied flatly. "I care only about getting out of here alive."

"They asked for the silver," Catherine said. Her almond eyes gleamed. "Let them have it."

"Exactly," Jean-Patrice said, struck by the fierce justice of this. "What do you think, Hyppolite?"

"They will kill us in the end," Hyppolite replied. "We may as well die fighting in the open air as be caught like rats in here."

Jean-Patrice turned to Raymond. "Are you with us?"

Raymond looked sick, but he shrugged as if to indicate he had little option but to agree. "It's all the same to me," he muttered.

"Schultze?"

The German rolled his eyes. He scrawled in his notebook:

I AM INJURED.
I NEED MEDICAL ATTENTION.
HOW WOULD I SURVIVE?
WHAT WOULD I EAT?

"We can buy milk from the natives on the river. And fruit, to make juice. You won't receive any medical treatment from the Fang, Schultze. Nor will they feed you any more diligently than we will. Our only hope is to get you to Libreville."

IT IS THREE HUNDRED MILES, Schultze wrote.

"I know that. You must make up your mind whether you are coming with us or whether you will entrust yourself to the mercies of the Fang. We don't have much time. If we don't act now, while they are feasting, we'll lose our opportunity forever. We must prepare. There is a lot to do."

I WOULD HOLD YOU BACK, Schultze wrote sadly.

"No. Injured as you are, you are our doctor. We need you with us." Schultze appeared to take some heart at this. He made a gesture indicating qualified assent. "Then let us begin," Jean-Patrice said.

21

In the strong room, he and Catherine sorted through the coins. Those which appeared most suitable from a ballistic point of view were the old Austrian thalers bearing the formidable bust of the Empress Maria Theresa. However there were also some suggestive American trade dollars, some Spanish five-peseta pieces and a number of battered British crowns, all heavy and solid. They counted these into a sack which would be rolled up and rammed down the barrel of the cannon. Upstairs, Hyppolite was disabling the rifles which would be left behind. Raymond, under the supervision of Schultze, was assembling provisions for the journey.

"Are you afraid?" he asked Catherine.

"Not while you are with me," she said.

He looked at her. She was very tired. Her eyes were swollen with crying and her mouth drooped at the corners. But he thought her lovelier than ever. It was an opportune moment to apologize for his gaucheness. "I was very wrong to say what I did," he said. "Please forgive me."

"That seems like a long time ago."

He leaned forward and kissed her cheek. "I want to survive this. I hope you do, too. When it's all over, I will make it up to you, Catherine. I don't mean just the cruel thing that I said. I mean what other men have done to you. I'll take away the hurt." He held the sack for her to pour the coins into. "We'll go to Leopoldville and find your daughter."

She smiled slightly. "She won't want me now."

"Oh, she will. I can assure you, from personal experience, that you are what she thinks about, day and night." He saw the expression on her face. "It's what orphans do. We dream about our mothers." He weighed the sack. "Still a pound short. We'll have to use some of the small coins, too."

They carried the sack of coins and the keg of powder upstairs. They could hear the Fang merrymaking in the distance and smell the roasting flesh of the poor Askari. But it would soon be dawn and there was no time to be lost.

They slipped out of the Residency by the light of the moon. The garden was deserted but for the dead men. A large night bird flapped away from one of the corpses, which had apparently been providing its dinner. Jean-Patrice and Hyppolite worked quickly on the cannon. They pushed the powder charge carefully home, followed by a patch of wadding made from an old shirt of Jean-Patrice's. The bag of coins was rammed in next, followed by a final, tight piece of wadding to stop it from falling out during the transportation of the cannon.

It was heavier than Jean-Patrice had remembered, especially without Narcise and Hyacinth to assist them. He and Hyppolite were powerful men, but it taxed their strength to move the thing. They put their shoulders to each wheel and heaved the weapon forward. It trundled along reluctantly, sticking in the soft earth, occasionally lurching ahead when it met a declivity. The squealing of the wheel hubs was distressingly loud but it was too late to think of oiling them. Perhaps it would be mistaken for the cry of frogs or insects.

Raymond, Catherine and Schultze followed, carrying their baggage and leading Chloë. The night was a hot one. Jean-Patrice felt the sweat burning his eyes and pouring down his back as he threw his strength against the sullen weight of the gun. Clouds of insects, attracted by their sweat, stung their necks and glued themselves to their faces.

They approached their target with agonizing slowness. The only safe route to pursue was a zigzag one, moving from one hut to the next, resting their aching muscles for a moment in the darkness before moving on. The revelry was at its height. The fire was now a mountain of glowing red coal, pouring out heat. The voices of the men were thick with alcohol. Gasping and panting in the shelter of a hut, Jean-Patrice tried to calculate the optimum range. A hundred yards would allow the shot to spread well; but if they could not guarantee accuracy, everything would have been wasted. It would be better to try for fifty, if they dared get so close. He peered around the wall. They also needed a field of fire clear of huts and trees, which would not be easy to obtain.

"There's a flat top on that rise," he said to Hyppolite. "If we can get her there, we'll have a clear range downhill. What do you think?"

Hyppolite nodded. "Very well. We can try."

"The others will wait here. The position is rather bare. We don't want to expose everyone to more danger than necessary. Let's just catch our breath."

Hyppolite looked at the sky. "It's getting light, Jean-Patrice. We haven't got time to rest."

The East was indeed lightening with a coy flush. "Then let's at least swap wheels. My shoulder is raw." They began lumbering up the rise. It was crushingly heavy work. He would have pressed Raymond into helping them but that he did not trust the man not to betray them in an attempt to save his own skin. He had given Schultze strict instructions to shoot Raymond down at the first false move.

Inch by inch they heaved the gun up the mound, their feet slithering in the sand, the iron rims of the wheels cutting their shoulders cruelly. They grasped for support at roots and saplings where they could. At one point, the weapon began to slide sideways, almost rolling disastrously on its flank. It was Hyppolite's strength which saved it from going over and crushing Jean-Patrice. They hauled it back into position with great gasps and grunts which Jean-Patrice devoutly hoped the enemy could not hear. The sky was brightening with what seemed like unnatural speed; their progress was far too slow. A pink light had already begun to touch the tops of the trees. If only they had started an hour earlier, he thought in anguish.

The ground leveled out at last. They were reaching the top of the mound. Sprawling on the earth, Jean-Patrice peered over the edge. As he had thought, the place gave a good vantage point from which to fire. If only they could get the gun set up and trained before they were detected. The Fang appeared to have started to eat their ghastly meal. They were crowding eagerly around the spit, their weapons laid aside.

"Now's our chance," he panted to Hyppolite. "We'll never have another one half so good."

Working like fiends, they manhandled the gun into place on top of the hill. There was no vegetation except some spindly shrubs up here. They were in full view of the enemy. There was no choice but to concentrate on the work and ignore their exposed state. Now a serious problem presented itself: although the barrel could be elevated, there was no mechanism for it to be depressed. It remained pointing obstinately forward. Their silver charge would fly harmlessly over the heads of the enemy, to expend its fury uselessly on the dark and brooding cliff on the other side of the river.

"Shit," Jean-Patrice hissed. "We'll have to dig."

They got on their knees and each began to dig earth

away from the wheels with their hands, like a pair of dogs at a rabbit hole. Their nails broke and the skin was torn from their fingertips. The barrel sank slowly as they labored. The gun had only the most primitive of aiming systems, a foresight near the muzzle which had to be aligned through a back sight at the breech. Jean-Patrice kept pausing to check this with one eye squeezed shut until it appeared to him the weapon was trained on the huge bonfire, which was the focus of all the activity below. "Stop digging," he commanded Hyppolite. "If she goes too far down, we'll never get her up again!"

He had spoken too loud, or perhaps his voice had carried downhill; one of the Fang turned and looked up at them. Jean-Patrice saw the astonishment settle over the man's features.

"He has seen us," Hyppolite said unnecessarily.

Jean-Patrice took the fuse from his pocket and unrolled it. He attempted to insert it into the touch-hole. His hands were shaking so wildly that the powder he had twisted into the cord scattered all over the dull bronze. He could barely get the thing into the hole. There was a shout from below, then another.

"Eh, blanc," a hoarse voice called. "What you doing up there, eh?" There was some drunken laughter, then the boom of a musket being fired. The ball howled between Hyppolite and Jean-Patrice.

"Hurry, Jean-Patrice," Hyppolite said, his jaw clenched.

"I'm doing my best," Jean-Patrice panted. "Lie down!"

"I am fine where I am. Just hurry!"

"My hands are trembling!"

At last the fuse was in the touch-hole. He struck a match and applied the blue flame to the fuse. A few sparks spat out of the cord. It began to burn. They had done it. The die was cast. A sense of great peace, or perhaps a surrender to the implacable force of destiny, overcame him. He and Hyppolite stood side by side, staring down at the Fang, who stared back up at them, both sides motionless. In fact, nothing appeared to be moving in the world except the wisp of smoke coming from the fuse, which rose straight up in the still air for a while, and then faded away to nothing. They waited.

"Jean-Patrice," Hyppolite said, "the fuse has gone out."

Jean-Patrice had noticed something else. The creature that had been roasted on the spit did not seem, in the dawn light, to be a man after all. It was not quite the right shape. A fresh hide was pegged out on the ground near it, bearing the number 5 branded on the rump. The Fang were not preparing to eat one of the slain Askaris after all, but the official calf, which they had found and murdered during the night.

"That is an outrage!" Jean-Patrice exclaimed, his bloodshot eyes stretching wide.

They were enveloped in a thunderclap which squeezed their hearts and shook the earth beneath their feet and thrust their eardrums into their brains. Regaining his senses as he staggered away, Jean-Patrice saw that the Fang camp had vanished under a pall of black and grey smoke. The cannon was also gone. Unsecured, it had flown backwards down the mound, leaving in its wake broken saplings and the deep ruts of its wheels in the soft earth. Hyppolite pointed. It lay half-buried at the foot of the hillock, its muzzle still pouring smoke.

Deafened, they made their way through the battlefield murk, trying to discern the results of their shot. It was a world without form or inhabitants, though fire rained down. A strange figure emerged out of the clouds: Schultze, his shirt front clotted with his own gore, his India-rubber elephant's trunk dangling, his Mannlicher in his hands. As they watched, he paused and assumed a military position with one foot forward and the rifle to his shoulder. He took aim at something and fired. They heard the shot dimly, as at a great distance. He nodded to them, reloaded and proceeded on his way, vanishing into the fog.

Jean-Patrice stumbled in the opposite direction, searching for Catherine. It was essential they get to the dugouts and paddle away from this place before the surviving enemy recovered their wits. The ghostly shapes of huts appeared. Some, he saw, were smoldering, their palm frond roofs kindled by cinders falling from the sky. Their cannon shot had blown the coals of the Fang bonfire into the air, with the effect of a small volcanic eruption, explaining the quantity of dense smoke that swirled everywhere and the glowing ash that continued to rain down.

He found her at last, behind the hut where he had left her. She was squatting beside their baggage, holding tight to Chloë, who appeared to be very shaken. She had her hands over her ears, her eyes wide and frightened. He embraced them, half-crying in the relief of finding them again. She was saying something to him, but he could not hear her.

"They've killed the official calf," he bawled at her. He could not make out her reply, but she was pointing her finger urgently in the direction of the river. "Yes, yes," he shouted, "we must get away. I am a little deafened. Where is Raymond?"

He saw her lips moving but her voice was only a thin buzz. She made gestures indicating that he had fled, she knew not where.

"Very well. Let's find Schultze and Hyppolite and set off." He hoisted the gorilla into his arms and took Catherine's hand. They made their way in the direction of the river. There seemed to be rather a lot of flame and smoke in the village now. He could see one or two roofs burning in earnest. He was experiencing severe pains in his ears; perhaps his eardrums had at last given way under the assaults they had experienced during this frightful night. The effect was to make his balance precarious. And Chloë was heavy. He found himself staggering from time to time, aiming in one direction but being carried by his legs in another. Catherine had to haul on his arm to steer him.

Black whirlwinds of smoke overtook them, blotting out the path ahead and choking them. Then a gust of wind cleared the air a little. Jean-Patrice found himself at the edge of the Fang camp. The ground was pock-marked with little craters, the banana grove in shreds. Far fewer of the Fang had been severely injured than he had anticipated. Some were bleeding profusely. Others appeared to have been struck by the smaller denominations and were less incapacitated. It was difficult to estimate how severe a blow he had dealt the tribesmen, but he had certainly failed to inflict mass death on them. He was rather relieved than otherwise, although there was now the inconvenience that some, at least, were bent on revenge. He saw a man, seated on the ground, pick up his musket and aim at them. There was a plume of smoke. He had the sense of something flying past his head at great speed. Catherine jolted him into action, breaking his trance. They hurried toward the river. Looking over his shoulder, he could see that others were firing at them, or preparing to fire.

He had begun to hear things, but not the sounds of the empirical world. His head was filled with the throbbing of some demonic orchestra, produced by his damaged eardrums. He was reminded of the overture to a Wagner opera, The Valkyrie, which he had heard performed in Paris a year or two earlier. He had been very impressed by it. One day he must go to Bayreuth and see the whole thing. The pain in his head was sickening. His chest hurt. He coughed heavily and spat mingled soot and blood. The river appeared through the smoke, its surface glinting in the early morning sunlight. At the landing, Hyppolite was already waiting. He was standing thigh-deep in the shallows, holding the mooring lines of the two remaining canoes. He had pushed all the others out into the channel, to make pursuit more difficult; they were now spinning at a distance downstream. He waved frantically to hurry them up.

They stumbled down the bank and threw their baggage and the spare rifles into one of the dugouts. "Where is Schultze?" Jean-Patrice shouted at Hyppolite.

Hyppolite shrugged impatiently. "We must go," Jean-Patrice faintly heard him reply.

"We can't leave him!" He helped Catherine into the canoe and looked back. Smoke was roiling into the sky from the roofs of the village. He could see the orange flames leaping upward briskly. "Good heavens," he muttered. The whole of Bassongo might well burn down, like a miniature Pompeii. In his somewhat exhausted and dazed state, the comparison haunted him, lodging in his brain. The Fang bonfire, of course, was Vesuvius. The river stood for the Bay of Naples. He and Catherine were ancient Neapolitans, fleeing in their boats across the Mediterranean. Like the Wagnerian overture in his ears, this was a convenient refuge for his mind, but there were more serious issues at hand. He could see one or two Fang tribesmen appearing through the smoke now, carrying muskets.

Hyppolite grasped his arm and indicated the enemy. "Most of them are still alive!" he shouted.

"I know. Perhaps we should have used the cutlery, after all."

"We must go, Jean-Patrice!"

"We can't leave Schultze." He drew his revolver and fired a shot at the approaching tribesmen. They scattered. But a spout of water erupted next to one of the dugouts, evidence of returned fire. "Lie down in the canoe!" he yelled at Catherine. She obeyed, holding Chloë in her arms. He searched the banks for any sign of Schultze. Where was the wretched man? He fired another shot at the enemy.

"Maybe he is dead already."

"No. There he is."

MARIUS GABRIEL

Schultze had finally materialized, plodding doggedly out of the smoke with his rifle in one hand. He was carrying his medicine bag in the other. Over his shoulders he had slung his shotgun and various knapsacks. His white suit, though bloodstained, made a glaring target. Jean-Patrice could see Fang musketeers mustering from the wreckage of their camp and leveling their weapons at the German. He blazed away at them with his revolver in an attempt to deflect their intentions. Hyppolite, more systematic, picked off a man carefully with his rifle and reloaded. Nevertheless, smoke squirted from several of the Fang guns towards Schultze. He stopped in his tracks. Jean-Patrice held his breath, thinking Schultze must be hit. But the doctor put down his bag, turned to face the enemy and adopted his firing stance, one foot forward, the rifle to his shoulder, like a lead soldier. The Fang scattered. They had evidently learned to appreciate the accuracy of Schultze's Mannlicher.

"Come on, Schultze," Jean-Patrice screamed. Schultze made a weary gesture and proceeded in his unhurried way towards them. The Fang were now firing at the dugouts again. Fountains spouted from the river. Jean-Patrice reloaded his revolver, noting that he was not as cool under fire as he had been when this entertainment had started yesterday. His nerves had begun to fray. He dropped some of the bullets and then found difficulty in closing the chamber since he had loaded badly. He began to cough again and spat out a quantity of blood. He had probably strained his lungs pushing the six-pounder up the hill. He felt weak and ill.

At last Schultze reached them. He looked very tired. Jean-Patrice saw that, incredibly, he was carrying the *Liber Libidinorum* under one arm. They helped him into Hyppolite's canoe. He sank down onto his back with his Mannlicher beside him, holding the medical bag on his chest. Jean-Patrice pushed the dugout away from the mooring. Hyppolite began to paddle with great energy

254

downriver. Jean-Patrice pushed their own canoe away, then clambered in, his weight almost upsetting the boat. He looked down at Catherine to see that she was unhurt and then began paddling after Hyppolite and Schultze. Something struck him a glancing blow on the left arm. Luckily not a bullet, perhaps some wadding from one of the muskets. He glanced over his shoulder. The Fang had come down to the water's edge and were staring after them. They had stopped firing and showed no inclination to enter the river. Behind them, Bassongo was alight. Black smoke towered into the sky. He paused in his paddling to look at the scene. It occurred to him for the first time that he would never see this place again. It might even cease to exist; unless a kindly rain fell soon, the village was doomed. The dugout was now in the channel. Pulled along by the current, it began to slide swiftly toward the sea.

A patch of colour on the bank caught the corner of his eye, a green frock with a design of red roses. It was Sophie, standing on a rock, watching them go by. She had not been eaten, after all. What her fate would be, nobody could say; but in that, she shared the common condition of all humanity. Cheered by the sight of her, he waved. She half-raised her hand in return, her eyes fixed on his. He must look to her like the little wooden European in the toy he had given her, he thought.

At the same moment, he had another thought. He suddenly knew why her mother had said it was all her fault and her father had been so angry with her, why they had beaten her and pushed her away. He could see it in her face. It had always been there, he simply hadn't understood until now.

Had she put the viper in Joliet's bed because he'd made her abort her pregnancies? Because she was maddened by the endless extracurricular activities detailed in the leather journal? Had he hurt her by some selfish sexual brutality? Had the oganga wipoga commanded her to do it as a punishment for a blanc who broke the rules? Perhaps for all these reasons. He would never know.

They watched one another out of sight.

22

It was Catherine who pointed out, once they had rounded the bend in the river and were on the next reach, that he had been shot twice. He'd been aware of considerable pain in his shoulder while paddling the dugout but had attributed that to bruises and sprains sustained while maneuvering the six-pounder. He hadn't noticed that his shirt was stiff with dried blood. He was continuing to cough up a quantity of scarlet froth.

Three miles or so further down the river, they steered the dugouts to a sandbank and beached them. All was quiet. She helped him take off his clothes and examined him with great care. He could see one of the wounds well enough; what he'd thought was a piece of wadding had actually been a musket ball, which had pierced his upper arm and was now wedged between the big muscles there, causing him great pain. The other ball had struck him high up on the right shoulder and was lodged under the shoulder blade. Both the arm and the shoulder were severely bruised and swollen. He was starting to feel as if his upper body were being crushed in an iron vice. Every breath stabbed him like a sword.

Schultze got wearily out of his canoe and looked at the

wounds. He produced his little notebook, which he had carefully tucked into his top pocket, and wrote:

THE BULLETS MUST BE REMOVED!

"Can't it wait until we are further away?" Jean-Patrice asked.

EACH ONE BREEDING
COUNTLESS STAPHYLOCOCCI
UNTIL DISINFECTED & CLOSED

he scrawled. He began to dig in his bag. Jean-Patrice's hearing was returning slowly. The Wagner was fading and he could hear the song of birds all around. He looked at Catherine. Her face was so fresh. "I'm glad we're alive," he said.

She nodded. "So am I."

"Although I have the feeling that our troubles are just beginning. We might wish that we were dead by and by."

He sat on the sandbank where Schultze indicated. The doctor peered at him rather myopically, having lost his glasses, then unceremoniously dug into his arm with the forceps, much as Jean-Patrice had once dug into Adeline. Jean-Patrice roared in pain, trying to get away from the infernal implement but Hyppolite threw his arms around him and held him fast while Schultze probed. Jean-Patrice ground his teeth as he felt the steel poke into the swollen fibers of his arm. It felt as though the forceps were red-hot and scraping against the bone. The pain intensified until he felt he could not bear it any longer. A final blinding burst of agony and then Schultze sat back. He was holding a misshapen lump of lead in the forceps, turning it from side to side to study it.

"It's all in one piece," Hyppolite said. "That is lucky. And they were using small bullets. A big one would have taken off your arm."

Jean-Patrice was still panting, his mouth open, tears streaming from his swollen eyes. Catherine wiped the sweat from his brow with her fingers. "I didn't make half so much fuss when I was in labor," she said reprovingly.

"Oh, God," he muttered. The initial operation had in some way blunted his senses. He sat with his head hanging dully and tried not to whimper as the doctor swabbed the wound with iodine and sewed it up.

"He wants you to lie down," Hyppolite said, "so he can extract the other bullet."

"Oh, God," he said again. He lay face down and naked on the silvery shingle, his head turned to one side. He could see a distant, dark smudge above the forest where Bassongo was burning. Hyppolite sat on him, making him groan. "You are not a lightweight, you know," he said.

"You would do the same for me, Jean-Patrice. And you are no lightweight, either."

He felt Catherine sit on his legs. Then Schultze began to dig in the wound. It swiftly became unbearable, a hole being burrowed into the centre of his being. He bellowed at the shocking pain, then was ashamed at his own bawling. He managed to remain quiet for a while. Then the torment took a new direction, wrenching at his nerves. He begged for mercy, for two minute's respite, for morphia, for chloroform. He had heard of men begging like this during surgery. With some part of his mind he listened to his own babbling, recognizing it as tallying with what he had heard. Soon he would start sobbing and calling on his mother, whom he could barely remember. It was shameful. They should have given him something to bite on, a piece of leather, anything to silence him. He dug his fingers into the sand and clenched his teeth and tried to remain silent. The implements gouged and tore at his flesh. He squeezed his eyes closed, managing to suppress any sound except gasps. The world became red and black by turns. The dizziness was welcome. He hoped it would carry him away to Lethe, the river of forgetting.

At last he felt the tugging of the gut thread in his muscle and knew that Schultze was sewing him up. He started coming back to himself. He had been in some Homeric vision, he realized, some crimson passage or other remembered from his schooldays describing how bronze weapons pierced Greek flesh on the beaches of Troy, singing of the sorrow and rage of warriors. Poetry was usually better than life, he reflected. It was neater and less painful, and it rhymed.

He felt Chloe's leathery fingers stroking his face. He opened his eyes blearily and spat blood. The world was unnaturally bright. Schultze and Hyppolite were peering down at him. "It is finished, Jean-Patrice," Hyppolite said. "You did well." They went down to wash their arms in the river.

"Have they really finished?" he mumbled.

"Look." Catherine's hand was cupped in front of his face. In her pink palm were five or six bloody fragments of lead. "Dr. Schultze was so clever. He found all of them."

"It felt as though he were digging them out with a shovel."

"Oh no, he was very delicate," she replied seriously. "Two of your ribs are broken. That's why you were spitting blood."

He raised himself slowly, feeling groggy. "You needn't sound so happy about it."

"The wound in your back is deep. If you weren't made like an ox, it would have killed you. Why do you pull that face?"

"Oxen have no testicles," he said.

"Forgive me. I can see that you have yours." She held a flask of water to his lips so he could drink. She threw the pieces of lead away, rinsed her hand in the water and showed him her empty, glistening palm. "There. It is done." She washed the blood off his body and helped him to dress. His arm was bound up and there was a dressing on his shoulder but they did not have enough bandage to strap up his ribs. He would have to suffer that as best he could. Hyppolite squatted beside Jean-Patrice.

"We can't stay here, Jean-Patrice."

"I don't think I can paddle, Hyppolite, at least until tomorrow."

"She can paddle." Jean-Patrice had noticed that Hyppolite seldom looked at Catherine, or mentioned her name. "The current is strong here. It is just a question of steering away from the banks. You can lie and rest. You have broken bones, Jean-Patrice. That makes a man weak. I must stay with the German. He is also injured."

"I am easily able to paddle," Catherine said simply. "Go, Hyppolite."

Schultze offered Jean-Patrice the morphine syringe. "I think it would be best," Jean-Patrice said. Schultze injected Jean-Patrice's arm and then his own.

They clambered back into the dugouts and pushed off, Hyppolite and Schultze going on ahead. Jean-Patrice was aching terribly now. His arm and shoulder were almost too stiff to move. He felt weariness overcome him. He put his back against the bags in the front of the canoe, facing Catherine. She paddled with easy grace, her slender arms strong and supple. He rocked to her rhythm, finding it almost sexual. His eyelids grew heavy as lead.

"Sleep," she commanded. He gathered the gorilla in his arms. The morphine, mixed with God knew what other drugs, rose in him like a dark tide. He closed his eyes. The swaying, gliding motion of the canoe carried him away and he slept.

When he next opened his eyes, he saw the afternoon sky above him, blue patches framed with white, wet cloud. He watched it for a while, wondering whether he were dreaming, whether all the memories that drifted through his mind were also dreams. The world came back to him slowly. He lifted himself to look at Catherine. She had taken off her blouse to paddle unrestricted by clothing.

Her naked breasts were high and round, paler than her arms, her nipples dark stars that drew his eyes. She smiled at his expression. "You must not stare at me like that, Jean-Patrice, or you can paddle yourself."

"But you're so beautiful."

"I haven't undressed to amuse you. My clothes were chafing me. Look the other way."

He found the water flask and drank. "I feel very stiff. Tomorrow I'll be stronger." He turned to look down the river. The other dugout was not in sight. "Are they far away?"

"I don't know. Hyppolite doesn't like me. He blames me for everything. He thinks I tempted Father Jacques, like Eve with the apple. They'll wait for us when evening comes."

Chloë lay in the bottom of the canoe, her eyes half-closed, sucking her thumb rhythmically. It would be interesting to note down, he thought, all the human conduct she exhibited. The chattering of teeth, embraces, sucking the thumb – all the behavior of a child. Could one classify the intellect of the animal in these terms? Assigning to her, say, the intelligence of a three year-old? But then there was the difficult question of speech... Dreamily, he watched the banks glide past. "These trees tower to such immense heights that at times it is dizzying to look up at them," he said.

"You should sleep some more, my dear."

"When I came up the river in the gunboat, these trees horrified me. Everything about the river was horrible to me. Now I see how beautiful it is."

"Do you?"

"The first gods were trees. The first sacred place was a grove. Only when man learned to cut the trees down and make lifeless columns of them did trees stop being sacred. Then they became incomprehensible and frightening. Relics of a past we preferred to forget. Then the forest stopped being magical and became terrifying. It became the dark and evil woods of Lafontaine and Grimm."

"Try to rest, Jean-Patrice."

"This world is not simply primeval, Catherine. It is prelapsarian. Life surges from the earth, majestic and beautiful. Look at these perpendicular torrents of sap and xylem, exploding into clouds of chlorophyll as they reach the sun! Do you know who Darwin was?"

"Father Jacques told me something about Darwin."

"I can imagine what the good Father Jacques had to say. Did you discuss Darwin before or after he impregnated you?"

"You are cruel!"

"I think the question is a fair one."

"We discussed very little after he impregnated me, as you put it," she said in a low voice.

"Ah, well, you see, evolution had already run its course by then. I hope at least he recognized that The Origin Of Species is as great a volume as the Bible. From it, one understands that these trees are locked in mortal combat, one with another." He clasped his two hands together. "They are fighting for light and air and water. For the materials of life. Yet the struggle is so noble compared to the bloody struggles of men. It is without sin. It takes eons to accomplish a victory." He looked at her with large, drugged eyes. "And the victories of evolution seldom result in the death of an adversary. No, the result is usually another adaptation for the vanquished, a higher rung on the ladder of evolution. You see the beauty of it?"

"I think so."

"Evolution tends towards perfection. But man is different, my beloved. His wars are nasty, brutish and short. There is nothing at the end but devastation. He is capable, bug that he is, of destroying all this in a generation." He turned his head to look at the green forest which slid past on either bank. "Every tree, every elephant, every butterfly."

"A generation will pass and all this will still be here,

Jean-Patrice."

"I'm not so sure. My superior in Libreville believes that in fifty years, Africa will be a paradise on earth. But what if it is a hell, instead?"

"It can be neither a hell or a heaven. It can only be something between."

"But what did we achieve in Bassongo?" he asked restlessly. "We inoculated a few hundred people and then burned down their village."

"They'll rebuild it. To make a house like that takes only two days."

"We shot those men with silver coins."

"They shot you with lead bullets," she pointed out.

"That's what I mean!" He raised himself, agitated. "That's what I'm referring to, Catherine! A pointless exchange of cruelty and violence. What does it mean? What did it achieve except suffering and death?" Tears spilled down his cheeks.

She stopped paddling and came forward. She knelt in front of him and put her arms around him. She drew his head down to her breasts. He smelled the warm, clean smell of her sweat, tasted the salt of her skin. "The morphine is upsetting your emotions. Sleep. It's best."

It was early evening when he next surfaced. The canoe was sliding along a silvery reach of river as smooth as a mirror. Everything that was reflected in it seemed even more perfect than the original. He roused himself. An immense silence was around them. No bird cried, no monkey whooped. She had covered her breasts again. Perhaps he had only dreamed that part. "How do you feel?" she asked, her voice quiet, as though she feared to disturb the great hush.

"A little shaky. But not so drugged. I think I talked a lot of nonsense, earlier. Forgive me. You must be so tired."

"I hope we find Hyppolite and the Doctor soon. I would like to rest."

He touched her arm and felt her muscles trembling with tiredness. "Give me the paddle. Lie down for a while. I'm much stronger now."

She surrendered the paddle to him when he pressed her and curled up next to his legs as he took up a position on the thwart. The current was strong; as Hyppolite had said, it was principally a question of steering the canoe away from obstacles. Despite his bravado, he found himself badly crippled with both sides of his body damaged and grunted with pain as the water pulled on the oar.

"Were you really so stoical while you were in labor?" he asked her.

"No. I only said that to make you feel braver. I gave birth alone, in the bush. I didn't want anyone to know or hear. I thought they would take the baby away from me. Or even kill her. But I screamed and cried, as all women do."

"My poor Catherine."

"It's all over, now." She smiled up at him. "I was very ignorant. Do you want to know how ignorant I was? I didn't even know there would be a cord. I was educated by the nuns from my childhood. They didn't tell us about anything like that. If I'd been like the other village girls, I would have gone to initiation camp and the old women would have told us all those things which girls need to learn." She laughed softly. "I found there was a rope coming from inside my body, tying Élise to me. I thought it was a divine punishment, and that I would be connected to her like that forever so that everyone could see how I had sinned. I didn't know what to do. I was dreadfully frightened."

"What happened?" he asked.

"I was alone with her in the forest for a long time, almost too weak to walk. I fed her from my breasts — I knew how to do that, at least — and made a nest in the grass and slept with her. When I woke up, the oganga wipoga had found me."

"That old hag?"

"Hush," she said, laying her fingers on his lips, as she had done before. "She hears everything."

"How had she found you?"

"They say she smells the blood of each birth. She wasn't so blind in those days, and she cut the cord for me and helped me with the afterbirth. If she hadn't come, I might have stayed there like a fool until some animal found us." She looked up at his face. "I shouldn't tell you these things."

"Why not? I want to hear everything about you."

"Women are not as simple as men, Jean-Patrice. We always have many complicated things in our past." She pointed. "Look."

In the gathering dusk, a pinpoint of red light had appeared. He steered towards it. There was a long, sandy spit in the middle of the river, with hummocks of grass and trees growing upon it. Hyppolite had beached his dugout here and had built a fire. When they'd pulled their own canoe up on the sand, Jean-Patrice went to help him search for dead wood in the dying light.

"We must keep a fire burning all night," Hyppolite said. "There are crocodiles and hippos in the river. The hippos are more dangerous than the crocodiles. They can bite a man in half. Tomorrow we must stop earlier in the day and gather enough wood to last all night."

"How is Schultze?"

"He slept all day."

"So did I. I'll be better tomorrow. Have we anything to eat?"

"A bag of plantain meal. The woman can make fufu."

"She has a name," Jean-Patrice said mildly.

"I know her name."

"Why are you still angry with her, after so many years, Hyppolite? She was only seventeen when it happened."

"Among your people, a female of seventeen is a child. Among my people, a female of seventeen is a grown woman. Most already have a child at that age. Some have two."

"A female of seventeen taught by nuns is different from one raised by a proper mother. It was not her fault that she was beautiful."

Hyppolite had been tearing dead branches from a tree. He turned a grim face on Jean-Patrice. "If you think she is beautiful now, you should have seen her at seventeen," he said.

Jean-Patrice was struck by his tone. "Did you know her well?" he asked.

"She was like the full moon. All the men went to the mission to look at her."

"Even you?"

"Even me," he said with a bitter smile.

"And that was why you became a Christian?"

Hyppolite did not answer for a while, ripping at the dead wood with his great strength. "I asked her to marry me," he said at last.

Jean-Patrice paused with his armful of kindling. "I see."

"She would not even listen to me. The nuns said she was reserved for higher things. And then she started to grow a big belly. We saw what sort of higher things she was reserved for. She would not say who the father was. But when the child came, everyone knew. There was no other white man in Bassongo." The branch came away with a splintering crash. Hyppolite threw it onto the ground and began to break it into smaller pieces. "She went to the oganga wipoga. You understand? She was saying to all the world that she had left Jesus and the white man's god."

Jean-Patrice stood in silence, listening and watching. "And the priest killed himself?" he asked at length.

"The priest took a gun and killed himself. Do you know why?"

"Because he'd sinned?"

"No. Because she would not come back to him."
Wood splintered in the darkness. "Love is a viper that
bites men and has no cure."

"The same viper has bitten me."

"Everyone can see that, Jean-Patrice."

"It can't be easy for you. I'm sorry."

He chuckled. "What should I do? Kill you and carry
her away in a sack?" The velvety darkness had settled
now. Hyppolite had become a shape made of liquid
shadow. His voice was husky. "You are the first man she
has smiled at in seven years."

"I don't know what I would do," Jean-Patrice said
slowly, "if she ran away from me and would not come
back."

"None of us know what love may make us do." His
tone changed, becoming steadier. "We have enough wood
for the time being. Let's go back."

"We need to find milk and fruit for Schultze. And
Chloë needs to find the leaves she likes."

"I have not seen anyone on the river all day.
Tomorrow we'll pass a little fishing village. They will sell
us food."

"What sort of place is it?"

"Very small. A few huts."

"Are the people good?"

Hyppolite shrugged. "Sometimes."

They sat beside the fire while the fufu cooked. That
immense stillness hung all around them. It was not the
stillness of a closed room or of deafness, but the stillness
of a great space where nothing stirred. The stars burned
down from a clear night sky. Their blue fires seemed to
hiss. The slightest sound echoed and carried across the
water. The plop of a fish or the fall of a branch resonated
and gathered an awful significance before it faded away,
leaving speculations spreading like ripples. Schultze
looked very tired. Twenty-four hours had now elapsed
since he'd received his injury. He had brought some

bottles of wine with him from the Residency. These, poured into his funnel, and morphine, injected into his veins, were all that were sustaining him. He had allowed nobody to look at his wound. It was still bound up with the napkins from the Christmas dinner, now filthy rags. Jean-Patrice had taken a decision.

"The journey to Libreville will take at least ten days," he said quietly, "and that is if we do not lose our way or meet with some other misadventure. By then you may be dead, Schultze. The journey by canoe, with its inevitable stresses, will break down even your iron constitution." Schultze nodded his assent wearily to this. "If we find any settlement with the slightest appearance of civilization," he went on, "we will leave you to be taken care of there and send help for you once we reach Libreville. You'll be better resting in some hut than journeying on this river. We will leave money to pay for your care. The gunboat will come for you. Then we'll all meet up to drink a bottle of champagne in Libreville. What do you think?" Schultze nodded again, closing his eyes. They sat without speaking, each aware of the unlikelihood of any of them surviving to meet in Libreville.

The fufu was bland but filling and welcome sustenance. While they ate, the noises of the night began, quite suddenly, as though the curtain of a theatre had risen on a bustling scene. Frogs, insects and other nocturnal creatures began to shrill; bullfrogs rattled loudly to one another up and down the banks. Fish began to feed; the river plopped and splashed as they rose to snatch at flying things.

Jean-Patrice patted at his pockets and realized he had left all the cheroots behind in Bassongo. "It's a filthy habit," he said without much conviction. "Here is a perfect opportunity to give it up."

They slept in the canoes, agreeing that whoever should be awake would feed the fire to keep away predators. Chloë lay at his back. Catherine crept into his arms. Her small body molded itself so perfectly to his large one. She laid her head against his breast, her hands folded together under her chin. "Are you comfortable?" he asked.

"I feel like a little frog, sitting on the branch of a big, strong tree."

He smiled. "That is very poetic."

"Do you think they are coming after us?" she whispered.

"I don't know. Perhaps they'll get frightened and go back to their village."

"Perhaps. The Fang move their villages often. Perhaps they will go far away and never come back."

Some large creature swam past them in the darkness. They could hear its breathing and the ripple of water along its flanks. It went by, swimming upstream on some urgent business of its own. Catherine put her leg over his, hooking her heel behind his knee, and pulled his thigh between hers. Heat flooded into his loins at the intimate contact. He felt himself swell and grow erect. After a moment, she reached down and laid her hand on his erection. She made no effort to excite him. Her hand was still, as though touching some talisman that could protect them both; or perhaps her touch was a promise, a consolation, a reassurance. She drifted quickly into sleep, her hand still upon him.

They made an early start, even though a heavy, white mist hung on the river. The possibility that the Fang were pursuing them could not be ignored. They ate the cold remainder of the fufu and paddled silently down the stream through the dense curtains that barely stirred at their passage.

Jean-Patrice had slept badly. His arm and shoulder were, if anything, even more painful this morning. He and Catherine shared the paddling, changing places every hour. The heat of the day built up. Dark masses of forest began to appear through the mist as it lifted. The world was silent.

At mid-morning they reached the village, no more than a dozen huts scattered along the bank, overhung with plantains and palms. The place looked deserted until Hyppolite shouted a greeting. People emerged from the huts, thin and languid, staring with dull yellow eyes at the dugouts. Hyppolite waded ashore and talked with them for some time. Jean-Patrice saw the villagers gesturing with skinny arms. At last, Hyppolite came back to the dugouts.

"They've had fever here. But they say the sickness went away a week or more ago. I think it's safe. It's lucky, in a way. They've been too sick to fish and they need money. They'll look after Dr. Schultze. They have goat's milk and they'll make fruit juice. I've told them the whites will reward them if he survives."

They helped Schultze ashore. He was installed in the largest of the huts, on a low bed, with his medicine bag beside him and his Mannlicher on the other side. Jean-Patrice was reminded uncomfortably of some Teutonic knight being laid in his final resting place, with his sword and shield. Catherine showed the women how to feed him. They gave him some fresh goat's milk.

There was little to buy at the village, only some bunches of plantains and a bag of coarse maize flour. A woman also gave them a calabash of a sour, buttery confection made from the goat's milk. They divided the provisions up among the two canoes, in case they were separated.

Jean-Patrice led Chloë along the bank until she found a tree she liked. She tore off a branch and sat down for one of her long, slow feeds; but there was no time for that. Jean-Patrice gathered as much of the green stuff as the canoe could hold, so that she could continue munching all day.

When the time came to part, Schultze took out his notebook and began to write with his silver pencil, his longest communication yet:

THESE PEOPLE HAVE MALARIA.
I HAVE SALTS OF QUININE.
A FEW GRAINS
ARE SUFFICIENT TO DISPEL THE FEVER.
I WILL CARE FOR THEM &
THEY WILL CARE FOR ME.
GOODBYE, MY FRIENDS.
IF GOD WILLS IT, WE WILL
MEET AGAIN SOON!
IF NOT, WE WILL MEET AGAIN LATER,
AT SOME YET WIDER & DEEPER RIVER!
IT HAS BEEN A PRIVILEGE TO SHARE
THESE ADVENTURES WITH YOU.
GODSPEED!!!
AND DO NOT FORGET YOUR FRIEND
WHO AWAITS YOU ON THIS LONELY SHORE,
FRIEDERICH SCHULTZE.

"I hope you don't suffer too much boredom until we return for you," Jean-Patrice said, trying to encourage the wounded man.

Schultze patted the *Liber Libidinorum*, which lay beside him, perhaps to suggest that its pages would make the hours light, or perhaps to symbolize the resurgence of life over physical decay.

He produced the morphia syringe and gave Jean-Patrice a last, very large injection, a parting gift to make the day's paddling less painful. He also gave them a bottle of iodine, his shotgun and a bandolier of cartridges. Catherine cried as they left him and Jean-Patrice felt a knot forming in his own throat. However, Schultze's generous injection soon began to take effect, bleaching the colour out of his emotions and taking the pain from his wounds. He paddled steadily, his mind entering rich realms of speculation again.

23

Hyppolite glided on ahead of them. His canoe was lighter and his arms were stronger. He was soon out of sight. In these reaches, the river sprouted dozens of islands down its centre. Some were long spits covered with abundant vegetation, others mere sandbanks strewn with rocks. At each of these places they had to choose one or another of the channels, taking the risk that some submerged rock or sunken tree might rip the bottom out of their dugout. The sun beat down like a hammer. Catherine covered her head with a cloth.

Sprawled upon a sandbank, its jaws gaping, they came upon a huge crocodile. There was no option but to pass within a few feet of the monster. As though with instinctive knowledge of the danger, Chloë hid in the bottom of the canoe, covering her face with her hands and keening. Jean-Patrice froze in his place. The animal was as long as their canoe, easily able to upset them and devour them both if it so chose. Jean-Patrice observed it with the clarity of hallucination. Its eyes were malachite, green and mottled, the pupil an unpitying obsidian blade. The cavernous throat was colored like a papaya inside. Small birds were busy in its mouth, pecking at the shreds of its last meal, which were lodged, rotting, between its fangs. It did not stir its jagged and armored limbs as they slid past.

"That was surely the god of the river," he said, when they had left the beast behind. "And we are those birds, allowed to hop up and down in its jaws, until it decides to swallow us."

She peered at him from under the sunshade she had made, smiling. Her face was pearled with sweat. "The morphine makes you say strange things."

"I have been thinking of Darwin again. About how I may snatch you from these jaws."

"The jaws of the crocodile?"

"The jaws of this Africa." He paused. "No, more than that. The jaws of this slow and snaking river of evolution."

"I don't understand you."

He gazed around with morphine-glassy eyes. "Look at this world, Catherine. It is at the beginning of time. Nothing has changed since the Creator first breathed life into it."

"Father Jacques taught us that one can believe either in Evolution or in Creation," she said. "Not in both."

"You must have had some interesting conversations with Father Jacques," he retorted.

"He was no less an educated man than you are, Jean-Patrice."

"By the way, do you ever visit his grave?"

"No. Why?"

"Well, I think he is still trying to run after you."

"What do you mean?" she asked uneasily.

He chuckled. "Let us just say, non requiescat in pacem. But let us assume, for the purposes of argument, that I was not an educated man like Father Jacques but an African like you. Or rather, like one of those Fang warriors we fought, my hair stiffened into zigzags with clay and a bone through my nose. Not so long ago, not to put too fine a point on it, I was not much different from Chloë over there." He looked at the gorilla, who was placidly browsing on her mountain of leaves and smiled. "Through some accident of fate – let us suppose that my canoe is washed out to sea and that the current carries me far – I find myself emerging on a shore in the Northern world."

"You mean France?"

"Yes. There, certain developments take place. My black skin grows pale under a milder sun. My woolly hair uncurls itself and grows long and fair. My eyes change from brown to clear blue. The cold obliges me to abandon my custom of going around stark naked and barefoot. I make myself boots and fine clothes. I encounter natural advantages – horses, cattle, iron in the rocks and wheat in the fields. I learn to dominate all these things and make myself master of new sciences and new arts. I evolve into a new being. You see?"

"I see," she said in a flat voice.

"My nature evolves from simple forms to more complex forms, from lower forms to higher forms." He held up his hand. "Then, by the same quirk of fate, except now reversed, I am washed back up this crocodile river to the place where I was born. There I find you, in puris naturalibus, still in much the same state as I once was. Nevertheless, I fall in love with you, of course. And now I want to take you back with me and show you the great cities that I have built. How do I go about it? How can it be achieved without the long process which I have described? How can your adaptation be accomplished in only one lifetime?"

"This is a very charming story," she said in a clipped voice. "Have you heard what your cousins, the Belgians, are doing in the Congo? How they rape and torture and mutilate women? How they cut off heads and put them on stakes? How they brand men with red-hot irons and hack off children's hands with bush knives? All these actions are no doubt evidence of their higher evolution."

He was taken aback. "This does not enter into the story I am describing."

"My daughter is there," she said. "So it enters into my story."

"That also is beside the point."

"Perhaps you can spare me the point altogether."

"I didn't mean to offend you."

Her eyes glistened darkly. "I never thought to hear you say such things, Jean-Patrice."

He smiled benignly at her. "You don't understand. Or perhaps I phrased it badly. I did not mean to say that you cannot evolve, Catherine – merely wondering how swiftly you will be able to do so."

She picked up the spare paddle and in one swift movement brought it cracking down on his head. Stunned and in considerable pain, he fell off the thwart and sprawled among Chloe's leaves, almost upsetting them into the river. The gorilla hooted in alarm. His long legs were tangled in the baggage, trapping him. He clapped his hand to his head and found his palm wet with blood. Groaning, he managed to sit up and saw she had taken his place on the thwart and was paddling smoothly. Even the morphine could not dull his headache.

"This does not incline me to withdraw anything I have said," he groaned.

"Don't talk to me," she said briskly.

"You don't have to paddle," he said, holding his aching head in his hands. "I can do that."

"I would rather be eaten by a crocodile than be rowed by you. Now be silent."

She was quite capable of giving him another swipe with the paddle, so he obeyed. He allowed himself to be enveloped by the morphia haze, self-pity forming a kind of abstract lump in the throat.

Plant nature was easier to understand than human nature. He stared at the banks, his mind losing itself in the infinite varieties of vegetal form. The leaf was the

GABON

common currency, but what a variety of denominations there were! Leaves as big as sails and leaves smaller than a mouse's ear. Leaves like ladders and leaves like boats. Warlike leaves that were lanceolate and hastate and subulate. Gentle leaves that were pinnate and lobate and palmate. Fierce leaves with divaricate spiniform teeth. And everything wound about with fronds and tendrils and lianas, knotted together with vines and creepers, studded with crimson thorns and yellow flowers and purple berries; it was bewildering and wonderful, a vast society of living beings interdependent on one another. And somewhere in this green world, Man had a place. Or Woman, in the case of Catherine. A kingfisher, brilliant blue and yellow, burst from the bank and plummeted into the water, emerging with a pewter fish in its beak.

He glanced hesitantly at Catherine's back. He longed to point this out to her but he had made a faux pas. He was aware that he had been unwise in his speech, but he was struggling to grasp at just why and how he had offended her so bitterly.

The morphine had enlightened his thoughts. His brain felt like a crystal cave, studded with brilliant and lucid notions. It was only a question of expressing them in language transparent enough to be understood. He cleared his throat. "Was I wrong to point out that the Africans are at a different point on the evolutionary ladder from the Europeans? That does not seem to brook any argument. But I'm sorry if I offended you." There was no response from her. He thought for a while. "Evolution takes some strange paths. After all, one can look at the Dinosaurs, those terrible reptiles of the Mesozoic age. What have they become, in the end, but the harmless birds? Who could have predicted such an outcome of natural selection?" He laughed. She made no reply of any kind. "Or let us consider Chloë, munching on her leaves over there. At some distant point, she and we shared a common ancestor. Yet look at us now, how far apart we

277

have grown!" His smile became a frown. "Your remarks about the atrocities of the Belgians were very upsetting, Catherine. I am not responsible for the behavior of King Leopold. Nor am I responsible for the forced-labor gangs in this country. In fact, I abhor—"

He broke off. She had laid down the paddle and, without looking at him, curled up in the front of the canoe to sleep. He got onto the thwart and took over, looking around. The afternoon heat was immense. The river was widening steadily, spreading into a low valley and turning from a stream into a sheet, its surface brilliant as steel under the colorless dazzle of the sky. On this lagoon, which he could not remember from the upriver journey in the gunboat, birds wheeled in great profusion, especially herons and ducks. He picked up Schultze's shotgun and loaded it. Allowing the canoe to drift, he sighted at the biggest flock he could see and fired. He was gratified to see a bird fall from the air. Catherine and Chloë both leaped up, staring in fright.

"I've shot a duck," he said. "Sorry to frighten you."

"You idiot," she said furiously. "Haven't you taken enough lives?"

"We have nothing to eat tonight but fufu," he pointed out humbly.

"And you're too evolved to eat fufu, of course." She lay back down without another word.

"While you're awake," he said, "I'll try and bag another one. There isn't much meat on a wild duck." He paddled over to his kill and recovered the duck, a handsome brown bird with a black face. His second and third attempts were misses. He looked anxiously at Catherine, knowing she was in a fury with him. His fourth shot brought down another duck. He collected this one as well, a black bird with a white face. Chloë shrank away from the dead things, muttering in dismay. "You can sleep in peace, now," he said to Catherine. "Got two." She made no response.

He paddled on, the canoe crawling across the lagoon, which had little current. An hour passed. Up ahead, he could see that there were several islands, shimmering in the heat haze that hung above the water. Something glinted in the sun. It was Hyppolite, beached at one of the islands, waving his paddle to attract their attention. Jean-Patrice rowed in to the beach and greeted him. Catherine sat up and looked around. Hyppolite was stripped to the waist, rinsing his arms and chest in the water.

"From here onward, the river is very complicated," Hyppolite said. "There are many routes, many islands and swamps. All of them lead to the coast. If you follow the current, you'll get there. But there are always choices. It will be impossible for you to know which one I've taken — and I am now much faster than you are. I cannot always be waiting for you." He stood up, water streaming from his glistening, muscular body. "I suggest that we split up, Jean-Patrice. We have nothing to gain by trying to stay together. The sooner I can reach Libreville, the sooner I can get help for Schultze. What do you think?"

"I agree," Catherine said, before Jean-Patrice could answer. "The best idea is to split up. I will go with you, Hyppolite." She gathered her bags and got out of the canoe.

Jean-Patrice felt as though he'd been struck in the heart. "Catherine!"

"As the more evolved species, you do not need my help." She turned her back on him and began stowing her things in Hyppolite's canoe.

Hyppolite watched her in surprise. "What has happened between you?" he demanded.

"He has been explaining to me how superior his race is to ours. He should be able to manage alone."

"Catherine, don't do this," Jean-Patrice said.

"You don't command me any longer," she said. "We're in Africa, the world at the beginning of time, before there was Monsieur or Madame."

279

"I am not commanding you. I am asking you."

"And I'm refusing."

"He is injured," Hyppolite pointed out.

"Yes, and you're uninjured," she replied. "You're better able to look after me. Natural selection demands that I go with you."

"He needs someone to put iodine on his wounds."

"He'll have to manage that by himself," she retorted.

"Please, Catherine," Jean-Patrice said in a tight voice, "this is not a very amusing joke."

"I'm not joking," she replied icily. "Hyppolite, let's go."

Hyppolite stared at Jean-Patrice steadily, standing with his legs apart in the shallows, his powerful arms hanging by his sides. His machete was thrust at an angle through his belt. His gaze had become heavy and glittering, as it done once before, in Bassongo, when he had asked why Catherine was in Jean-Patrice's bed. "Is it agreed, then?" Hyppolite said. "The woman comes with me?"

"No! I don't agree!" Jean-Patrice said.

"What do you say?" Hyppolite asked Catherine, without talking his eyes off Jean-Patrice.

"I want to go with you. The white man can go alone. I have had enough of white men."

"You are one," Hyppolite said to Jean-Patrice, "and we are two. We are in the majority."

"Catherine, let me speak to you alone." Jean-Patrice moved to go to her, but Hyppolite stepped in front of him, blocking his way.

"She has already spoken, Jean-Patrice."

Jean-Patrice might have been a match for the corporal once, but in his present condition, he had no chance in any kind of fight. Hyppolite could cut him down in a second and leave him here for the crocodiles. "What will I do without you?" he pleaded with Catherine.

"Natural selection will produce the correct outcome," she replied. "Give me Chloë. I will take her."

"No! She's mine! Leave me that, at least!" Only

shreds of his dignity were left him. His anguish and desperation were so great that he was thrown back on the banal. He picked one of the ducks out of his dugout and gave it to Hyppolite. "This is the bigger of the two. You take it." Hyppolite nodded his thanks and tossed the bird into his canoe. "And we'll share the flour out in three equal parts."

"I will find food," Hyppolite said shortly. "Keep the flour. We'll go. There are still two hours of sun. Try to follow us, Jean-Patrice."

"I'm too slow," Jean-Patrice said. "My wounds are very painful." He glanced at Catherine for some sign of compassion, but her face was stony. "Perhaps I'll spend the night here."

"As you please. Follow the current, Jean-Patrice. It will take you to Libreville." Hyppolite pushed his dugout into the water with easy strength and climbed in. With a few strokes of the paddle, he turned the boat around and set off. Catherine did not look back. Nor did Hyppolite.

24

Jean-Patrice sat on the sand, staring across the lagoon. The morphine was wearing off. His detachment was evaporating pari passu. A frightful reality was coming in like a dark tide. He thought back over the things he had said to Catherine this morning. The first spasm of wretchedness shook him. Had he really said those things? It seemed incredible now that they had actually passed his lips. He had never held such views. He had never said such things in his life before. Was the behavior of Europeans in Africa evidence of a higher state of evolution? Of course not. It was as though the morphine, mixed with other and unknown poisons, had taken him over, silencing his real voice and allowing someone else to speak through him, a repulsive individual whom he only vaguely recognized. He saw in his mind some apish, balding old obscurantist with a long beard and a sneer, bearing a faint resemblance to Darwin, but hideously distorted by lust, hypocrisy and complacency. That was the owner of the voice which had spoken through him.

The drugs had poisoned him. They had not made a crystal cave of his mind at all. They had turned it into a dusty cellar full of rubbish, ghosts and moldering skeletons. She had been right to flee from him in outrage. Another spasm made him tremble. Nausea and pain hunched him over. The morphine concoction had done something terrible to him. Could he persuade her of that?

A new and horrible thought struck him. Perhaps she believed that the morphine had revealed his true opinions? In opio veritas! It must have appeared to her that the drug had stripped away some veneer, revealing the sneering, patronizing pseudo-Darwinist who was the real Jean-Patrice Duméril and who espoused such offensive opinions.

He had spoken to her of race in evolutionary terms! Practically called her a monkey to her face! Wondered aloud whether she was fit for civilized society! He beat his forehead with his fists in an agony of remorse.

He would never find her again. She and Hyppolite would vanish into the maze of waterways between this lagoon and Libreville. Even if he survived the next two hundred miles, he had lost her forever. Hyppolite had waited for her seven years, as Jacob had waited for Rachel. Now, at last, she was his. Her belly would swell with Hyppolite's children, surrounding her year by year as she withered into a toothless mammy with flattened dugs.

He struck his brow again. How could he think in such terrible terms? The pseudo-Darwin was still in his brain, sniggering from behind a bookcase. Why could he not free himself of these bigotries, this language of a Simon Legree at the auction block? Was racialism so entrenched in his soul that he could not rise above it? He had never even seen an African until he'd stepped off the *Marmotte*. Those he had met since had been noble or ignoble in exactly the same proportion as Parisians or Berliners. Yet somehow, they had been his subjects and he an overlord, treating them as children. Where had all these bigoted ideas come from? Perhaps one drank them in with the air one breathed, ate them with one's lunch, like Schultze's staphylococci. They took root without one noticing them.

And then, when an African took a pot shot at one, one was ready to spit out the fully-formed disease: calling them savages, brutes, beasts. From there it was only a step to the atrocities of Leopold in the Congo. Why, slavery, colonialism itself, were only possible if one believed that a dark skin made a man a beast.

He did not believe any of that. What had led him to breathe the idea that Catherine was a less evolved being than he? All he'd meant to say was that he wanted to marry her, and was anxious that she should be happy in France. That was as far as he had meant to go. The morphine had said everything else.

Loss, loss, loss. He had lost all the most important things in his life. He was reduced to this Robinson Crusoe island, a ragged man sitting weeping on an alien shingle, abandoned even by Friday. Hitting his head with his fists brought a kind of relief but also gave him vertigo. He lay on his side and wept for a while. Chloë, agitated by his misery, tried to comfort him. She bent over him, stroking his face and grunting. When this failed to produced a response, she puckered her lips and kissed him gently on the cheek. He opened his eyes. It was another human-like form of behavior to add to the list. But he was no longer compiling lists.

He got up and wandered aimlessly around the island, picking up such dry wood as he could find. The sun was sinking low. Thousands of birds drifted in the golden light, casting long shadows. He stood staring at the overwhelming abundance of life. A pair of waterbuck waded past his island at a distance of a hundred yards or so, their lyre-shaped horns held proudly erect, their step strong and purposeful.

It came to him, sorrowfully, that this was already a paradise on earth. It needed nothing that the white man could bring to perfect it. The white man could only make it worse. The black man lived within it harmoniously, producing little damage. Whereas the white man, hungry for ivory, gold, rubber and other riches, never intended to live in it. He wanted only to plunder it. He wanted the black man to continue grubbing in what was left of it, cultivating the white man's crops, each Beti or Fang becoming an organ of a greater France, laboring to send a capillary trickle into the stream which would become a river, a torrent, a hemorrhage of wealth.

As the darkness settled, he cooked the duck over the fire. He missed Catherine dreadfully. He wanted to tell her that he had understood something at last, something important. He wanted to tell her that he loved her. It was too late for that. This Africa was too vast for his love.

He had never felt more lonely in his life. His epiphany had not brought him any comfort. Nor had he cooked the duck very well. It was an unsuitable bird to try to roast over a few damply smoldering twigs. Half of it was blood and the rest cinders. It tasted very fishy. He gnawed at the carcass and then crept into the dugout with Chloë, his wounds aching terribly, longing for a cheroot.

He set off early the next morning, stiff and wretched. Schultze's morphine had left his system completely. He was depressed and in pain. The sun had not yet risen, but a chorus of birds echoed across the lagoon, a symphony of honks, squawks, whistles, shrieks and deep, reverberating booms. He threaded his way through the islands, heavily set upon by biting insects, which raised red weals on his face and arms. The bites were maddening. He scratched intemperately, finding his own flesh and blood under his fingernails, which were now growing rather long and black. Chloë had eaten all her leaves long since. She would soon be hungry.

Despite Hyppolite's assurance that the current would infallibly lead him in the right direction, he found it difficult to discern a current anywhere. When he stopped paddling, his canoe would simply drift to a standstill, or gyrate in aimless circles, or glide to the nearest island and nudge its nose into the mud. The water was warm and slimy.

"Twenty million years of bird shit," he informed Chloë. He paddled steadily but became convinced he was progressing round and round the same group of hummocks.

A vast, maroon face surfaced near him, ears twitching, bulbous chocolate colored eyes staring at him. Backs and heads rose all around him like islands. He stared at the hippos in frozen dismay. One opened cavernous jaws at him, wide and deep as the grave, except colored like a guava inside and studded with curving yellow tusks like stakes. He had read of the violent fury of these beasts; how they would charge a boat and break it in half like a twig and kill the occupants with terrible bites. But these specimens appeared placid. They watched him drift through their midst, occasionally snorting or champing the weeds in their mouths. He did not begin paddling again until he was a long way past them.

Later in the day, he passed more crocodiles, sprawled on the mud banks. They made no movement. It was hard to tell whether their stony green eyes were watching him and their frightful mouths leering at him, or whether they slept the dreamless sleep of millennia, until one scuttled off the mud with indecent haste and sank under the tepid brown water on some bloody errand. Should he fall in the lake, he thought, he could expect little mercy from these saurians.

The heat was crushing. He found himself drifting off at the oar, his brain cooking in his skull like a tortoise on the coals. His eyes were swollen with bites. It was hard to keep them open, even with the fear of the crocodiles ever-present. He wondered how Catherine was faring, whether Hyppolite had taken advantage of her in some ungentlemanly way.

"But Hyppolite is more of a gentleman than I am," he pointed out to Chloë. He imagined them gliding along cool, ferny banks, laughing together at him, at his absurd notions of racial superiority.

He forced himself to direct his thoughts away from her and towards his present necessity. He had little food, only some maize flour to make porridge and some rancid curd from the fishing village. He had seen no human presence since yesterday. The duck had not been a great success. But he decided to try another one. He loaded the shotgun.

"Forgive me, Chloë," he said wearily, "I must commit more murders." He set off in pursuit of waterfowl. A couple of lucky shots secured him two rather small birds with attractive black-and-white markings. He stowed them in the canoe and paddled onward.

By mid-afternoon, he was very tired and hungry. He had made little progress that he could see. He had probably done no more than row himself around the lagoon, like a bug on a plate. He shipped the paddle to rest his shoulders. For once, however, the dugout did not come to a standstill. It kept moving, slowly but steadily. He had found a current of some sort. Hope awoke in him. He let the boat drift, watching the islands ahead intently.

The canoe gathered speed. Ahead, he could see a waterway opening between bushy banks. Praying that it was not a dead end, he steered the canoe into it. Trailing his fingers in the water, he found it was cooler now, not so viscous. Soon, he was gliding along a stream with great trees on either side. He had finally managed to leave the lagoon behind. He began to sing, his voice hoarse and unmusical, but triumphant. He might soon find Catherine and Hyppolite!

He beached for the night on a sandbank where piles of driftwood had collected, bleached white as bones. Chloë found a tree she liked and began to tear off branches. Mindful of last night's failure, he decided to try a different approach with the duck. He plucked and cleaned the bird, revealing a rather scrawny fowl inside the abundant feathers, and wrapped it in a large, banana-like leaf. Then he dug a hole in the mud and buried it ceremoniously. He piled driftwood on the grave and built a crackling fire. He sat on his hunkers to wait, watching the river go by with reddened and swollen eyes. To survive, he thought. That was the way to win Catherine back. To arrive in Libreville, cool as a cucumber, alive and laconic – that would be magnificent. That would show her he was a man. A tropical flower in his buttonhole and a calm smile on his sun-bronzed lips. He touched his mouth and felt the skin hanging off it in rags.

He threw more wood on the fire. Darkness settled. Sparks flew up into the blue-black sky. Things were biting him again. He scratched and swatted. The bullet wounds felt very tight now, the skin around them hard as a drumhead. He hoped that was a sign of healing and not of infection. The sun had burned him. His head ached. His belly was so hollow that he was able to rest his chin on his knees. Crabs emerged from the river to snatch at the innards of the duck which he had thrown into the shallows. He dozed a little.

When the fire burned down, he moved it aside carefully and dug up the duck, burning his fingers and muttering to himself. He unwrapped the parcel and picked at the steaming flesh. It was cooked through. He ate voraciously, though the meat was gamey. He began to feel better. As he came to himself more, the thought of Catherine awoke in his mind. He ached for her. It was a physical ache, a pain in his chest, like a metal skewer through the heart.

He paused in mid-chew, his mouth open, staring into the dark unseeingly. This was exactly how he had felt about Justine. Another hopeless love had taken over his life. He had learned nothing. Nothing at all.

He built up the fire. He and Chloë huddled by it. Now he was too tired to think or feel any longer. There was only fear. Fear of the dark and of the beasts and men in it who might find him. He whispered a few prayers. Then he got into the dugout and slept with the gorilla in his arms.

He was awakened in darkness by the rain. His fire was out, the ashes hissing. He lay huddled in misery, pelted by heavy drops, aware that the dugout was filling with water. This was a new refinement. After an hour, a dim grey light revealed heavy mist all along the river. The rain fell without haste or pause. He roused himself. His injured arm showed an ugly aspect, swollen and red, the bandage stained with dark oozings. He removed it, wincing. Pus was seeping from between the stitches. The wound had not even begun to close. The lips looked puffy. Judging by the heat and pain in his back, the other wound was in a similar condition. He felt feverish. He was at a low point. Chloë was soaked, her fur dripping, but seemed not to mind. She peered sadly around her with clear eyes, sniffing the air with her huge, flat nostrils.

He tipped as much water as he could from the dugout and launched himself back on the river. He did not feel like eating. The rain had not lowered the temperature at all; it was, if anything, even hotter. The river was dark and foggy. The rain that beat into his face made visibility even poorer. His wounds were too painful to allow him to paddle, so he restricted himself to steering the canoe away from the banks as the current pulled him along. He was feeling increasingly feverish, his head aching and his body hot and cold by turns. He was starting to shiver. The rain appeared interminable. Among the snaking, woven patterns of the jungle, his eye was caught by something belonging to man: squares. A hut, half-buried in banana trees.

His heart thudding, he steered to the bank and drew the canoe up out of the water. He called a hoarse greeting. There was no reply. Cautiously, he peered into the open doorway. The dwelling was empty, abandoned. Nothing remained in it but an armful of reeds strewn on the floor. The bitterness of the disappointment almost made him weep. One side of the roof had fallen in and was open to the rain, but the other side still offered shelter of a sort. He carried his gun and the rest of his meager possessions in from the dugout and lay down on the reeds. Thunder rumbled all around. He closed his eyes and thought of Catherine, who should have been his playmate in paradise.

The storm lasted much of the day. It grew even darker. Rain poured down in sheets. Each peal of thunder shook him as if he were a pea in a drum. The thunder was very close, unimpeded by any human or natural dispensation. If it wanted to shatter him, it would do so. Chloë, shaking in terror, clung to him with her long arms. He did not have the strength to console her.

When the tempest receded, he tried to rouse himself to make something to eat. He found he was too weak to get up. His legs would not support him. The pain of his wounds was fading, but there was no strength left. Strength and pain went together, he realized. While you were strong, you felt pain. When the pain was taken away, the strength went, too.

He turned his head to face the doorway of the hut. Evening lay on the river like a silver spell. Water still dropped from trees and gurgled through countless rivulets into the main stream, but the world was at peace. His eyes travelled slowly from leaf to leaf, capturing each crystalline raindrop as it fell.

"This is paradise," he whispered. "But there is no place for man in paradise."

It was another important revelation. He wanted to record it. If only he had a little notebook and a silver pencil, like Schultze! Paradise existed, but one could not live in it. One either died in it, as he was doing, or one found the way out and escaped, as Hyppolite and Catherine had done. He was the serpent, still wound around the tree of knowledge; they Adam and Eve, running away hand and hand, lucky to be alive.

There were so many ramifications to this thought. It had profound implications for the philosophy of human development. If he was correct, then humanity tended not towards perfection, but towards increasing imperfection. Man would continue to make his world more complex, more chaotic, less perfect, less beautiful. He had been right. Paradise was doomed. It was inevitable.

A line of glistening termites hurried over his arm, intent on their business. Chloë sat among a pile of leaves, eating in her slow and steady way. She could feed herself here. She was a legitimate tenant of Paradise. He was becoming very ill. His limbs were shivering uncontrollably. His blood was icy. He felt that if he were to cut a vein, it would emerge half-frozen, like red slush. His teeth were chattering. His clothing was soaked but there was nothing dry in the world with which to cover himself.

He lay in the same position, his eyes opening from time to time to see how the light ebbed out of the day. Night fell. The darkness was absolute. No stars hissed. The moon had hidden herself.

During the night he dreamed he heard light footsteps and distant singing, as in the fairytales of his childhood. But he returned to consciousness the next morning to find himself as alone as ever. He could not see Chloë. He peered at his arm. The wound had broken open in the night, the flesh tearing away from the stitches. Pus oozed.

He turned his head. He could see now what the termites were making. They were building a Joliet near him, a Joliet of red mud. Each little creature, hurrying with a crumb of moistened earth in its jaws, was obeying the will of some fat, invisible, underground queen, carefully depositing its contribution, plastering it in place, scurrying away again. The mud Joliet was still faceless and crude, but it was taking shape. The limbs had been roughed out (he noticed that the left leg was still missing, though there was no need for a crutch, as the mudman had grown a root-like penis, reaching to the ground, on which it supported itself quite adequately). He turned his gaze away from the horrible thing, willing it to melt back into the earth.

He spent the morning sleeping intermittently. While he was awake, he thought back over his life. What had been the sum total? Had he done more good than harm? If there was to be a judgment, then it would depend upon that. On whether he had contributed as much as he had taken. It was a difficult calculation. He had made some people happy. He had loved some women and given them joy. He had taken his work seriously. He had also been selfish, vain, demanding and cruel. He had been destructive and thoughtless. He had caused some hundreds of souls to be inoculated against the smallpox. He had shot certain individuals in various ways, deliberately and with ingenuity. As far as The Reckoning went, it was a rather difficult outlook. But he had not been a bad person, overall. Or so it seemed to him.

"Are you adding it all up, Jean-Patrice?"

He became aware that Catherine was beside him, sitting with her arms around her knees, staring at the river. He tried to touch her, but he was too weak to move.

"Beloved," he whispered.

"You have misunderstood the nature of evolution," she said, "despite the silver medal you won for your essay."

"Forgive me," he replied.

"You misunderstand Africa. But then, you misunderstood yourself, long before you even came here. You, the silver medalist, habitué of the opera and the theatre, the symphony and the lofty, echoing public library, a man of culture and taste!"

He groaned in misery.

"Do you remember the Abbé Fouquet, your old headmaster, whom you once thought the cleverest man on earth? Do you remember how he would send you to fetch books from his shelves? How old were you, then? Perhaps nine or ten? Not much taller than that shotgun of Schultze's, at any rate. You would drag the ladder to the bookshelf and clamber up it, one step at a time, and pull out some dusty tome of sermons or theology for the old man. Did you think that the sweetest fruit grew on the highest branch? Did you think those little wooden steps led anywhere? You have begun on the wrong path and you continue on it, one step after the other, until you run out of steps and you fall. You lie here now, disintegrating into the fabric of Africa, and you have learned almost nothing."

"I have learned to love you," he croaked.

She turned her face to him at last. Her eyes were golden, like those of a beautiful serpent. "That, at least, you have learned. It is not very much. Half of it is self-love."

"The other half is pure!"

"And what have you brought here that is worth anything, Jean-Patrice? What, in that iron trunk of yours, which sunk so deep into the river mud, has survived you?"

"The vaccine!"

"We had no need of the vaccine until you brought the smallpox," she replied. "You came with disease and bronze and gunpowder and the books you drew out of the shelves for the Abbé Fouquet. Everything lies rotting in the forest now. Including you."

"I tried my best, Catherine!"

"Did you learn nothing the day we fired the pots, Jean-Patrice? You wanted to cut down the trees. Didn't you see then that the wood was just enough to make the flame, the flame just enough to bake the pots, the pots just enough to carry the water and cook the fufu? Didn't you realize that more than just enough is too much?"

"It should have been different."

"How could it have been different? You came looking only for what you could steal and take away with you. Your brothers took the ivory and the timber. You wanted to take me. I was your personal plunder."

"You were more than that."

"Father Jacques told me that I was a precious vessel of

the spirit of God. His voice would tremble when he spoke to me. I could see the blood rushing up and flying away under the white skin of his face. His hands would shake when he reached out to touch me. He always drew back. At first. I thought that the spirit of God was moving in him. I did not doubt. But he, too, had failed to understand himself long before he came to Africa. When he finally gathered the courage to take off my clothes, he told me that I was an animal, a seething pit of lust, a fountain of wickedness. He said I had tempted him beyond endurance and that the Devil was in me. Then he raped me."

Jean-Patrice managed to raise his trembling body on one elbow and reached for her. "Forgive me."

"He never found himself, in the end," she said. Her golden eyes, oval instead of round, looked into his. "He wanted to be forgiven. He wanted to see his child. He wanted me. He wanted to be healed. But it was not in my power. He took his pistol and shot himself through his ignorant heart." She rose to her feet. "The forest is a maze. If you find your way through it to me, I will know that you truly love me." A vast crocodile, the spirit of the river, nosed out of the current and clambered ponderously onto the bank. She took her seat on it, as on a throne. The crocodile slipped into the water again, bearing Catherine on its back. They sailed down the river and were gone.

When he next looked at the red mud Joliet, he was horrified to see that it had developed considerably. The face was now almost complete – and leering at him. The surface of the thing was active, restlessly crawling. Each crumb of wet mud was mobile, jostling its fellows, so that the mudman's skin was constantly changing, developing wrinkles or warts, the eyelids flickering, the tongue licking the mud lips. It could not yet move, being rooted to the earth, but it was clearly alive. It was observing him. More than that, it was asking to be acknowledged by him, wanting him to listen to it.

Another day passed and then another night. Now and then Chloë ambled up to him, patting him with her gentle hands and grunting. Then she would wander away. Now that he was dying, she seemed to be growing indifferent to him. Perhaps she was growing accustomed to a life out of human houses and human ways, becoming an animal again. When he died, her last tie with the human world would be gone.

He received another visitor at twilight: Justine, strolling along the riverbank, carrying a paper lantern. She wore a gauzy gown which floated about her, a sash tied round her waist with a bow at the back. Her hair was gathered in wavy masses at the top of her head, drifting around her temples artlessly. She greeted him with a mischievous smile. She held up the lantern, which glowed waveringly in the dusk.

"Do you remember the night the fireflies appeared?" she said. "We slipped away from the drawing room, you and I, left Maurice with all those stuffed shirts and wagging jowls – poor Maurice – and went into the garden."

"I remember," he said.

"We took one of the children's paper lanterns. You held it while I chased the fireflies and tapped them into their paper prison with my fan. We incarcerated them there and put them to hard labor. Remember how the lantern glowed? Wasn't that lovely! Wasn't it cruel!"

"We released them in the end."

"What a charming light they gave. They switched themselves on and off like gaslights I was afraid they would set the paper alight. You said I was silly." She imitated his diction. "The phosphorescence is produced by a chemical reaction, my dear. There is light but no warmth. Luminosity without combustion or sensible heat."

"We kissed behind the convolvulus."

"The odorous moonflower gave out her rich perfume,"

she agreed. "There was warmth but no light. Combustion and sensible heat without luminosity. You hoisted my skirts and we made love like mad things, gasping each other's names. We could hear the chatter from the house. We laughed so much afterwards. You examined my face by the light of the firefly lantern and said I was more beautiful than the moon."

"We took the lantern back to the company to explain our absence. Everyone said oh! and ah! We saw them whispering and staring at us. I wondered how many had guessed. I wanted them to guess. We released the fireflies at the window and drank champagne all night. I was the last to leave. As I stood on the doorstep, waiting for my fiacre, Maurice said I was an asset to the Bureau. He seemed happy that we were lovers."

"Is that what you thought?"

"I thought he was glad it was I and not someone worse."

She laughed. "Who could have been worse than you? You were like one of those bad-tempered boys who gets angry during a game and says he is being cheated and turns it into a fight where noses bleed and eyes are scratched."

"It stopped being a game."

"Not to me. Don't think that I didn't know I was your firefly," she said, sitting on a fallen tree a little distance away from him. "It gave me no pleasure to lead you on such a chase, Jean-Patrice. I had no choice but to fly. To see you stumble and fall was terrible to me."

"You laughed at me."

"I laugh at everything. Do you think I took pleasure in your ruin? I loved you. It was all I could do to save myself from that same ruin. When they sent you to Africa, all the fireflies escaped from my lantern. The moon went out, the moonflower folded up and her rich perfume was gone. Maurice blamed me. Everybody blamed me. The garden was desolate."

"For a while."

"Everything is for a while, Jean-Patrice. Nothing lasts."

"But you are all change, Justine. You are never constant."

"Nor is the moon, and yet she is changeless."

The red mud Joliet had now achieved the dimensions of a large termite mound. Its surface still writhed. Veins and rootlets had grown on the limb-like penis which burrowed into the ground. The face was in constant movement, the lips squirming, the eyes rolling. He dreaded that it would find a voice and speak to him, confiding in him the muddy secrets it held. Already, the distorted arms were able to move independently, shedding red splinters of earth. It no longer needed the termites, which had vanished. It was able to rearrange its constituent molecules at will. It would be able to uproot itself soon and walk the earth.

"Look at that! Isn't it awful?" She did not reply. It was growing dark. He could hardly see her any more. "Don't go!"

"You chased me because you wanted to pull off my wings, as barbarous boys do in your youth. A butterfly without wings is just a bug."

"How can you accuse me of that? I never wanted that!"

"Then you wanted to put me in a lantern so I could glow only for you. What you loved about me was the very thing you wanted to destroy."

"Not destroy – possess!"

"You loved me because I came when you called. I came because Maurice gave me freedom. That binds me to him forever."

"Forgive me," he whispered, understanding.

"I absolve you of being yourself." She glimmered for a while, smiling, fading. Soon only the lantern was left, a faint phosphorescence in the night. Then it dissipated and was gone.

He opened his eyes languidly after one of his deep,

deep plunges into unconsciousness. His slow gaze encountered a splash of colour. Fruit. Something had fallen from a tree. He smiled slowly. When he focused his eyes better, he saw that the fruit had not fallen from a tree. A banana leaf had been laid at the doorway of the hut and the fruit had been set out upon it. Some red, ribbed berries. Three bananas. Could Chloë have done this? He wondered whether it was another dream. The fruit was just within reach. He stretched out his arm and closed his fingers around a berry. He did not have the strength to peel a banana. He brought the fruit to his mouth by degrees. It was tart, fibrous. He absorbed it slowly and then slept again. When he awoke, he ate some more of the berries.

He heard a soft whisper. The mud Joliet had found its tongue at last. He turned his head unwillingly to look at it. It was monstrous now, a leering, obscene mudman, thrusting its penis into the earth, looming against the sky. The mud voice was insinuating, persuasive.

"As you are now, I was. As I am, you will be."

"I will never be like you!" But he thought of the real Joliet's emaciated body. That was indeed how he would soon look. The ligaments and integuments would give way. The bones would separate and settle into the mould. Insects would clean them. The earth would absorb everything that he had been. A leaf would sprout. Then another. He would become part of the fabric of Africa. And termites would carry his crumbs away to build a tower of ugliness.

He lay with his eyes half-closed, feeling his empty stomach react to the fruit. The sensation was not altogether pleasant. It made its way downward, becoming more urgent. His bowels began to cramp. Perhaps the gift had been a trap, to poison him. Groaning, he forced himself to move. He crawled out of the hut and squatted at the edge of the river to relieve himself. He looked around to see who might have brought the fruit. He could see nobody. There was no sign of Chloë. He washed himself and crawled back into his hovel.

That had exhausted him. But after a while he found he felt better, not worse. The berries had cleansed him. When he had rested, he ate the rest of them and also a banana. He had one duck left. He placed it on the banana leaf, hoping it would be an acceptable thanks-offering. The evening closed in. The darkness of the night fell over the river. He lay in a state somewhere between sleeping and waking. It rained for a while, the drops pattering among the leaves.

Deep in the night, he heard music again. Some simple stringed instrument was playing a repetitive refrain, the notes grouped closely together, like the song of an insect or a bird. A voice carried the melody, sweet and plangent. When the music faded, he wept for the sheer beauty of it, longing for it to begin again.

He awoke at another time and heard what he thought was the sound of small feet moving around his hut. He was afraid yet expectant. He called out. The footfalls were silenced at once. He did not hear them again. He slept deeply after that.

In the morning, the duck had been taken but there were more gifts on the banana leaf: a handful of seeds and nuts, some shiny fruits like damsons, more bananas. There was also a calabash filled with some sour-smelling liquid. He sat in the doorway of his hut and ate the fruit. The fermented stuff in the calabash tasted bitter but was refreshing. He drank it all. The handle of the calabash was made of twisted and plaited grass. He examined it with wonder. It was something so simple, yet so elegant and functional. He could never have adapted his imagination or his fingers to the fabrication of such a thing.

He searched the surroundings with his eyes, but could see no trace of whoever might have left these things. It was as though the forest itself had sung and dropped fruits in his lap; or spirits, which could not be seen, but which laughed at him invisibly. He had not seen Chloë for two days now.

The red mud Joliet no longer spoke to him. Its moist, granulated skin was beginning to harden. It could no longer move so freely. The mouth still leered at him and the hooded eyes still stared, but it appeared to be ossifying, or fossilizing. He was relieved.

His back was wet. He reached behind himself, feeling his ribs and spine bony under his questing fingertips. The wound in his shoulder had broken open, like the one in his arm, and was discharging pus and blood. But the tight, hot feeling had faded. He was content to sit blinking at the river, allowing his body to expel the poisons in it.

He had not seen anyone on the river since leaving Bassongo. He must be on some lesser branch of the river, he thought, some route not travelled by rafts and dugouts. He chewed the nuts and seeds, one by one. He was very feeble, but he no longer thought about dying. He felt no urgency about anything, not even about reaching Libreville and seeing Catherine again. He felt that he was part of the riverbank, like the hut, a battered and somewhat disintegrated object which nevertheless was entitled to a small place in the fabric of things.

When the sun was at its hottest, he took off his clothes and washed himself in the river. The purulence was not pouring out of him so abundantly, now. He rinsed the wounds in the clear brown water and then applied the last of the iodine as best he could. He went to lie down in the shade of the hut. There was work to be done in simply breathing, blinking, feeling the blood flow in his veins. The body was a rhythm. Its fibers pulsed and relaxed, its liquids flowed and ebbed, it had cycles of sleep and waking. It was important not to interrupt any of these processes, but to exist in harmony with them.

The mudman was no longer a figure of terror. Its resemblance to Joliet was not apparent any more. The surface, hard as baked ceramic, was abstract. There was no face, no rooting penis. It was simply a termite mound that looked rather like a man when seen from the corner of one's eye.

Before he went to sleep, he left some more return gifts for his night visitors. He laid some of his plantains on the banana leaf; also the last of the goat milk curd. Perhaps they would allow him to see them tonight. Perhaps they had learned to trust him.

He was wakened from dreams by the music. Tonight they sang in harmony, a haunting melody with a catch that was repeated again and again, some voices taking it up as others were ending it. He listened, entranced, to the choir. The voices were childlike, yet some wavered like the voices of the very old. For some reason, the music brought his mother and father into his mind. He remembered them only as dim forms. To have lost them so young had been the event that had most deeply shaped his character. He wept for the second night in a row, wishing things had been otherwise in his life.

A moon had risen, slender and golden, like the body of a young girl. Against the reflections on the river, he thought he saw figures moving, little people gliding out of the forest. They appeared naked; he could see breasts and buttocks. He called to them but knew in his heart they would never approach him. They were too wise for that. They had been willing to help him, but not to risk the contamination that hung around him.

In the dawn, he found more fruit on the banana leaf. It had been tied up in a bark basket, as though for a journey. The suppuration in his wounds had almost stopped. He felt clear-headed, his strength returning. He loaded everything into the dugout.

He had no farewell gift to leave, which grieved him. Perhaps his departure was all they desired, the only true gift he could offer.

He searched for Chloë. At last he saw her, sitting some

distance away on the bank, surrounded by leafy branches she had torn down to browse on. She no longer seemed hideous or grotesque to him. Rather, she was strange and wonderful and utterly disconnected from him. He hesitated to address her.

"Chloë, I'm going," he said. "Will you come or will you stay?"

She watched him, her leathery face impassive. He climbed into the canoe. She made no move to follow him. He did not blame her.

"Goodbye, Chloë," he called. He found himself crying like a child. He launched the dugout and paddled out into the channel. He set off into the maze that was the forest. Blinded by tears, he calculated the days in his mind. It was New Year's Eve, the last day of the nineteenth century.

25

He could not be sure of the exact date that he reached Libreville, since time had become far less important to him than space, and he had abandoned his efforts to keep a calendar. In point of fact, he had reached the coast earlier, but the stream he had travelled on decanted him several miles north of the estuary, and he had to walk through the mangroves for four or five days to reach the town, assisted by a young fisherman who offered to carry his baggage. This last stage of his journey almost finished him off.

He entered the sleepy little town, hobbling. His shoes had rotted away, so he had wrapped rags around his feet. The dagger-like roots of the mangroves had pierced these easily. His hips, buttocks and knees were covered in sores from kneeling in the canoe, so his progress was slow.

Oddly, he attracted little attention at first; his sunburned skin, ragged hair and long beard made him appear like a marabout or some other wandering holy man. He moved among the groups of idle Africans who drifted through the public places. Nobody made the assumption that he was a Frenchman until he appeared in Malherbe's office, asking to speak to the Director.

Malherbe emerged, crisp and starched in his tropical

uniform, and stared blankly at Jean-Patrice. "Yes?"

"It's me, Monsieur de Directeur."

Malherbe's expression changed. "Duméril?"

"Yes."

"My God." Malherbe pulled out a chair for Jean-Patrice, who lowered his thin frame into it by degrees. He stared at Jean-Patrice with an expression of incredulity. "May I ask – where have you been?"

"Making my way here from Bassongo."

"All this time?"

Jean-Patrice attempted to smile. "The forest is a maze, did you know that? I had no map. I think I have taken a rather ... a rather meandering route."

"Do you know what the date is?"

Jean-Patrice thought. "I believe it must be ... the late part of January."

"It is the end of March. The twenty-eighth."

Jean-Patrice made a gesture. "I devised a system ... carving lines on the ... the wood of the boat. Sometimes ... I suppose it seemed irrelevant."

"You are exhausted and weak. I will call the doctor at once."

"Please ... one moment."

"What is it?"

He swallowed. "Catherine."

"You mean the woman? She and the corporal arrived two months ago, Duméril. They confessed to having abandoned you in some swamp. You have been given up for dead weeks ago!"

"But ... where is she?"

"They are in prison, my dear fellow, charged with your murder. The corporal is in the dungeon of the fort, under close confinement. She is in the jail for native females, on a regimen of hard labor. Please sit back down, Duméril, there is nothing to be achieved now."

"But I am alive!"

"So I see. The most urgent question at the moment is

a visit to the doctor."

"I must speak to her!"

"And so you shall," Malherbe said soothingly, pushing him back into the chair. "You would not want to distress her unnecessarily? Your appearance is that of Orson, the wild man of the woods. You are not really a fit spectacle for the public gaze, and the public will wish to gaze. The best policy, I think, is to install you in a room in the hotel where you can receive the attention you require as to medicine and hygiene and be allowed to rest."

"A message."

"You have my word. A message will be sent to them both before the hour is out, telling them that you are alive."

He had to be satisfied with this. He allowed Malherbe to wrap him in a blanket and take him to the hotel. He was dazed, now. His senses were confused. The news of his arrival was already spreading like wildfire. A small crowd had gathered in the barroom to discuss the event. They thronged the doorway, craning their necks to watch him hobble up the stairs, supported by Malherbe.

"I drank with him the night he left," a red-faced man said hoarsely. "A lion of a man he was, then. Look at him now!"

Jean-Patrice was lowered into galvanized tub of hot water, gasping as it scalded his many sores. "Have you sent the message to her?" he demanded of Malherbe.

"She abandoned you to die," Malherbe said in his dry way. "She admitted as much herself when she arrived here. Her breast-beating did not convince the authorities. Had you not fortuitously arisen from the grave, she and the corporal would both now be facing the gallows. I have sent the message. But why do you care about her?"

"She is all the world to me."

Malherbe raised his eyebrows. The doctor arrived and dosed Jean-Patrice with laudanum. As the paregoric spread through his brain, he gave a great sigh and closed his eyes. The native servant was able to wash him undisturbed. His nails were cut. His rags were burned. A barber arrived, carrying towels and a bag. Jean-Patrice's beard was carefully shaved, revealing once again his familiar features, though thinner than they had been. His hair was washed and cut. He was bandaged and put into bed, where he lay with half-open eyes, staring at the window.

"Are you more comfortable now?" Malherbe asked.

"Very. Who will pay…?"

"You have three months of back pay outstanding," Malherbe said. "I will try to persuade the lieutenant-governor to free it for you. Your friend Tosti is now district commissioner at Bassongo."

"I'm glad." Jean-Patrice slept for two days, waking only to be fed on soup or other invalid dishes. On the third day, he felt his strength return. He rose from his bed and dressed in the clothes he had been lent and went to raise the issue of Catherine with Malherbe once again.

"There was a misunderstanding, Monsieur le Directeur. Not an abandonment."

"You will have ample occasion to comment on that in your report," Malherbe said, "and at the enquiry."

"But in the meantime, she has been put to hard labor. There is not even a charge against her. It is very unjust."

"It's out of my hands," Malherbe shrugged. "The lieutenant-governor decides these things."

"She is an educated woman who can read and write. She has been a teacher and is, moreover, an artist. This is a great cruelty."

Malherbe's own wife was a teacher, an artist and a mulatto, and perhaps this softened him. He eventually persuaded the lieutenant-governor that Catherine should be put to lighter duties, but could not secure permission for Jean-Patrice to see her yet.

Jean-Patrice began to write the report which the lieutenant-governor had ordered. The attention he was receiving daily was shocking to him. His arrival had produced the electrifying effect of a resurrection, since he had been counted among the dead for so long. He had travelled on minor branches of the river system and had not been seen at any of the villages where the traffic passed. There were no reports of a solitary white man in a dugout canoe. The logical assumption was that he had died. Of course, he had received a considerable amount of spontaneous help from non-commercial natives on his route, without which he would certainly have died. As it was, he suffered remarkably few permanent impairments to his health. In after years he was seen to be a little thinner, a little quieter, a little slower in his speech. But that was all that could be seen from the outside.

The endless questions bewildered him at times and he did not know what answers were expected of him. Crowds of Europeans were overpowering to him, now. He found that he had to escape from any room where more than two or three men were gathered. The smell of tobacco and alcohol were nauseating. Loud voices or hearty laughter rattled his nerves. Though commanded by Malherbe to rest, he found the inactivity intolerable and fidgeted uneasily. The need to travel, to journey each day, had imprinted itself so deeply in his soul that immobility was the cruelest of torments.

He broke free of the invalid regime that had been imposed on him and took to walking around Libreville for hours each morning and afternoon, looking neither to left nor right, simply impelled by the requirement to move forward. People pointed him out to one another. In the article which later appeared in *Le Figaro*, this withdrawn demeanor of his was cited as part of his heroic mystique, and a cartoon, purporting to show him hugging his breast and brooding over a slain cannibal, was given prominence. The truth was that he did not care to look at anything in Libreville. After the river and the forest, everything there was a disillusionment to his eye, squalid and small.

He received part of the pay that was owing to him. He made repeated efforts on behalf of Catherine and Hyppolite, but since he himself was now the subject of an enquiry, his influence was slight. Hyppolite, now on the lesser charge of desertion, remained in the dungeon of the fort. Jean-Patrice was not permitted to see him. No new charge had been specified against Catherine – she was of secondary interest – but she remained incarcerated in the Native Jail nonetheless, now on what were called "light duties." He was forbidden to communicate with her in any way. However, he found a prison guard, an Mpongwe with deep tribal scars on his cheeks and forehead, who was willing to be bribed. He paid the man to smuggle in healthy food for Catherine, parcels of fresh fruit, bread and other things. He had no way of knowing whether the packages ever reached her. He asked the man to try to get him into the prison to see her.

The news from Schultze was heartening. He had been picked up by a river steamer, and had reached Libreville in February in relatively good health. He had returned to Europe by boat and was said to be making an excellent recovery in Bavaria and to be working on a prosthesis for his shattered jaw, made from leather, steel spring and India-rubber, which he claimed would allow him to speak and eat with at least some degree of normality. Jean-Patrice obtained his address and sent him his shotgun, together with a letter detailing some of his own adventures, which was later published in the *Münchner Zeitung* in a translation made by Schultze himself.

At length the need to keep moving ebbed out of his system and he was able to sit for a couple of hours at a time, finishing his report and reading weeks-old copies of newspapers from France. The twentieth century had arrived without the floods, comets and other catastrophes which had been prognosticated. Civilization as it were crept over him by degrees. He began to lose what men described as his "long stare," that searching for the horizon that dismissed everything in between. He even took up cheroots again, though he now had more pleasure from staring at the smoke curling from the end of his cigar than from puffing at it. He ate sparingly, sometimes pausing for so long over his plate, apparently gazing at the food upon it, that his dining companion or the waiter would have to jog him into resuming his meal. He slept little and did not touch alcohol. Despite this Spartan regime, his strength returned. He had turned twenty-eight somewhere along the river and he was still young. He began to recover his leonine appearance.

He searched for cheaper accommodation than the hotel and found a small house on stilts near the beach with a palm thatch roof, two cool rooms with windows facing the sea and a small kitchen where he could prepare the simple food he was now used to. He paid his bill at the hotel and moved out. The stilt house suited him perfectly. He took up one of the rooms. The other waited for its occupant. He liked the constant murmur of the sea and the sound of rain on the roof. The street was little-visited by Europeans, which he also liked. He could walk along the beach and see only Gabonese fishermen. He could buy fish and vegetables for a few centimes every day. Just enough.

The children of the street approved of him, and would bring him shells and other objects they found on the beach. He bought some paper and began to write. He composed a few letters to friends at home. Then he began to write down some of his thoughts about Gabon and his experiences in Africa. The stilt house had a small veranda, and he took to sitting there with his writing, staring out across the sea while he reflected on the little unsolved mysteries of Bassongo: why had Sophie put the viper in Joliet's bed? Had she meant to kill him? Or just to frighten him? Had the oganga commanded it to save the souls of the women Joliet took to his bed illicitly? Or was it a personal revenge, the furious cruelty of a wounded woman's heart?

Had Raymond sold her to the Fang out of frustration at his relationship with Catherine? To be eaten? Or to try and save her from a living death in Bassongo? Would she find a new life with a new tribe?

How far had Father Jacques climbed out of his grave? Was he by now crawling imperceptibly towards the village, looking for Catherine with empty eye sockets? Or had some animal by now made a meal of his chalky bones?

Was Joliet still hobbling around the village, disguising himself as termite nests or dead trees? How was Tosti, who was now district commissioner there, coping with the ghostly and human perils of Bassongo?

In the meantime, the lieutenant-governor read his report. A second report was sent down from Bassongo by Tosti. A boat arrived from Senegal, bearing an investigating lawyer appointed by the Navy, named Petit. A special hearing was scheduled for the 10th of April. Its findings would be sent to the Minister of Colonies. Tosti wrote Jean-Patrice a private note which cautioned him against the lawyer:

My dear Duméril,

Happy as I was to succeed you so quickly (you remember I gave you six months?) I was desolated to do so on the basis of your early death, so your resurgence gives me enormous pleasure. Bassongo is not in such a bad way. You have not actually ploughed it with salt, at any rate. A few more months will work wonders. And of course, I continue to do what I can for you! I have favored you in the report I made — send me some decent cigars and cognac, if you please. I have made myself comfortable enough here and feel that the position suits me. There are many advantages. Beware of Petit. He has a reputation for cleverness and will probably be vicious. I leave you in the wolf's mouth.

Michel Tosti.

Shortly before the special hearing began, the scar-faced Mpongwe guard arrived at his house and told him that he could visit Catherine. He could see her immediately, the guard said, but there were restrictions. The meeting would be very short. It would take place in the prison work room. He was not allowed to approach closer than three yards from her bench and she would not be allowed to stop working. The guard also insisted on a payment of twelve francs, a week's wages, in cash. Jean-Patrice accepted these conditions without hesitation

26

The guard led him into the jail. The place was a filthy
dungeon whose smells and sights were vile. Half of it was
given over to a laundry where the women washed naval
and military uniforms, laboring over choking vats of lye.
Other women sat on the floor repairing shoes, belts and
other leather accoutrements. All wore the same shapeless
grey uniform, their feet bare, their heads shaved. Many
appeared to be diseased. He shuddered to think she had
been confined in here for two months, his bright
Catherine, with her burning sensibility. Once inside the
courtyard, he was made to wait for half an hour beside a
vegetable garden where inmates worked, manuring the soil
with stinking buckets of their own dung. At last the scar-
faced guard bawled for him insolently. Jean-Patrice went
through the doorway and found himself in a low-ceilinged,
crushingly hot room where female criminals worked,
sewing uniforms. The place smelled of greasy clothes and
sweat. He looked for Catherine. She sat at a trestle table,
wearing a coarse grey dress, her feet bare, like the others.
Her head had been shaved. The native guard lounged and
picked his teeth idly at the window.

The sight of her acted on him strangely. She did not

look up and perhaps it was as well, since he felt his head spinning and his heart faltering. He was so dizzy that for a while he thought he might faint. It was hard to remember who he was or where he was. He groped to a bench opposite her. The giddiness passed off slowly. She continued to pull thread through the button she was sewing, her eyes downcast; but her breast was heaving quickly.

"Catherine," he said quietly, "I haven't seen you in three and a half months, except in dreams. Will you not look at me?" She seemed not to have heard him, but at last she laid her hands down and allowed her eyes to lift. As soon her gaze met his, she began to cry. Tears streamed down her face, splashing on her dress. She made no sound. "Don't cry," he whispered, unable to touch her.

"You look so thin," she said. "When they told me you were alive, I thought it was a trick." She wiped her cheeks, her fingers shaky. "They say you've been sick."

"I was just tired." He gazed at her as though he wanted to devour her with his hollow eyes. "I am still a little weary, but I assure you, my heart is singing at seeing you alive and well."

"I am alive. I am not well."

He looked at the other prisoners, who worked on their piles of uniforms like exhausted automata. "After the enquiry, you'll be released from this place."

"I have not been well since we parted, Jean-Patrice. The world was a prison when I thought you dead. The prison is a paradise now that I see you alive."

"My journey took a little longer than yours, that's all. Have they ill-treated you here?" he asked.

She seemed to struggle for a moment. "They whipped me."

"Oh, Catherine!"

"They said I had murdered you, Jean-Patrice. They stripped me naked in front of the whole prison, even the men. They whipped me until they believed what I told them." He covered his face, trying to shut out the vision. "Why did you remain on that island?" she burst out. "If you had followed us, all would have been well. Didn't you know that an hour after we parted, I would have come back to you?"

"No," he said, "I didn't know that. I had said terrible things to you."

"They are things that many people think."

"I do not think them. I have never thought them. The morphia made me say and imagine many things that were not part of me. I am ashamed now that they ever passed my lips. I ask for your forgiveness, Catherine."

"What are my tears to your blood?" she replied quietly. "I had nothing to forgive but an insult and I have forgiven it long since. You have to forgive a betrayal that might have taken your life."

"I thought you would never want to see my face again."

"I see nothing but your face, awake or asleep." She stared at him with eyes that seemed huge in her thin face. The guard looked over his shoulder and uttered a laconic command in his language. She picked up her work and began to sew. "My heart was breaking when we left you. As soon as the sun set, my madness was over. But it was too dark to look for you. At dawn we went back. We found your island and the fire you had made, but you were gone. We searched the lagoon for three days, through all of those islands. Once we heard the sound of a distant shot. Hyppolite fired into the air every half-hour after that, but there was never an answer. We thought you must have gone past us and reached the river, so we followed as quickly as we could. But nobody had seen you on the river. We stopped at every village."

"The stream I took carried me away quickly. It was not the right river, of course. It took me a long way north of where I should have been. I heard none of your signals. And soon after that I got a fever and had to rest on the bank for some days."

314

"I deserved the whipping, Jean-Patrice. I minded only being laughed at by the men. I thought I had killed you. I told them that."

He sighed. "You should not have said any of that. At the time, I thought I deserved what you said and did. I still think so. I was very grieved to have lost you to Hyppolite."

"Lost me to him?" She raised her eyes to his swiftly. "Is that what you thought?"

"It's what I dreaded."

Her forehead creased in compassion. "Ah, Jean-Patrice. You understand me very little."

"I fear you are right."

"I'm sorry I gave you any cause to think that of me. I was angry, but my feelings cannot change."

"You make me ashamed again. But also happy."

"Forgive me, Jean-Patrice."

"I forgive you freely. I saw you in the forest, Catherine. You appeared to me, or at least a vision of you appeared. You talked to me about how little I knew myself, about Father Jacques. You told me that he raped you."

She shook her head. "No, Jean-Patrice. He was a gentle, sensitive man who fell desperately in love with a very young woman. Perhaps I could have saved him, but I did not know how. We made love only once and then we avoided each other. But when I became pregnant, nobody could do anything to save him – or me. What else did I say to you in this vision?"

"You said the forest was a maze, and that if I could find my way through it to you, you would believe that I loved you."

"It was not me who said that, either. I know that you love me. Or that you once loved me. Perhaps something has died between us."

"But perhaps something else will be reborn."

"Yes," she whispered. Her eyes were on her sewing

again. Her face, like his, was thinner. Despite that, her beauty struck him as it had done the first time he had laid eyes on her.

"Please look at me. Never mind that fellow."

"I can't look you in the face, Jean-Patrice. But I want to say something, if you will listen."

"I am listening."

"Do you remember the day you rode up to my house, and found me making pots?"

"I'll never forget it."

"You looked at me in a way no man had ever done. Your face was full of tenderness. You looked at me as though you knew me and cared for me. I could tell that you desired me. I wanted to be desired by you. You looked at my pots and you could see me in them. You wanted the one that had come fresh from my hands. I was so happy. It was like a declaration of love. When I pressed my thumb into the rim, I thought, I am pressing my imprint on his heart, let him come back to me."

"And I did."

"Yes. But I was always afraid to believe that you thought of me as I wanted you to. I have been wanted by others whose desire was not what I desired. I wanted you to love me forever. When you began to talk that way on the river, saying that I was primitive—"

"Catherine!"

"Let me finish. When you said those things, I wanted the boat to sink under us and for us both to be drowned at that moment. I thought you were telling me that I had been wrong to hope, wrong to dream."

"No."

"Our life can never be easy, Jean-Patrice."

"But apart, it will be impossible." The guard was beckoning him urgently. He rose. "I've written a report which exonerates both you and Hyppolite of any blame. However, your own statements, when you arrived in Libreville, may be regarded as evidence of some guilt. The fact that you were whipped shows you spoke under duress. You should say as little as possible. If you have a chance to speak to Hyppolite, say the same thing to him." He paused, but she did not, or could not, look up at him. "Goodbye, Catherine."

The guard grasped his arm and hustled him out of the place. Having seen her had satisfied him in one way; he had ached for the sight of her. In another way, it made him burn for her, to have her in his arms, to kiss her face. He was filled with uneasiness and anxiety. His heart had become a question. He sat on the veranda of the stilt house all night, thinking of her and listening to the restless waves.

His Sunday morning walk the day before the special hearing took him to Sainte-Marie, the cathedral, which stood opposite the port. Despite its grand title, it was a quaint, low structure erected on the masts of old ships that had served their last commission. He paused at the door and then walked in. A straggling queue of men littered a side-aisle, waiting to make confession before Mass. He joined them, not certain what his motivation was. It had been many years since he had last taken Communion. Perhaps he felt that there was something to give thanks for and also imminent danger to ward against. He eyed his companions, most of whom were employed in the civil service or the export companies, thinking what a rascally lot of fellows they seemed to be. Scruffy, unwashed, with leering mouths and guilty eyes, sporting pimply cheeks and greasy hair, they looked more like the habitués of some provincial brothel than the advance guard of a great civilization. What a dreary load of sins they must have brought along with them to deposit here.

At last it came his turn to enter the confessional. Jean-Patrice knelt by the grille, crossing himself. "Forgive me, Father, for I have sinned in thought, word and deed—"

"Yes, yes."

"I am truly penitent—"

"Yes, yes, yes. Go on."

Jean-Patrice thought for a moment, wondering whether to begin. Perhaps it was best to begin at the beginning. "I have been guilty of adultery."

"With aboriginal women?"

"With a Frenchwoman, Father."

The priest appeared astonished. "Here?"

"No, no, in Paris. More than one woman, in fact. It is many years since my last confession."

The priest grunted. Through the mesh, Jean-Patrice could see he was resting his head on his hand, his thumb and two fingers sinking into his fat cheek. "Go on."

"I have committed murder."

"Of aboriginals?"

"Yes."

"How many?"

"I am not sure, Father. I fired on them with a cannon."

The grille was pulled open with a rasp, revealing the curate as a tubby man with a red face, spreading cheeks, bulging black eyes and richly dyed chestnut hair. He stared at Jean-Patrice with an appearance of wildness, as though he had already heard more than he could cope with that morning. "You are that man, that man—" He snapped his fingers and grasped at the name. "Duméril."

The anonymity of the confessional seemed to have fallen by the way. "Yes."

"You appear to be a most imprudent individual."

"Yes, Father."

"Good Heavens. So it's you." The priest looked him over and seemed disappointed to find that Jean-Patrice had not horns and a tail. "What else have you done?"

Jean-Patrice was more cautious now. "Those are the salient sins, I think."

"Surely you have committed sins of impurity with aboriginal women?"

"No, Father."

"Why do you hide your transgressions? Do you think

God does not see?"

"I haven't been with native women. Not in that sense."

The priest frowned suspiciously. "In what sense, then?"

Jean-Patrice hesitated. "I am in love with a native woman. I want to marry her."

"Marry? Are you mad?"

"Perhaps I was. Not any longer."

"Are you in a state of sin with this female?"

"No."

A fat finger was wagging. "Young man, I most earnestly advise you that it would be far better for your immortal soul to enter a state of sin with this female than to marry her and destroy yourself. Sins can be forgiven and washed away. Marriage cannot."

"But I love her."

"Don't be a fool, Duméril. Do you not see the atrocious example you would give? Your father was no doubt a decent man. Do you want to see little brown Dumérils scratching in the gutter, shaming his name by carrying it on their woolly heads? Sins committed here have a special dispensation. You understand? Take a mistress if you must, but do not compromise yourself and your country in this way."

"Does murder have a special dispensation here, too?"

"We are among savages," he retorted. "This is not France." He looked at his little clock and sighed in exasperation. "If I had known I would be confessing the whole of Gomorrah, I would have started earlier. Do you sincerely repent your transgressions?"

"Yes, Father."

"Say as many Hail Maries as it takes to bring you to your senses. Remember the purity of the Mother of God when you are next tempted to sin." He began muttering the absolution very fast, reaching *ego te absolvo*. The plump, white fingers sketched a cross over his head and then waved him away impatiently, closing the grille. Jean-

Patrice walked back past the line of lounging men, sensing that they were muttering about him to one another. He felt lighter in some ways, heavier in others. He sat at the back of the church to await the Mass, but he did not take the Communion wafer. He did not feel that he had been absolved of anything that mattered and he doubted whether he ever could be.

Coming out of the cathedral, he felt a touch on his arm. He turned to see a handsome, lean, olive-skinned woman with black ringlets, wearing a cream dress and a broad-brimmed hat, cocked up on one side. Her eyes were very dark. "Monsieur Duméril?"

"Yes."

"I am Marie Malherbe. The wife of Director Malherbe."

"Enchanted." Hiding his surprise, he raised her hand to his lips.

"My husband never attends Mass. He professes to be an atheist. But I seldom fail. Perhaps you will do me the service of walking me home?"

"I should be delighted." He offered his arm and she took it in her lean fingers, which were clad in white gloves. She had a fine profile, with a large mouth and a rather aquiline nose. It was odd to think of the leathery Malherbe conjoined with this elegant and exotic woman, who could be no more than thirty-five. "How did you know me?"

"You had been pointed out to me. 'Mad Duméril,' you know."

"I have gained worse titles in this country. The people of Bassongo called me Culblanc."

She laid white kid fingers on her lips to stifle a laugh. "My husband has spoken to me of you. I feel I must tell you that he intends to do all he can for you at the special hearing."

"I'm very much obliged to him."

"He finds you an interesting case. I was sure I should also find you interesting, which is why I was so bold as to engage you outside the Cathedral."

"I am very glad you did. It is no hardship to walk with a beautiful woman on a Sunday morning."

She smiled to herself. "I should have known you even if you were not pointed out to me."

"How?"

"They say you are like a lion, and you are. A lion which caresses and has velvety paws. I am sure it would be hard to resist you if one were a young gazelle."

He was taken aback. "I assure you, I am tame."

"And I am no longer a young gazelle." She paused to tie the strings of her hat against the breeze which blew in from the estuary. "My husband tells me you are connected with a Beti woman?"

"Yes."

"Usually, when a white man is connected with a black woman, it is something not to be mentioned."

"In my case, I should be happy to shout it from the roofs of Libreville."

"The roofs of Libreville are not so very high, but I admire your sentiment. You care for her deeply?"

"Sometimes it seems to me that I have hardly known her long enough or well enough to be in love. And no sooner did I acknowledge my love for her than we were separated. And yet I am certain that without her, my life will be deeply unhappy."

"You intend to make her your wife?"

"If she will have me."

"My mother is Mpongwe. My father was an English trader. Their marriage was extremely unhappy."

"Are you about to deliver a solemn warning, Madame Malherbe?"

"Would it make any difference to you if I did?"

"I would listen with great attentiveness. And while I listened, I would think what a remarkable and interesting person you were, and consider what a lucky thing it was that your parents married."

"Ah. Another velvet caress. But I was not about to deliver a warning. I was about to advise you not to listen to warnings."

"I have made that my life's policy," he said gravely.

"My parents' unhappiness had very little to do with the difference of race, even though most of the world turned its back on them. Much of the world turns its back upon my husband and upon me."

"The back of the world is usually the best part of it to see."

"One comes to think like that. I don't know if it is true. A marriage of which the world disapproves is a difficult path, Monsieur Duméril. It requires constancy. To be constant, one must be sure of one's love. No spectacle is more ridiculous than that of the couple who have married against the world's advice and who then seek the world's pity when love has fled."

"No spectacle is more beautiful than that of two people who love one another in spite of the world's disapproval."

"Like Romeo and Juliet? I do not care about the world, personally. My sisters and I are very like my mother. We Gabonese women are proud. We never forget an insult or a slight. Now, Monsieur Duméril, in case it has escaped your attention, that is a warning."

"I take it to heart."

"My husband does not care, either. I take care that he does not care, if you understand me. He is an uncommon man. He may give the impression of coldness, but he loves Africa. That is unusual among the whites who come here. Most hate Africa. They are here only for profit and are glad to do as much damage as they can while they make it."

"I have seen that," he replied gently.

"Do you know what the real treasure of Africa is?"

"Yes," he said. "It is the Africans."

"Ah." She patted his arm with her white-gloved hand. "I am very sorry to hear that your intended is in prison."

"It's quite a recommendation, in its way."

"Have you seen her?"

"Yes, thank God. Two days ago."

"And how is she bearing up?"

"She is very strong. But she is undernourished. And – and she has been whipped to make her confess to my murder."

"Black skins were made to bear stripes, it seems. She had already confessed, my husband tells me."

"Yes, unfortunately."

"She may be sent to a worse prison."

"I know that."

"And how long will you wait for her?"

"Until the moths have eaten my mane and all my fangs have fallen out."

"Let us hope it does not come to that." She stopped. "This is my street. That is my house, with the white balconies. No, you need not walk me to the door. But I hope you will call, you and your intended, when all this is over?"

"You have my word."

"Then I thank you for the use of your arm, Monsieur Duméril, and I restore it to its owner."

He tipped his hat and watched her walk away, her slim figure swaying in the ivory silk. Malherbe must indeed be an uncommon man, he thought, or else a very lucky one.

27

The audience chamber was stiflingly hot. It had a large window which looked out onto the lieutenant-governor's garden, with its emerald lawn and its clump of palm trees. One side of the window was open and the blind was drawn to keep out the sun. Everyone present wore formal clothing. Jean-Patrice sweltered in a dark suit with a waistcoat and a necktie. The lieutenant-governor, Petit and Malherbe sat in a triumvirate at a single table at the window, reaping the benefit of such slight breezes as might arise, as well as having the light at their backs. There were a dozen chairs, all of which were filled by civil servants, and a small desk for the secretary. A bench was reserved for the natives in the case. Catherine and Hyppolite sat between a white corporal and four black guards. Hyppolite appeared unchanged but Catherine looked grey and exhausted. She sat with her eyes closed most of the time, her shaved head drooping. He felt she was ill, but he was not allowed to approach them.

The lawyer, Petit, was a wizened man with a long, narrow nose and arched nostrils. He did not direct his glance at Jean-Patrice but sat with his arms folded. He had an ironic smile, which he used to good effect even before the proceedings opened, sneering elegantly at everything that was said to him by raising his upper lip in such a way as to expose his canines, and lowering his lids over his pale green eyes.

The lieutenant-governor rapped on the table with a gavel and the murmur in the room was stilled.

"This special hearing is opened on this 10th day of April, 1900. The events under investigation took place while Jean-Patrice Duméril was district commissioner of Bassongo during the last three months of the previous year. We may dispense with any other formalities. Maître Pierre Petit will begin the questioning."

Petit spoke, revealing that his voice was thin and nasal. "Approach the bench, Duméril." Jean-Patrice rose and stood in front of the table. Petit looked up at him with his gooseberry eyes. "Before we begin, is there any statement you wish to make?"

"No, Monsieur."

"You wish to produce no preliminary assertion? Such as, for example, an affidavit of hereditary insanity in your family?"

There was a ripple of laughter. Despite himself, Jean-Patrice felt his cheeks colour. "There is no insanity in my family."

"Indeed? Then we are to take it that you were in full command of your senses when these—" He picked up a sheaf of papers and then tossed them down. "—these revelries were enacted?"

"I believe myself to have been as sane then as I am now."

"You appear sane enough, it has to be admitted. I wish to be certain, however, since some of the passages in your own report seem to belong to the annals of the celebrated Baron Munchausen, rather than to a sober civil servant." There was more laughter. Petit evidently enjoyed it, waiting until the last chuckle had died away before continuing. "Do you have syphilis?"

"No," Jean-Patrice retorted angrily.

"I cannot see what that question has to do with the subject," Malherbe said dryly.

"Very well. To begin with, help us to understand the nature of your duties at Bassongo."

The next two hours passed in a minute examination of the first weeks that Jean-Patrice had spent as District Commissioner at Bassongo. Petit's questions were steady and searching. Jean-Patrice made no effort to hide the shock of Hugo Joliet's death, his initial difficulties in beginning the inoculation program, his slowness in finding and training a vaccinator. He was aware that Petit was attempting to paint a picture of an idle man lazing in a backwater sinecure, doing as little as possible in an office that involved minimal duties. He readily admitted his inexperience and even his unsuitability for the job.

"If you had so little aptitude for the task," Petit pressed him, smiling thinly, "why then did you apply for the appointment?"

"I wished to expand my horizons."

"In what sense?"

"I suppose I had a taste for adventure."

"Indeed? That is often a euphemism used by young men who have already had so many adventures in their native country that it has become rather too hot for them."

"I bow to your superior experience, Maître."

"There are many paths where a young man may stray. Let us mention, for example, drink. There is also the getting of money by dishonest means. And, of course, there are the ladies. You are aware of all these pitfalls?"

"I am aware of them," Jean-Patrice said.

"I hope you are not one of these young men, Duméril, one of these loose fellows who seem to populate the colonial service so extensively, who are packed off from France in disgrace to inflict their vileness on a hapless native population?"

"I suggest that the last comment should be removed

from the record," Malherbe put in.

"Strike it," the lieutenant-governor ordered.

"Well, then," Petit said, "let us content ourselves with agreeing that you enjoyed a promising career in France before you suddenly developed this unaccountable taste for adventure and plunged into a remote corner of deepest Africa. Please explain to us the origin of your quarrel with the Fang."

Jean-Patrice sensed that Petit was now moving in for an attack. "I don't think 'quarrel' is an appropriate term. The Fang were aggrieved because members of their tribe were being captured and put to forced labor on the road. Where," he added, "conditions were of such brutality that—"

"You are aware," Petit cut in, "that the levying of compulsory labor gangs is quite legal in Gabon?"

"Legal and just are different concepts."

"Leave the law to me," Petit advised, "and let us forget the labor gangs. Confine yourself to answering the question."

"There was a misunderstanding. The head servant of the Residency, Raymond Mbangu, accused some men of having stolen his daughter, Sophie. These men also killed Ndoumou."

"The imbecile," Petit put in, consulting his notes.

"Yes. The imbecile. I demanded the return of the girl and imposed a fine for the murder of Ndoumou. Mbangu had lied to me, however. He had sold the girl as a concubine or slave."

"Why did he lie to you in this way?"

"I believe it was to punish me for not accepting the girl as my mistress. She had been the mistress of District Commissioner Joliet until his death."

"Strike that reply from the record," the lieutenant-governor said laconically.

"You are aware that, in a statement made to District Commissioner Tosti, Mbangu denies all this? He accuses you of having purchased some ivory from the men and then having demanded the payment back in order to line your own pockets."

"That is very plausible, if you trust the word of a father who would prostitute his daughter to one man and sell her to another."

"That comment will also be struck from the record," the lieutenant-governor commanded.

Petit shrugged. "Very well. Then it will be fair to say that the quarrel between you and the Fang was a personal one, instigated by you yourself?"

"That is not fair. I have explained the origin of the quarrel, as you call it."

"Let us move on. Describe to us the events of Christmas day, 1899."

Jean-Patrice requested a glass of water before continuing. The room was becoming hotter and more airless. He had still not recovered his stamina fully, and he was beginning to feel dizzy after standing for so long. He composed himself and described the unexpected arrival of Schultze, the preparations for the Christmas dinner and the initial shot which had wounded the German. The room became silent as he described the development of the siege, the exchanges of fire and the horrible death of Narcise. He gave an account of the escape from the Residency in the early hours of the morning, the dragging of the cannon to the little hill, and its discharge against the enemy.

Petit was laconic. "You do not deny, then, that you loaded silver specie to the value of some five hundred francs into a six-pounder and then fired it at the Fang war party with gunpowder?"

"I do not deny that."

"Kindly explain to us how you came to this choice of projectile."

"I was afraid that the cutlery might get jammed in the barrel."

The laughter which followed this statement was loud enough to make the lieutenant-governor rap the table with his gavel. "Your humor is misplaced, Duméril," he growled.

"I am not attempting to be humorous, your Excellency. I was under siege. I had with me an injured German civilian, two native civilians and my corporal. I had been issued with a cannon and two kegs of gunpowder, but no shot. If I had been able to obtain chains, scrap iron or any other such material, I would have used that. As it was, I was compelled to make use of what was at hand. I considered the cutlery, but was anxious that it might burst the barrel, since the gun was rather small. The silver was a good choice."

"Good?" Petit said sharply. "Good in what sense?"

"In the sense that it saved all of our lives."

"It was a very expensive means of saving lives which some might say did not have any great value," Petit retorted.

"If it comes to that," Jean-Patrice replied, "I believe that life has no value at all in the commercial sense. It cannot be estimated. No sum you care to mention can ever purchase life. Therefore no sum can be too great to save a life. But having seen Narcise cut down in front of me, I was under no illusions as to the fate which awaited us all at the hands of the Fang."

"You are a heavy drinker, are you not, Duméril?"

"Not as a general rule."

"Come, come! Your reputation as a drunkard was well-established before you even set foot in Libreville. You were soused every day on the *Marmotte*. Your fellow passengers recall that clearly. Do you wish to deny that?"

"No."

Petit leaned a sharp elbow on the table, directing a scornful smile at Jean-Patrice. "I put it to you that it was Christmas Day. You had received a visit from a congenial spirit, Dr. Schultze, who had brought with him an immoderate quantity of alcohol – cases of fine Hock, schnapps and so forth. You became wildly intoxicated in the company of this German reveler. In your maddened state, you began an altercation with a group of savages, whom you had earlier swindled. In the course of this fracas, Dr. Schultze was injured. It now seemed fitting to you to stuff several pounds of Government silver into the cannon and discharge it at your enemies – the symbolism would have appealed to your drunken imagination – thus also burning down the little town which had been entrusted to your care." He threw his pen down with satisfaction, looking around the chamber with hooded green eyes to see the effect he had created.

"That would indeed have been a devilish Christmas entertainment," Jean-Patrice said gently. "However, the events of the evening consisted of a desperate struggle for life and death, rather than a farce. Neither Schultze nor I were drunk."

This calm statement produced an effect which Petit did not like. "So you say."

"I swindled nobody. My corporal, Hyppolite Mokamo, will confirm that during the siege, the attackers expressed their anger at Raymond and asked for him to be sent out to them so that they could punish him."

"Mokamo will no doubt say anything you desire him to, since his liberty depends on your evidence."

"Mokamo has always been a trustworthy officer in my experience."

"If indeed the Fang guaranteed your safety if you would hand over Mbangu, why did you not do so?"

"Because I feared he would be killed and eaten."

"Ah, how dramatic. In fact, these fearsome cannibals turn out not to have eaten any human being at Bassongo, is that not true? Not even the Askaris of the good Dr. Schultze, who attacked them without provocation?"

"Dr. Schultze might argue that having his jaw shot off was provocation enough. As for the cannibalism, I was mistaken about that. But there was a smell of roasting flesh—"

"Which turned out to be the smallpox calf, did it not?"

"Yes."

Petit examined his papers. "It is an interesting point that this animal produced greater havoc on the Fang than your cannonades, Duméril. According to the figures supplied by District Commissioner Tosti, consumption of the infected animal resulted in generalized vaccinial eruptions which have killed four men and incapacitated eight more. An unspecified number continue to suffer from scabs of varying degrees of severity."

"The meat was probably under-cooked," Malherbe put in. "Or they may have drunk the blood. According to Tosti's report, they regarded the calf as magical and hoped that eating it would confer protection against evil spirits on them. They probably held a ritual of some kind."

"That is beside the point," Petit said. "He didn't kill a single savage with all the silver coins."

Jean-Patrice cleared his throat. "I am glad of that. I didn't really want to kill any of them, only to stun them for long enough to make an escape."

"The point I am trying to make is that he claims to have discharged a year's worth of trading dollars in one blast, to little effect except that he burned down the town."

Malherbe put on his steel-rimmed spectacles and consulted some papers. "Some of it has been recovered, Maître. Almost eighty francs' worth from the banana grove alone. Some thirty francs' worth from the limbs of the wounded – so it has to be admitted that he did hit some of them."

"That leaves most unaccounted for. Monsieur Duméril, can you assure us that you loaded the full weight of silver into the six-pounder? Is it not likely that you slipped some of it into your own trouser pockets, you and Schultze? Say a pound or two apiece?"

"We would have found it difficult to escape with a

pound or two of silver in our trousers, Maître. I was considering the silver in ballistic terms at that point, not in pecuniary terms."

"Well, let's leave that aside for the time being," Malherbe said. "Coins are still being handed in at such a steady rate that District Commissioner Tosti has employed the local blacksmith to spend one afternoon a week hammering them flat again. It may well be that a majority of them will eventually be recovered. Let us consider the beneficial results which Duméril's actions have had on the community of Bassongo. Natives have been flocking into the area steadily for many weeks."

"Scavenging for silver," Petit snorted.

"It is true that Bassongo is now being called The Silver River. But those who arrive bring willing hands. While I am vehemently opposed to enforced labor, let it not be ignored that recent arrivals in Bassongo have provided scores of laborers for the road from Medoneu and the lumber camps. The burning of the village, of course, was directly due to the huge fire which the Fang had built near the huts. It is they who are responsible, not Duméril. Bassongo was in a very dilapidated state, as I saw with my own eyes on my last visit there, with many deserted dwellings disfiguring the town. The empty and broken-down houses have now been rebuilt, in great measure by the arrested Fang, whom Tosti has put to work. The population has swollen greatly and there is demand for new housing. Trade has increased. The market is thriving. The police force is up to full strength. The Americans are opening a mission there even as we speak. The Catholics intend to follow. What was once a moribund and forgotten corner of the province is becoming a thriving metropolis."

"Don't get carried away, Malherbe," the lieutenant-governor growled.

"But Excellency, all the evidence indicates that a renaissance is under way." Malherbe made a gesture with one of his dry flippers. "One can see the discharge of Duméril's cannon, freighted with precious metal, as an almost divine act, investing the trees, the river, the very soil with treasure. It is like the shower of gold with which Jupiter impregnated Danaë. It has brought fertility and prosperity to what was once barren. It was a scattering of precious seed which will engender a bounteous harvest in years to come." There was a ripple of amusement at Malherbe's flight of rhetoric, but he had not done, yet. "And let us not overlook another great benefit, the pacification of the Fang achieved by Duméril. This particular group had been terrorizing the area for many years, committing atrocities against whomever they chose. To them, Duméril's cannon was a thunderbolt of vengeful justice. Those who were not raked with the silver were poisoned by the calf. They have limped away, chastened men, to whom the name of France is now synonymous with terror."

"Bravo, Malherbe," the lieutenant-governor said ironically. "Do you have anything else to add, or can we return to the terrestrial plane? The hearing is adjourned for lunch. We will meet again at three o'clock."

28

Jean-Patrice had been hoping for a moment to talk to Catherine, but she and Hyppolite were hustled away to eat at the jail. He was tired. He would like to have taken one of his brisk walks to clear his head. He found that a solitary meal had been prepared for him in the next room. He sat at a little table, grateful for a glass of wine, but unable to eat the fufu and tinned beef which had been supplied. As he sat, staring into the glass, the door opened and a man appeared.

"Am I intruding, Duméril?" The stranger, wearing a soiled white linen suit, did not wait for a reply, but took the chair opposite Jean-Patrice and lit a cigar. There was something familiar about his shabbiness, his seamed face and his brown teeth. "Montpelier," he said, supplying the name which Jean-Patrice was groping at. "We shared the passage out."

"Of course. I recall how you tried to advise me, the morning after I got so drunk. How are you?"

"Business is booming. I'll be retiring in a couple of years. Thought I would look in on you. That little rat Petit has been trying to dig up any dirt on you he can find in Libreville. I wanted to assure you that the remarks about your drinking didn't come from me. There's always someone willing to dish the dirt on a fellow white man for a few francs." He squinted at Jean-Patrice through his tobacco smoke. "So this is how you ended up, eh?"

Jean-Patrice smiled slightly. "Well, I hope this is not quite the end."

Montpelier grunted. "I've worked in one of those inland stations. Spent ten years there. Something of a record, you know. White men don't generally live longer than a year there. I know what it's like. I know what goes on there. Hell on earth."

"Oh, I don't know. I was getting to like it."

"You weren't expected to like it. You weren't expected to come back. You gave them quite a turn, crawling out of the jungle like that." He chuckled. "Most of us in that room are behind you. And you're lucky old Malherbe likes you. Me, I'm getting out of this place. Going back to France to spend my savings. A nice little place in the country, some fat white pigs, a fat white wife. Eh?" He winked.

"I wish you happiness in your retirement."

"I advise you to do the same. They say you want to marry that woman in there? Don't ruin your life. She's a pretty piece but I will tell you this, that nobody in the civilized world will ever see in her the qualities that you do. They'll only see a black skin. It'll be just you and her forever. And if they try to send you back up the river, refuse. You've done your time. Get out now."

"You see no future here?"

"Not any more. The good days are over. Call 'em bad days if you will. The blacks are getting richer and bolder every day. They want to take over." He gestured with his cigar. "One fine day, there'll be a black fellow sitting in the governor's chair. Life will get complicated. Go home, Duméril. You're not suited for this country." He checked his fob watch. "Almost three. You're back on stage in a few minutes. Finish your wine. You'll need it."

The company reassembled, bringing a smell of food and alcohol with it. Petit resumed his questioning in the same sneering tone, now concentrating on the journey back to Libreville, asking Jean-Patrice to account for the weeks he had spent in the forest.

"I'm not sure I can account for them," Jean-Patrice said wearily. "Each day was like the day before. Sometimes the streams I took would end in swampland or would simply peter out. I would have to paddle back up to find the last branch. That was exhausting. Sometimes I would meet natives. They were invariably kind to me. Almost always they fed me, sometimes they would allow me to sleep in their huts. Most of the time, I was quite alone. Many days would pass without the sight of a human face or the sound of a human voice. It is surprising how one can come to miss the company of—" Unexpectedly, he found that his cheeks were wet with tears. "Pardon me." He fumbled for his handkerchief.

Malherbe rose to his feet. "I, for one, have heard enough. I think it is clear that Duméril behaved with exemplary resourcefulness and bravery, under very trying circumstances. He escorted his companions to safety at great personal risk. He has suffered to an extraordinary extent. He bears two wounds from Fang muskets and endured a three-month journey, alone, through forest where few white men have ever penetrated. To hear him mocked and abused in this tribunal, where he should be garlanded with honors, is extremely painful to me and should be painful to any gentleman here who has a drop of French blood in his veins."

There was a murmur of sympathy from the rest of the room. A dark line of red touched the lean cheekbones of the lawyer. "It is not my intention to mock or abuse any person," Petit said shortly, "simply to get at the truth."

"The truth is that this young man, sent on an almost impossible mission, has returned in triumph. He was charged with the inoculation of a remote tribal population.

With the help of his gallant young female assistant, who now sits before you in chains, he succeeded beyond any expectations." Necks craned to look at Catherine, who raised her head slowly.

"Stand up, child," the lieutenant-governor commanded. Catherine rose to her feet, revealing that she was not actually in chains, though barefoot and wearing her grey prison garb. "How many did you inoculate?" he asked.

"I don't have my records with me," she said in a low voice, "but I think the total stood at three thousand, one hundred and thirteen."

"Vaccinated by your hand?"

"With help from Jean-Patrice – from the District Commissioner – at times."

"You call him by his first name?" Petit interrupted sharply.

"In private, yes."

"You are his mistress, then?"

"That question will be struck from the record," the lieutenant-governor said.

"I am not his mistress," Catherine said quietly.

"The report of Raymond Mbangu says that you are his paramour, his 'native wife,' if that term accords better with your feelings."

"None of the terms you use accord with my feelings," she said, looking him in the face.

Petit showed his canines. "Did you not share his bed?"

"No."

"So Mbangu is lying when he says that on one occasion you did not leave Duméril's bed for three days?"

"I spent three days in his bed, Monsieur, but he was not in it with me. I was very ill and he cared for me like a mother."

"Like a mother?" Petit laughed. "That is a very odd way to describe the robust Monsieur Duméril."

"I know of no other way to describe the tenderness and love with which he looked after me," Catherine said. The room had become deathly quiet, the attention of everyone present concentrated on her. She stood with her hands at her sides, looking calmly at Petit, almost seeming to smile slightly. The prison had taken the bloom from her skin, but her beauty had become in some way refined, more luminous.

"You use the word 'love?'"

"Yes."

"But when he was ill and it came your turn to care for him, you did not behave like a mother. You behaved more like a viper. You abandoned him to his wounds and the wild beasts."

"You are right to castigate me, Monsieur," she replied, even more quietly. "I can never forgive myself for that."

"Ah. You are not his lover, but you love him."

"Yes."

Petit was pinching his lower lip, regarding her balefully. "Does he love you in return?"

"That is for him to say."

"But you believe he does?"

"You must ask him."

"Very well." Petit turned to Jean-Patrice with his thin smile. "Do you love this woman?"

"Yes," he replied. There was a complete silence in the room. Nobody stirred. He opened his mouth as though to add some explanation but found he had nothing else to say.

"Were you not surprised, then, when she abandoned you, alone, wounded and defenseless, in a swamp?"

"It wasn't a swamp. It was a lagoon. And there was no abandonment. We simply misunderstood one another as to the route we were to take. None of us reckoned with the complexity of the river system. We thought there was one river, when there were in reality dozens. We became separated. By my own error, I took the wrong course. And I was not alone. I was with a gorilla."

Petit was startled out of his sneer for once. "A gorilla?"

"Chloë. She was Hugo Joliet's pet. A young female."

"And where is this animal now?"

"She left me one day on the river."

"You have some difficulty in retaining the loyalty of females, it seems," Petit said derisively. "Your version of the events differs substantially from her own account."

"She blames herself unnecessarily. The relation between us has not always been easy. The relation between a white and a black must always, I believe, be beset with difficulties in Gabon. But I intend to ask her to be my wife. She has already been whipped in prison. If she continues to be incarcerated, I believe that no human purpose will be served except in making two souls very unhappy."

Three pairs of eyes stared at him from the bench – Malherbe's with something like pity, the lieutenant-governor's with dry displeasure, the lawyer's with disdain. Petit turned back to Catherine. "You hear what he says. Now will you please explain to us your relationship with Hyppolite Mokamo?"

"I have no relationship with Hyppolite."

"Indeed? Let the corporal stand." Hyppolite rose to his feet. His face, with its tribal initiation scars on each cheek, was impassive. He stared ahead of him without expression. "He is a fine, big fellow, is he not?" Petit said. "Between him and Duméril there is not much to choose for physique. Your taste in men is to be commended. You are a beautiful woman, so of course you have your pick, not so?"

"I don't understand you."

"The corporal has been your suitor, has he not?"

Catherine hesitated. "He asked me to marry him. But that was many years ago. And I refused."

"And yet you and he have been living in the same village for all these many years."

"One does not leave one's home because a neighbor proposes."

"According to Raymond Mbangu, there was more than a proposal."

She compressed her full lips. "I am starting to detest the name of Raymond Mbangu, Monsieur."

"As well you might," Petit said sarcastically. "I put it to you that while making the journey to Libreville by pirogue, you and the corporal decided between you that the white man, Duméril, was slowing down your progress. Dying, in fact. Rather than care for him, as he once cared for you, you determined to throw your lot in with Mokamo, your former lover and the man of your own race. You abandoned Duméril to die in a festering swamp, thereby conserving your rations and lightening the burden upon yourselves. It was thus that you arrived here safely in a few weeks, whilst Duméril, your erstwhile beloved, crawled through the forest in agony for three months."

Catherine did not answer at once. She allowed her eyes to drift around the room, finally settling on Jean-Patrice. "I see white faces and black faces here," she said quietly, "but I see only one face that I love. To me it belongs to no race except the human one."

The muttering in the room was interrupted by Hyppolite. "I would like to speak."

"Let him speak," the lieutenant-governor said.

"She loves him," he said in his deep voice, "as he loves her. They quarreled out of pride. The medicine which the German gave him took over his spirit and he said things he did not mean. For an hour she was angry. We became separated because of it. She made me look for him for three days in the lagoon and then every day on the river, after that. When we reached Libreville and found he was not here, she wanted to turn around and go back for him. I stopped her. No decision was taken to abandon anyone. Our lives are sometimes shaped by foolish things, which begin with a word and end with blood. That is the way of it." He gestured at Petit. "This Monsieur need not turn it around with his words any longer. It is no more difficult than that."

"You were negligent of your duty," the lieutenant-governor said harshly.

Hyppolite lowered his head. "Yes."

"You should not have let a woman's temper lead you astray."

"I was wrong. It is true that I once loved her and perhaps for a moment, I dreamed—"

"We are not interested in your dreams." The lieutenant-governor examined the watch in his vest pocket. It was now late afternoon and the shadows were growing long in the room. He consulted briefly and inaudibly with Petit, then with Malherbe. "I think the corporal is right. We need not turn this matter around any longer. Strike everything that was said by Catherine Atélé and Hyppolite Mokamo. It is not relevant. I will make a report to the Minister and he will decide on any action which must be taken. In the meantime, pending the Minister's decision, Catherine Atélé is at liberty. Hyppolite Mokamo will be returned to the fort and will remain incarcerated until the Minister takes a decision. Jean-Patrice Duméril will be paid the salary that is owing to him and will continue on sick leave and on full pay until otherwise decided. The hearing is concluded."

The meeting broke up. Bemused, Jean-Patrice allowed his hand to be shaken by various strangers who declared that he had acquitted himself well. He tried to make his way towards Catherine, but too many people were blocking his way. Petit passed by and patted him familiarly on the shoulder. "My job is to throw as much mud as possible and to see how much sticks. It's nothing personal. No hard feelings, I hope."

"And now what happens?" Jean-Patrice asked.

The other man shrugged. "Now a wait of two or three months until word arrives back from the Minister. Be prepared for a reprimand or a commendation. Then you cannot be taken by surprise either way. Good luck,

Duméril." He put his hat on his head and departed.

Malherbe appeared from the throng, folding his steel-rimmed spectacles into his breast pocket. "A long day, Duméril. It may have seemed to you a pointless ordeal, but that is often the way of these enquiries."

"I don't know how to thank you, Monsieur le Directeur."

"The truth is that I did not expect you to vaccinate a single individual. I was pleasantly surprised. I understand you have met my wife?"

"Yes."

"She has asked you to pay us a call. You and Mademoiselle Atélé together, of course. Shall we say Sunday afternoon at about four?"

"I should be delighted."

Malherbe nodded and passed on without further comment. At last, Jean-Patrice saw Catherine, standing alone near the doorway. Hyppolite and the guards had gone, leaving her there. He went to her. "Well, my dear," he said gently. "They have done with us, it seems."

She looked up at him with her almond eyes. "I have no clothes but this sack, and they say I must return that. I have no money. I have nowhere to go."

"You could come with me. I am not much better off than you, but I would count myself immensely rich in having your company."

She smiled. "I could go a little of the way with you, I suppose."

He offered her his arm and she took it. He escorted her from the lieutenant-governor's mansion, barely aware of the stares that followed them. "I have taken a little house on the beach," he said. "It's very simple. There are two rooms. I have left one of them for you. The street is quiet and you can watch the sea from the veranda. Nobody will bother us there."

"We have been in different prisons," she said. "It will be strange for both of us to be free."

"I've been waiting for you a long time," he said.

She laid her shaved head on his shoulder for a moment. "I feel so ugly, Jean-Patrice."

"You are beautiful to me." They walked through the sunset to the sea. He led her up the stairs into the little house and showed her the rooms, the shutters that opened onto the beach. She stood at the open window, staring out at the golden sea. He watched her profile, marveling that she was here, marveling at her. "Are you hungry? Can I make you something to eat?"

"I would like to swim in the sea," she said. "I would like to feel clean again."

"Then come." They walked to edge of the sea, where the breakers rolled in from the west. She stripped off her dress and threw it onto the sand. She was naked beneath it. She turned to him, smiling into his eyes, and spread out her arms so he could see her body. He saw the scattering of shiny disks left by the vaccine on her ribs and belly. He saw the grim lines of the whip, with a raised weal where each stripe had crossed another. He saw the dark emblems of her sex, the stars of her nipples and the triangle at her loins. He saw the curves of her flesh and the frame of her bones. He saw the strength of her and the beauty of her. He saw how she had survived brutality and betrayal and had come to him, scarred but still beautiful, still fertile, still brimming with life.

She turned so he could see her back, where the marks of the whip multiplied across her rounded buttocks and over her strong thighs. He saw how she had suffered for him, as he had suffered for her.

He undressed for her and showed her his own scars, the places where the canoe had rubbed him to the bone, the marks left by the musket balls and by the forest's thorns and claws. She touched them with her fingertips, then took his hand and led him into the sea.

The water was warm with the day's sun, foaming around their ankles, then their hips, then swallowing them into its kind body. They floated, the rolling of the waves pushing them together until they were in one another's arms, his thigh sliding between hers. He felt her against him, soft and hard, yielding and demanding. He kissed her mouth. She drew away from him, smiling.

The sun went down swiftly. It grew dark. She would not put on the prison dress again so he gave her one of his shirts to wear when they got back to the house. She curled up, watching him as he cooked a fish over the charcoal.

"Tell me what happened to Chloë."

"She stayed with me until I got so ill. I lay in a broken-down hut for a few days. She found some trees that she liked and sat near me until I was strong again. When I left, she stayed behind. She wouldn't get into the canoe. I cried when we parted."

She touched his hand. "She's where she belongs."

"And now we must find where we belong." He fanned the charcoal to make it glow. "I don't know how to make sauces," he said. "This is the way I learned to cook fish on the river. It will be a very plain meal."

"I cannot imagine how you survived, Jean-Patrice."

"The people who helped me gave me fufu and maize porridge, or fruit. I learned to throw scraps of fufu in the shallow water and then catch the crabs when they came. Sometimes I caught frogs. Not all of them are good to eat. Some taste bad. The same with the fish, some are very bitter. I was often so sick after eating something bad that I could not paddle, and had to drift along helplessly. I had Schultze's shotgun and sometimes I was able to shoot a bird, once a monkey. Then I ran out of shells. I didn't eat once for four days. I thought I was going to starve. A fisherman gave me the fish he didn't want – it was half-rotten, all bones and cartilage, but I ate it like a wolf." He smiled. "Now I don't care what I eat any more."

"I am the same. The food in prison smelled so bad that we often preferred to go hungry than eat it. When you started to send me food, everyone was excited. I had to share each package with the women in my cell. They all said that my lover must be rich. I said that you were not my lover, but my friend."

"I hope I am both."

"They meant that I was a kept woman, and you were the man who kept me."

"I hope to be the man who keeps you," he said gravely.

She looked at him with smiling eyes. "Are you sure you want me? I am not an easy person, Jean-Patrice. I was once innocent. I am no longer like that. You may find me difficult and obstinate."

"You are a starchy schoolmarm. I am quite familiar with your obstinacy. In my experience, obstinacy must be met with patience, and I have learned to be very patient. I am changing, Catherine. When I left France, I was absorbed utterly in myself. I look back at what I was and am ashamed. I thought of nothing but my own comfort. Coming to Africa should have been the great adventure of my life, but I thought of it as a penance. I am not yet what I would like to be, but at least I have realized that I am ashamed to continue being what I was." He turned the fish over carefully to cook the other side. "You are the most interesting woman I have ever met. You fascinate me. I would like to spend the rest of my life learning about you."

"And what if you don't like what you learn?"

"I want only to be close to you. I expect nothing else."

"But you are free, now. Bassongo was a kind of prison for you. You were so lonely there. I cannot help thinking that is why you are drawn to me. Now that you are free, I may not seem so interesting to you."

"I would like to think there is more than that," he said quietly. "We have suffered for each other. And here we are."

"Yes, here we are." She paused for a while and then spoke in a quieter voice. "If this is really what you want, Jean-Patrice, then I want it, too."

"It is all I have thought about for many months."

She was silent as he served the fish. They sat together and ate. The sound of the sea was in their ears. When they had eaten, he washed and cleared the kitchen. "You're very neat," she said.

"What goes on in my head is so complicated that I like the house to be orderly," he said. "Let me show you your room." He led her to the second bedroom and showed her the low bed, the simple furniture. "Tomorrow we will get you some clothes and whatever things you need."

Her eyes seemed to be wet with tears. "I need very little."

He touched her cheek. "I dreamed of seeing you here."

"I will try to make you as happy as I can, my beloved."

Jean-Patrice took her in his arms, holding her close, feeling himself tremble. "I have been thinking about our future for so long. We'll go to Leopoldville and find your daughter. I have my back pay, now. I can afford the journey. You should at least meet her. Perhaps you will want to take her with us when we go."

"When we go where?"

"I think we would have a better future in France than here. Here, we will always be put in a certain category. Your people and my people will both laugh at us. In France, there is no category for us to belong to. We would be ourselves, unique."

"Do you truly believe that?"

"You don't have to give an answer now. We can think about it and talk about it before we take any decisions. You must be tired. I'll leave you to sleep." He released her at last.

"No. Please don't ever leave me again." She sat on the bed and took his hands, drawing him down to her.

29

The Malherbes' house was bright and filled with the laughter of children. For such a leathery man, the Director had produced remarkably fine daughters.

"One sees the influence of my wife," he pointed out, in response to a remark made by Jean-Patrice. "I can claim little credit for myself." Jean-Patrice watched the girls helping their mother, and thought with shame of how he had once imagined the futility of Malherbe's domestic life. They served tea in the English style, with pretty china and little cakes. When the tea and the milk and the sugar and the lemon and the little cakes had been distributed to the utmost satisfaction of all concerned, the girls melted away to practice on the piano. It could be heard, discreetly muffled, in a back room. Marie sat beside her husband and considered Jean-Patrice and Catherine with her dark eyes. She had assumed the authority that the old married person has over the newly betrothed.

"Well, Gaston, I cannot remember having seen a handsomer couple," she said decisively. "Can you?"

"Mademoiselle Atélé is certainly a handsome young woman," Malherbe replied in his dry way. "But I am no great judge of male beauty. To me, Duméril merely looks very large and very pleased with himself."

"Exactly like a lion which has caught and eaten a young gazelle," she agreed.

"One cannot help feeling that good fortune continues to accompany him," Malherbe observed over his teacup. "He is one of those young fellows who evidently have only to stretch out their hands to encounter a pearl."

"I am not so sure that he would agree with you," Catherine said. "He tells me I am starchy and a schoolmarm."

"I suppose Gaston has the same complaint," Marie replied.

"I have not complained thus far, my dear."

"You would not use the term 'starchy,' I suppose, since you like your dinner hot and your life comfortable. But you have certainly called me a schoolmarm."

"And so you are."

"The amount of starch in a schoolmistress is in direct proportion to the good behavior of her charges," Marie said.

"But it is not necessarily a desirable quality in the companion of a man's life," Jean-Patrice pointed out with a smile.

"It depends on how you define 'starch.'"

"Well," he said, "a certain quality of stiffness, formality or primness, I should say. Perhaps even of severity. I am not sure how to define it, but when I begin to feel like a ten-year-old boy, I know the quality is present. There is a certain tendency towards irony, too. When I first introduced myself as the District Commissioner of Bassongo she replied that she did not think I had fallen from the moon."

"It sounds as though you have begun well, Catherine," Marie said, pouring more tea. The two women wore day-dresses in the flowing, flowery Parisian style that had just arrived. Jean-Patrice had warned Catherine that Marie Malherbe was fashionable and she had prepared herself to good effect in the Libreville shops.

"I don't think I'm capable of being severe with Jean-Patrice any longer," she said gently. "I once called him a boy, because he fired off a cannon in my ear, but that was long ago."

"Was this the inoculation-cannon or the silver-cannon?"

"The inoculation-cannon. I didn't expect it to be quite so loud. But he exceeds my expectations in everything he does." She smiled at Jean-Patrice with soft eyes. "I find myself in a constant condition of awe these days."

Marie glanced at her husband with a sparkle in her eyes. "What will be the result of the enquiry, Gaston?" she asked him. "What can they expect?"

"The corporal will receive at least six months for desertion of his superior," Malherbe replied. "By the time the decision arrives, he will already have served his term, and in all probability will be set free. Duméril may be reprimanded for the destruction of the silver and his career in the civil service will possibly end."

"But he was acting in self-defense."

"The government of France is essentially secular, my dear, I am glad to say. However, if there are divinities, they consist of the glorious franc and her hundred loyal centimes. Sins committed against this pantheon are not pardoned easily. Nevertheless, I would hazard a guess that the wounds he received in service will entitle him to retire with a pension, which will be a great advantage. He will be able to seek employment advantageously elsewhere."

"And where will he seek employment?"

"That is up to him. Africa offers a great many opportunities to an active and resourceful young fellow such as he."

She turned her black eyes back on Jean-Patrice. "Do you hear, Mad Duméril? You are active and resourceful. I can assure you that Gaston does not bestow such praise lightly."

Malherbe shrugged. "My dear, those are qualities which might be demanded by any burglar."

"According to Maître Petit," Jean-Patrice smiled, "I am a syphilitic drunkard and a thief."

"High praise, from a lawyer," Marie said. "What are your plans now, my dears?"

"We are going to be married," Jean-Patrice said.

"When?"

"In a week or two."

Marie opened her eyes wide. "That is rather precipitate, even for 'Mad Duméril,' is it not?"

"There is a reason," he replied.

Catherine put down her teacup. "I have a child, a daughter. She was born when I was eighteen. She was taken by nuns to Leopoldville. We are going to find her, if we can, and take her back. It will be much easier if we are husband and wife."

Malherbe showed no emotion, as usual. "If there is anything I am able to do for you, please let me know."

"Thank you," Jean-Patrice said. "You have already been kindness itself. There is another reason for a quick marriage. The longer we remain betrothed, the more we are subject to pressing advice that we should not marry. It becomes tedious. Neither of us have any family in the world, so it will be a very simple ceremony."

Marie folded her hands. "So! Another mixed marriage in Libreville. What advice can we offer them, my dear?"

"There is no advice that can be offered a young couple on the brink of matrimony. Their future depends upon them alone. But we can offer our good wishes."

"I can offer more," she said. "Because I am a believer, I can invoke the blessings of my Creator. And we can offer to act as witnesses to their marriage."

"We would be honored," Catherine said. They became engrossed in plans for the style and place of the wedding, whilst Jean-Patrice and Malherbe were sent outside to smoke peacefully in the garden and admire the sunset.

"You seem in harmony with the world," Malherbe remarked.

"I cannot recall any occasion when I have had less to say for myself," Jean-Patrice said.

"Married life offers many advantages," Malherbe replied equably. "One of them is the opportunity to indulge in prolonged periods of silence. No-one questions the muteness of a married man. It is accepted with compassion and respect." He puffed on his cigar. "The missionaries inform me that they intend to erect a memorial at Bassongo to Father Jacques Delacroix, who died there a few years ago. There was some little mystery over his death, but he is now to be regarded as a martyr, it appears."

So Father Jacques had been caught absconding from his eternal bed, and had been tucked in once again by firm, kindly hands. Probably for the best. "He was the father of Catherine's child. He died by his own hand."

"Ah. I had understood something of the sort. The Church sometimes leaves us its little problems to resolve in Africa."

"I will be overjoyed to become a father to her child. It is not a problem to me."

Malherbe inspected the ash of his cigar. "You are a decent man, Duméril. You deserve your luck."

It was evening by the time Jean-Patrice and Catherine said goodbye to their hosts and left the house with the white balconies. Marie Malherbe watched from behind the lace curtain in her parlor as the couple walked down the street. She seemed to be waiting for something. When she saw them pause at the end of the street, almost out of sight, and turn to one another, she held her breath. She saw Catherine raise her face to Duméril, and saw him bend down tenderly to her. She let out her breath in a long sigh.

"Are you satisfied with your observations?" Malherbe asked her, clearing away the tea things.

"I had a little wager with myself that they could not

wait until the end of the street before kissing one another. They look at each other with such eyes, Gaston. Can you remember being so deeply in love as that?"

"I am not aware that I have stopped feeling that particular emotion," he said with equanimity.

"Perhaps it is the flaming newness of their love that so enchants me," she replied, drawing the curtains on the evening. "I hope that life is kind to them."

"I hope so, too," he replied.

30

When Jean-Patrice next saw Justine, it was in the Jardin
des Tuileries, during the summer of 1902. He heard
someone call his name and turned to see her hurrying up
to him, breathless and laughing.

"Jean-Patrice! I knew it must be you!" She embraced
him, bringing a wave of her familiar scent to his nostrils.
He looked down into her face, bemused. She was very
pretty. She had changed her hair; it was redder, curlier. It
suited her. She wore a grey dress with a white shirtwaist,
in the new fashion. She had on a straw hat with fluttering
ribbons. "How marvelous to see you! You look so well.
And so distinguished! People said you had settled in
Gabon."

"No, I am back in Paris."

"For good?"

"For good, I think."

She held him at arm's length. "You look wonderful.
And such a beard! Africa has made you into a Ulysses."

"I have had many travels, it's true."

"Of course we heard all about your adventures. It was
in the papers here. I cut out the articles and the cartoons
and pasted them in a scrap book. You must come and see

it!"

He did not know what to say. He smiled at her, shrugging. "I am sure they made it sound much more interesting than it really was."

"But you were injured, surely? Shot twice by cannibals, they said. You had to retire from the foreign service."

"I was awarded a decent pension, at any rate. It is a great help." Over her shoulder, in the distance, he could see the sunlight glinting on the blonde heads of three of her children. They were clustering around a man – not their father – seated on a bench with one leg crossed over the other. She followed his gaze.

"That is their Uncle Charlie."

"Uncle?" he repeated.

"A sort of uncle, one might say, at any rate." She smiled. "I wrote to you at Bassongo. I don't know if you ever received the letter. You did not reply."

"I answered it in my mind."

"Ah! I did not receive that message!"

"Perhaps it's just as well."

"I said I was sure you would return to France a hero. And you have. You see? I was right."

"A sort of hero, one might say, at any rate."

Her eyes danced. "You always made me laugh, Jean-Patrice. Did you forget about me, out there in the jungle?"

"I had dreams of you," he said.

She held his eyes. "Ah, Jean-Patrice. You loved me so much, once upon a time."

"Yes. I loved you so much."

"Why didn't you tell me you were back in Paris?"

"The burned child dreads the fire."

She made a face. "And how do you fill your days, my dear?"

"I have a shop. A tobacconist's. In Montparnasse."

She looked blank for a moment. "A tobacconist's?"

He was amused at her expression. "Yes. *La Tête de la Négresse.* I sell pipe tobacco, cigars, cigarettes, cheroots, cigarette cases, pipes. All that sort of thing. I make up special mixtures for discerning customers. It is expensive, but worth it." He presented her with a card. "You must tell Maurice."

"Maurice has had a stroke," she said, looking at the little square of pasteboard abstractedly. "He is almost paralyzed and is not allowed alcohol or tobacco."

"I am sorry to hear that," Jean-Patrice said sincerely.

"The doctors say that he cannot last much longer. I will be a widow, Jean-Patrice." She made a gesture of touching her eyes with a handkerchief although they were quite dry. "A wealthy widow, at least. Maurice has shown me his will. It is very generous." She glanced into his eyes for a moment with a touch of her old allure. "But a tobacconist's – in Montparnasse – I am not so sure about that, my dear. Does it pay?"

"Oh, yes. It's quite a popular establishment. I like the area. Artists and intellectuals are to be found in every café. I suppose I count myself among them, now. I write for the newspapers, reviews of art, music, the theatre and such things. My pen name is *l'Africain*. I am working on a novel, too."

"But how extraordinary! You have become a Bohemian!"

"Oh, I am thoroughly bourgeois. My wife is far more interesting than I."

Her eyes widened. "You are married!"

"Yes."

She appeared wounded, though perhaps it was only coquetry. "Oh, Jean-Patrice! What is she like, in one word?"

"She is rather hard to describe in one word."

"Is she a modern woman? Does she work?"

"She is the most modern woman imaginable. She works. She is an associate of Ambroise Vollard's gallery in the Rue Lafitte."

"The art dealer? But he is a dreadful fellow!"

"You know him?"

She tossed her ringlets. "He is that boorish creature who is always throwing paint in the public's face. He advances anarchists, Impressionists and madmen of that sort."

Jean-Patrice was amused by her vehemence. "Anarchists do not cherish the same ideals as Impressionists, my dear Justine. Kropotkin cannot be categorized with Van Gogh and Gauguin."

"They all belong in an insane asylum, along with the Catalan nationalists and the Russian revolutionaries."

"Well, perhaps."

"And I may tell you, since you are to be trusted, that the police have thick files on most of them!"

"But of course they do. The Préfet de Police is well-known to be a connoisseur of modern art."

She made a face at him. "You know very well what I mean."

"Yes, I do. As a matter of fact, Vollard is not a madman at all, but a very shrewd fellow. I am sure he will be exceedingly rich one day."

"Good luck to him. And what does your very modern wife do in his very peculiar establishment?"

"She is a specialist in African masks and sculpture."

Justine raised one penciled eyebrow. "Primitive art! How fascinating! And are there buyers for her totems and fetishes?"

"It seems so. Many of her clients are themselves artists or poets. She has just sold a very interesting collection of masks to the young Spanish painter, Pablo Picasso."

"A Spaniard?" she said dismissively. "I have never heard of him."

"Perhaps you may, one day. I think he is a kind of genius. We have bought two or three of his works. It will be interesting to see what influence the African artifacts will have upon his art. Such small things sometimes cast long shadows."

"Well, I will be sure to notice him if I should meet him walking down the street wearing feathers and a savage's war mask. And your wife procures these objects from Africa?"

"Yes. She is also a ceramicist. Our domestic arrangements call for us to each pursue at least three careers. We make enough to send our child to a school where she is taught the same subjects that boys are, and that does not come cheap."

"You have a child already!"

"A girl of ten."

"Ah, your wife was a widow, then. I should like to meet this extraordinary woman, Jean-Patrice. There are so few extraordinary women in Paris nowadays."

"You have your opportunity now." He gestured. Justine turned. Catherine was walking across the lawn towards them, with Élise at her side. They both wore pale yellow tea dresses, Catherine wearing a hat, the child bareheaded. Élise carried a little sailboat which she had brought to float on the pond.

Justine still had one of his hands in hers. She dropped it now and laid her fingers on her lips. "My God." She stared blankly as Catherine approached.

"Catherine, this is Justine de Marigny, the wife of my former chief. Justine, this is my wife, Catherine."

"Enchanted," Catherine said., holding out her hand, which Jean-Patrice loved so much, with its rosy palm and its smooth, soft brown skin.

"But," Justine stammered, "you are – you are—" Justine became speechless. Catherine merely nodded and smiled sympathetically, as she always did, when confronted with this reaction.

The women touched fingertips. Justine recovered herself sufficiently to utter some conventional greeting. She turned on Jean-Patrice a swift look that was half-appalled, half-amused. "I had no idea," she said in a low voice, though she did not elaborate on just what it was that had so astonished her. For a few moments, they stood together exchanging pleasantries about the day, the sunshine, the flowers, the progress of the summer. Then Élise tugged gently on Jean-Patrice's sleeve.

"Papa," she whispered. "The boat."

"Forgive me," Jean-Patrice said. "As you can see, the captain is calling and our ship is ready to set sail." He lifted his hat to Justine and took Élise and Catherine by the hand. They walked away to where other children clustered with their boats along the wall of the circular pond, whose central fountain threw up a constant jet, rising into the unclouded sky, falling back onto the glittering surface.

Afterword:

The remains were discovered by Schultze in 1901, during the expedition funded by the *Münchner Zeitung*. Jean-Patrice had achieved a fame in Germany greater than that in his own country, and colored with less irony, due in large part to the writings of Schultze himself, who had depicted Jean-Patrice in a particularly noble light, where French journalists had turned him into a figure of fun. The Bavarian newspaper had taken Jean-Patrice to its heart, as newspapers do when circulation is boosted by a surge in public sympathy. The editor had nourished the idea among his readers that the former District Commissioner of Bassongo might be found alive, perhaps even turned into a god-king by some lost tribe of the deep forest; but as Schultze privately declared, that idea was poppycock (*papperlapapp*).

That Schultze could enunciate this word was a tribute to the efficacy of his prosthesis, designed and in part constructed by himself. The soft rubber "lower lip" was a particular stroke of genius, making it possible for him to pronounce plosives like the letter p from behind the convincing brown beard.

It was the loneliness of the spot which enabled the identification to be positive. As Jean-Patrice had himself realized during his last days, he had entered a particularly obscure stretch of the river system, one unfrequented by European traders and relatively uninhabited by natives. In the broken-down hut, Schultze found his own shotgun (a handsome Kronengewehr with Krupp barrels) together with some bottles and coins, all of which would have been plundered long since on any other part of the river.

The bones themselves were scattered along quite a wide stretch of the riverbank and were as clean as if they had been boiled. The very modern young woman journalist who had accompanied Schultze, and who always wore a daring cream riding habit with jodhpurs, boots, a veil and a pith helmet, excitedly mooted the possibility of a ritual killing and cannibal feast, conducted perhaps by the notorious Leopard Men. Once again, it was Schultze who dispelled the fantasy, retorting "bosh" (*quatsch*) and pointing out that the disarticulation was the work of rodents and other scavengers, who had picked Jean-Patrice's bones clean of flesh post mortem and had strewn them along the bank.

Schultze's experience of pathology was invaluable here, enabling him to find, identify and assemble some sixty percent of Jean-Patrice's bones. They made an affecting sight when laid out on a sheet of canvas. The lady journalist, scribbling in her notebook, recorded both her own tears and the interesting remark of Dr. Schultze that he would have known these bones anywhere by their size (Jean-Patrice had been over six feet tall) and the bullet wounds to the humerus and scapula, where the fractures had not had time to knit before death had supervened and put an end to all organic processes save those of dissolution.

"Duméril had evidently spent some days at the site before departing this life," the journalist wrote. "One wonders what thoughts and dreams went through his mind during this lonely vigil, as the lamp of his life burned ever lower."

Setting up her camera (a Reitzschel "Clack") she took various photographs of the scene, including the bones, the remains of the canoe, the hut, the expedition's river steamer, the assembled black porters and a panoramic view of the river, with Dr. Schultze sitting on a fallen tree trunk in the mid-distance, cupping his prosthetic chin thoughtfully in his hand.

The editor of the *Zeitung* had decreed that, in the eventuality of a dead Duméril, the mortal remains should be brought back to be interred in Munich. It was predictable that this provocation should lead to a newspaper war with various Paris journals, especially *Le Figaro*, which dropped its ironic tone and demanded that M. Duméril, whom it now described as The Hero of Bassongo, be laid to rest in French soil. In these furious exchanges (which were very good for circulation on both sides) could be seen some of the nationalistic enmities which were to reach their apotheosis during the Great War which lay in the future. For the present, the long white bones were packed away in a crate, each one labeled carefully by Schultze.

Conscious that time was money, and weary of Gabon by now, the lady journalist suggested an expeditious return to Libreville. Schultze, however, demurred, insisting on taking a long walk along the riverbank with his shotgun, "for old times' sake." And, as he later remarked, "it was a jolly good thing I did."

If it was the same gorilla (and it was a female of the right age, showing little timidity with humans) it was the most faithful of Jean-Patrice's female companions, for it had apparently haunted the place of his death for something like a year. Discovered by Schultze munching leaves in a clearing, the solitary animal allowed him to approach close enough to establish a rapport. Trembling with excitement, he was able to lead it back to the steamer, where an injection of morphia soon sedated it. It remained in this twilight state during the trip back to the coast, roused only to partake of a little fruit now and then in order to keep body and soul together.

As Schultze had predicted, the dissection catapulted

him into medical history. First published in German but soon also in French and English, the painstaking work, with its superb attendant photographs, many taken through the microscope, was a classic of its kind. This, together with his work on the parasites causing elephantiasis, resulted in a Professorship at the Ludwig Maximilian University in Munich and shortly thereafter, the directorship of the School of Tropical Medicine attached to the same institution. Schultze served there until 1915.

During his retirement, the publication of the *Afrikanische Kamasutra* in a deluxe private subscription edition brought in a supplement to his already liberal pension and royalties. Many copies were burned by the Nazis during the 1930s and the book is now very rare.

Jean-Patrice Duméril's remains were interred with some ceremony in a cemetery in a Munich suburb, which was hit by a stray bomb during the 1945 raids. The gravestones were scattered, and in the general re-interment, the original plot was lost.

ABOUT THE AUTHOR

Marius Gabriel served his author apprenticeship as a student at Newcastle University. To finance his postgraduate research, he wrote 33 Mills & Boon romances under a pseudonym. His identity as a man had to be kept secret until he turned to longer fiction under his own name.

He is the author of 9 sagas and historical novels, including the best-sellers "The Mask Of Time," "The Original Sin" and "The Seventh Moon." Cosmopolitan accused him of "keeping you reading while your dinner burns." He very seldom burns his own, being an enthusiastic cook, as well as an artist and a musician.

Born in South Africa in 1954, he has lived and worked in many countries, and now divides his time between London and Cairo. He has three grown-up children.

His latest novel, "Wish Me Luck As You Wave Me Goodbye," is published by Lake Union.

21936770R00217

Printed in Great Britain
by Amazon